Revenge on the Fly

Revenge
on the
Fly

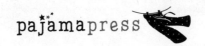

Sylvia McNicoll

pajamapress

First published in the United States in 2014

www.pajamapress.ca info@pajamapress.ca

 Canada Council Conseil des arts
for the Arts du Canada

 ONTARIO ARTS COUNCIL
CONSEIL DES ARTS DE L'ONTARIO
50 YEARS OF ONTARIO GOVERNMENT SUPPORT OF THE ARTS
50 ANS DE SOUTIEN DU GOUVERNEMENT DE L'ONTARIO AUX ARTS

The publisher gratefully acknowledges the support of the Canada Council for the Arts and the Ontario Arts Council for its publishing program. We acknowledge the financial support of the Government of Canada through the Canada Book Fund for our publishing activities.

Library and Archives Canada Cataloguing in Publication

McNicoll, Sylvia, 1954-, author

    Revenge on the fly / Sylvia McNicoll.

ISBN 978-1-927485-56-9 (pbk.)

    I. Title.

PS8575.N52R48 2014   jC813'.54   C2013-908414-2

Publisher Cataloging-in-Publication Data (U.S.)

McNicoll, Sylvia 1954-

    Revenge on the Fly / Sylvia McNicoll.

[224] pages : cm.

Summary: In 1912, twelve year old immigrant William Alton's adoptive city offers a prize for the child who can improve sanitation by killing the most flies. William first sets out to win to avenge the sickness and deaths of his mother and sister, but competition with classmates almost makes him lose sight of the contest's real goal.

ISBN-13: 978-1-927485-56-9 (pbk.)

1. Social values – Juvenile fiction. 2. Emigration and immigration – Juvenile fiction. 3. Flies as carriers of disease – Juvenile fiction. 4. Competition (Psychology) – Juvenile fiction. I. Title.

[Fic] dc23 PZ7.M3543Re 2014

Image credits: Shutterstock/©Everett Collection (boy), Shutterstock/©akiyoko (jar), Shutterstock/©irin-k (fly), Shutterstock/©Africa Studio (fly), Shutterstock/©Reinhold Leitner (fly), Shutterstock/©LeksusTuss (sky). All other images Shutterstock.
Cover design: Rebecca Buchanan
Interior page design: Martin Gould

Printed in Canada by Webcom
www.webcomlink.com

Pajama Press Inc.
112 Berkeley St. Toronto, Ontario Canada, M5A 2W7

Distributed in the US by Orca Book Publishers
PO Box 468 Custer, WA, 98240-0468, USA

MIX
Paper from
responsible sources
FSC
www.fsc.org **FSC® C004071**

 **ANCIENT FOREST** ™
FRIENDLY

For my favorite bug lovers—
Jadzia, William, Violet, Desmond, Fletcher, and Hunter

Chapter I

"Not a word to the doctor about your mother." Father frowned as a woman left the ship's examination station weeping. The doctor had boarded at Rimouski and set up shop in the corner of the dining room. Between the row of tables and the wall, the line of passengers inched forward. "Or your sister."

I nodded in agreement, didn't trust myself to speak. I wasn't some small child—I knew how much depended on this visit to the doctor. Father had been talking about it since we left Liverpool last Saturday night. I knew what I should and shouldn't say. Besides, we rarely spoke about Mum and Colleen, almost as though they never existed. Sometimes I just wanted to scream, *Why my sister? Why my mother?*

Not today though. As usual, the motion of the ship was making me ill. Up...down, up...down. The waves heaved all 14,500 tons of the *Empress of Ireland* as if she were no more than a feather. I only wished I could wait outside on the deck so I could see the open waters and breathe in the cool salt air.

After a day and a half of heavy fog, the air had finally cleared too—perhaps I would even spot land.

"They'll send us to the quarantine station if they think we have the consumption," Father continued, as if I didn't know.

Ahead, smelly old Mr. McNiven, our bunkmate, turned to us. "Grosse Île, huh! You don't want to end up there, lad. My grandfather died on that island. Of the typhus."

The dining room grew hotter, too many people and tiny windows that let in no air. My mouth went dry. I held my head to make it stop spinning.

"Yer not going to be sick now, Will. We're so close." Father gripped my shoulders. "Take a deep breath."

I did, but I took in the leftover aromas from breakfast—stew and onions and oatmeal—combined with Mr. McNiven's sweat and tobacco odor. The smell made everything worse.

"Grandfather was a healthy man, too, till he boarded the ship," Mr. McNiven warned.

"William doesn't have the typhus. He's just seasick," Father said firmly.

I wanted to break away, to run outside and grip the rails tightly so that I could hold on to my breakfast, but Father kept his hands on my shoulder.

Mr. McNiven shook his head. "Seven days at sea and he still doesn't have the stomach."

As if any length of time could make me comfortable with

the rolling and churning. We'd set sail the last day of May and the mighty *Titanic* had sunk just the month before. Wasn't the fear of the sail enough to make anyone ill?

"Never mind." Father stared into my eyes. "Look at me, Will. Think of Uncle Charlie. We're going to see him in a couple of days." Father smiled wide and happy and I almost managed to smile back. You wanted to believe him when he grinned like that.

Besides, I missed Uncle Charlie. With no children of his own, he'd always been generous with his gifts and time. He was the adventurer I looked up to, our lucky uncle.

"Charlie and his grand house. A job for me, a new school for you. Opportunities, just waiting."

I looked into Father's gray eyes and knew I couldn't let him down.

A family walked past us then, a mother, a father, a boy, and a little girl, curly haired and smiling. She was older than our Colleen and as she skipped her brother gave her a shove. I frowned. I wanted to be that boy. I would never have shoved Colleen. I would have taken my sister's hand gently and kept her safe on this rolling ship. I swallowed hard. We should have been that family. Uncle Charlie had sent money for all of us to come. We should be here together. Instead, Father spent Mum and Colleen's ticket money on medicine.

An annoying buzz in my ear made me wave my hand at

my head. I felt the whir of a fly against my fingers and shuddered as it flew away.

"Next!" an impatient voice called from the corner.

Mrs. Gale with Baby Maureen in her arms took her place in front of the doctor and the line inched forward again. The doctor peered into Maureen's ears and into her throat. With her black hair and dark eyes, Mrs. Gale looked like Mum, and they had often been mistaken for sisters back in London, where we had moved when I was eleven.

There had been no jobs anywhere in Ireland for Father, and he and Uncle Charlie schemed to get to Canada. Only first we headed to England to save money. In London Mum had cleaned with Mrs. Gale and Father had worked the docks. When Colleen was born, I was already ten and could help look after her.

Only then my sister turned sick. Six months old, a round-cheeked baby with dimples, Colleen was cooing and laughing one moment and sick with a fever the next. It wasn't like what Mum had. Colleen never coughed. But she quickly changed overnight, grew paler and thinner, too weak to even cry. Nothing stayed inside her. Within three days she died. Mum had needed Mrs. Gale's help and friendship more than ever.

Yesterday, Baby Maureen had woken with a hot forehead.

The doctor examined her now and shook his head. Mrs. Gale pleaded with him but he just shook his head again. She turned and ran down the center aisle. Dad stepped out of line to catch her.

"We have to get off the boat," she told Father. "We're going into quarantine."

He put his arms around her and she collapsed into them, Baby Maureen and all. "There, there." He spoke quietly as she cried, and frowned as he patted her back. After a few moments he changed his tone, put a smile into his voice. "Perhaps it will all turn out for the best." Couldn't he force cheer into the darkest moments. "With the care of those doctors on Grosse Île, the little one can get better again."

Mrs. Gale looked up at him with a sudden spark of hope in her eyes.

He stroked the locks on Baby Maureen's head, his lips smiling along with his voice. "God willing, we will see you both in Hamilton."

Mrs. Gale believed that smile too. She blew her nose and pushed her shoulders back. "Do you think Charlie can hold that job for me if we're late?"

"Oh, to be sure. Likely there will be an even better post by that time."

"God bless you both." Mrs. Gale turned to me and touched my cheek. Then, holding Maureen to one side, she hugged me fiercely. She smelled like Mum too, sweet like heather in spring. When she broke away, she looked straight into my eyes as if trying to memorize me.

I wanted to hold onto her forever. Despite what Father

said, there was a good chance we would never see each other again. Weren't we always having to say goodbye to the people we loved? I tried to memorize her face too. My own mum's features were fading on me. I kissed the baby's hot cheek. "Goodbye," I whispered.

She turned away and headed outside for the waiting boat to take her and Maureen to the island.

I couldn't let myself cry. I was too old for that. But who else could help me remember Mum now? We didn't have anyone left, only Uncle Charlie in Hamilton. "Why does everyone we know get sick?" I asked, swishing at another stupid fly.

"Because everyone we know is so stinkin' poor." For a moment, I heard something hard and bitter in Father's voice. Then he shook his head and took a deep breath. "But that can all change from here on in, Will. You go to school long enough and maybe you'll learn a better answer."

The lurch of the boat made my stomach turn.

Mr. McNiven stood in front of the doctor and the doctor listened to his chest with a stethoscope. He nodded.

"Next!"

Our turn. Father pulled me along and I grabbed at a chair to steady myself.

"Your name and age?" The doctor asked. His voice sounded as tired and faded as his gray hair.

"William Alton, twelve, sir."

"Very good." He peered over his papers at me. "Come closer. Have you always been this thin, lad?" he asked as I stepped toward him.

I stared at him, not saying a word. What if I answered the wrong way and we had to get off the *Empress*? I had to swallow hard to keep my oatmeal down.

"It's just the rough sail," Father answered, a broad smile on his face. "He's been seasick the whole trip, Doctor. But he hasn't had the diarrhea at all."

The doctor stood and frowned at my face. "No spots," he said. He touched my head. "No fever. Breathe in, lad," he commanded as he listened to my chest. "Cough for me."

I managed a small cough despite the rocking boat. This morning's porridge tickled up the back of my throat and as I swallowed, it felt as though a piece of straw had lodged there. I coughed again and couldn't stop.

The doctor watched me with narrowed eyes.

"He had his vaccination for smallpox back in England," Father said.

We both knew that coughing wasn't a symptom of the pox. But it was for what Mum had. In the middle of the night she couldn't stop. I would wake up to the sound and pray to God to help her catch her breath. And then in the daytime, she hacked until she spat up blood. Coughing was a sign of consumption, what my friends at school had called the white plague. Being pale and thin was too.

I tried to breathe and calm the tickle down.

"Here, have some water." The doctor held out a glass.

I drank and managed to stop the cough, but not the sick feeling.

"Did you spend any time with that child I just saw?"

Baby Maureen, limp and pale. I'd just kissed her goodbye. I'd also played with her in the sandpit on Monday to give Mrs. Gale a bit of a rest. The baby had laughed and flattened the tower I'd built her. "No sir. I said hello to her mum from time to time, is all."

The doctor watched me still. If he thought I was sick our whole trip would be delayed—and that was at best. At worst, we could die on Grosse Île, like Mr. McNiven's grandfather.

The doctor shook his head and stamped a paper. "You're fine."

"Thank you, sir. Thank you."

"Now you. His father I presume?"

Dad had no trouble with the examination. I rushed down the aisle and out the room the moment the doctor finished. Across the mahogany deck I raced to the rail, and released my porridge into the St. Lawrence River.

Ow, ow, ow, the seagulls called. And it all did hurt, so badly.

I took a deep breath and tried to be more like my father. Brave, cheerful.

After all, we were *this* close to the new life we had dreamed about as a family. We just had to get to Uncle Charlie and the job he had secured for my father. I wiped at my mouth and looked out at the endless water. I shook my head then forced myself to look up at the clouds instead. "We're going to make it, Mum. You made us promise, and so we must."

Chapter 2

Sometime after tea, we finally docked in Quebec City. Passengers emptied from the rooms and halls of every level of the ship onto the decks, eager to see this new country or perhaps just to set eyes on land again. The city rose up high above us like a paradise. Rows of houses lined the curl of the cliff from top to bottom. "It's so grand," I told Father as we stood near the rail. I breathed in the harbor smells of seaweed and sewage but also a hint of something more pleasant. I sniffed again, nose toward the hills. Pine? Earth? Or perhaps just wishful thinking. "Look there, Da! There's even a castle!"

"Château Frontenac, my son. A hotel for the wealthy. Get your schooling and perhaps you will stay there one day." Father clapped his hand on my shoulder.

"When can we leave the boat?" I asked.

"Captain said tomorrow morning," Mr. McNiven grumbled from beside Father.

"No!" Land was so close, and we'd waited forever to get to our new home.

Father nodded. "I'm afraid he's right. We need to go through immigration and board a train. Too late for any of that now."

No matter, just one more day till we saw Uncle Charlie again. We stayed on deck till the last rays of sunlight melted into the water. Then we made wishes on the stars: that there would be no more sickness in our family, that Father would do well in his new post, and that I would become someone important some day so I could always look after the people I loved.

That night I could hardly sleep for the excitement.

Early next morning we grabbed our luggage and headed out. Down the gangplank we shuffled with people ahead as well as at back of us.

As my feet touched the solid ground at the bottom, I wanted to stop for just one moment to enjoy the feeling, but passengers jostled at me from every side, their suitcases nudging my legs and hips, moving me forward. Still, I could breathe and swallow and nothing was backing up my throat anymore. "We live here!" I swung my arms around and knocked off a young boy's hat. "Sorry."

"Look out below!" a man's voice bellowed.

I glanced up. A net of baggage swung high above our heads and dropped down onto the dock.

"Hurry now, Will. We need to queue up for immigration."

If only we could stay in one place just for a little while.

In the end, I got what I wanted but didn't like it. We waited three and a half hours in a hot airless shed for our turn with a clerk. I had hoped for a quick train ride to my new home and my favorite uncle, but when we finally boarded our train, Father explained that Canada was huge, and we needed to travel another couple of days to Hamilton. I blew out a sigh of disappointment.

Still, once we boarded the train and began the next part of our journey, the movement of the wheels beneath my feet felt more familiar and friendlier than the rolling of the *Empress*. *Chh-chunk, chh-chunk, chh-chunk*, they whispered at me. My eyelids drooped. Only the wooden bench biting at the back of my knees kept me from falling asleep. When I did fall off the bench, Father spread his coat on the floor and I curled up there.

Later I awoke and crawled back on my bench to look out the window. The train passed a forest of tall pines and a rushing stream. And then another and another. The wildness and bigness of it all made my heart pound harder and faster. So much of everything, except people.

"Where does everyone live, Da?"

"In the cities, just like in England," Father answered.

"Just like in England," I repeated to myself, only I secretly hoped everything would be so much better.

Then we stopped in such a city, called Montreal, and needed to switch trains to get to another called Toronto. We shuffled through the dark smoky tunnel from one car to the next. The only people we saw were our fellow travelers.

This next train provided padded seating, much more comfortable. The journey continued on throughout the night and with only a window of inky blackness to stare at, I leaned on Father's shoulder and fell fast asleep. Father shook me awake in the morning so that we might switch trains one last time.

"I'm starving, Da," I told him as we shuffled through the tall halls. The footsteps of the hundreds of our fellow passengers echoed against the high ceilings. How many were arriving from another land, like us?

"We'll stop here then," Father said, directing me over to the small corner diner in the station. "Just something light, mind. We don't want to spoil our appetites for the feast Charlie surely has planned for us."

Or run out of money, I thought. We ordered sweet buns and tea.

Sitting on a spinning stool, sipping and eating, I carefully held the seat still by bridging one foot against the counter. No more movement if I could help it.

"One last train ride and we'll be there," Father told me as he laid down some money to pay the bill.

"How long, Da?"

"An hour and a bit, no more, I promise."

I stayed awake for the last leg, counting trees until I lost count. One last beautiful lake, and then through a long dark tunnel.

"This is it." Father patted my knee.

Back under the open sky, the train chugged slowly to a halt. I peered through the window hoping to see Uncle Charlie in the huddle of people waiting. No luck.

"Our boat was delayed a day by the fog, don't forget. We may have to go find him," Father told me.

He hoisted down his large black suitcase and I struggled with the brown one that used to belong to Mum. We stepped into the hot sun and crowds, heard the familiar *clackity-clack* of hooves and I breathed in the smell of steaming manure. Ah, horses. Much better than musty life jackets. Not so different from London, then. My feet rested on firm and steady ground, this time for good I hoped.

I peered around. The station was a huge gray stone building with a tall round tower. Another castle-like building. Sure, weren't there more of those in Canada than in England and didn't that bode well! Even ordinary travelers got to live like kings.

As I watched, a trolley car stopped at the tracks, let some passengers off and took on some more. No Uncle Charlie among them.

I shielded my eyes and searched some more. He should have been easy to spot. Like Father, he was a big man with large feet and large hands who stood tall over the crowds, but unlike him, Uncle Charlie had red hair.

Something jabbed me in the back and I spun around. Uncle Charlie? No. It was the tip of an umbrella belonging to a woman with three young children bunched into her large skirt.

I swished a few flies away from my face.

Someone knocked my head. Again I turned. This time, it was a short, dark-haired man with a large sausage, waving hello to his family. I tried to move out of his way and bashed one of the woman's children with my suitcase. "Sorry," I said as the boy bawled to his mum.

On the far end of the platform another man held a sign: *Laborers Wanted. No Irish.*

I stared for a moment. In London they didn't like the Irish either, but this was a new land. Nodding toward the man with the sign, I grumbled. "You said it would be different here."

"Don't worry yourself, Will. I don't need a job; Charlie has one for me." Father stepped down into the road alongside of the platform and I followed, not wanting to lose him in the crowd. We walked toward a boy near the station who was waving a newspaper in the air and calling, "Read all about it. Looking glasses banned from the *Titanic*."

Father bought one from him. The story was about the investigation of the ship's sinking.

"Do you think anyone on the *Empress* had binoculars?" I asked him. Would they have even helped in that fog we sailed through the last few days, I wondered.

"Oh, to be sure. They never make the same mistake twice, Will. We were perfectly safe."

"Mind the wagon," a man in a uniform warned us.

I dodged out of the way, careful with my suitcase this time. The man guided the wagon, piled high with trunks and bags, to a horse-drawn carriage parked at the side of the platform. Another carriage already loaded with luggage and travelers pulled away. Slowly, all the people seemed to drain from the platform. But still no red hair anywhere.

Father dug his fists into his hips and shook his head, frowning. "Surely he read about the shipping delays. He must have just been held up."

We stood all by ourselves now, track stretching in front and behind of us as far as the eye could see. It felt so lonesome and endless.

"Good day to you," a voice called. A man jumped from the train waving. Mr. McNiven!

I was even glad to see the smelly old grump.

"Do you have a position yet?" Father asked him.

"Not here. I'm traveling on. Headed for a farm out west."

"But you worked the docks."

"Did. Don't want to anymore." Like Father, Mr. McNiven had been forced to strike for higher wages since the middle of May.

No one dared to cross picket lines, no matter if they had mouths to feed and bills to pay. If they tried they were called scabs and sometimes even beaten. With no further money coming in, Father knew it was our last chance to leave. He had booked our passages and Mr. McNiven had done the same.

Mr. McNiven threw up his hands. "In Winnipeg they're begging for farm hands, so that's what I'm going to be. You?"

"My brother has a post for me in a livery. I'll be doing blacksmith work too. He should be here any moment." Father peered out into the streets. A wagon rattled by us.

Mr. McNiven raised his eyebrows as he looked around. "If he isn't here by now, do you suppose he's really coming?"

"Of course! I have his letter right here saying so." Father's brow furrowed as he patted his shirt pocket. "Well now. That's odd." He rooted in his trouser pockets.

"Why don't you get back on the train with me?" Mr. McNiven asked. "You can stake a claim for land if you like. Raise your own horses instead."

Father shook his head. "He'll be here for us any minute.

Besides, we need to live in the town, close to schools. I want a proper education for William."

"Can't say as I blame you." Mr. McNiven shook his head as the train whistled. "Just want to stay put myself. This country is too big, if you ask me." He climbed back on and as the train pulled out he saluted Father from the window.

We stood alone on the platform, four thousand miles away from home. Not a soul here we knew except for Uncle Charlie. Even the paperboy was leaving.

"You there," Father called to him. "Can you direct us to a good place to eat?

The boy grinned and pointed. "Down James Street over there on King. Look for the Waldorf Hotel. My mother works there. They make great apple pie."

"Thank you." Father raised his cap. Then he turned to me. "We'll leave word for your uncle with the ticket clerk. He'll likely be waiting for us by the time we finish our meal."

While Father went in to speak to him, I stood watch over our suitcases, all the while searching for Uncle Charlie. Father took forever but still no one came for us. "Come along then," he said as he stepped out of the station. "We'll feel better after we've eaten."

We walked in the direction the paperboy had shown us. The street was quiet now that all the wagons had pulled away. The sun felt hot on my head but we didn't have far to go before we spotted the Waldorf. Sure, wasn't this hotel almost as grand as that Château in Quebec; four stories high and arches over the doors. We couldn't have enough money to stay here. I didn't think we had enough to dine here either. Still, my morning hunger had returned. The sweet bun had only been a stop gap after all.

Inside, a large chandelier fair blinded me but Father led me to the dining room and told me to order whatever I wanted. Then, over a plate of hot roast beef with potatoes and gravy, he read the newspaper. "Sure, isn't this the land of opportunity. There are seven jobs listed here." He tapped it with the back of his hand. "Mind, most are asking for boys."

"I can work, Father."

"No!" he said sharply then grabbed my hand. "I promised your mum," he said more gently, and smiled. "Don't worry. Charlie will show his sorry self." Father called to the waitress and she came around. "Can we have some coffee and some of your wonderful apple pie?"

Father's smile and the apple pie made me feel like there wasn't anything we couldn't conquer together. As we ate, he circled rooming-house adverts in the paper. "It's getting late, and dashed if I remember Charlie's address without that letter."

Uncle Charlie. I remembered the day he left—I cried harder than when my mother died. But he had taken my chin in his hand and looked directly into my eyes. "I have to do this, Will.

But we'll be together again. I'll come and get you myself if yer old man doesn't bring you to Canada."

So why wasn't he here, I wondered. Why hadn't he at least left word somewhere? What if we never found him?

Finally, Father folded the paper and stood up. "Right. Off we go." He left some coins on the counter.

Back at the train station there was still no Uncle Charlie outside, nor any word from him inside, so we headed off. "Can you manage?" Dad asked as I struggled with my suitcase. "I'd like to save the wagon fare for room and board."

I nodded and we walked, Father looking back all the while. "'Tis a fine joke your uncle is playing on us. We owe him one for this." He sighed. "Let's try the boarding houses over this way, shall we?"

At the first house, Father rapped out a tune on the door. "We've come about a room," he explained to the tiny gray-haired lady peering from behind her door.

"All full up," she said, closing it quickly.

"But there's no sign in the window, Da," I said.

Father shrugged his shoulders and we continued on.

At the second house a young girl answered. "Sorry. Too late. Happens whenever the train pulls in." At the third and fourth houses the answer was the same. None of them had signs in the window either.

"Is it because we're Irish?" I asked, wondering how the

rooming-house people could even tell when we'd scarce had a chance to get a word in.

"No, I don't think so. This part of town is Irish. Corktown, it's called. The last one listed here says it's on Park Street." Father's brow furrowed as he looked around. "Excuse me kind sir," he called to a man walking by. "Can you direct us to this address?"

The man tipped his hat and squinted at the newspaper advert. "That's over near Central School, back that way." He pointed up the hill.

"Thank you, thank you!" Father clasped the man's hand and shook it. Then he turned to me. "Near Central School! Your Uncle Charlie said Central was the largest public school in Upper Canada. And the room is only a dollar per week. It's like it was meant to be!"

Full of new hope, we retraced our steps quickly past the train station and up the hill till we saw a large, fine building.

"That's the school!" Father exclaimed. "This street must be Park"—he pointed—"and that's the place."

Tall with dirty red bricks and a long flight of steps to a gray door, the fifth rooming house seemed to be the ugliest building in the area. As we climbed the blistered wooden steps, the boards creaked as if in pain. I pointed to a fly struggling in the spider web that stretched across the front window.

"It will have to do. Just for a little while. Till we find Charlie." Father knocked on the door once gently, and then again, harder.

I couldn't walk any more. My arms felt stretched out of their sockets as they had both taken a turn with Mum's brown bag. I wiped at the sweat from my brow. The soles of my feet burned.

No one answered.

Finally, a thin witch-like woman opened the door and scowled at us. Yes, she had one room left. "*Une chambre,*" she told us.

Relieved, I set my suitcase on the porch even as she stared me up and down and shook her head. "*Pas de garçons.* No boys."

My father's grin dropped off his face and for the first time that long day, I could see that he was as weary and as frightened as I. He snapped back in an instant. "Ah, but give us a moment, will you, dear woman?" Removing his hat, Father took a deep breath, smiled, and bowed. "*Bonjour,*" he started, "*je m'appelle* Arthur Alton. This is my son, Will, a good lad." He reached out his hand to shake hers. "And you are?"

"Madame Depieu." She took his hand, but she shook her head at the same time. "The boys, *ils font trop de bruit et la saleté.* How do you say this in English? They make too much noise and dirt."

"My Will's different," Father said, patting my shoulder as he spoke. "Since his mum died, he's all grown up. My mate, as it were. Don't you worry about him at all."

"*Bien non.*" She touched her pointed nose and I worried she was casting a spell to make us disappear. Instead, almost as bad, she began closing the door.

Just as fast, I stuck my foot in front of it. I had no idea what I was doing, but to be sure I wouldn't be the cause of us not having a roof over our head. I stared at the fly in the spider's web, trapped with nowhere to go. Didn't I know just how he felt? I looked up at Father and he winked at me. For his sake I wouldn't cry.

Instead, I straightened my shoulders and made myself stand tall. Our dream of a new life in Canada started today, right this moment at this rooming house. If I could make it past that immigration doctor, I would make it past this woman. "Please, Madame. I can clean for you. I helped my mother all the time."

She tilted her head, her chin jabbing at me. "*Vraiement?*"

I nodded and tried to smile the way Father always did—big and broad and as bright as the sun.

Madame Depieu sighed. "*Eh bien.* I give you a chance, since we have the one room. This week you can stay. Two dollars for the both of you. I make the breakfast and the *souper*. One chance and that is all!" She huffed as she swung open her door.

Father wiped his shoes carefully, and I did exactly the same. I tried to step lightly as I followed him in. Only one chance and at double the regular price. *Crash!* The suitcase hit the stair rail.

Madame Depieu's eyebrows shot up like broomsticks. "*Fait attention!*" she commanded.

"Sorry." Mine wasn't the only gouge out of the baseboard running up the stairs, and greasy spots along the ivy wallpaper showed where others had groped their way along the wall, but I wasn't about to point that out. I wasn't going to do anything to make her change her mind about us staying. I didn't touch the wall myself.

"I have the modern conveniences." Madame Depieu said as we reached the top of the stairs. She pointed to the far end of the hall. "Over there is the water closet you share with the other men. Your room is on the side."

A water closet! As soon as she left us, I had to peek in this amazing little room. On the floor sat something that looked like a large chamber pot. Above it hung a box, and from the box dangled a chain. They'd had one at the mansion Mum had worked at in London, but I'd never visited it. At our flat, we'd used an outhouse. "Imagine not having to go outside in the cold, Father!"

He smiled. "Ah, it will be grand, Will."

Our room was small and hot and smelled of vinegar and onions, and the flowered wallpaper was water stained around the window. Next room over some men laughed loudly and the wall thumped. Sure, couldn't grown men make all the noise they wanted. Madame Depieu wouldn't toss *them* out.

Father said we should turn in early—it had been a long and tiring day— so I used the wonderful toilet for the first time. It roared and whooshed when I pulled the chain. Later, as I squeezed up close to Father in the small bed, it roared and whooshed as the other men used it, one by one, and the pipes gurgled long after. The noise made it hard to sleep and I lay awake wondering about Uncle Charlie. Could I last in this house till he turned up? *Set your mind to it,* a voice inside me said. I wanted to think it was Mum. "I will do it," I replied. *I will be so good that Madame Depieu will wonder what she did without me.*

Chapter 3

First thing after breakfast, Father pulled me outside. "What a fine school you will be attending!" We both looked toward the two-story oatmeal-colored building, the one we'd spotted yesterday on the way here. A tower stood at the front flanked by two walls of windows.

"This is it, my boy!" Father clapped his hand on my shoulder excitedly. "Your mother would be so pleased. Such a wonderful opportunity and so close."

We crossed the street together and climbed the cement steps to the large oak door, removing our hats as we stepped into the building. Father asked at the office for the principal and was introduced to Mr. Morton, a tall mustached man with gray eyes. I shook his hand as well, and he squeezed mine too hard. Still, his silver hair hung in his eyes like the mane of a horse and somehow that made him seem friendlier to me. Didn't our whole family get along well with horses, after all.

We sat down in front of Mr. Morton's desk. "Young William should be in junior fourth form, correct?" he asked.

Father and I both nodded.

"Has he had his smallpox vaccination?" Mr. Morton asked.

"Before we left England," Father answered.

"Wonderful. Your son will be in good hands." Mr. Morton stood, and it was clear my time with my father was over.

Before he left, Father handed me a bag. "Your lunch. The witch made it for you." He smiled that wonderful grin that promised gold at the end of the rainbow. "I'm going to get a job today...so I will not be around to eat with you." He chucked me under the chin. "And you're going to get an education. It's what your mum would have—" He broke off and started again. "It's what your mother wants for you. Do well."

"I will. Goodbye, Father." I felt a pang at seeing his back as he headed out the door. School had never given me any problem back in England. I knew my numbers and letters. Everything would go just fine here too. But Father and I had been together night and day nigh on two weeks. What if he disappeared like Uncle Charlie? Then I would have no one left.

Mr. Morton cleared his throat. "Well, my boy." He clapped his hand on my shoulder. "Come with me."

Together we walked down a long, dark hall. Even though I was tall for my age, Mr. Morton towered over me. It was like walking with a giant through his castle. Finally, we stopped.

"This will be your classroom." He knocked on a door and a younger man with dark hair answered. "Mr. Samson, this is your new pupil, William Alton. Just landed from England."

Mr. Samson nodded, guided me in and shut the classroom door again. "Welcome, William."

Just as in London, the classroom had three walls of blackboard and one of windows. At the front, near the right-hand corner, a portrait photo of King George watched over us. Next to it, in the center, hung a large Union Jack. A map of the world lay unrolled over the board. Pink colored the parts of the British Empire, and I felt happy to see all of Canada in that bright happy color. No matter how far I was from Ireland, or London for that matter, I was still standing on British soil.

Still, rows of unfamiliar faces watched me as I stood in the front and the teacher introduced me. "Class, this is our new student, William Alton, all the way from London. I know you will do your best to welcome him." He turned to me. "You can share Fred Leckie's desk, over there."

Mr. Samson showed me to a double bench attached to a desktop by black wrought iron. Just as in England it was bolted down, only in London I sat by myself. "Fred, you will be in charge of looking after William and showing him around."

Dressed in a fine linen suit with a wide square sailor collar and blue bow, the boy looked me up and down with hard eyes, a creamy smile across his face.

My own brown shirt and britches suddenly felt coarse and itchy, and sweat trickled down from my armpits. Nevertheless, I grinned back at Fred.

His eyes glittered with something fierce that certainly wasn't welcome. He turned away.

Had he made up his mind about me already? Did I not seem worthy of his time or friendship? I looked around and felt the atmosphere grow cold. The other students took their cue from Fred and stared hard or turned away.

"Class, take out your readers and turn to page seventeen." Mr. Samson pulled a book from the shelf behind his desk and brought it to me.

I opened it up to the correct page.

"Ginny." He turned to a freckled girl with long sand-colored braids who sat in the next row. "Would you start us off by reading the poem?"

Ginny stood up hesitantly. She placed a forefinger on the page. "The Lamb," she read as she moved the finger along. She paused, flinging one braid behind her shoulder. "By William Blake." She looked up and around as though waiting for someone to disagree with her. When no one did, she continued, her finger sliding beneath the words. "Little lamb who made thee..." Back in London, we had already read that one. It was about God and how he made lambs and children and provided for both.

Beside me Fred sneered at her as he flung an imaginary braid of his own behind him. What did he not like about Ginny? She read well enough, if not with a lot of feeling. Perhaps, like me, she didn't quite believe Blake's words. God didn't provide equally for all children. Fred did all right but Ginny certainly didn't. Her dress looked old, patched in two places with a hem sagging. And hadn't we had lamb chops on the passage over? Lambs fared even worse than children.

Knowing the poem so well did make me feel ahead of the class. Maybe in Canada I would lead the others and earn even higher grades. That would make Mum happy. I sighed.

The room grew hotter and the air felt heavy. A cluster of flies buzzed around the window. Finally, Ginny sat down and we turned the page to a story called "Lost at Sea." Mr. Samson called on a boy named Harry to read. Harry sounded each word into separate syllables, slow and painful.

It could have been an exciting story—the ship crashed into a rock in the fog. Instead I watched as a lone fly landed first on Fred's arm, then Harry's nose, and finally on Ginny's desk, where she whacked it with her reader.

Mr. Samson raised his eyebrow and, frowning, pulled a rag from his desk and handed it to her to wipe off the book.

At least she had felled the creature. She handed the rag back when she was done. Finally, I could concentrate again. Did the captain in the story use a looking glass? Or were binoculars banned from that voyage too? Harry paused and stumbled, so I read ahead.

I needed to know if the captain escaped—the one on the *Titanic* went down with his ship, after all—and if I waited for Harry, I might fall asleep before I ever found out. When Mr. Samson called on Fred, it was obvious that he had read ahead as well, because he had lost the class's place in the story.

"You know you should be following along," Mr. Samson scolded. "Stand up, please."

Ever so slowly, Fred lifted himself from the chair. A smirk stretched across his face and his lips pulled down from one corner. The teacher didn't seem to notice. He just turned his attention to the next reader, a girl named Rebecca. She wore large blue ribbons in her hair that exactly matched her eyes. Rebecca read smoothly and even dramatically. I quickly flipped back to find her place in the story and followed along.

"Thank you, Rebecca."

She sat down.

"Fred, do you feel you can concentrate on the task at hand now?" Mr. Samson raised an eyebrow.

Same smirk, but Fred's small nod satisfied the teacher.

"You may sit down, then. Why don't we hear from our new student next. William?"

I stood quickly and took a breath. After Colleen died, Mum grew weaker and weaker, until she could no longer work.

Finally, she took to her bed. I would read to her from a book the lady of the manor had given her as a parting gift—*Jane Eyre*. The words were difficult but I added expression as best I could to make the story come alive. It was one small thing that I could do to try to make her happy when there was no joy left in her. In those final weeks, the daily storytelling had turned me into a very good reader.

As I began the passage where the lifeboats were lowered, I could sense that the class was watching me. The room grew silent. The first mate called to the captain to leave and even the flies at the window stopped their buzzing. When the ship slipped below the surface, I looked up to see my classmates staring wide-eyed. When the captain gave his place in the lifeboat to a child, I heard Rebecca sniffle. I finished—the captain and all hands were lost. I sighed. It made me glad to be off the *Empress of Ireland*.

"Well done!" Mr. Samson clapped and the class joined in. "This is the way you all should be reading."

I smiled and looked around. Even though my clothing was shabby, perhaps now they would all know I was no slouch.

Ginny eyed me like a cat does a bird. Rebecca smiled back warmly.

Fred elbowed me hard as I sat down. "Show-off."

Fair enough. Perhaps I had been showing off just a little. The elbow in my ribs caused me to slump. Maybe that would make Fred happy.

Next, Mr. Samson loaned me one of his pens so that I could copy out the week's words with the rest of the class, ten times each, to practice penmanship and learn spelling. The pen was full of dark ink and I had to write quickly and evenly so as not to bleed heavy drops of blue on the page. As I finished copying the last word, Fred knocked into me. The page tore.

I kicked him under the desk.

When Mr. Samson walked around he suggested I stay in at recess to redo the page.

I sighed but did not tell on Fred. The sun blazed outside, and without any friends at this new school, it was no great hardship to give up recess anyway.

But then, later in drill class when we were lined up in rows, Mr. Samson demonstrated how to swing our Indian clubs up and over our shoulders. Somehow Fred managed to bash my arm with the wooden pin.

"Ow!" I couldn't help crying out this time. I gripped my throbbing arm.

"Fred, what have you done?" Mr. Samson asked.

"'Twas an accident, sir. I'm sorry," Fred told me, extending a hand. But his smile showed me that it had been deliberate and he jabbed and jostled me enough during the rest of the day to let me know that he considered me his enemy.

Just before dismissal, Mr. Morton appeared at the door of the classroom again. When Mr. Samson stepped out to speak to him, the class became restless. Fred threw a crumpled bit of paper at Rebecca and Harry pulled at Ginny's braid till she hammered him. Harry roared and the other boys laughed at him.

"I have an announcement," Mr. Samson said as he returned to the class. He held up his hands till there was complete silence. "We have an important guest coming to visit tomorrow and he will bring news of an exciting opportunity for all of you. You can be a hero to your city, vanquish disease, and win great prizes too. Be sure to wash well, clean your nails, and dress in your best. Class dismissed."

Vanquish disease? I forgot all about Fred's torment. I had felt so helpless watching Mum and Colleen fall ill and die. Hadn't I wondered a thousand times over whether there was anything I could have done—anything anyone could have done—to have prevented them from getting sick, to stop them from dying? I'd felt the same way on the boat, when we'd said goodbye to Mrs. Gale.

Would tomorrow bring the answer I had been looking for all this time? Would I finally learn how to defeat disease? It might be too late for Mum and Colleen, but there were surely others who could be helped. The thought brought a smile to my face, and as I filed out of the class—my first day over and done—I remembered the rest of Mr. Samson's words. Prizes. What exactly might they be?

Chapter 4

Eagerly, I rushed down the hall and out the door, ready to run back to Madame Depieu's rooming house to tell Father what little I knew about the exciting opportunity. Outside the school building I paused for just a moment to get my bearings. Just then I heard Father's voice, calling from the other direction.

"Will, over here. Across the street. Look this way!"

The church stood directly across from the front of Central School. But his voice seemed to be coming from the castle-like manor next to it, which faced the back of the school. Could it be?

Were my ears playing tricks? Or maybe he had found Uncle Charlie, and that was his manor. Oh, to live in that castle! I crossed at the corner and headed down the street.

"In the back at the stable." Father stood, waving, by a small building behind the manor.

I ran across the lot, then over the street and through the

yard to throw my arms around him. "Where's Uncle Charlie?" I asked as I pulled away. "Did you find him?"

"Not yet. I found work instead," Father explained. "Just now I am seeing to the owner's horses, Beauty and Blue. Come and have a look."

"Can you be a blacksmith here?" I asked, confused. The post Uncle Charlie had for him was supposed to give him a trade, a future.

"No. For now, I took the position of servant and stable hand." We walked into the stable, where an empty carriage stood. "Mr. Moodie owns this grand mansion. He calls it the Blink Bonnie." Along the wall hung tools, several polished harnesses, and a saddle. "This morning I went door to door, looking for odd jobs, and was lucky enough to find him at home."

"Why didn't you try to find Uncle Charlie instead?" I didn't look at him, didn't want to be fooled by a smile. Instead, I stood on my toes to see the horses in their stalls.

"I checked back at the train station and there was no word." Father's voice was low. "We've run out of money, Will. Without board, Madame Depieu will surely turn us out."

"She'll turn us out soon enough anyways. She hates boys! If you had found Uncle Charlie, we could move in with him."

"*Whisht*! William, we don't know what's happened with him. What if there's been an accident?"

What if he's dead? I couldn't bear to think it.

Father took a deep breath, put his hand on my shoulder and squeezed. "Mr. Moodie has also bought a new motor car. If I stay, he's promised I can train to look after it. No matter what's happened to Charlie, we have a future here and we're together. That's all that matters." He let go of me then and chucked me under the chin. "Talk to me as I finish up." He led a large chocolate-colored horse out of its stall, and tied it to the carriage. "You can watch Beauty here while I muck out her bedroom."

I reached up and patted the horse's warm smooth nose. "Tomorrow someone important is going to come to school to tell us how to stop disease," I called to Father. "There's going to be a contest too, with prizes."

He ducked his head from around the stall. "See there. And you wanted to go out and get a job. Education pays, my lad. And so quickly!" He grinned. "Go fetch my paper off the counter there and read to me."

I picked up the newspaper, climbed up onto the carriage, and read to him about a flood in Buffalo, Wyoming. Walls of water had carried off several brick blocks and wrecked a number of buildings.

By the end of the story, Father had finished the stall and he called me over to the sink. "Let's wash up. Madame Depieu owes us supper and I expect she will not hold it for us if we are late."

I pumped the water for Father and he pumped for me. Sharing a brown bar of soap to scrub our hands, we also washed our faces and the backs of our necks so that we would feel cooler.

After drying off, we headed from the Blink Bonnie past the back of the school, down Park Street, and past a row of tall red-brick buildings till we hit the ugliest and dirtiest, our rooming house.

We climbed the creaking stairs to Madame Depieu's house.

The witch poked her head out the door. "Take off your shoes!" she screeched. "I don't want the dirt on my stairs."

We did as she commanded, even though the steps looked none too clean.

At the top landing, she grabbed my arms and checked my hands. "*Pas mal.* Help me serve up supper."

I saw Father bristle, but I knew we had nowhere else to go so I shrugged my shoulders and gave him my biggest grin. He smiled back instantly.

I brought plates of food and heavy jugs of water to the table. We ate hard potatoes and carrots and stringy meat that didn't quite taste like beef. I only hoped it wasn't horse. I'd heard that some of the French enjoyed eating their mounts. After supper I cleared plates and helped clean dishes. Would this be the way I spent every evening? I went to bed exhausted. *It doesn't matter*, I told myself. It was only for a short while. Till we found Uncle Charlie. And, as Father said, we were together, and that was all that mattered for now.

Next day at school, despite the oppressive heat, the class hummed with excitement. Mr. Samson told us to study our spelling words till our guest arrived. "Quietly," he added. Still, pencils rattled and books dropped. No one could settle. When Harry fell out of his seat, Mr. Samson slammed a ruler across his desk. "All right then. Since you all know your words so perfectly, we will have a spelling bee."

Back home, we'd enjoyed spelling bees on the odd Friday. Because I could often picture the words in my head from all of my reading, I usually did brilliantly.

Mr. Samson divided the class—Fred on one team with many of the boys, and I on the other with Rebecca and Ginny and the rest of the girls. We stood along the front blackboard.

"Shoveled," Mr. Samson called to Harry. He stood on Fred's side.

Not an easy one, for sure. Harry shuffled from foot to foot, repeating the word. He looked, big-eyed, toward Fred.

"No helping," Mr. Samson warned.

"S...h...," Harry paused. "A?" he asked.

Mr. Samson shook his head and Harry sat down. "Copy it out one hundred times so you will know it next time."

On our side, Rebecca repeated the word and spelled it easily. Our next word was *barrel*. Ginny pronounced it in two syllables, as though listening to the sound each part of the word made. Reciting the letters took equally long, and her golden-brown eyes looked skywards the whole time. When she hit the first *r*, she paused like a wagon stuck in a rut, and then, bump, she gave the second *r* and the rest of the letters. After she finished she repeated "barrel" with some attitude. "So there!" When Mr. Samson nodded, she beamed, like the sun from behind a storm cloud.

I wanted to applaud.

"*Consider*," Mr. Samson called out for Fred.

Smiling, he immediately launched into spelling it. "C...o...n...s...i...d...e...r."

There was a gasp. Mr. Samson raised one thick black eyebrow. Fred's face fell as he realized his mistake.

"Consider," Mr. Samson repeated. "You need to *consider* carefully before you act. Fred, you know you have to repeat the word before spelling it. You may sit down."

A nervous twitter from the girl next to me made Fred glower my way.

I tried hard not to smile and add salt to his wounds. My turn at it. "Consider," I repeated. "C...o...n...s...i...d...e...r, consider." No double letters to think about; it would have been an easy word even if Fred hadn't given me all the letters. I spelled the word by the time he reached our desk.

He slammed his body down on the bench, making everything on it jump up.

Mr. Samson shouted at him, but a knock at the door interrupted any attempts at discipline. Mr. Samson opened it and Mr. Morton stepped in. He nodded.

"Our guest has arrived," Mr. Samson announced.

Everyone cheered except Fred.

"Quickly, class, line up!" Mr. Samson commanded.

The spelling bee lines shifted to the door, and Mr. Samson led us to the end of the hall and up the staircase, Harry and Fred bringing up the rear. Through a set of double doors into a large auditorium our line marched, picking out and sitting down on hard wooden chairs.

Students chattered among themselves nervously as they settled. An important visitor was speaking today, after all. A teacher hissed, "Shhh!"

Up on a stage in front of us, and next to Mr. Morton, stood a worried-looking younger man in a dark suit, checking his pocket watch.

Was this the man who would give us the secret to vanquishing disease? Would he give me the answer to the question that troubled me most?

When everyone was seated and had stopped talking, Mr. Morton introduced the man. "Girls and boys, join me in welcoming the city of Hamilton's esteemed health officer, Dr. Roberts." Mr. Morton began clapping and we all joined him, stopping when he cleared his throat to continue. "Dr. Roberts is here to talk about an important threat to everyone's well-being. I know you will give him your fullest attention. Dr. Roberts?" He gestured toward the man and we all applauded together till Dr. Roberts stared us down.

After the room had quieted down a second time, he unrolled a large poster inch by inch, revealing a drawing of a huge fly. The creature had hairy black legs and feelers that seemed to grow from cherry-pit eyes. Dr. Roberts called one of the taller older boys to the stage to hold the poster up for him.

The fly on the poster had its wings spread across the chest of a smiling sweet child. A little baby girl, just the way I remembered Colleen—or was it Baby Maureen from the boat? Their faces had blurred into one in my mind. Across the top of the picture the words read, *Kill the Fly and Save the Baby*. I felt my face grow hot.

Dr. Roberts finally spoke. "The importance of cleanliness cannot be underestimated in keeping the citizens of our city healthy. Boys and girls, we must dispose of our garbage carefully and keep our streets and alleyways clean in order to avoid our worst enemy."

He knocked the back of his hand against the drawing of the fly. "This seemingly harmless insect loves excrement and rotting food. It lands in it, lays its eggs in it, and then, boys and girls, it lands on your food."

Next to me, a girl gasped and looked sick.

"Not only does it land and walk on your bread, it spits, defecates, and wipes its legs on it."

Shrieks of horror came from the younger children in the rows ahead of me.

"And so the fly spreads germs. If it doesn't immediately poison our food, it kills us by giving us horrible diseases. Typhoid, consumption, summer complaint—the fly spreads them all, leaving dead babies and adults in its wake."

Why hadn't someone in England shared this information with us? My mouth went dry and I found it hard to breathe. In everyday life, the insect was so common and insignificant. Blown up large on the poster, however, it was easy to see it as a menace. Something that small had killed my mum and sister. We had so many of them in the flat; it made sense that they were the cause. To think, I hardly bothered swatting at them, either. I was so poor at it.

There were many on the boat too. Sweet Baby Maureen. If just one had landed on her bottle of milk it could have caused her illness. I squeezed my eyes shut so that my tears wouldn't spill. No family anymore save for my father. And no Mrs. Gale with us either, all because of this disease-spreading menace.

"The fly is our worst enemy." Dr. Roberts looked straight at me as he continued. "And as such, it is everyone's duty to swat and kill these death carriers. Boys and girls, we are declaring war on the fly." Dr. Roberts shook his fist in the air.

"Hurrah!" I cheered along with the rest of the students and teachers in the assembly.

"And I am here to announce an exciting competition that the *Hamilton Spectator* is sponsoring. Beginning June 15 and ending July 6 we will be counting how many flies you catch each day. And the winner—the boy or girl with the most dead flies—will receive fifty dollars." There were second, third, fourth, and participation prizes, too, ranging from twenty-five dollars down to two.

But that first prize was easily a few weeks of Father's wages back in England. Twenty-five weeks of board with that witch Madame Depieu, only we wouldn't have to live with her anymore! We could rent a furnished house for a month and even more.

"We are not the only city to declare war. Many towns across Canada have already done so, as have cities in Europe and Australia. Cleveland, Ohio, in the United States of America, has successfully vanquished the foe and declared itself a flyless city. In addition to rewarding fly catchers, we are also holding a composition contest. Convince others to kill flies in an essay and you could win one of two prizes of five dollars."

Students cheered less for this proposal. I could understand why! Putting words on paper couldn't be half as satisfying as smashing down the miserable creatures that had caused my family so much grief.

To my left, Fred pounded his fist into his hand. "I'm going to win," he declared, his usual creamy smile stretching across his face.

Why would he even bother? It was clear his family had plenty of money. I looked across at his smug face and recalled his behavior when he had to sit down in the spelling bee. He'd made a stupid mistake and instead of laughing at himself, he had sulked. Such a poor sport. Did he need to win to keep himself above everyone else? How unfortunate for him, because I wasn't going to allow him his victory. Father and I needed those fifty dollars. And it wasn't only about the money for me either. I wanted to kill every last fly to avenge my mother and sister's deaths.

Chapter 5

For the first part of recess, we remained inside the classroom, eating whatever snacks we had brought from home while Mr. Samson visited the staff room. Fred stood up the moment Mr. Samson left the room. Good, I had the desk to myself. I took out the only snack I had, the sandwich Madame Depieu had made me for lunch. Lard on rye. For the second day in a row. She'd complained both times to Father that she wasn't getting paid extra for *le garçon* and she shouldn't be put to this extra expense, never mind that she was charging us double the usual room fee. Nor was I getting paid for helping her with serving supper or clearing dishes. I had to bite my tongue not to tell her where exactly to stuff her sandwich.

But now the salty fat on the heavy bread tasted wonderful and I only wished she'd made me two of them.

Rebecca smiled at me from her seat and nibbled at a cookie. It was a friendly smile that gave me light and hope, almost like Father's grins.

"I'm going to win that fly-swatting contest, Rebecca," Fred boasted loudly, waiting till she looked his way to leap onto his chair and then on top of our desk. He reached up with a rolled notebook to swat one flying near the light on the ceiling. Then he caught the body and dropped it into his pencil case. He raised his arms in the air as if commanding an audience to applaud. Then he stepped down and grinned at her in particular, as though waiting for her to swoon.

"All those germs. Are you going to wash your hands?" Rebecca asked him.

"She's right," I added, disregarding his sudden scowl. "That fly wiped his feet in dung, after all." I wrinkled my nose and winked at Rebecca. She giggled.

I chuckled too. Having a laugh on the well-dressed boy who looked down on me felt grand.

He stared at his fingers, his scowl buckling. The other students stopped to watch what he would do. If he washed his hands, he would be carrying out a girl's orders. He glanced up at Rebecca again, his scowl straightening.

"No need to wash. I'm done eating anyway." Suddenly, he grinned. "But I have this offer..." He held up an orange. "To any of you who promises to bring me one hundred flies tomorrow, I'll give you a piece."

At least three boys jumped from their seats to line up for wedges of the orange.

He turned to me. "What about you, rooming-house boy?"

How had he known? Was it the way I dressed or my sandwich? "I'm not a rooming-house boy."

"You came from Depieu's boarding house. I saw you this morning."

"That's just until our own house is ready." It wasn't entirely a lie. When Father found Uncle Charlie, or Uncle Charlie found us, we would be moving in with him.

But right now Fred's orange looked good. The color of a sunrise, Mum had said last Christmas when Father bought her one. She'd shared it with me and the sweet juice had run down my chin.

If I could bite into one of Fred's bribes, maybe I could taste our last Christmas all over again.

Ginny stepped forward to beg a piece of orange.

Fred sneered at her. "Ginny Malone, you'll never catch a hundred flies by tomorrow. Go away."

She stared hard at Fred for a moment. Then she pulled off an elastic band from one of her braids. Carefully she stretched it across two fingers and pulled at it with a thumb and forefinger. She aimed the band toward the window, where a cluster of flies buzzed lazily. *Whap!* Three dropped from the glass.

I grinned. The rest of the class went silent.

Ginny pulled the band off her other braid and repeated the movement. Another group of flies fell.

"I'll have them for you by the end of recess. Save me a piece of that fruit." She walked closer to the window, curled her hand into a fist, and studied the cluster. Suddenly, her fist snapped out quick as a lizard's tongue.

Nothing buzzed in that corner any longer. Ginny dropped the flies into her own pencil can.

Fred turned to me again. "So, rooming-house boy, what do you say? Going to let a girl beat you at this?"

"No one's going to beat me, I assure you," I answered him. "But why would I give my catch to you? I don't want any food you've plastered your dungy fingers on."

Ginny Malone twisted her head around, interrupting her hunt. She squinted at me. For a freckled girl she could carry quite the mean look. Her lips pulled into a sneer.

Perhaps I'd said the wrong thing. After all, she and three other classmates wanted that orange, touched by fly-germ fingers or not. I hadn't meant to insult them. Wouldn't I have grabbed at a piece myself if I really thought Fred would let me have it?

"Citrus gives me a rash," Rebecca sighed, fluttering a pleated paper at herself like a fan. She winked at me and I assumed she was fibbing to annoy Fred.

"Me too," I squeaked in a girl's voice, happy that at least one person in the class was on my side against the braggart. I fanned myself with my hand and batted my eyelashes.

Rebecca giggled, showing a lovely milky-toothed smile.

Perhaps she would be my only friend in this school—in this whole country even. I smiled back at her.

Later, when no one was watching, I walked to the waste paper basket and took out a piece of Fred's orange peel just to smell it. Ahh! Piney like Christmas. I couldn't help myself. I took a small bite and chewed at the bitter spicy skin.

"Garbage picker," one of Fred's followers cried.

"I need the peels to catch flies," I lied.

"Well, it's mine," Fred exclaimed. He dashed over and snatched it away. "If you want to make any money from this contest, you should sell your catch to me, 'cause you don't stand a chance at winning. Not while I'm entered."

"We'll see about that," I told him, and grinned as broad as Father always did when he wanted everyone to be sure of him.

When Mr. Samson returned, we were sent outside for the rest of recess. Just a few trees grew along the grounds of Central Public. Most of the property lay wide open with plenty of room for a soccer or rugby match. Still, no one really wanted to play any games. The girls and boys all scattered looking for likely fly homes. Two boys fought over the dustbin and knocked it down. Three other boys ran for a steaming manure heap in the street left by the horses drawing the ice wagon.

I would have run after it myself but Rebecca strolled alongside of me under the shade of the trees.

"My father tells me flies are attracted by white surfaces," she told me. "Milk, for example. That's why babies get sick so frequently."

Smart as well as pretty, I thought.

"Just because your father is a doctor doesn't mean you know everything," Ginny growled. *Slam*! She swatted her shoe against a cluster of flies on a nearby fir tree. She peeled them off to collect in her bag.

Rebecca smirked. "Maybe not quite so hard, Ginny."

She glared at Rebecca. Without the elastics, her braids were unraveling like fraying rope.

Suddenly, her hand snatched out into midair.

Rebecca flinched.

Ginny smirked now. Then she uncurled her fist and smiled at the dead thing in her hand. "Rebecca Edwards, with milk or no, you will never catch as many flies as I."

"Oh, but I don't want to. You can have all your dead bugs and Fred Leckie too as far as I'm concerned."

From the skin beneath the fray of her braid right up to her forehead, Ginny flushed a bright red. She fancied Fred, did she? So it was clear, make an enemy of Fred and you made one of Ginny too. Still, I felt sorry for her. Did she think she could ever catch enough flies to make him stop sneering at her?

Chapter 6

At the end of the day Mr. Samson held up a hand as we stood in line to be dismissed. "Ladies and gentlemen, it is only the thirteenth of June. You have two more weeks of school and three weeks to the end of this competition. Pay attention in class and save your fly-killing efforts for after school, better yet for summer vacation. Please file out in an orderly fashion."

The students ahead of me fair flew from the building. They likely had friends to play ball or ramble the park with, whereas I had nothing but this competition. I crossed the street to the Blink Bonnie and headed directly for the stable.

Father was brushing Beauty, the chocolate-colored horse. When she snorted at me, flicking her black tail, flies scattered into the air.

I stared after them, wondering how best to catch them. "Hello, Father."

Father turned to face me. "Hello, Will. What the devil are you looking at?"

I pointed at the deadly pests. "Dr. Roberts told us *they* cause all our diseases."

"Flies?"

I nodded. "There's a fifty-dollar reward for the student who kills the most of them."

"To be sure, that is a lot of money."

We watched as the flies settled back on Beauty's rump. As I stared at those flies, Dr. Roberts' words rang in my head. *Typhoid. Consumption. Summer Complaint. The fly spreads them all, leaving dead babies and adults in its wake.*

Suddenly, I felt a murderous rage the likes of which I'd never felt before. If I'd had a gun, I would have shot the insects right then and there. "Imagine, those stupid flies made Mum and Colleen sick!"

Father came over then and wrapped me in his arms. "Ah, Will, hard as it is for us to accept, perhaps it was just their time."

I broke away from his embrace, shook my head, and bunched my fists. "I mean to make the flies pay!" I shouted. Then I took a deep breath to calm myself. I told him about Ginny Malone swatting the insects with her hair elastics.

He chuckled at that.

"Some of the boys—and Ginny—can catch them with their bare hands. I...I've never been able to do that."

Father raised his eyebrows. "You should always try to use your head over your hands, my boy." He picked up a newspaper from the seat of the carriage, rolled it up and smacked at the wall of the stable. Three flies dropped. "Newspapers are great for expanding your mind...and killing insects."

I reached down to pick them up.

"Go find something to put them in first. Look in the garbage shed outside."

I stepped out of the stable where dark green grass grew. To the left a big stone church bordered the property. Walking 'round the back, I saw yet another small wooden building that might have been a shed for Mr. Moodie but a home for others, certainly for the flies. I heard the buzzing before I even unlatched the door. Another good spot to kill flies. A group of them continually circled and landed on top of a smelly trash bin. I spotted a large brown-and-yellow container at the top of the pile marked *Magic Baking Powder*. That was a great name. In my mind I turned it into *Magic Fly-Killing Powder*. It would be my lucky container. I picked it up and removed the top. Then, quick as Ginny did, I squished a fly with the lid, scraping the body off into the tin.

"That will teach you to kill babies."

The insect looked like a raisin with wings, not very deadly at all. I trapped a few more with the lid, then flipped them into my hand and squeezed them dead. "That is for baby Colleen." Five flies dead already. Fred Leckie had a promise of four hundred flies just in payment for the orange slices he gave out today. Of course, these five in the can wouldn't be enough to win, but according to Dr. Roberts each one of them might have laid five hundred eggs within the next three or four days. I tried to picture the five hundred flies and ended up shaking my head to get rid of the thought.

I headed back into the stable and picked up the flies Father had felled.

"Do you need to have killed them yourself?" Father asked.

"The prize for the most flies is fifty dollars and another boy is hiring everyone in class to kill flies for him."

"Never you mind what the other children do. There are plenty of flies in here for you to kill all by yourself."

As he watched, I dropped his flies into the dust bin in the corner.

"I will give you my weapon though." Father handed me the rolled-up newspaper.

As I swatted, Father mucked out the stalls, shoveling manure into a large barrel. "They like to lay their eggs in the dung," Father explained. "As long as we clean up the manure within the week, we kill a lot of the maggots."

One horse snorted when I smacked the newspaper roll against his stall door.

"You gave old Blue a start there, Will. Can you swat more gently?"

I tried. It was easier to get a less-squeezed body into the can anyway. The *Magic Baking Powder* container was almost full when Father said we needed to go. If I had counted right, there were 385 flies in there.

We washed up under the pump and headed back to the witch's house again. This time we climbed the stairs in our sock feet, carrying our shoes so there could be no complaint.

"*Vite, vite*. It is time for supper," she scolded, "and you did not help today!"

The beefy smell of stew made my mouth water. She rushed us to the dining room where the other eight boarders already sat. They shoveled their food in quickly, grunting, and stopping only occasionally to drink.

Madame Depieu banged a bowl of stew in front of me. Just as she had yesterday, she twisted my hands around to check them. "*Pas mal*. That is good. I run a very clean house and I like my boarders to be clean too."

Father gave me a wink and a shrug. I knew we had nowhere else to go so I just ate. What little meat I found was stringy. There were far more potatoes and carrots than anything else. When I spooned up the last potato I saw a large chunk of pepper in the bottom of the bowl. At least I hoped it was a chunk of pepper. But when I nudged the black speck I saw that it had wings.

Chapter 7

I swallowed hard. Madame Depieu claimed to run a clean house. But there, bent legs in the air, lay the proof otherwise. Had I already eaten flies that I hadn't noticed? If so, would I get a fever like Baby Maureen on the ship? Even if I hadn't eaten any, surely the dead one stuck in the gravy had flailed around, spreading deadly germs with his hairy legs. I sighed. If I was going to get sick and die, I wanted to leave this earth victorious, beating Fred Leckie out of a winning spot in the competition. I carefully picked the fly from the bowl. Maybe I hadn't killed this one on my own, but I would keep it anyway. It would make 386 flies in my *Magic Baking Powder* can.

I couldn't help staring at the bowl and the streaks of brown gravy clinging to it. Ordinarily I might take a slice of bread, soak up that gravy, and eat it. But today, instead, I wondered just how attractive this stew might be as a fly trap.

I stood up as Madame Depieu started clearing the table.

I began taking the dishes into the kitchen, keeping my dish to the side. Finally, I grabbed the dustbin.

"*Mais*, what are you doing?" she asked.

"Taking out the trash."

"Very well. Put it in the alleyway in the back."

Carefully, when Madame wasn't looking, I grabbed my bowl with its thick puddle of gravy. It was awkward, carrying both the bag of garbage and my fly trap to the heap of trash in the lane. After setting down the garbage, I found an out-of-the way place to put the bowl. Immediately, a thick black fly flew toward it, landed, and began floundering. Its legs twitched. I could have almost felt sorry for it, but for my mother and sister. Instead, I smiled. Three hundred eighty-seven.

"Will! Good news! I found your uncle's address in my suitcase," Father called from the back door. "Come along. We'll try to find him!"

I ran to join him and we headed out the front.

"If we find him tonight, who knows? Maybe we can stay with him and not have to deal with the good madame." Father held a map. "One of the men drew this for me. See here. We need to travel north for three blocks and then west to this park."

We walked past my school and then turned north. The houses here were fine, two stories, and red brick. One day we would own one just like these. Perhaps my fly winnings could act as a down payment. We passed a grocery store and then Father pointed. "Look, there's the fire station."

I watched, hoping for an alarm so I could see the fire brigade in action. I stepped into the road.

"Watch out!" Father's arm flung me back, away from the corner. A gleaming black motor carriage turned in front of us. To the right, two horses pulled the trash wagon, slowly, *clip-clop*. They hadn't immediately noticed the motor car either. Suddenly, one horse rose up on his hind legs, the whites of his eyes showing. Terrified, he whinnied. The carriage shimmied back and forth, looking as though it would tip.

The man driving the carriage raised his whip. He looked as frightened as the horse.

"Easy boy." Father stepped into the street and grabbed the reins under the horse's throat. "Steady there," he said, his voice soothing the horse enough that it allowed its hooves to touch the cobblestones again. He patted the animal's neck. "There, there." He stroked the other one. "You are both fine. You may not like those motorcars, but you have to get used to them. " He dropped the reins again and then stepped back.

The driver of the wagon thanked him and Father tipped his hat. "My pleasure."

"Do you think cars will replace horses?" I asked as we crossed the larger main street and continued along.

Father shrugged his shoulders. "That would certainly make a cleaner city. Sweeter air too. But I would miss them."

We passed a garage and carriage company, a tire firm, an umbrella store, and a jewelry shop. Just like London this city, only less crowded. Past a hair dressing salon, a tailor, a laundry, and furniture store. We walked by A. H. Dodsworth Funeral Emporium. Even in Canada people fell ill and died.

We continued walking, passing several beautiful buildings as we made our way.

"Banks," Father answered the unspoken question. "So many of them, and so grand!"

"Look there!" I pointed ahead toward a statue mounted high over an island of parkway in the middle of the busy street.

"That's Gore Park," Father read from his map. "Not far now." We crossed to the white concrete walkway that wound around the statue and I stopped at its base to stare upward. Queen Victoria, complete with crown and scepter. *Queen and Empress, a model wife and mother*, the plaque beneath her read. Mum had been far more beautiful. I tried to replace Queen Victoria's face with hers but I couldn't do it. I didn't remember Mum's well enough.

"Will?"

I dropped my eyes and saw the flowerbeds of pink and white blossoms. "It's all so beautiful." Farther ahead, a huge fountain spilled water up and out of a two-tiered stone urn. "Can we walk through there?"

"Only halfway. That street over there should be Charlie's." We continued beneath the trees, a soft spray from the fountain cooling us. Along the right side of the park, street cars jangled by. Along the left, motor cars rumbled and horses clip-clopped as they drew their carriages. A few queued up close to the edge of the park. A black one whinnied and stomped his front hooves.

I stopped to admire him and then turned again.

Up ahead I saw Mum walking with a little girl at her side, one hand draped at the back of her shoulder. She used to put her hand, just like that, on my back! I squinted at the little girl, perhaps three years old. Yes, that is how old Colleen should be now. There must have been some mistake. They were not dead at all! I felt like I might float away. Here they were, alive and well in this new country, this new wonderful park! Hadn't Father said she would be waiting for us in the new country?

Then the mother and daughter came closer and I saw, of course, that she wasn't Mum at all. Still, the way she held the little girl was so like Mum. I gritted my teeth for wanting someone to hold me that way right then and there.

"Come along, Will. Why are you dragging your feet?"

"That woman...," I tried to explain.

Father turned his head. "She wears her hair the same way as your mother, and her gait is similar, isn't it?"

I squeezed my eyes closed so that nothing could spill from them and nodded.

"I see her everywhere too, lad. Mr. McNiven told me that it was perfectly normal. As time goes by we will see her less and less."

I shook my head. I was already having trouble calling up Mum's face. Mr. McNiven might be right, but it didn't give me any comfort to know she would fade from my memory.

"We can only hope that in a while it will not pain us so much." Father squeezed my shoulder and we kept walking. I leaned into his hand, grateful for the comfort of his touch. "Just think, we'll be seeing your Uncle Charlie soon!"

The thought brought a smile. To see even one familiar face would make things a lot better. I hurried alongside of Father.

We made our way past a few stores and another fire station, down three more blocks and then, finally: "Over here. Number 192. This is where he lives! Come on, Will!" Even after the long walk, Father sprinted up the stairs and knocked on the door.

It was a fine new gray building. Even if it meant a longer walk to school, I could hardly wait to move here. No Madame Depieu to deal with, and Fred Leckie could no longer make fun of where I lived.

The door opened and a very tall woman frowned at us. "What do you want?"

"My brother, Charles Alton, resides here." Father stepped forward so that she could see him better. "We have come all the way from England to visit him. Can you tell him we have arrived? There was apparently a mix up in the dates of our arrival."

The woman frowned and shook her head. "Charles Alton. No. No one by that name lives here."

"What? But see here, this letter..." Father took a folded piece of paper from his pocket.

She raised an eyebrow as she looked at Uncle Charlie's letter. "I am not certain why he would use this address on his post to you unless he was hiding the true circumstances of his life here."

"But why would he do such a thing?" Father asked.

She shrugged her shoulders. "Perhaps he is in jail for drunken behavior. You Irish and your spirits."

"Neither my brother nor I drink," Father told her.

The tall lady smiled as though she were reassuring a child. "Well, sir. I surely do not know where your brother is. Good day." She tried to close the door.

Father threw his foot in its path. "He was a big man, red hair. You cannot have forgotten him."

"Sir, kindly remove your foot or I shall call the police."

"Please." Father took a deep breath and lowered his voice. "If a man by that description should come here, can you tell him I work at the Blink Bonnie?"

She gave him a cold stare until he pulled his leg back. Then she slammed the door.

Father continued to stare at the closed door, his face turning as gray as a tombstone. He took a deep breath but did not muster a smile. Finally, he shook his fist at it. "Liar!" he gasped.

We were done for if even he couldn't make light of this.

My heart fell. There was nothing left for us here. What would we do now? Was Charlie's yet another face I would never see again? My stomach squeezed together till I could feel my supper back up into my throat. Father continued to stare at the closed door. Suddenly, I knew I would be sick. I ran down the stairs and threw up into the grass.

My father came after me. "It will be all right, Will," he said, gentle as though he were soothing a horse. I felt his hand rubbing my back. "You are going to school. I have a position. We can find a better place to live. If we are careful with our money, we can buy a place of our own."

I straightened. "But what happened to Uncle Charlie?"

"I don't know." Father frowned and shook his head. "But there has to be an explanation for his disappearance. And I won't rest till I find it."

Chapter 8

Walking back, we passed the same establishments as before, only Father chattered about them as though he could charm something wonderful out of this terrible turn of events. I went along with it, same as I always did, hoping against hope he was right.

"A. M. Souter and Co." Father read the name of the furniture store with a forced brightness. "Do you know—the owner had an article in the paper that would interest you. He suggested a rather ingenious method for catching flies."

I no longer had to pretend interest. "What method?"

"He claimed that he used a vacuum cleaner and that the suction power attracted the insects."

"Do you suppose Madame Depieu owns a vacuum cleaner?"

"I know you will think of a way to find out." Father winked.

Turning south again toward the rooming house, I spotted a small black-and-white dog sniffing around a trash pile.

Suddenly, the dog leaped up and snapped at the air. What was he doing, I wondered.

The dog landed again, jaws shut around something.

"Finnigan, give!" a girl's voice commanded.

The animal ran back down the street. I watched him meet up with a young girl wearing a gray dress that drooped at the back of her knees. One of her boots opened into a flap at the toes. Near this boot, the dog spat something on the ground, wagging his tail.

I noticed sloppy braids hanging from the girl's faded bonnet. She bent down and picked up something tiny. I sighed. Trust Ginny Malone to have a dog trained to catch flies for her. The dog didn't care about the torn boot or drooping old dress. It just gazed up at Ginny with admiration and loyalty.

"It must be ever so nice to have a dog," I called to her.

She turned toward me and gave me her stare. The one that made her eyes squint and her nose wrinkle, a stare that was far too hard for those friendly-looking golden freckles.

"School mate?" Father asked.

I nodded.

"She's a tough one."

I shrugged and we walked on.

Back at the rooming house, I ran through the hall, calling Madame Depieu.

"*Trop de bruit*. Quiet, quiet!" she came out of the salon.

"What is it that you wish?"

"To help you clean, of course. My father and I have returned. Can I vacuum your halls?"

"*Eh bien.* I do not spend the money on the fancy gimmicks. But I do have the mop and a bucket. And you can wash my kitchen floor."

It was worth the try, I thought as I swished the wooly gray mop along the tiled floor. When I spotted a group of flies swirling near a corner, I swung the mop, splat, and caught another two.

"*Mais, qu'est-ce que tu fais?*" Madame Depieu came running as I collected their bodies.

"I am just ridding your kitchen of these disease-carrying bugs!" I told her.

She squinted at me, one hand on her hip.

"We learned it in school. They walk in horse patties and then they walk in our stew."

"*Voyons.* See that you kill these flies with less noise and"— she pointed at the suds splattered against the wall—"less mess."

"Yes, Madame." Meanwhile I counted in my head as I put the flies in my pocket: 388, 389.

Next morning I tiptoed out the back door to look in on my stewy fly trap near the trash. I scooped out thirty-one winged terrors, and found an empty Ovaltine jar in which to store this latest catch. Four hundred and nineteen, I thought to myself, smiling. In my mind I pictured the spotted dog Finnigan leaping up and snapping at the air. A fly-catching dog! How far behind would I fall if Ginny Malone gave all the insects both she and her amazing animal caught to Fred Leckie?

Thinking I would catch some more with my bare hands, I scrambled up the fence at the back of the trash pile to reach one.

"What are you doing?" Shrill and close, Madame Depieu's voice startled me.

I stumbled into the mess, all the trash clattering down around me.

Madame yelled now. "This is what I get. I say no to the children, especially no to the boys, and you say to me you will clean. I give you chances after chances, *et regarde*, what do you give me, *un autre grand* mess!" Her hands flapped as she gestured at the toppled garbage. "And you steal my good plate. Always you Irish give me the trouble."

"We do not steal," Father came from behind her now.

I picked up the dish and stood up. I held out the empty fly trap to her. Much as I disliked Madame Depieu, I had to think quickly so that Father and I would not be tossed out onto the street. "I am so sorry. I remembered this morning that I had seen a dish of yours in the garbage. Maybe when you scraped the bowls, you accidentally dropped one?"

Madame Depieu's mouth dropped.

"So I rushed to retrieve it as I had seen the trash wagon and feared for your dish."

"You better clean up again before you head off for school," Father said.

"Certainly, Father. Let me just put all this garbage in order."

Madame Depieu's mouth still gaped. I had a feeling that if she came to her senses before I scooped the trash back into the square bin she would throw Father and me out, so I worked quickly. Then I went to the pump inside the kitchen and washed up. I collected my lunch from inside and carried off my jar of flies.

"You're not stealing my Ovaltine. Isn't it enough your father insists I make you lunch?" Madame Depieu said when she saw me leaving.

"It's just an empty jar, Madame," I answered.

She caught my hand and pulled it up to her eyes so she could look in the jar herself. "*Des mouches!*" she exclaimed and made a sour face.

"Yes, yes. I found them all in your stew. See you after school!" I ran out the door before she could say anything further.

Many children were already heading toward Central Public. I spotted Ginny holding the hands of a small girl and boy.

The girl sported the same loose braids as Ginny, and the boy's knees, poking out from beneath his pants, were dirty.

I frowned. What it must be like to have a sister and a brother. I wanted to call out for her to wait, but I remembered her scowl. Instead, I hung back a bit and walked a suitable distance behind them.

In the classroom I stored my jar of flies—421 of them now—along with my hat and lunch in the only wooden slot at the back of the room with no name on it. I frowned as I placed the jar on the shelf. Fred Leckie's slot was adjacent and even the sight of his name soured the morning for me.

After we sang "God Save the King," recited the Lord's Prayer, and read the scripture for the day, we watched and listened as Mr. Samson cleared his throat and addressed us. "I think it admirable the enthusiasm with which this class has undertaken to rid the city of Hamilton of flies." He looked around. "And I know I said you should confine your activities to outside the classroom. But we do seem to have plenty of the menaces flying around here. I think we can organize a civilized attack on them in the classroom. Do you agree?"

Our voices answered as one: "Yes, Mr. Samson."

"So...to that end, I want you to raise your hands if you intend to participate in the competition." All hands shot up except Rebecca's. "Good, that makes forty-eight students and we have twelve days left of school. Miss Edwards..."

"Yes, Mr. Samson."

"You will make a chart assigning four students a day to fly-catching duties. We will have two morning fly killers, who will kill all the flies in the classroom before the others arrive... and we will have two lunchtime catchers. How many catchers does that make...Ginny?"

Ginny chewed at the end of a braid. "Forty-eight."

"Correct. So, Miss Edwards, please make the chart. How long will it take for all of these students to have a turn, Master Leckie?"

"Till the end of school, sir."

"Correct."

Fred gave me his smug smile.

"During the balance of class time, no other students will move to catch any insects. Is that clear?"

Again the group answered as one: "Yes, Mr. Samson."

Fred raised his hand.

"Yes, Master Leckie?"

"I would like to give my time slot to Ginny Malone." By now Fred must have recognized Ginny's superior fly-catching skills.

Ginny smiled, something I had never seen her do before, and it opened her face like a flower. Ginny might look sloppy with her loose braids and worn clothing, but her eyes had a golden fire when she was happy. And at this moment, that golden fire lighted on Fred.

I felt sorry for her. You couldn't help whom you liked.

"Admirable of you to be so generous with your fly-catching time slot, Master Leckie." Mr. Samson raised one shaggy black eyebrow at Fred. "But everyone participating will take their own turn."

"Yes, Mr. Samson."

"While Rebecca prepares our chart, the rest of you will turn to page fifty-three in your arithmetic book. You will copy out problems one to seventeen and solve them."

Desk drawers opened, papers shuffled, pages flipped. Finally there was a quiet scratching of pencil tips against paper.

I was calculating sums when I heard Rebecca's voice.

"Sir, I have the chart prepared."

"Excellent. Which two students should be up catching these deadly insects today?" Mr. Samson asked.

"William Alton and Henry Best, sir."

It made sense, Alton and Best, *a* and *b* being the first two letters of the alphabet. Still, every head seemed to turn to look at me. Fred Leckie's glare carried a warning.

"William and Henry, since you missed the opportunity to catch flies this morning before everyone arrived, would you care to take your turns now?" Mr. Samson asked.

I knew I couldn't say no, but I wanted to. I didn't need everyone watching me. Why did no one enjoy spying on Henry? I looked around for a fly-swatting tool of some sort.

No newspaper anywhere. What would Mr. Samson say if I used my notebook? I frowned. He wouldn't like fly-smeared sums. Instead, I picked up the wooden ruler from the ledge of the chalkboard and headed for the window. *Slap*! I missed the fly buzzing there. *Slap, slap*, I missed two more times.

Fred Leckie snickered.

I flung down the ruler and swatted with my hand. Missed again. The tiny menace dove for me, buzzing just beneath my nose. I sneezed twice.

My sneeze splatted the fly against the glass.

The whole class laughed now.

I felt my face growing red, but I snatched up the body anyway.

"William," Mr. Samson called. "Henry."

"Yes sir," we answered together.

"I have reconsidered. You will take your turn at recess instead, please."

"Yes, sir." I sat down, happy to stop flailing for an audience. Between now and recess I wouldn't get any better at fly catching, but at least fewer people would be around watching and laughing.

Fred snickered. Henry smirked too.

I sat at our desk and turned slightly, smiling back at Fred as if I didn't have a care. Let him think I was no match for him in this competition. If he let his guard down, it would only help me.

At recess, Fred again offered up his orange in exchange for flies.

I inhaled the smell but swallowed the longing.

"I have two hundred flies here for you," Ginny said.

"But I only have one piece left," Fred told her.

"You can owe me the rest then." Ginny blushed and looked at her shoes as she placed her can of flies on Fred's desk.

If only she had glanced up for a moment, she would have seen Fred's lip curling. He sneered at her messy hair and holey boots. I had heard him make fun of them when Ginny was out of earshot. Fred gave her the orange segment without another word and Ginny smiled as though she carried away a piece of the universe.

Just then a fly landed on Fred's desk. "Rooming-house boy! Here! Kill it! Go ahead!"

This time I looked in the wastepaper basket for a weapon. Nothing there to roll up. I walked over to the desk, willing the fly to go somewhere else before I got there, but it didn't. I stopped and stared at it. Then fast as a whip I snatched at the bug. Faster still, it flew up ahead of my hand.

"See there. He cannot catch a single fly!" Fred held himself around his middle he was laughing so hard.

"Neither can you," I said. I couldn't stop myself. "But at least I am not a cheater. All the flies I do catch are on my own."

I turned and walked away without looking back. I didn't want to see his face or anyone else's.

Chapter 9

I caught another twenty flies and stowed them in my Ovaltine jar, giving it a jiggle. Four hundred and forty-one—not a bad number considering how bad I was at catching them with my bare hands. Also considering I couldn't hire helpers. I scrubbed my hands in the boys' room and finally headed outside onto the schoolyard.

What I saw made me wish recess was over. There, strolling together as if they were meant for each other, were Fred Leckie and Rebecca Edwards. I swallowed a hard lump of disappointment. What could she possibly see in him? She was far too sweet and smart to be spending her time with such a mean boy just because he dressed well. I'd thought maybe she and I would be friends. Now I wasn't so sure... Certainly no one else paid me any attention. All the other students were busy catching flies as usual except—I looked over the yard a second time—where was Ginny Malone?

At that moment a fly buzzed by and I followed it with my

eyes. Up and up into a tree—there I noticed a leg hanging over a branch, the foot of which wore a telltale flapping boot.

"Why aren't you out there catching more flies?" I asked Ginny Malone.

"Come up here if you want to talk to me," she grumbled back.

It was the usual sneering tone she used on me, but I thought I heard something more forlorn in it. I looked up into the tree and wondered if I felt like climbing, only to be spoken to like that. But what else did I have to do? I had no other friends besides Rebecca and if she preferred Fred to me, I didn't want the others to see me moping about. So I caught a branch and swung myself up, scrambling to a spot next to her. "You're so good at killing the creatures. You should enter the contest yourself instead of giving all your flies to Fred."

"My brother and sister never tasted orange before. I want them each to have a piece."

"And you think Fred will pay you." I shook my head.

Ginny shrugged her shoulders then stared at Fred as he walked with Rebecca.

"It doesn't matter. People like us never win."

Certainly, all the illness and bad luck that followed our family made Ginny's words seem right. But hadn't we come to this new country for better opportunity? Sure, wasn't anything possible in Canada? "I'm going to win," I told her. I watched

Rebecca too. She didn't seem unhappy to be walking with Fred. "What do you even see in him?"

"Ha! I could ask the same of you over Rebecca. Look at him! Hair freshly combed and slicked back, clean new clothes, never mended. Why, his shirt doesn't show a mark on it and it's white." She sighed. "Someone with a life like that. . .if I could get him to like me back it would make me feel. . .richer." She looked at me directly now. "Tell me you don't feel the same way about her."

It was true that I liked Rebecca's long golden hair and the large ribbons, like blossoms, that secured it. Her hands were dainty and pale with pink nails that had milky half moons. I liked that she didn't rush about trying to kill flies, but mostly I enjoyed the fact that unlike all of his "paid" friends, she stood up to Fred—or had till now. I changed the topic of conversation. "You have a great dog. How did you teach him to catch flies?"

"Finnigan? He comes by it naturally." Ginny smiled a little then. "When we found Finn my pa said he was not going to be able to feed another mouth. So Finn catches mice and squirrels and flies when pickings are slim. He offers me his other catches too. Of late, I have just asked him for his flies."

"Hmph. I would never starve my dog for the likes of Fred Leckie!" I told her.

"If he wins the contest, he said he would bring me a whole orange. Besides, Finnigan doesn't starve. I give him some of my supper."

"You could probably buy at least a dozen oranges with the prize money if you went for it yourself."

"Fred's father brings citrus in all the way from California. Besides, I told you. I can never win. Neither can you. Fred, with all his money, will always find a way to beat us."

I shook my head. "Not this time." I knew I would have to think of a way to catch vast quantities of flies if I wanted to overtake Fred. But I would work at it and I would win.

I looked at Ginny for a moment. When she smiled, she was just as pretty as Rebecca, but with dark hair and golden eyes. And with those freckles, she was perhaps more interesting. "Tell me something," I said after a while. "How can you catch flies with your bare hands?"

Mr. Samson stepped out the door into the schoolyard just then, shaking a bell to signal the end of recess. Ginny looked like she was going to ignore the question as she slid off the side of the branch and then jumped to the ground. I jumped too but it was a harder landing. I rubbed my backside and heard the familiar sound of Fred's donkey laughter.

Ginny's voice cut through. "Wait till the fly lands."

"What? But you snatch them from midair."

"That will take some practice. For now, approach the fly from the back. And only after it lands. Shoot your hand out above it. Then, when it flies up, you will have it."

"Thank you, Ginny."

Someone beside me snickered and made kissing noises, but I ignored the idiot. Instead, I spotted a fly on a tree trunk and tried out Ginny's advice. It worked! Inside my fist I held one of the creatures. I rushed to my cubby in the cloakroom to add it to the collection but when I reached in, I found only my hat.

I looked on the floor in case it had fallen out. Nothing. Not in the cubby to the left, or to the right either. I was sure I had stuffed it in with my hat. I looked in again. Still nothing. My jaw dropped. Someone must have taken my jar.

"What's the matter with you, rooming-house boy?" The tone in Fred's voice taunted. As he stowed his cap in the slot right next to mine, he raised an eyebrow and smiled.

"You know full well!" I said, giving him a shove. "You stole my jar of flies."

Fred shoved me back harder. "Why would I need to, Irish scum? There are plenty of others around to do my bidding!"

Irish scum. The words made lightning crack inside my head. In a flash I saw Mum's face on the day the undertaker came for Colleen. She couldn't give her up, not even to Mrs. Gale. I had to take Colleen away from her. Then Mrs. Gale dressed her. The man hadn't called us scum as he gazed at our pale, thin baby girl. Perhaps he had even meant to be kind. "Ah, you Irish. You'll have another one soon enough, even if you can't afford to feed it."

In the next instant my fists flew at Fred, knucklebones against cheekbone, hard against hard. Fred fell backwards and

I leaped on top, continuing to throw punches at his head. Fist against hard chin, then fleshy nose.

Suddenly, somebody hauled me up by the collar. Mr. Samson. "That will be enough, William Alton. You will report to Mr. Morton immediately."

On my feet again, it took me a few moments to slow my breathing down. Poor or not, my family was *not* scum. I felt the heat drain from my face and saw, now, the blood running from Fred's nose. Irish scum! I did not feel sorry. I felt satisfied.

But, as I walked the hall toward the office, the satisfaction drained away. What had I done? What if Mr. Morton expelled me? I wanted to run out the door instead of facing the principal. I hesitated near the office. It was close to lunchtime. Could I get away with leaving? Would Father find out?

I pushed through the door leading into the main office. The secretary there looked very busy. Good. If she ignored me until the noon bell, I could say I went to the office but no one attended to me.

Mr. Morton stepped into the hall to ring the lunch bell. I thought I could safely leave now and turned to make my way out. A hand suddenly gripped my shoulder.

"So, you were in a fight, William Alton," a deep voice said from behind me. "Step this way and we will discuss the matter further."

I had no choice but to follow Mr. Morton into his office.

"Take a seat, young man."

I squeezed around the small chair in front of the principal's desk, lowering myself into it with as little movement as possible.

Mr. Morton sat down, pushing his chair hard toward the desk. He folded his long fingers in front of him as he stared at me with gray horse-eyes. He didn't look especially angry, more like he was measuring me in some way. "Your third day here and already you scrap with another lad." Mr. Morton shook his head. "So. . . tell me exactly what provoked this attack. I hear that Fred Leckie did not raise his fists once."

I thought about staying quiet. No one liked a tattletale. But then, at this new school no one liked me at all. Even Rebecca preferred strolling with Fred. So I spoke up instead. "Fred stole my jar of flies."

"Ah, the fly-catching competition." Mr. Morton frowned as he continued to watch me. No hurried moves about him. He ran one hand through his mane of hair and sighed. "Mr. Leckie can be a troublesome chap, I will be the first to agree. But looking at him and then at you, do you really think he has any need to steal from your likes?"

I wondered at that for a moment. Fred wanted victory in this competition and if stealing assured him of the win, he would surely steal. But did Fred actually feel as though I was any kind of competition? Likely not. But then who else could it have been? "He called me Irish scum."

"But you are originally from Ireland, are you not? You came here from London, but you are Irish. Half the school is. Do you believe you are 'scum'?"

"No sir! That's why I fought him."

"But if you don't believe you are the film on top of a pond, you needn't have used your fists. If someone called me an elephant I would look askance on him, but I wouldn't feel the need to hit him. Why, it might justify his claim."

But we're poor, I thought. *My clothes are old. We live in a rooming house. Mum and Colleen might have lived if we weren't surrounded by filth and flies.* I couldn't smash being poor with my hands. Or disease. I couldn't wrestle the power of money from Fred Leckie's hands. But I could knock the smug smile from his face. Would Mr. Morton strap me now? Whatever the punishment, it had still been worth it.

"If I have my facts straight, you accused Mr. Leckie of being a thief and he, in turn, called you a name. The fact that he insulted your heritage is of some matter, but it is not of enough substance to excuse you of pounding at the young man's face.

"You will therefore sit down at the desk in the hall and write out a letter of apology to Mr. Leckie. Before you return to your classroom this afternoon, you will present this letter to Mr. Leckie, along with a copy to me."

Never, I thought. No matter what Father or anyone else did to me, I would never apologize to Fred Leckie.

Chapter 10

"Here is a sheet of paper, a pen, and an ink jar. Get to it, William," Mr. Morton said to dismiss me.

I stood up, but didn't say a word. I reached for the pen but then dropped my hand and fled the office. I walked straight out and across the street toward the rooming house. I knew I couldn't face Father at that moment. The other students had long made their way home for lunch by now—the streets were clear, although coming from the laneway in back of the rooming house, Ginny Malone wandered with her dog. I didn't feel like speaking with her either. Instead, I headed up the steps.

When I made it to the top of the creaking, peeling staircase, I needed to blink my eyes several times. Was I seeing things? There on the landing sat Father's black suitcase, and next to it my banged up smaller brown one. Had Father come and packed? Perhaps he had found Uncle Charlie. I dared to hope until I opened the door.

"You are home, good!" Madame Depieu snapped at me. "The week your father has paid for is almost up. I wish you to leave."

"Why?" I asked. My hands started to sweat.

"I run a clean house. I told you I don't like dirty boys. Then what do I find but another jar full of the disgusting *mouches*."

I tried to understand what she was saying. Where would we go? "You are putting us out on the street?"

Madame Depieu's voice rose a pitch. She wagged a finger in my face. "I gave you the chance. But again and again you bring noise and filth into my house. Tomorrow when the train comes in, I will have the opportunity for more respectable guests. I need to clean for them."

"Where did you put my flies?"

"What do you mean, where did I put your flies? *Elles sont sales.* They do not belong in my house. I throw the can in the trash."

"But they were my property! I could win lots of money with them."

"Va-t'en!" she screamed at me. "Get out of my sight!"

I picked up our two suitcases and climbed down the flight of steps. I left both for a moment and ran around the back to collect my magic fly-catching can.

The trash was still piled high in the shed, but I saw no trace of the yellow jar. I started to remove garbage bit by bit, frantic to get back the collection of 389 flies I had worked so hard to catch. Then I stopped. Madame Depieu would have thrown it out today after breakfast sometime. I shouldn't have to burrow to the bottom. If the container was not at the top, it simply was no longer there.

I walked to the front again, picked up my suitcase and Father's, and headed for the Blink Bonnie. It was hot, heavy work, and I needed to stop every few moments. We had nowhere to live! I was stunned. Father would expect to have supper in another few hours, but Madame Depieu would not serve it to us—all because of me.

I walked a little farther up the hill. Even though it was bad news I was bringing him, he needed to know quickly so we could find another place to live.

"Father!" I called as I drew near the stable at the back. Instead, a plump short woman with a white bonnet peeked out the back door.

"Here now, stop your yellin'. Your father is working in the big house right now. Step in and you can have tea with him."

Back at school, lunch hour would be over by now. I was late anyway so I followed the woman down the stairs to the kitchen. I'd never seen so many cupboards, or pots dangling from the cupboards, in my life.

"Sit," the woman told me, pointing to a chair at a large wooden table. She brought a teapot, three teacups, a plate of scones, and some preserves to the table and then sat down herself.

"Milk and sugar?" she asked.

"Yes, please."

"Help yerself." She pushed the plate of scones toward me.

I couldn't believe my good fortune! I reached for one and smiled as my hand touched the firm floury edge; it was still warm. "Might I have some jam?" I asked.

"I told ye to help yerself."

I grabbed for the preserves before she could change her mind, spread the red berries on the scone, and bit in. I was starving, and the biscuit made me forget my troubles.

Till Father joined us. "School is over early today?"

I should have told him I had skipped out during lunch but he gave me no chance.

"I see you have met Mrs. Swanson, our cook. Mrs. Swanson, this is my son, William."

"Father, Madame Depieu kicked us out this afternoon because she found my container of flies under our bed."

Mrs. Swanson sputtered out some biscuit.

"What? You kept the flies under our bed?"

"Three hundred and eighty-nine of them. For the contest. But they are all gone because Madame threw them out. I checked the trash, but the container isn't there either."

"Finish your tea, Will. We need to get back to the stable."

Father gave me a sharp look, as though I wasn't to discuss the matter in front of Mrs. Swanson.

I savored my last bit of scone, wondering what my chances for a second were. Mrs. Swanson began clearing the table. No chance. I frowned.

Then suddenly she turned and handed me one. "For the road."

"Thank you, ma'am."

Just as Father stood up from the table, a loud mechanical roar started up. I jumped.

"That will be Ellie with the vacuum cleaner," Mrs. Swanson explained. "Mr. Moodie enjoys every new contraption there is out there. He has that new bicycle and a motorcar. Of course, he has his maids use the vacuum cleaner."

"I wonder how it works," I said, thinking about how Souter advertised the machine as a good fly catcher.

"You can ask Ellie to show you Saturday," Father suggested. "Come along now." I followed him up the stairs and out the door, through the back yard to the stable.

"I am sorry the witch found my flies, Da. Where are we going to sleep now? Any word from Uncle Charlie?"

"Yes."

"But that's wonderful! Can we move in with him tonight?"

"No. Unfortunately your Uncle Charlie is in St. Joseph's Hospital under quarantine for typhoid."

"But how did you find out?"

"I told Mrs. Swanson the story of that strange woman who denied that Charlie lived at her establishment and she explained to me how the same thing had happened to a friend of hers. She had gone to visit a sister, but the landlady at the rooming house claimed to have no knowledge of her. Her sister was in the hospital. None of them want to lose business over a boarder's disease."

"So you visited him at the hospital?"

"Actually, I walked over to the City Health Department, where they gave me a list of quarantined patients. Charles Alton was on the list."

"Is it bad, Father?" I swallowed hard. My lucky red-headed uncle, always ready for an adventure. How could he fall ill? "Will he die?"

"It's not like typhus, but it's bad. His fever can go high and he'll be laid up a month at least." Father winced as he shrugged his shoulders. It took him a few moments to form words. "I have heard that some people survive."

Up to now, our family had not had a good record with surviving illness. "What are we going to do?" I stared down at my feet and noticed that my shoe was beginning to split, just like Ginny's boot.

"We will pray for him, of course. As for ourselves, tonight we'll just bunk down in the stable. You can take the seat of the carriage, if you find that comfortable, and I will spread out on the floor."

Just then a fly landed on Father's arm. Without saying a word, I snatched just above it with my fist. I got it! It was a new start. One fly. Somehow, I would think of something to ensure that Fred Leckie would not win. For my family I would destroy the disease-carrying monsters. And if I could win the fly-killing competition, perhaps my Uncle Charlie could win his competition with typhoid.

Chapter II

The next morning I awoke with a stiff neck and cramped legs, wondering where I was. Then I heard the familiar snort of the horses and smelled their strong earthy scent. I heard my father's voice. "There you go Blue, enjoy your oats." For a moment I felt safe and warm.

Then another thought pricked at my conscience. The letter of apology for Fred! Because of our eviction from Madame Depieu's rooming house and the bad news about Uncle Charlie, the fight with Fred had slipped to the back of my mind. *Irish scum.* How could anyone expect me to apologize to someone who had called me that?

Right then and there, I knew what I had to do. I would not return to school. Instead, I would go door to door to the shops and factories close by and catch flies. If I spent the day working at it, surely I would have a chance at overtaking Fred.

I washed myself as best as I could under the pump and Father got us some tea and a scone from the manor for breakfast.

Then, just as usual, I left for school. I followed the same pathway as I had for the past two days, crossing between Blink Bonnie and Central Public.

When I arrived in the schoolyard, I intended to march straight on to the park with the marvelous fountain, where I thought I had seen Mum and Colleen. Only someone tapped my shoulder.

I turned. It was Rebecca Edwards. She wore a blue dress and matching bonnet, looking for all like a piece of heaven dropped out of the sky. She smiled and held out a large jar. "I caught these for you. The servants helped me."

I stared through the glass at the dead insects, the finest gift a girl had ever given me—the only present, in fact. "But how can I take them? I didn't catch them myself." Still, I couldn't help myself. I already had the jar in my hands.

"These will just replace those that were stolen from you by Ginny Malone."

"Ginny! But I thought it was Fred Leckie who took them."

"Well, of course he's the one to benefit from them. Certainly he didn't return them to you when he realized they were yours."

I smiled at Rebecca. Mostly I felt comforted to know that I hadn't lost her friendship, even if she had been walking with Fred yesterday. But I also realized how much this gesture meant, since she had never stooped to catch a fly before. I thought she detested touching them for the germs. I wanted to show my gratitude in some way. "Thank you, Rebecca."

"It was entirely my pleasure, William Alton." She leaned over and gave my cheek a quick kiss.

It felt wonderful. Tingly and warm. I felt happy for the first time since before Mum died. Here was a fair girl who had nice clothes and pretty hair ribbons. She was loved and well looked after. Nothing like any of the girls I'd ever met in London. With such a girl's lips touching against your skin, sure wouldn't anything be possible from here on in. "Rebecca, in order to return to class, I must write a note of apology to Fred for bloodying his nose." I shook my head. "And I just cannot."

"But, Will, you have to come back."

"Yes." I swallowed. "But there's something more. We found out yesterday that my Uncle Charlie is in quarantine with typhoid fever."

"No!" Rebecca clasped her hands to her mouth.

"So now there is even more reason for me to kill flies. I intend to take the day to kill so many"—I made a fist and shook it—"that I can vanquish disease. And hold my head up high when they count my numbers against Fred's—especially if I must write that apology."

Rebecca looked at me, blue eyes wide. "To vanquish disease, you will skip school. Are you sure? My father attended university many long years to do the same. Is it not simply so that you can beat Fred Leckie?"

I twisted my mouth as I thought about her question, and realized she was right. "He needs to be beaten," I finally answered. "I will see you on Monday."

"If not before," she answered.

Before, before. My heart thumped the double beat as I marched down Hunter Street. *Where would I possibly see Rebecca if not in school*? I wondered. Still, I hoped and my heart pounded harder.

I walked briskly, checking over my shoulder to make sure Mr. Morton was not in view, or worse, following. Then I turned north up the street. Beating Fred Leckie *had* become everything to me, I realized as I passed a gray stone mansion.

I sighed, looking at it. With two chimneys and many large, shuttered windows, perhaps that house was even Fred's home—if not then certainly one like it. I wanted Father and me to live in a house with pillars and a balcony over the entrance. I wanted to wear crisp white shirts and boots without holes and to eat oranges for a recess snack. I wondered what it would be like to have all of that and then wondered whether I would ever know. I sighed and then continued till I saw the park. Water spouts from the fountain were leaping toward the sky and made me want to reach up too. I could beat Fred Leckie, I knew I could.

Down the street, the first shop I stopped at had a window display of large hocks of raw red meat. A couple of flies buzzed near the windowpane. Even though a CLOSED sign still hung on the door, I knocked.

"Excuse me, sir. May I come in and kill flies for you?"

The man with the bloody apron around his neck looked more than a bit surprised. "Why? We use flypaper. I am about to change it now."

"Can I have your old one?" I asked. Taking these strips would not help in the war against flies and germs, only in the war against Fred. I hoped Dr. Roberts would count the bodies on the sticky tape if I brought it in.

"You can have all three. What is this about?"

I explained about the contest. I also asked if I could kill any flies loose around the shop now.

"Only until the shop opens at ten o'clock. We don't want the customers to see you in action. Mind you're careful that none of your victims fall into the meat."

With those rules in mind, I borrowed the butcher's fly swatter and set about annihilating all the flies in the store. I carefully slapped and caught the ones in the window first, then worked on the back room. When I finished there, I headed for the trash shed. I swatted at least fifty but one flew up and away. *Always wait till the fly lands.* Ginny Malone's advice came back to me. I frowned when her name came into my thoughts.

I could understand Ginny working for Fred—she couldn't help whom she liked—but to steal my flies right from the cubby at school was too great a betrayal for me to accept. I would show her that I could win despite her sabotage—that people like us did have a chance.

The creature circled and dove at me, back up and down, buzzing brazenly. "Well, I have had loads of practice now." I watched it do another turn in the air and then snatched where I thought it would fly next.

Nothing. Ginny was right. I let that method go for another day.

I collected 378 flies from the meat shop, a fairly good catch. If I continued swatting at this rate—and with Rebecca's jar added in—I would regain everything I'd lost and certainly give Fred some competition. Before I left, the butcher pressed a nickel into my hand. I smiled at it, imagining a whole bag full of hard butterscotch candy. I would eat them for lunch. No, I would save some to share with Rebecca—better yet, Ginny Malone's little brother and sister. Then she would see that she didn't have to steal my flies to gain Fred's favor. He wasn't the only person who could make treats possible for her family.

The next stop was a shirt manufacturer. The foreman I approached told me that they used Wilson's Fly Pads and did not need my assistance in getting rid of the creatures.

"Really, sir? May I see one?" I asked.

"There, on the window ledge. Go ahead. Mind you don't pester the ladies at work."

I walked quickly around a row of sewing machines to the window ledge at the back. There sat a round container with a picture of a fly on one side and a large hole on the other. It didn't look like a pad so much as a trap.

I heard the frustrated buzzing coming from the inside and smiled. I wondered how much the trap cost. The cluster of flies in the corner of the room I slapped and collected with my hand. When one stubborn fly escaped, I waited patiently till it landed on a sewing table. I guessed the direction of flight and scooped it from behind, slightly above the table, squeezing and dropping it in my jar. Just as Ginny had told me to do.

"Here now. I told you I don't need you to get rid of the little buggers," the foreman called. "I'm not going to pay you."

"My goal was to capture and kill more flies not to earn money." I walked back toward the front. "May I come back after school every day and collect the bodies from the trap though?"

He thought about that for a moment. "Don't see any reason why not."

"Good." I thought for a moment. Saturday was the official opening day of the competition, the registration, and the first count-in. "Are you open tomorrow? Can I come in at three o'clock?"

"If you like."

"Thank you, sir." I left with one jar full of flies and another just started. Walking away from Gore Park, westward, I visited a grocery store, two stables, and a furniture shop. As I walked by the chairs and lamps, I realized that this was Souter's, the store Father had pointed out when he spoke about the owner's unusual way of catching flies.

I stopped and the owner, Mr. Souter, came out. When I asked about his vacuum cleaning method, he insisted on demonstrating. I followed Mr. Souter to the back room. The machine looked like a broomstick stuck into a hatbox with a bagpipe attached. Mr. Souter pushed the machine toward the front window. There, he plugged it in and connected a hose.

Grinning, he switched the vacuum cleaner on and aimed the rubber tube toward a corner where two flies sat. The flies disappeared into the nozzle. "It's a Hoover Type O. Don't you think everyone should own one of these? For hygiene and health?"

"Certainly, sir. And I'll tell everyone to come here and buy one. May I borrow your machine to demonstrate to the other shop owners?"

Mr. Souter shook his finger at me. "I like the way you think, but I cannot loan it out like that. Once you borrow this machine, I will have to discount it as used."

"But you demonstrate the method with it, do you not?"

"Yes, but only in this store. We would discount it only a little and call it a demonstrator model."

I scrunched up my mouth. I didn't really understand Mr. Souter's thinking, but that happened to me often with adults. So I tried something different. "May I use the machine in your store only? And can I empty the flies into my container?"

"Certainly, my boy. And if someone comes in to shop, you can be the person who demonstrates." Mr. Souter smiled. "Check around all the windows and the back stockroom."

I agreed. The vacuum sucked noisily but successfully. I liked this new way of killing the creatures. No touching or squeezing needed. The nozzle aimed for the creatures and—*schlumpf*—they were gone. After I had visited the storeroom, Mr. Souter helped me unload the flies.

He also flipped me another nickel.

I filled two more jars but my stomach rumbled. I fingered the two nickels in my pocket. Should I buy myself something to eat? I didn't want to waste time shopping for food. And I imagined those butterscotch candies again. Later, I told myself, later.

For now, I visited the dustbins in the back laneway.

I killed and missed many flies landing and lifting off from the trash. It took forever. I needed to leave bait and traps everywhere to speed up the catching process. Every once in a while I tried to snatch the insects straight from the air like Ginny and her dog. Not once did I succeed.

I checked the clocks in the shops, and just before the usual dismissal time, trudged back to Blink Bonnie Manor using my regular route from school. I headed to the back of the building where I thought he might be working.

"Father?" I called when I saw him sitting on the carriage, a small leafless tree branch across his lap.

"Where were you today?"

My mouth dropped open. Hot as I was from fly catching, I suddenly felt my blood chill.

"Why did you not attend school?" Father leaped from the carriage and grabbed my arm, hard.

"I wanted to catch flies so that I could win the *Hamilton Spectator* competition."

"You missed school to catch flies!" he said, low and angry. He swung the switch in my direction. It whistled past my ear.

"I meant to tell you. I couldn't go to class unless I wrote a letter of apology to Fred Leckie."

Father swung the switch again, but it came nowhere near me. "You bloodied that lad's nose. Mr. Morton told me when I came to get you for lunch today." He swung again. This time he would have hit, only I ducked.

"You don't understand! He thinks he owns the world because his parents are wealthy."

"You must attend school!" He threw the switch at me and this time it found its mark.

"Ow!"

"I promised your mother!" He shook his fist at me and then buckled onto the floor, burying his head in his hand.

A promise to my mother. I watched, ashamed, as Father silently wept. It wasn't just because I had skipped school. It was his helpless rage at not being able to help my mother when she was sick. Or my sister. But he had made that promise about school for me and it was one thing I could help him do for Mum.

"Father, I will write the apology." I sank down on my knees near him and put an arm around his shoulder. "And I will return to school." I was willing to say anything to make Father stop crying. "I shouldn't have hit Fred Leckie." He didn't look up, so I kept talking. "He never stole my flies. And he called me a name because I accused him." I couldn't think of anything more to say. Instead I just leaned into him, still holding him with one arm.

"You must promise me to never miss school like that again," Father finally said.

"Never. I promise."

Father stood up and I followed. "We will not speak of this day again. I only hope your mother wasn't watching."

That night Father borrowed a bottle of ink and a pen for me as well as a few sheets of scrap paper. I began my letter to Fred several times. Each time, though, I remembered the satisfaction of pummeling the wealthy brat's face and needed to stop. I dearly wanted to be truthful. Finally, I ended up with this note:

Dear Fred,

I am sorry you called me a name that so incensed me that I smashed your nose with my fist. I understand now that you did not steal my can of flies from the cubby next to your own. I am sorry for assuming that you did. I do hope we can put this behind us and, I assure you, I will not punch your face again.

William Alton

I showed Father, who smiled at me for the first time since I had come to the stable. "Well done, son. *Incensed* is such a pretty word. You do turn a phrase nicely." He placed his hand on my shoulder. "If you get an education, I promise you will not spend your life endlessly apologizing."

I smiled back, then thought of something else I could tell. I wasn't sure how he'd take it but I knew it would make me feel better. "Da, today a pretty girl kissed me."

"Ah!" Father ruffled my hair. "Already you are finding your way in the world. See how the lasses will flock after you with a university diploma!"

Chapter 12

Happily, Father was able to secure us a servant's room in the Blink Bonnie. I enjoyed a good sleep sharing a bed and an eiderdown comforter with him. The next day, I woke early so I could visit all the shops and businesses I'd been to on Friday to collect even more flies. I bought milk with the money some of the shopkeepers gave me. Rebecca had said flies were attracted to white surfaces, and I certainly wanted the most irresistible bait I could find. Just in case, I added a little sugar that I borrowed from Mrs. Swanson at the manor.

When I returned awhile later to check on my bait, I found no flies. Mrs. Swanson suggested vinegar and honey and loaned me a little. I set it out immediately, but there was no time to wait and see whether it worked. Four o'clock was the time set for the opening of the competition and I wanted to be at the head of the line and needed to get to the health department early to accomplish this.

At three thirty sharp, I carried four cans and a paper bag with three strips of flypaper, all full of dead insects, up the stairs to City Hall, where the health department was located. So many stairs and three grand archways led to the main doors of the great building. Certainly I'd never entered the city hall in London. Didn't this entrance mark the beginning of better times for the Alton family?

I wasn't early enough. The lineup of children formed right from the front door. I joined it, craning my neck to see what was happening up ahead. Four men sat at a table, gloves on, counting. They worked quickly. One of them, Dr. Roberts—I recognized him from his visit to our school auditorium that second day—used a thin stick to group and count the flies, marking something on a paper for each cluster. When too many collected on top of the counter, he pushed them off into a large barrel.

Fred Leckie stood next in line and he lifted his containers, one by one, for Dr. Roberts.

"The highest count so far has been 1,200," the boy ahead of me said.

I watched as Fred emptied a jar marked *Ovaltine*, my jar from the cubby at school. Perhaps Fred had no idea that Ginny had stolen it to give to him. *Of course he knew*. Especially after I'd accused him of stealing it. My fingers curled into a fist. My letter promised that I would never hit Fred again. But I hadn't given him the letter yet. I could still sneak in a punch before I made the promise. What I saw next made me step out of line to do exactly that.

The second container Fred dumped was yellow and brown and marked *Magic Baking Powder*. My other container, the one Madame Depieu had thrown into her trash. I felt a hot red rage flash through me. "Save my place," I told the girl behind me and walked to the front. As I approached Dr. Roberts, I noticed Ginny and her dog Finnigan standing next to Fred.

I remembered the satisfaction of my fist hitting Fred's fleshy nose and raised my arm, ready to strike. Then I heard a soft voice. "Will!" it called. *Mum*, I thought immediately. I turned slightly and saw Rebecca walking toward me. In my mind, another picture formed. I saw Father, head in hands, kneeling on the stable floor. The only thing that had made him get up again was my promise to get an education.

If I hit Fred now, he would never accept my letter of apology. Instead, he would probably tell his parents and they would make sure Mr. Morton never allowed me back into Central Public. If I hit Fred now, I would let Father down and, wherever she was, Mum too.

That gentle kind voice belonged to Rebecca, not Mum. I glanced at her golden face, wide-eyed, mouth slightly open. I would not fight in front of her. Still, I shook with the effort of straightening and relaxing my hand. I brought my arm down and spoke instead. "Dr. Roberts, that container of flies was stolen from me."

Dr. Roberts looked up from his counting.

"I have never stolen anything in my entire life," Fred snapped, stepping toward me. "And I will not be accused by this guttersnipe." He shoved me.

I did not strike back, but I could feel my breath coming more quickly. My heart pounded at my chest and everything inside me raced, readying for a battle. Ginny stepped between us before Fred could shove me again. "Sir, I found every one of those flies in the garbage at the back of McNab Street."

Cleverly worded. I scowled at her. I had seen Ginny that day, walking the dog in the back alley. Finn must have sniffed the jar out. Ginny might have found them all in the trash, as she told Dr. Roberts, but they had been caught and killed by someone else. *Me!*

"Should we allow others to help the catchers?" Dr. Roberts asked one of his fellow counters.

Surely not the point, I thought, but right now I would take any ruling that would disqualify Fred's catch.

That man swept all the flies from his counter into another bushel barrel. Then he shrugged. "There is no way of checking who caught what. Really, the whole point of the matter is to rid the city of flies. It doesn't matter how that goal is achieved."

Dr. Roberts looked at me. "Look after your catch better,

son." He lowered his head and continued counting.

I turned away. Rebecca had told me Ginny was the one who stole my flies at school. But this time it didn't count as stealing—not if she just removed the Magic Powder jar from the top of the garbage. So why did I feel as though she'd kicked me in the stomach? Rebecca laid a hand on my shoulder, instantly making me feel better.

She smiled. "You may not beat him but you killed a great number of flies."

"I will beat him!" I answered more angrily than I had meant to. I saw her smile drop and forced my lips to lift into one. "Sorry! Come join me in the line. Someone is saving my place."

She strolled alongside of me back to my spot.

"Look here." I showed her my jars and bag. "I think I may just have more flies than Fred Leckie. Do you agree?"

At that moment, Dr. Roberts called out Fred's final number. "Two thousand two hundred."

How could that many flies even fit in Fred's containers?

Rebecca raised her eyebrows and repeated the number. "Do you still think you have more?"

I shrugged. My long strips of sticky flypaper should be good for several hundred. The line moved up and so did we. Fred, on his way out, stopped near us, Ginny Malone still at his side.

"Rebecca, why are you spending time with the likes of him? Why don't you join me for an ice-cream soda instead?"

As Fred smiled his smarmy smile at Rebecca, Ginny stood staring down at her dog. Suddenly, I wished I had bought that bag of butterscotches. Only why? Ginny had betrayed me in the worst way possible, choosing to help the rich braggart instead of me. I shook my head to rid it of the thought.

I dropped down to pat Finnigan. The dog licked my hand, but Ginny didn't say a word.

"Ice-cream soda with you?" Rebecca repeated the question back to Fred. "No time, I'm afraid. I may wish to kill a fly or two myself."

Fred's mouth betrayed his sour thoughts. "Your hands should never have to slap at such filth." The way he turned to look at me then, I wasn't entirely certain that he meant the flies.

Still Ginny looked up at Fred with sad adoring eyes. Fred thought her hands were just fine to kill the creatures. Ginny's hands, somehow, were less worthy of protection than Rebecca's. Despite her betrayal, I felt my heart tighten for her.

"You're right. I will write an essay for the contest instead," Rebecca said.

"Bah, the prize is only five dollars. Why bother?" Fred asked.

"Because I don't care about the prize. I want people to know about germs. To stay well," Rebecca answered.

Vanquishing disease. Wasn't that what I had always wanted too? To save someone else's mother or a little girl like my sister? But then the contest became about beating Fred, about that fifty-dollar prize.

"What good are words? Look at how money talks to everyone here." Fred gestured with his hand to the long line of children now leading outside the building.

"Words have power," Rebecca said. "It was Dr. Roberts' words that inspired them all to come today. Not the prize money."

I wasn't certain that that was true, but I'd rather side with Rebecca than Fred. "Rebecca is right. Not everyone is as greedy as you."

Fred stepped so close that I could feel his breath. "But you are, aren't you? And no matter how hard you try, I will beat you." Fred smiled, shoved me, and left, Ginny and Finnigan tagging after.

Would Ginny look back and give me one sign that she was sorry for all this? I watched for it. Instead, I saw Finnigan leap into the air and snap at something. He had caught another fly.

"Give, Finnigan!" Ginny bent down and held out her hand. The dog dropped the insect and she patted him. Then Ginny glanced back at me, hand on her hip, eyebrow raised.

Whatever did she mean by looking at me like that, I wondered, all spit and vinegar? Still, I smiled in spite of it. I shook my head. I liked this spunky Ginny way better than the hangdog one who kissed Fred's feet. "Don't waste yourself on him, Ginny Malone," I told her softly.

Chapter 13

As fast as the health inspectors counted the flies, I still had to wait over an hour till I stepped up to the counter with my catch. I counted along with the man at the front. "One, two, three, four..." all the way till ten and then he would mark a line on his paper. After ten marks, he struck through them and pushed the hundred flies into the barrel with his stick. One hundred, two hundred...the first container held six hundred flies. The second only five hundred. Two more cans.

Fred Leckie's count was 2,200. If each of my cans held 500, and the sticky strips held another 300, it would be enough to beat Fred. Beside me, Rebecca squeezed my arm. My heart beat a double thump as though I had already won. The third can held 450, but the inspector marked 500 anyway. The fourth held 530, but he marked 500. Two thousand one hundred flies. The sticky paper held at least 300 flies, I felt sure of it. A smile stretched my face, so big I felt my face might split open. I would win today's count!

"I cannot separate these flies from the paper. How do I count them?" The inspector asked Dr. Roberts.

Dr. Roberts shook his head. "We cannot count them. We decided for the last child that we would disallow flypaper. Traps are fine so long as we can remove the flies, but nothing sticky."

"Two thousand one hundred," the inspector called out. "Well done, William Alton. You are in second place."

The children in line cheered. Rebecca clapped.

So close! I cursed under my breath and turned to leave.

"Maybe you can beat him," Rebecca said, following. "If anyone can, I believe it will be you."

"Thank you for that," I said. I walked quickly, grateful that Fred was not still around to gloat.

"Do you want to go for a soda?" she asked me. "My treat?" Her voice was bright and the miracle of it was I knew it was a true invitation. Money didn't mean much to her. It never did to people who had lots. Still, I couldn't allow her to buy the soda for me. How would I ever be able to return the gesture?

"Can we walk instead?" I asked. "We can sit by the fountain in Gore Park."

"Surely, it's a fine day." She smiled at me and I smiled back.

"Let's go this way." I pointed down the hill.

As we strolled down the street, the sun shining warm on our shoulders, a pair of horses pulling a carriage clip-clopped ahead of us.

"How is your composition on flies going?" I asked Rebecca.

"Fine. Only I'm not certain I believe they cause all the diseases."

The carriage paused for a moment as one horse defecated on the street.

Such beautiful animals, such a large quantity of smelly dung. "What about the germs the flies carry?" I asked. "They lay their eggs in manure. If we wait a moment, you can see them land. I can also show you the maggots in my father's stable."

She chuckled. "You don't need to show me, William Alton. I have seen them enough. But what about the germs in the manure itself?"

"What do you mean?" I stared at the steaming heap in the street looking for the answer.

"Those same germs lie in the street every time horses pass. We can pick them up just from walking around."

Suddenly, I found myself lifting my feet a little higher. "But we wear boots. And we step around the manure if we can help it."

"Perhaps, but the rain washes the germs into the sewer. The sewer empties into the lake. And that's where we get our water."

"Ah, but the water is treated before we drink it."

"Mmm. Dr. Roberts warned my father that he found some

typhoid germ in Hamilton's water supply. To be safe, we should boil it."

I sputtered, "But that means Uncle Charlie could be sick from drinking the water."

"If he drinks tea and ale, perhaps not. And the city feels Dr. Roberts is wrong. Did you know over a hundred babies die every summer in Hamilton alone?"

"Not from the water. It's the same liquid all year round, after all."

"My father says it's from impure milk."

"Impure from flies, though!" I shook my finger. "The little buggers walk all over the milk. You told me so yourself."

She shrugged. "Maybe."

"There are more flies in summer and more babies die, it all makes sense," I continued. It had to be the flies—flies were something I could smash and kill, something I could control, something I could protect other families from.

"But it's also hotter in the summer. The poor can't buy enough ice to keep the milk from spoiling."

"What can anyone do?" I held my hand to my head, which felt like it was spinning inside. Then I saw a fly land on a lamp-post and ran to catch it. I watched the creature rub its front legs together then its back legs. Suddenly, my hand shot out, almost with a mind of its own. The fly lifted off right into my waiting palm. I felt the tickle against my hand and squeezed.

"Well done! You're getting so much better at it." Rebecca clapped my shoulder.

I slipped the creature into one of my empty containers. "Thank you."

She smiled. "The Babies' Dispensary Guild is collecting money so that it can supply pure milk at half the price to mothers in need."

"So collecting money is the ticket," I said. "Not flies. You won't be able to win the essay competition with that story."

"I suppose not," Rebecca answered, dejected.

What did she even need to win the contest for? Couldn't she buy anything she wanted at any time? "Listen, I believe flies must be part of the problem," I told her. "Don't you?"

"Yes, a part of it for sure."

"Well, make sure everyone who reads your story believes it too and you will have a winner."

"You are brilliant, Will Alton. Why don't you write an essay for the competition too?" She smiled, her beautiful milk-tooth smile.

Did she mean it? Should I write one? I'd rather help her with my ideas. Just like Ginny Malone, I thought. I was always telling her to kill the flies for her own entry into the contest. But because she liked Fred Leckie, she gave them to him instead. I turned to Rebecca. "I can't just write about them. Even if they are only a small part of the reason people fall sick, I need to kill them." We reached our turn and headed east. "I need to kill something to avenge my mother's death. And my sister's."

Rebecca stopped abruptly. She covered her mouth with her hands. "Your mum died? Your sister too?" Her eyes filled. "Oh, poor Will."

"I didn't mean to upset you." Watching a tear slide down her cheek, I felt my eyes fill too. "It's all right. I don't even remember their faces anymore."

"Oh!" She threw her arms around my neck.

My throat tightened. I cleared it and broke away from Rebecca. "So you see, using my hands makes me feel more like I am doing something." My fingers curled into fists.

She pulled a lace hanky from inside her sleeve and dabbed at her eyes. Even when crying, she managed to look pretty. "I do understand." She sniffed into her hanky. "Only, moving a pen over a paper is also doing something with your hand."

She was right. I smiled at her and she tried to smile back. We continued walking and crossed the road to the park. At the fountain, I had her laughing again as I told her about vacuuming the flies up from the window of Souter's furniture store. "He won't let me use it elsewhere. But I can 'demonstrate' on his premises."

"Too bad you can't borrow someone else's," Rebecca said. "I would loan you ours if I thought the housekeeper wouldn't notice and tell Mother."

"The shops are all closed Sunday anyway and I promised Father I would never skip school again." But the flies still buzzed around the stable even on the Sabbath, I thought as an idea began to take hold. And the maids in Blink Bonnie had no need for the Moodie vacuum cleaner on Sunday. Chances were, if I borrowed it tomorrow, they would never know it had been gone at all.

Chapter 14

Later that night, when the rest of the staff at Blink
Bonnie had stepped out for the evening, Father filled the large
tub left for us in the kitchen. The rest had all had their baths.
"Your turn first," Father told me. "Make sure to wash behind
your ears. I'm going to see about our clean laundry."

I stepped into the tub and sat down slowly. The water fair
boiled the dirt off of me. I steamed like a chicken in a pot. As I
passed the washcloth around the back of my neck and around
my ears, I wondered exactly where the maids kept the vacuum
cleaner. Was it in the cupboard next to the kitchen? Would I
even recognize it, if I saw it? Did they all look like Mr. Souter's
Model O? *I'm clean enough,* I thought, and climbed out of
the tub, wrapping a towel around myself. Ducking around the
corners, I found the closet and carefully pulled open the door.

There it sat, a hatbox bagpipe Model O. I didn't want to
chance dressing first and sneaking it out to the stable. I listened for any noise. Nothing. None of the staff or the Moodies

seemed to be around. Father might be gone for awhile putting our laundry away. Quickly, I grabbed the handle and pulled it out. It was awkward, keeping the towel up with one hand and first pulling, then pushing the heavy machine with the other. I needed to haul it up the stairs to the back door and free one hand to open it. With my hip I held it open and dragged the vacuum cleaner out. Barefoot, I stepped on a sharp rock and cursed.

I let go of the machine and hopped on one foot.

Somewhere someone laughed, but when I looked around I saw no one. I could have sworn it sounded like Fred Leckie's stupid donkey bray. I had to have imagined it. If it were Fred, wouldn't he stay around to make fun of me some more? No one behind the stable that I could see. No one on Bay Street. I had to hurry. I lifted the heavy machine the rest of the way and hid it behind the carriage. I smiled as I rested for a moment; this was the miracle that would help beat Fred. I dashed back inside, and down the stairs. I heard Father's footsteps and hopped into the tub again.

"Almost done?" Father appeared from the hallway. "I have your clean night shirt here."

"Just a minute." I dunked myself, sputtered, then climbed out, wrapping myself in the moist towel, still dripping.

"Well done. Dry yourself off better. How the devil did the towel get so wet and you're still not dry?"

I shrugged as I rubbed the towel across the back of my shoulder. "Father, you know I won't ever miss school again, but might I skip church tomorrow? I have a new method to catch flies that I want to try." I slipped the nightshirt over my head.

"No, son. Tomorrow we are going to pray for your Uncle Charlie's recovery."

"But I could do that just as well from the stable as I caught flies."

"I think it might be easier to communicate with the Lord in his own house. St. Mark's is only a few steps away, Will. It will only take an hour of your time. We cannot visit Charlie because of his quarantine, but we can do this one thing for him." Father cuffed my chin gently and smiled. "Now you'll excuse me while I take my bath."

Of course I couldn't tell Father that I wanted to use the Moodie vacuum cleaner on the flies while the staff and owners were out of the house. I'd just have to get up earlier than everyone else so that I could vacuum up the flies in the stable. "Yes, Da," I answered and headed back to the room we shared off the downstairs hall.

Even as I shut my eyes to sleep, I tried to keep my ears open for the sound of the birds. At the first chirp, I would get dressed quietly in the hall so my father wouldn't wake up. *Keep listening, keep listening, you have to do this to beat Fred Leckie,* I told myself but it only served as a lullaby.

In my dreams, I saw Fred Leckie at the counter of the health department, rubbing black threadlike arms together, one over the other. His nose, still swollen from my punch, became a stinger, his eyes, huge discs. "Dr. Roberts! Dr. Roberts! Look at Fred," I called to the health officer. *Why does no one but me see? Fred Leckie is part fly!* I ran to the front of the line and shouted to the fly counters that they couldn't let Fred win.

Dr. Roberts merely shook his head. "A fly most certainly can enter the contest and win. Who best to kill others of the same species?"

I opened my mouth to argue, but then woke up. I rubbed my eyes and listened. Birds. I rushed to the window and parted the drapes, and sunlight streamed in. Another cloudless, hot day. I gathered my pants, overshirt, and shoes and tiptoed out the door. My heart beat hard as I dressed in the hall. Then I raced down the stairs and out the back.

In the stable, I connected the rubber hose and then plugged in the machine, just as I had in Souter's furniture store. Pressing the on switch hard, I made it roar to life. One of the horses whinnied in protest. "Shh, shh, Beauty. I'm just ridding you of those fly menaces."

I yanked the machine to the corner and aimed for some flies. Unfortunately, some hay was sucked up too. *No matter, I'll remove it when I remove the flies*, I told myself. Still, my heart continued to thump wildly in my chest. What would

Mr. Moodie do if he knew one of his stablehands' son was using his cleaning instrument in this way? This was foolish, I thought, Father might lose his job. *Schlump*! I vacuumed up about ten insects in the window before they could flit away. How satisfying! I smiled. Five windows and all the corners done now. Did I dare to head to the dust bin? No, better not. Instead, I carefully emptied the flies, pulling them out through the bag opening. It was disgusting work, and a considerable amount of fluff and dust came out as well.

There had to be about two hundred of them. I stashed the jar carefully on a shelf and then began dragging the Hoover back.

Wait! What was that noise? A bark? It didn't matter if a dog was disturbed. I hurried the machine back into its place just as Mrs. Swanson rounded the corner.

"See here! What are you doing up so early? There is no food in there for you to steal."

"No ma'am. I was just admiring the vacuum cleaner. I've never seen one before."

"Go on with you. You can't fool me. Here have a scone." She pitched me a small baked bun. "That's all you're getting for another hour yet, mind!" She sounded harsh but her face looked kind.

I munched as I headed back to our room. I slipped into the room and lay back on the bed, dozing happily.

Later, I enjoyed porridge with Father and then together we left for church. St. Mark's was the large red-bricked building with steeples and stained-glass windows just next door. "Father, it's so close. Surely my prayers from the stalls will make it to the Lord while I catch flies."

"You're keepin' me company, not another word about it," Father warned. As we walked, people passed us on their way to the Presbyterian church several blocks past the school. Others joined us heading in the same direction. I told Father how Fred Leckie had beaten me by a hundred flies in Saturday's count.

"But you did marvelously well!" Father said. "I'm proud of you."

"I don't know if I can win if he keeps coming up with new ways to cheat."

"Ah, but you already have beat him. You know that in your heart. Fair and square you caught 2,100 flies, whereas he needed some 500 of yours to come in first place." Father put his arm around me as we entered the church and slid into a pew.

Dark and quiet, the air felt a bit cooler and smelled like old books—I could almost believe prayers could be heard better from here. Other people must have felt that way too, as they crowded in.

Father knelt onto the wooden trestle and bowed his head. I knew he was praying for Uncle Charlie.

I joined him with my own prayers. I squeezed my eyes shut

tightly as though that would help two prayers come true. I tried to see my uncle's face in my mind, but just like Mum's it was fading. "Please let Uncle Charlie live. We need him right now." I felt a slight tickle on my nose, a brush of a feather or fur, or...I opened my eyes...the wings of a fly. "Dear God," I added. "Help me kill every fly in this city and win the *Hamilton Spectator* competition."

Chapter 15

Early Monday morning, I recopied my note of apology to Fred Leckie, twice, on two cream-colored sheets of stationery Father had borrowed from Ellie, one of the maids at the manor. I looked at both copies when I finished. On one, the dot over the *i* in my signature appeared as more of an ink blob. That one would be for Fred, I decided. The other, the more perfect one, I would hand to Mr. Morton when I entered the school. Before I left, I asked Father where best to store my latest stock of flies. Father unlocked a cabinet above the harness hook and placed my three cans there. "No one can steal them from you now, my lad," he told me as he turned the key again.

I nodded and smiled. I had a good feeling about the competition. "Bye Father!" I called as I waved goodbye.

"Learn well, Will," Father returned and waved back. "Make me proud."

I will do that, I thought as I began walking. *When he sees my name in the paper for killing the most flies, he'll be so happy.*

And I'll give him the prize money so we can buy a home. When I crossed the street and reached the front of our school, I saw Ginny and Fred arguing on the sidewalk, her brother and sister flanking her.

"You said you would give me those orange pieces today," she yelled.

"I never said any such thing. I told you I had run out. You were the one who assumed I would pay another day."

"You're just a big cheat!" The little boy beside Ginny rushed Fred, only Fred ducked and shoved him as he flew past. The boy landed in a heap on the grass.

Ginny, in turn, shoved Fred and he fell to the ground too. "Touch any of my family, will you! You'll never see another fly from me. And you certainly won't win if I can help it!"

I was too thunderstruck to feel happy about her announcement. I hurried on to get to the principal's office and turn my apology in.

Rebecca joined me.

"Hello, Will." She beamed at me.

I grinned back at her, speechless with delight for a moment, then I frowned. "I won't be going straight in to class. I have to hand in my apology first."

Her smiled tugged downwards, but her fingers touched my elbow gentle as butterfly wings. That touch made me feel lighter, if only for just a moment. "I'm sorry you have to do that, Will."

I shrugged my shoulders. For certain I dreaded the reckoning also. "See you later," I told her as I turned off for the front entrance of the school. Rebecca continued to the yard at the back.

Up each stair, my heart beat a double time. As I reached the office door, it raced like a drum. My face felt warm and my mouth as though it had turned to paper. The secretary asked me to wait on the hard chair at the front of the office. From there I sat through morning prayers and songs, feeling warmer with each minute that passed.

Finally I stood up. "Could I just leave these letters for Mr. Morton and see him when he is not so busy?" I asked the secretary.

"No," she answered without looking up.

I sat back down and counted dead flies in my head to pass the time. When I reached four hundred, as if called forth, one live one flew in front of my face and over my head. I leaped up to catch it.

"Step into my office, William Alton," Mr. Morton's voice boomed.

The shock of the sudden command made me loosen my fingers and with that, the fly buzzed off. In a daze, I followed the principal, and when I stood in front of his desk, held out the two letters of apology.

Mr. Morton ignored my outstretched hand and the contents. Instead, he slid open a drawer behind the desk and pulled out a thick black strap.

"I let you go over fighting with Fred Leckie because I thought the letters of apology would be a worse punishment for a lad such as yourself. Normally, fighting would have earned you four strokes across your left hand."

I swallowed and dropped the letters on the desk.

"But you skipped school on Friday. Your behavior becomes worse and worse." Mr. Morton stepped around his desk, strap curled in his fist. "You have earned six strokes. Hold out both hands."

I did as I was told and Mr. Morton crossed them, palms up.

"After each blow, you will switch hands."

I nodded and Mr. Morton raised the strap high in the air. Then he brought it down hard. The air whistled and the rubber slapped across my hand. The sting burned from my palms right up my wrist. My eyes filled. I thought I could endure the pain. But the humiliation! Knowing I was in the wrong and deserving of this, I remembered Father kneeling on the stable floor, crying, and blinked hard to keep in my own tears. Trembling, I switched hands for the next blow. *No one is watching, you big baby. No one needs to know.* I switched hands again. By the time the strap stopped falling, my hands and wrists looked as red as the slabs of meat that hung at the King Street butcher's window.

Mr. Morton stared straight into my eyes. "Now you will go to your class and bring Mr. Leckie back here."

"Yes sir." I rubbed my hands against my sides as I strode down the hall. The door to the classroom was open, but as I entered all my classmates looked up. I folded my arms across my chest, but could see that only drew stares to them. "Mr. Morton wishes to see Fred Leckie." I saw Fred go pale. He looked afraid, and I felt pleased for myself as well as for Ginny and her brother. I uncrossed my arms so Fred might anticipate and fear more clearly a similar fate.

In her seat, Rebecca gasped.

Fred stood up and marched out of the room ahead of me. I turned and followed him past the lockers, through the door, and past the secretary. Fred hesitated by the open door of Mr. Morton's actual office.

"Come in!" the principal's voice boomed. Mr. Morton walked over and closed the office door behind us. "Sit!" he commanded. He handed Fred one letter of apology. Mr. Morton himself sat behind his desk again and appeared to read his copy. I couldn't help noticing that the strap lay on top of the papers on his desk. He had not put it away yet. I looked from the strap to Fred and watched as Fred took it in too.

"I find this letter satisfactory. I think you should accept the apology, Fred, and promise not to hold a grudge against William." The principal stared at Fred, who simply stared back. Mr. Morton reached for the strap.

"I accept William's apology and promise not to hold a

grudge," Fred repeated quickly.

Mr. Morton slid open the drawer and tucked the strap in again. "Shake on it, gentlemen."

I winced as Fred gripped my sore hand hard and pumped.

"Good. You may return to your classroom."

Fred rushed ahead of me, not speaking a word.

Mr. Samson also gave me lines to write: *I must come to school each and every day.*

During both recesses and lunch hour I stayed behind to fill ten pages with them. As I scribbled away and the other students passed my desk, items mysteriously appeared, an apple, a piece of hard candy, and three dead flies. Getting the strap seemed to have earned me some new friends. I tucked the candy into one pocket, the flies in the other. Then I bit into the apple as I continued to write. The juice squirted up my face. The strapping had been almost worth it, I thought as I chewed and wrote some more. I bit again and again, till I found myself gnawing at the core. Finally, I ate that too. I was still starving. But before the end of the second recess, the pages were full. I walked over to my cubby for more food.

"What in..." Inside my cubby was a rusty old can full to the brim with dead flies. There had to be at least four hundred. "Ginny Malone," I whispered. "Ginny?" I called out loud. I shoved the can back into the cupboard, grabbed my lunch, and ran outside to join the others. I looked around the playground but then remembered to look up. And there it was—her boot sticking out from a branch in a tree.

"Thank you," I told her as I swung myself up.

"I'm sure I don't know what you're talking about." She didn't even look my way. Then she turned, wiping her hand across her nose as she sniffed. "Did it hurt much?"

I wanted to brag that, no, it didn't hurt at all. But her eyes searched mine for truth. "Like the dickens. He gave me six blows but I had to stack my hands so it stung them both and right up my arms."

She nodded and sniffed again. "He strapped me that way last week."

"But you...you're a girl."

"The only girl in class who's ever been strapped." A tear slid down her nose and she wiped it away.

"But why?"

"My little sister was sick, so I needed to stay home and look after her. My ma had to go to work."

"Did you tell him?"

"I couldn't. I didn't want Ma to get into trouble. The truant officer has already stopped at our house—last time I stayed home a week to watch my brother."

I pulled out my sandwich from my lunch bag. Mrs. Swanson had sliced her homemade bread thickly and had covered each piece with butter and cheese. I separated the two halves and offered Ginny one. She shook her head. I reached into my pocket and took out the candy. "For your sister?" I passed it to her and she finally smiled—like the sun peeking from behind two clouds. But the smile disappeared almost immediately. I saw where she was looking. Fred Leckie had sat down beside Rebecca.

"I knew he'd never love me, but I'd hoped he would at least respect me." She sniffed again and wiped beneath her eyes. "Instead, he cheated me."

"He's a fool. And he doesn't love her either," I answered Ginny. "He only loves himself."

Another wipe of her hand against her nose, and another sniff, "But you like her better too."

"Well, you didn't give me much reason to like you! Till now all you've done is steal from me!"

She turned her nose up, proud again.

"I like you different is all," I continued, but found it too difficult to explain further. Rebecca, with her proper manners and pretty clothes, was easier. Wild-tempered, freckled Ginny was harder but perhaps more interesting. "Why don't you take the can of flies you gave me and enter yourself?"

"I don't know what you're talking about," she said firmly, her eyes drilling me.

"Next catch then. Respect yourself first, Ginny Malone, before you expect others to." Uncle Charlie used to tell me that back in England when I had moped over being teased about my Irish accent. Other times he'd advised me to know my own worth. He'd touched my chest where my heart was. *Remember what's inside you.* I finished the rest of my sandwich and we sat together in peaceful silence till the bell rang.

That afternoon, the line snaked from the City Hall door down the stairs and around the corner. Could it be that even more children had found out about the contest and wanted to enter?

"Where did all these children come from?" Rebecca joined me in line. "They must have queued up early. Did they all skip school?"

"Still ten minutes till opening, too," I told her. I didn't have nearly as many flies as on opening day. But I'd had three days to catch before the Saturday count. Today I'd only had a day and a half of swatting. Still, no one had stolen from me either, and I had Ginny's rusty can full.

The line moved forward suddenly. The ten minutes were up. As on Saturday, Dr. Roberts had three assistants helping count the flies. "Four hundred!" one of the assistants called.

"Two hundred," another shouted.

"Five hundred," Dr. Roberts countered.

"Three hundred," another assistant yelled out.

"It certainly looks as though you'll have many more flies than they do," Rebecca said.

I smiled when I heard others had smaller catches as well. As we waited, I heard similar totals again and again.

Suddenly, someone shoved into me so hard I was spun around. My cans dropped and I dove for them as Fred Leckie bolted past. "Wait your turn!" I called after him but to no avail. Someone allowed Fred to sneak in ahead of him. I scooped the flies back into the can.

"Seven hundred," Dr. Roberts' voice called. The line moved again.

A few minutes later another voice called, "Eight hundred."

I stared at my cans, calculating. I had to have close to a thousand there. The line moved again.

"One thousand, one hundred!" Mr. Roberts shouted. "Mr. Leckie here may end up having the best catch today again."

Of course! I frowned, waiting for Fred to pass and gloat, but he didn't. An hour later when I finally shuffled forward, placing my cans on the counter, I saw Fred hovering to the side.

He's waiting to see if he beats me, I thought with some satisfaction. I watched Dr. Roberts group his flies in tens and mark them on paper. Ten, twenty, thirty...all the way to a thousand. It was as I thought. I had over a thousand. But did I have a hundred or more over?

One thousand ninety, one thousand one hundred—and Dr. Roberts continued. "Our new high scorer today is William Alton, with 1,300 flies."

I grinned as the lineup of children applauded. Only one person did not clap or smile.

Fred Leckie stepped toward me.

I tried to walk through him. "I promised I wouldn't hit you again. But get out of my way."

"You're cocky now, rooming-house boy. But you'll drop out soon enough."

"Never. I'm going to beat you Fred Leckie."

Fred walked alongside me, shoving me as we went. "I saw you with Mr. Moodie's vacuum cleaner. You were taking it to the stable to catch flies, weren't you? Moodie's a friend of my father. I wonder what he'll say when he hears how you used his equipment."

Rebecca spoke up. "You wouldn't tell on Will. That is too low even for you."

Fred paused for a moment, looking at her. If anybody could change his mind it would be her. But instead, he smiled. "Oh, no?" Then he turned to me and sneered. "If you don't quit, rooming-house boy, I'm going to report your antics to Mr. Moodie. I will win this contest. What is your answer, William Alton?"

Chapter 16

My hands curled into fists, but I knew I couldn't use them. Seeing Fred's creamy smile and narrow-eyed look, I had no doubt he would tell Mr. Moodie about me vacuuming up flies from his stable. And then what? Would we lose our room? Would Father lose his job, too? Did I have the right to risk any of that? I lifted my chin high as I thought about it. "Drop out? Why ever would I?" I asked Fred. "Mr. Moodie knows about the vacuum cleaner. He suggested the idea." It was a bluff, but I added a smile as bright as Father's as I stared Fred Leckie down.

First person to blink would be the one to give in, I thought, so I willed myself to keep my eyes open and to betray no emotion.

Fred's smiled dissolved into a sneer. He looked away. "I guess we'll see about that," he mumbled as he walked off.

"Will, Will?" Rebecca shook my shoulder.

I stood still, in shock.

"Good for you! You certainly got the upper hand."

"Whatever have I done?" I finally gasped. "I'm not sure Mr. Moodie even knows I live with Father in his house. If he finds out what I've done with his vacuum cleaner..."

"Mr. Moodie doesn't know?" Rebecca's eyes widened.

I shook my head.

"It's all right, Will, really," she hastened to calm herself. "As long as Fred believes you, he's never going to bother informing him."

"You're right. I know you're right," I said as we stepped out of City Hall into the bright sunshine.

"Do you want to go to Gore Park?" Rebecca asked.

Sitting by a water fountain with a pretty girl whose eyes were the color of the sky—there was nothing I would rather do. But I shook myself. "No, no, I can't." I needed to go straight home, to be by myself and mull everything over. "Right now, Fred *seems* to have backed down," I explained. "But he'll get angry again when he remembers my win today. At that point, he may tell his father about the Hoover, and his father may tell Mr. Moodie. I need to do something and do it right now. Before Mr. Moodie finds out."

"All right then, William." She looked disappointed, which made me feel better oddly. It was nice to know she'd really wanted to spend time with me, and wasn't just trying to make me feel better. We walked more quickly down the street toward the neighborhood where both of us lived. At least I lived there for now. Once Mr. Moodie learned the truth, who knew where Father and I would find a home next.

I said goodbye to Rebecca and headed for the back entrance, down the stairs into the kitchen.

Mrs. Swanson stood at the counter, placing a teapot and cup on a large silver tray.

"Mrs. Swanson, how do I get to see the master?" I asked. If I made my case to him before he heard about the vacuum cleaner from someone else, if I begged forgiveness, if I offered myself up as free labor for something...well, I didn't know what exactly would work, but I would try anything to get Mr. Moodie not to send us packing.

"You *don't* get to see him," she replied. "He's a busy man. You need to make an appointment and in order to do that, you must have important business—adult business," she emphasized, "that you need to tell his secretary about in advance." She filled a plate with peas, beets, mashed potatoes, and a pork cutlet. She placed the plate next to the tea.

I followed Mrs. Swanson to what looked like a closet. "Kindly open that door for me, would you?" she commanded.

I did as she asked and she put the tray down on a shelf inside. She reached for a rope next to it and began to pull on it, raising the shelf and the tray.

"What are you doing?" I asked.

"Have you never seen a dumb waiter before? I'm sending Mr. Moodie's dinner up to him."

I grinned. I had seen a dumbwaiter before, where Mum had worked in London. "Is Mr. Moodie dining alone this evening?" I asked.

"In his den, as he often does. He likes to have peace and quiet when he eats."

"You're a busy woman, Mrs. Swanson. Where is his study?"

"No, Will, you cannot possibly disturb the man while he is eating."

"Please, Mrs. Swanson, you don't understand. If I don't speak with him this evening, it may cost me and my father our lives." I tugged at her apron in desperation.

She made a face as if discovering a bad smell in her kitchen. "What could possibly be so urgent..."

I saw a weakening in her mouth. "I'll run up the stairs, grab the tray, and take it to him. I'll tell him I stole it from the dumbwaiter. That you had no part in it."

Her mouth twisted downward. I took my cue and began running toward the stairs. Mrs. Swanson didn't follow. Good. I took the stairs three at a time and burst into the main hall, searching for the dumbwaiter. It should be at the other end, judging by its position on the bottom floor.

Yes, yes—there on the far side was a rather smallish door. I ran to it, pulled it open, and saw the tray. I pulled it out.

Now where was Mr. Moodie's study? I heard talking from what I thought might be the dining room. I looked into another large, beautiful salon complete with a fireplace and a piano. The huge mirror above the fireplace reflected back my face, pale with frightened gray eyes.

What was I thinking? What would I even say? The next door over was closed. I knocked.

"Come in," a deep voice answered.

I took a breath and shifted the tray into one arm as I twisted the knob and pushed the door open with my shoulder.

"What's this?" A silver-haired man with a gray paintbrush moustache folded up the newspaper he was reading, placed it near the edge of the large dark desk, and peered up at me.

"Your dinner, sir," I answered quickly as I set the tray down in the center of that desk, on the only clear spot I saw. As I looked up, I saw we were surrounded on all sides by shelves of leather-bound books. Could anybody read all those in a lifetime? Mr. Moodie must be absolutely brilliant.

The man continued to stare at me. "Where is Jessica tonight?"

"Please, sir, if you mean your maid"—I looked quickly toward the door—"she may catch up to me any moment. I'm sorry to disturb you, sir. But I didn't know how else to see you. And I have a most urgent matter to discuss with you."

Mr. Moodie took off his glasses. "Sit down, boy." He gestured to the chair opposite him.

It felt like I was facing Mr. Morton all over again, only there was no strap in that middle drawer. I stared down at Mr. Moodie's wide hands and clean, squared-off fingernails. Instead, Mr. Moodie wielded something much worse: power over my destiny, mine and Father's. Finally I sat. "Sir, I borrowed one of your machines without asking."

"One of my motorcars?" Mr. Moodie ducked his head back.

"No, no!" I gasped.

"My bicycle?"

I shook my head. "Your Hoover O vacuum cleaner."

Mr. Moodie's bottom lip dropped. It looked as if he was going to speak but the words didn't form.

"I didn't break it. I didn't even dirty it. I promise, sir."

Mr. Moodie tilted his head. "What...what did you do with it?"

"I vacuumed your stable."

"I'm sure Beauty and Blue appreciate a clean stall but..." Mr. Moodie scratched his chin. He didn't look particularly angry; if anything he looked amused.

"I wanted to catch flies for the *Hamilton Spectator* contest."

"With my Hoover?" Mr. Moodie sputtered.

"Mr. Souter does it all the time," I quickly explained.

The sputtering turned into something else. Was he choking, I wondered. His vest shook. He covered his eyes with his hand.

No, not choking. Laughing. Mr. Moodie was laughing. "Ah, yes, that is something Mr. Souter would do," he said as he pulled out a white handkerchief from the jacket hanging on the back of the chair. "Anything to sell those machines." He carefully wiped at the corners of his eyes.

I dared to smile for the first time. No one would fire anyone while laughing, would they?

"And so, does it work? Are you winning? Tell me about it."

"Well, sir, I'm not particularly good at catching flies with my hands, so I have to keep trying different methods. But yesterday, I held the highest count, so I think it worked pretty well."

Mr. Moodie nodded. "Very good. What is your name lad?"

"William Alton."

"Arthur's boy." He tapped his glasses with a finger. "He told me you were a bright lad. And I think he is right. Now, why did you take it upon yourself to confess at this particular moment?"

I frowned. I didn't want to bring up Fred Leckie and our quarrel. After all, Fred's father was supposed to be Mr. Moodie's friend. Fred was his kind of people. I was just the son of the hired help. I chose my words carefully and explained how someone was pressuring me to pull out of the competition by threatening to tell.

"And you refused to knuckle."

"That's right, sir." I winced. "I told him you had given me permission."

"But you lied." Mr. Moodie watched me.

I took a deep breath but it didn't help with the boulder sinking inside my guts. How could I have told Fred the truth? The lie had been my only shield against him. Looking at Mr. Moodie, I understood that shield would now be held against me. Mr. Moodie would classify me as a liar.

Chapter 17

"I am sorry. The lie just came out of me before I could think of anything else. Fred...er"—

I mumbled over the name to cover up—"that boy was so insolent and I've promised not to fight with him..."

"Ah, Fred Leckie." Mr. Moodie smiled. "I've wanted to smack that lad sometimes myself. Well, you must promise me never to use my Hoover in the stables again. Can you keep a promise though, lad?"

"I can, sir. Really," I answered. "I never lie unless it's absolutely necessary."

Mr. Moodie tilted his head to one side. "Well, then," he said. He stood and reached out his hand. "You don't think it's necessary to lie to me, do you?"

"No, sir." At first I didn't know what to make of the outstretched hand. Then I realized I was to shake it. I grabbed hold and Mr. Moodie pumped.

"I'm sure, William Alton, you will go far in life. You're

going to be a wealthy man some day."

"Thank you, sir." I thought it was meant as a compliment.

"Now you will excuse me as I get to my dinner."

"Of course, sir." I continued to stand there.

"Is there something else?" Mr. Moodie asked.

"Well, sir. If you are finished reading your newspaper, might I have it?"

Mr. Moodie's eyebrows shot up. But wordlessly, he picked up the paper and handed it to me.

"Thank you, sir. Enjoy your meal." I took the *Hamilton Spectator* and backed out of the study.

What had I been thinking? Sometimes I astounded even myself with my nerve. I narrowly escaped getting Father fired and then I ask for the man's paper? Without a vacuum cleaner, however, I'd wondered how I would manage to kill flies in the stable. I had remembered how Father had rolled one and effectively swatted some.

I headed back down the hall and stairs to the kitchen. Mrs. Swanson folded her arms across her chest when she saw me, frowning. "What did the master say?"

"He said I would become a rich man someday." I shrugged my shoulders and tried a smile on Mrs. Swanson.

"That is if I let you live!" She unfolded her arms and shook a wooden spoon at me. "Go wash up for your supper."

I went outside to the stable, put down the paper, and pumped water over my hands. The coldness on my palms refreshed the red-hot sting left over from this morning's session with the principal. I lathered them well and rinsed. Then I wiped them dry on my pant legs and returned to the kitchen. When I found a place at the large table beside Father, I realized how much things had changed since we left Liverpool. Food in front of me, same as Mr. Moodie's, and a fine roof overhead. I already felt like a rich man.

Father accompanied me to the stable afterwards. I rolled up one section of Mr. Moodie's paper and began swatting, holding a large can beneath as I did so that I would not have to pick up the tiny dead bodies.

"Watch your step there, Will," Father called as he shoveled around me.

I looked down and saw the mound of manure in front of me. It glistened with the blue backs of at least twelve flies. I couldn't very well smack them with the newspaper. How could I capture those?

Father shoveled up the manure before I could come up with an idea.

"Father, what do you do with the manure?"

"A little goes in the garden. The rest gets carted away by the farmer on Tuesdays and Thursdays at the end of his day at the market.

"And the flies lay their eggs there, so their babies must go to the farm too?"

"I suppose, Will."

I continued killing the insects around the windows and against the stalls, thinking.

Father picked up the section of the *Hamilton Spectator* I'd left on the seat of the carriage. "Why, Will, your name is in here. See here?" The page Father held up indeed listed the names of all the boys and girls who had brought in a catch on Saturday. Too bad it publicized Saturday's numbers, because Fred Leckie's name was on top. Beneath him, W. Alton was listed with my catch of two thousand flies. "Well, my son, we come to this country not even nine days and already you're making your fame and fortune."

I grinned. First Mr. Moodie, now Father—both of them had to be right. I would become a wealthy man someday in this country. And it would all start when I won this competition.

The next week didn't go so well though. To begin with, right on Monday, when I visited the same stores and factories to rid them of their pests and raise my count, I found other boys had already visited. "What was the name of the boy who came in and killed your flies, Mr. Souter? Or was it a girl with long braids and a dog?"

Mr. Souter shook his head. "Not a girl. But I couldn't tell you the name. I thought he was you or one of your friends."

I had to change locations and look for flies in factories and stores farther away. It took time to walk to these areas and I needed to introduce myself and establish trust all over again. Of course, I promised Father I would only pursue the creatures after school. In order not to have my clients stolen from me a second time, I changed locations every day now, too. Even though there was less and less time to catch flies, the new areas provided a good supply. My count fell only slightly lower than Fred Leckie's and he had a whole army helping him.

"Nobody expects you to beat Fred Leckie. You're doing very well for yourself," Rebecca told me. "Why don't you enter the essay contest with me? Fred's never going to enter that competition."

Words, words, words, such a waste of energy, I thought as I listened to Mr. Samson on the last day of school. But I remembered Father's compliments on my apology letter and his pride at seeing my name in the *Spectator*. I remembered the walls of books surrounding Mr. Moodie, all full of words. I remembered Mum, too, suddenly and strongly. "Isn't that a pretty story," she had said one day after I had finished reading. The pain of the fleeting memory seared at my heart, but then it faded to a warm glow.

"Class dismissed," Mr. Samson said after we had recited the Lord's Prayer. "Have a good summer. See you next September." Everyone in the class stood up and cheered.

"Want me to show you some places where you can catch more flies?" Ginny Malone asked as we stepped outside the door.

"Are you going to show Fred as well?" I raised an eyebrow at her.

"He shoved my brother. I'm not helping him anymore." Ginny stopped and smiled then. "So if you're not too afraid, you can meet me at the market, at York and James, nine o'clock tomorrow morning. Look for the Buttrum's stall. They'll have a good cabbage supply."

She flung her braid back and grabbed left for her little sister's hand and right for her brother's. Together they marched down the street's incline back to Corktown, leaving me wondering if I could trust her.

"She's a strange one, that Ginny Malone," Rebecca said as she caught up to me. "She can be mean, but with her own brother and sister...she's gentle."

Rebecca and I continued together up the street. The Blink Bonnie came before her house. Really, I had no idea where Rebecca lived, only that she kept going. "Will I see you tomorrow at City Hall?" I asked.

"Of course. I'll be there to cheer you on."

I turned off and headed for the stable.

"Well, there, Will." Father gave me a slap on the back. "We should perhaps look for a new home this weekend."

"What? I thought Mr. Moodie accepted my apology. He can't go back on his words now."

Father's eyes narrowed, his brows instantly furrowed. "Now what exactly are you blathering on about?"

"I cleaned the stable with Mr. Moodie's Hoover on Sunday. But it was all right. I just had to promise not to do it again." I stared into Father's steel-colored eyes. "It *is* still all right, isn't it?"

"Yes, I believe so. Will, it's got nothing to do with you." Father shook his head. "It's your Uncle Charlie."

My heart began drumming. "Is he..."

"He is still alive and that in itself gives us great cause for hope." Father smiled. "But we should be prepared that if he recovers, he won't be able to work for a while. We can't expect Mr. Moodie to put us all up, now, can we?"

I shook my head. "We should buy a house, Da. Next week I'll win the fifty-dollar prize and we can use it as down payment."

"That's a fine idea." Father tousled my hair. "But just in case we'd better look for a couple of rooms to rent. We don't want Charlie rotting in a hospital bed waiting."

Father didn't believe I would win, I could tell. I thought for a moment. "Do you mind if I don't come along to look? The landladies we meet never seem to like children that much. And I want to keep catching flies for the contest."

"Probably for the best, you're right." Father shook his head. "But you must promise to keep yourself out of trouble."

"Of course," I answered, even as I crossed my fingers behind my back. I had decided to meet Ginny Malone tomorrow morning. If anyone could help me win, she could. Only I wasn't sure that I could stay out of trouble.

Chapter 18

I could smell the market from a block away. It had an earthy odor of animal manure mixed with cabbage and kale. As I approached, I could hear squeaks and squalls and grunts. At least thirty wagons lined both sides of York Street in front of the market building. Another twenty circled the center aisle of stands sheltered only by awnings. As I peered around the huge skirts and hats of the women shoppers, I could see baskets filled with carrots, broccoli, heads of lettuce, and other green leaves that I didn't recognize. Where were the horses? Each wagon must have been drawn by two of the manure-producing beasts. Still, I couldn't see any, and they would certainly be where the flies buzzed. I also couldn't see Ginny Malone or her little dog anywhere.

"Excuse me, excuse me," I said as I squeezed between the shoppers. I would start at the end near the building itself and work my way around. I needed to find Buttrum's stall, where she had said we would meet.

It all took my breath away. Flies buzzed dozily over the chickens squawking in the crates at the first stall. I wanted to begin swatting, but I knew it was past nine o'clock already and Ginny might give up on me if I didn't find her. As I passed the fish shop, I smelled our trip across the Atlantic again. From a bed of ice, silver-scaled creatures stared back at me with glassy dead eyes. Flies landed, rubbing their legs together and plotting their next plague. It set my teeth on edge. All the people buying and eating this food, would they all be victims of summer complaint or consumption or something? Were these flies really poisoning everyone?

Something knocked into me then. When I looked down, I realized it was Ginny Malone's little sister. Grinning, gap-toothed, she held out a handful of dead flies and I allowed her to dump them in the pail I had brought for this purpose today.

"And what's your name?" I asked.

"Bea," she said as she led me to her sister. "And my brother's name is Ian."

Ian gave a little wave and a big grin.

"Took you long enough," Ginny complained. "Isn't this a great fly-catching spot?"

I heard a loud squealing from the stall with the Buttrum banner hanging over it. A huge pig took offense to Finnigan sniffing at its crate.

"Finnigan. *Psht,*" Ginny called, and with a sharp bark, the dog dragged himself away. Head hanging for one moment in shame, Finnigan shot up suddenly, snapping at the air. "Finnigan, give!" Ginny bent over and held out her hand. The dog seemed to kiss it. "Here," she dropped the body in my pail.

"But you need to start your own can. You and your sister and brother need to enter the competition yourselves."

"We want you to win," Ginny said. "I want to show Fred Leckie he can't shove the Malones around."

We passed a stand displaying a small basket of oranges on the table. A wild squawking interrupted our discussion.

"Finnigan, get away from those chickens!" Ginny snapped her fingers twice and the black-and-white dog scampered toward her. "Hurry," she told me. "There are even more flies where I'm taking you."

I trailed beside her but for a moment lost track of Bea. Then I heard someone yelling. I turned and saw a man waving a shovel in the air as he chased after little Bea, who held something orange in her hand. Ian dashed back and cut in front of the man, tripping him and sending him flying.

I fingered the coins in my pocket. It was the money I had earned from fly catching last week. I knew what I needed to do, especially since we wanted to linger in the market and catch a few thousand flies today. I walked purposefully over to the man sprawled on the ground and held out my hand to help him up.

"I'm sorry sir. Did my friend forget to pay you? How much do we owe you?"

The man scowled so hard his moustache entirely swallowed his mouth. "Fifty cents," he growled, ignoring my hand.

Such a horrific amount of money for one piece of fruit. I was at least ten cents short. But now Finnigan ran up and began barking and growling at the fruit seller still on the ground. "Here," I said. "It's all we have. Or do you want your orange back?"

I watched as the market vendor studied the coins. "The oranges were a special display. I got them from Mr. Leckie himself. He won't like being cheated," he grumbled. "I should call the cops is what I should do."

Suddenly, Finnigan leaped forward baring his teeth and growling low in his throat.

The vendor scrambled to his feet and stepped behind a crate. He glanced at the change in his hand again. "I suppose it will have to do since she touched the orange and all."

"Thank you, sir." I nodded and strode away with Ginny. I had nothing left now, but it didn't matter. Stuffed in my pocket was a sandwich Mrs. Swanson had made me. I wouldn't starve. After all, I had wanted to buy Bea some butterscotch candy with the money anyway. Instead, she got the orange wedge that was promised Ginny, the one she had intended to give to Bea and Ian, only Fred Leckie hadn't paid up. That wedge and a few more. I grinned.

Ginny didn't stop or turn my way but I heard her anyway. "Thank you." I saw the pink flush on her cheek.

Bea and Ian ran through the crowds toward the end of the block.

"Where are they going in such a hurry?" I asked. "Do they know I've paid and they don't have to flee?"

"It doesn't matter. They're heading for the largest supply of flies in all Hamilton."

"Better than around those pigs and chickens?"

"Oh yes! See those three buildings over there on the corner of Merrick?"

"Yes."

"Those are the stables for all the market horses, the farmers' and the customers'. Hundreds of them there. And my brother Tom looks after them. He'll let us in. And only us."

I grinned as we walked to the first building. Ginny knocked and a tall freckle-faced boy with long arms let us in. "Don't disturb the horses, mind!" he told us, holding up a warning finger. With black hair and coal-dark eyes, he looked nothing like his sister except for the freckles.

I followed Ginny and her sister and brother in. The stable was oven-hot and reeked of manure—the perfect home for flies.

Side by side in the small stalls, the horses shuddered and snorted as the winged creatures landed on their flanks. When the giant tails swished them away, they flew over the piles on the ground, laying more and more eggs. Perfect, I thought again. Ginny was right, we would kill enough flies to win here.

"You can each have a fly bat," Tom told us, handing Ginny and me a stick with a piece of screen nailed on one end. He handed Bea and Ian their own sticks too. "This was how the original fly swat was made—one of the farmers told me. The air holes in the screen help you swat with speed. And the flies don't see it coming."

Ian slapped against the wall, hard and quick. But I could see the look of determination on Bea's face. She resembled Ginny for a moment, as she gazed at a cluster of flies on one of the horse's necks. She raised her fly bat high and then back. As she snapped it forward, I grabbed for it even quicker so that I caught it mid air. The horse threw back its head with a loud whinny.

"What did Tom say, Bea? No disturbing the horses!"

She stuck her bottom lip out in disappointment.

"Easy boy," I crooned at the animal to calm it down.

"Watch where they land outside the stalls," Ginny told her sister.

The four of us spread out and swatted. I felt the sweat roll down from my face and from under my armpits. It must have been the hottest day of the year. Over the *slap, slap* of the fly bats, I heard Ginny humming. The tune sounded familiar. I felt my heart swell and pound a little slower and harder. "What is that song?" I asked her as she dropped a handful of flies into my bucket.

"Don't you know it? It's 'Sweet Molly Malone.' We figure it was written about one of our relations!"

I frowned. "I had forgotten it. My mother used to sing it to us. I don't know if I remember the words."

Bea approached me with another handful of flies. As she dropped them in my bucket she sang in a sweet little girl's voice:

In Dublin's fair city,
Where the girls are so pretty,
I first set my eyes on sweet Molly Malone,
As she wheeled her wheelbarrow,
Through streets broad and narrow,
Crying, "Cockles and mussels, alive, alive, oh.

The chorus came back to me then and I smiled and joined in:

"Alive, alive, oh,
Alive, alive, oh"
Crying "Cockles and mussels, alive, alive, oh."

I stopped when Ginny joined in on the next verse with her sister. Though we walked to opposite ends of the stable, and slapped at the flies, their voices rose together in a wonderful sweet harmony.

She was a fish monger,
And sure 'twas no wonder,
For so were her father and mother before,
And they each wheeled their barrow,
Through streets broad and narrow,
Crying, "Cockles and mussels, alive, alive, oh!"

I joined in on the chorus again but found myself choking up. Tom sang with them instead, deep and low, and when they hit the final verse, I remembered suddenly and sharply the words, and when exactly my mother stopped singing that song to us.

She died of a fever.
And no one could save her,
And that was the end of sweet Molly Malone,
Now her ghost wheels her barrow,
Through streets broad and narrow,
Crying, "Cockles and mussels, alive, alive, oh!"

Tears streamed down my cheeks. It was the day my sister Colleen came down with that fever. Mum had started singing the song as she rocked my sick little sister, but she had stopped before she hit the last verse.

Chapter 19

"You don't have to cry," Bea said as she tossed more flies into my bucket. "Look, your pail is almost full."

"Don't be daft, Bea." Ginny dropped her voice and directed her words at me. "You've lost somebody then, have you?"

I could only nod. I knew if I forced myself to speak I would bawl like a babe.

Ginny squeezed my shoulder. "Let's stop for a bit to eat."

"Let me put something over your pail so you don't lose your catch," Tom said kindly. He cut some screen from a bolt he had leaning against the wall. With a piece of rope he secured the screen over the top of the pail.

"Thank you," I finally spoke.

Ginny took her sister's hand and mine, and called over her shoulder, "Come on, Ian." She whistled for Finn.

We stepped outside into slightly cooler air.

I looked around. The streets in front of the market were crowded with even more carriages and people. Two motorcars tried to make their way through the crowds with no luck. Shiny and black like bugs, they crawled along, honking loud and hard. "Does it never rain in this country?" I asked. "It hasn't the entire two weeks I've lived here.

Ginny shrugged. "Usually, it does. And we need some soon or we'll boil to death." She dropped my hand and fanned herself with her fly bat.

"There's not one spot out here where we can sit and eat!" Ian complained.

"Why don't we eat in Gore Park?" I asked. "There's benches and shade."

"And a water fountain," Ian chimed in.

"Anywhere to get out of this blasted heat," Ginny said. We strolled down the hill together, Finnigan at Ginny's heels. At King Street, we turned and crossed the road.

I grabbed the bench closest to the fountain in hopes of feeling the spray, or even the coolness of the air that had been close to the water. Placing my fly bucket on the ground under the bench I bit into the cheese sandwich Mrs. Swanson had prepared for me. Ginny took out what looked like crusts and passed them around to her brother and sister. From underneath the bench, Finnigan let out a disappointed growl.

I noticed how little Ginny had kept. She couldn't possibly feed Finn too, so I held out a piece of my own sandwich for the dog. Finn happily grabbed it from my fingers.

Even with the occasional hot breath of wind, a fine spray of water did cool us. I sighed as I stretched my legs.

Someone tapped my hand with something wet.

"Have a piece of my orange," Bea said.

"It's his orange, anyway, since he paid for it," little Ian said.

"Never mind. That's very generous of you, Bea." I popped the wedge of fruit into my mouth and, closing my eyes, just let it sit there. I didn't even want to swallow the juice, just to savor the taste on my tongue forever. Christmas on the hottest day of the year. I couldn't see Mum's face anymore or my sister's, but I could feel their love as I slowly began to move the orange around in my mouth. Finally, after a minute, I knew I would have to chew it up so that I could breathe again.

I never expected what came next.

When I opened my eyes Little Bea and Ian were kicking off their boots. Before I could stop them, they made a dash for the fountain.

"Will they not get into trouble?" I asked Ginny as they climbed in.

"Look around. Do you see anyone?" She shrugged. "Besides, it's worth it to them. By the time anyone says anything, they'll be cooled off anyway."

When Ginny finished eating, she turned to me. "I'm going in too."

I watched, astounded, as she removed her flapping boots. Finnigan leaped in after her, barking shrill and high. The other two Malones were splashing and shrieking. I couldn't stand it any longer either. I took off my own shoes and climbed in.

The water sprayed down from the top two tiers and reached to midway up my shin. Bea kicked at it, aiming her spray at me and wetting me to my waist. I poked my head under one of the jets to let the water splash down over the rest of me. I watched as Ginny did the same and giggled along with her little sister. Sunshine, laughter, and a cold-water spring, could anything be finer?

I didn't even notice the uniformed policemen strolling toward the fountain till one of them grabbed my shoulder.

"Here now. No trouble. Step out of that water."

No chance of making a run for it, not with that iron grip, but I looked helplessly toward Ginny and hoped she and her brother and sister could. Instead, another policeman guided her out of the fountain too.

Finnigan, meanwhile, clamped his teeth on the back of that constable's pants and refused to let go.

How would I explain all this to Father when I'd promised him to stay out of trouble?

"Call your dog off, miss," the policeman commanded, Finn's teeth still firmly attached to him.

The other policeman seemed amused. *Laughing is not*

angry, I reminded myself hopefully.

"Let go of me then," Ginny snarled back at the constable. She was very much like a churlish little dog herself.

She wasn't going to help our situation any, so I reached forward and grabbed Finnigan. "Come on, I have a crust for you still," I promised the animal. The dog released his hold on the pant leg, turned his head as if to bite my hand but then instead licked it. I scooped him up in my arms and the police constable released Ginny.

There the four of us stood, without boots, dripping wet, like a bunch of drowned rodents. No wonder the one copper was laughing. Was this exactly what the police expected of Irish brats, I wondered, and what was their punishment for the crime of jumping into the city fountain?

"We don't have to take you to the station if you promise this is the end of it," the laughing policeman said. "No more swimming in the water fountain."

"Yes, sir," I agreed for everyone. "No more swimming indeed."

"So move along with you," the bitten constable ordered, swinging his arms as if to shoo us away.

I found a crumb to keep Finnigan quiet. Ginny's rebellious glare I could do nothing about. "Just do as the man says, Ginny. Please," I told her, quietly. "We need to catch more flies at the market anyway."

"Fine," she grumbled. "You can put my dog down now. Ian, Bea, come along. We need to get back to the market."

It was a slower walk to the livery this time. We were headed back to work again, after all, soaking wet and cooler. Tom took us to the second barn full of horses. He also loaned me another bucket to store the afternoon kill in.

Slap, slap, slap, no one hummed or sang. Still, I felt like I was part of a big family, all working together for one purpose. Over the next hour my arm became sore and my shoulder stiff so I switched sides. With the left half of my body, though, I was an even worse fly catcher. "All right, that's enough. I cannot swat anymore. We must have enough to beat Fred Leckie."

Bea and Ian cheered. Once again Tom gave me a piece of screen to close off the top of the pail. "Thank you. I'll bring this all back to you tomorrow." *There should be an easier way of beating Fred Leckie*, I thought as I stepped around a shovel. Suddenly, my heel slid over something smooth and soft. I felt myself falling backwards. No recovery was possible, but I flapped my arms desperately, trying to avoid what I knew was coming next.

Chapter 20

I was used to the smell of horse manure. It had hovered over the streets of London and even in Dublin when I was very little. In this hot, sticky weather, the air was ripe with it. But that didn't mean I wanted to have it on my clothes.

"Are you all right?" Bea asked.

"I'm fine," I answered, picking myself and my fly pails up. I wrinkled my nose at the sight of horse dung stuck to my boot and the back of my pant leg. "Is there a pump somewhere?"

Ginny snickered as she led me to the water supply. I pumped and ran the water over the bottoms of my boots as well as my leg. No trace of manure was left by the time I finished. Still the odor clung to me.

"Never mind. We should head for City Hall," Ginny said, stifling another giggle. "We want all these flies counted in. You don't want to leave them lying around all Sunday and Monday till the next count."

I nodded, even though it was Ginny who had stolen my previous stockpiles when I'd left them "lying around." Today's catch should prove the winning number, I thought. Perhaps it would even win me the competition. How could I chance fate like that—I needed to rush those pails in to the health department.

Ginny and I led the younger ones across the street to City Hall. The three of them looked quite bedraggled from their splash in the fountain and fly fighting in the barn and I'm sure I didn't paint any prettier a picture. Nevertheless, we all trekked happily to the health department. As usual, a line stretched out of the building. I joined it on the stairs.

"What's that smell? Did something die around here?" a boy ahead of me asked.

"The dog farted." Ginny dug her fists into her hips. "Would you like to discuss it?" Her eyes locked onto the boy's but he quickly turned to face straight ahead.

I wanted to run home and ask Father to help me wash my clothes and perhaps hang them in the backyard to dry.

After half an hour of standing, I heard Fred Leckie talking behind me somewhere. I turned and saw him strolling toward the front of the line with a couple of his friends, sure as always that he could buy himself a spot at the head. They carried a large bushel basket. Fred slowed down when he spied me and stopped. He scrunched up his cheeks and nose. "Ginny

Malone, why would you want to share a space on earth with this piece of horse dung. *Uh*, he even smells like it." Fred covered the lower half of his face with his arm.

"Better to smell like it than to act like it," she answered him back.

I smiled. I liked how she defended me more than I felt bothered about Fred's words. But then I heard Rebecca's voice. "William, William!"

I wanted to hide. She was wearing a rose-colored dress with matching ribbons. She looked like a flower and probably smelled like one too. I closed my eyes, willing her not to see me.

"He's with us," Ginny snapped at Rebecca.

I opened my eyes and saw Ginny with her arms folded across her chest. Rebecca stood facing her.

"Is he now?" Rebecca answered. Her nose wrinkled and she stepped back a bit. "I just want to hear the winning count."

"Suit yourself," Ginny answered. But she didn't move over so Rebecca could stand with me. Likely a good thing since she wouldn't know exactly where the smell was coming from.

Rebecca held her ground too.

I looked at the two of them, side by side. Although they were as different as the sky and the ocean, they were also as similar. Rebecca, in all her store-bought finery, put together so well and so beautifully, seemed soft and sweet. But she was strong just like Ginny.

And Ginny? For all that she looked like a stormy sea after her wash in Gore Fountain, and seemed as tough as a horse-shoe, her loyalty made her gentle and kind, just in a different way than Rebecca.

I realized I didn't want either one of them to leave. I sniffed at myself. I only wished I could have bathed and worn a new set of clothing.

Suddenly, a voice boomed out. "Listen to this, boys and girls. Fred Leckie has just turned in a record number of 19,600 flies!"

Ginny gasped.

Rebecca bowed her head.

I stared at the half-empty bucket and wished we had all continued to catch till it was full.

The line moved up. There were other high counts too: Alfred Feaver caught 10,200; George Rogers caught 15,000; Harry Roberts, 8,900.

Finally, I stood before the health officer with my buckets of flies.

"Would you remove the netting, please," Dr. Roberts told me. His eyes looked kind but he couldn't do anything to help me. He had to count what was there. I hoped I had at least 15,000 flies in the pails. That would be a respectable number. I took off the screens and gently placed the buckets on the table in front of the health officer.

"Thank you." Dr. Roberts took a deep breath and slowly poured out the dead insects. Then he counted, and counted, and counted—grouping them in tens, shoving them in to another bucket as he marked a cross on the paper.

I mouthed out the numbers along with him.

At the end, Dr. Roberts stood up. "Another astounding catch!" he called, and my heart stopped beating for a second so that I could listen. "Nineteen thousand, two hundred."

Four hundred short of Fred's catch.

"Oh," Ginny said from beside me.

"Don't worry, we'll catch more tomorrow," Ian encouraged.

"But we worked at it all day, Ian," Bea moaned.

Rebecca squeezed her mouth together so hard it looked as though it hurt. She hesitated, as if waiting might bring a different result.

"Without our help, I don't see how Fred managed to catch so many," Ginny said.

"I know how," Rebecca answered.

"How then?" I asked.

"His father made all the staff in his factory catch for him." Rebecca shook her head. "There is just no way he will ever let you win."

"*Let* me win?" I said. "There is no *let* about it. I need to think about this. But I will find a way to beat him."

Carrying my empty pails, I began to move toward the door.

"Will?" Ginny called. "Shall we try again? At the market on Monday?"

"Definitely. I'm not giving up yet. But I need to go home, Ginny. I need to see my father."

Walking into the Moodie stable, I whacked four flies on my arm. "Father, Father!" I called.

"What is it, lad?" He came out from the far stall.

I picked up the one fly I'd managed to kill and dropped it in my bucket. "Is there any way I can have a bath right now? I smell so bad, I'm attracting flies."

Father grinned. "Well, you think you'd be wanting to attract them so you could win that competition." He stepped out and wrapped his arm around my shoulder. "You don't smell like anything to me."

I grinned back. "That's because you've been working around Blue and Beauty. You can't have any sense of smell left." I also thought Father smelled a bit like horse manure himself.

"Come along. Let's wash up best we can at the pump or Mrs. Swanson won't let us into her kitchen."

I stuck my head under the cold water, then my arms and hands. I let the water run over my shoes again. I scrubbed with soap and then rinsed all over again.

"I'll take my shoes off," I told Father, and unlaced them and left them outside the door. Even my socks felt stiff with dirt.

"Just in time for tea, gentlemen," Mrs. Swanson told us as she set out plates of mashed potatoes and corned beef.

The wash at the pump must have worked; I only inhaled the aroma of her dinner.

My mouth watered. "It smells delicious. Thank you!" I slid onto the bench behind the table.

"You're welcome, Will. You're a good lad. Lots of people 'round here don't appreciate what I do." She looked from side to side at the other two maids sitting at their plates.

"Mrs. Swanson, young Will here was wondering if he could have a bath first after supper. He's been catching flies all day and caught himself in rather a stinky situation."

"Sorry, no. Jessica and Ellie are going out tonight and will have theirs immediately following tea. If you help draw the water, it will go much quicker though."

I agreed, and after eating and hauling the water to the large tub in the middle of the room, I decided to take advantage of my own smelliness. I headed back to the stable and waited outside Blue's stall, daring the flies to land on me.

Chapter 21

Four hundred flies short! I pondered the number Fred Leckie had beaten me by as I soaked in the tub much later. I'd sat outside in the stable most of the night, killing the winged creatures as they landed on me. First I had jeered at them, then I fell silent, waiting patiently, watching to see exactly when they began to rub their legs. Then, *zap*, I'd scooped them up, squeezing just tightly enough to stop the tickling movement. It had made me feel powerful.

Now an idea came to me.

Why should I chase the flies? Manure attracted them. I certainly didn't want any more on my body, but why couldn't I just take a few piles and spread them out some place where no one would disturb them? I could water the piles so they would stay nice and moist. If I took manure that already had maggots in it, I could screen the piles in to catch the flies as they were born.

As usual, when I was done bathing, Father used my tub water. But when Father finished washing himself, I dumped my manure-smelling pants into the water. After washing them out best I could, I hung them in the backyard over the fence near the stable and headed back downstairs for bed. The whole disgusting, smelly incident had happened for a reason, I thought. Now I knew I could win the competition. I could show Fred Leckie and I would help Father buy a home for us and Uncle Charlie. Feeling cheerful, I fell asleep easily.

Next day was Sunday and Father once again insisted I come to church.

I explained about how difficult it was going to be to beat Fred, how I needed all the flies I could get in this last week of the competition. "Father, I can win this. And you can have all the money for a house—you know, so Uncle Charlie can rest and not worry."

Father frowned, picked up his cup, and drained the last bit of his tea. "Charlie may need our prayers more than a new home."

"What? But you said he was getting better."

"It looked that way, but he has a cough now."

"The consumption?" My heart fell hard into the pit of my stomach.

"We don't know. But the fever's back." He set his cup back down and ruffled my hair. "So come on, be a good lad. Come with me and pray for your uncle."

I couldn't argue with Father. Even though I had prayed for my sister and mother and my prayers had gone unanswered, even though I felt tricked by and angry with God and maybe had earned God's disfavor because of these feelings—for Father's sake I had to go to church.

The building sat just next to Blink Bonnie; we didn't even have to cross the street. As fast as we left the Blink Bonnie, we were on the front steps of St. Mark's.

"Arthur Alton!" I heard a woman's voice call just as we were about to go up the stairs.

Father stopped and looked around. I saw her first and pointed.

Father turned to see her too. "Be careful!" he shouted as she ran across the street toward us.

A motor car veered to the right to avoid her and bumped over the walkway. The driver waved his fist.

But Mrs. Gale didn't seem to notice or care. She continued straight for Father. Her face seemed longer and thinner than when I had last seen her. Was it only two weeks ago? Certainly her cheekbones jutted out more so that her brown eyes looked sunken. Her arms and hands seemed at loss with her body. Long and moving...and empty. That's when it struck me. Where was Maureen? Mrs. Gale threw herself into Father's arms, sobbing. "My baby's gone. After we left the boat, she only lived one more day."

So Baby Maureen had died in quarantine. Everything inside me turned cold.

"Ah, the poor lass." Father patted her back.

I couldn't think of what to do or say so I just stood there helplessly.

"Have you had anything to eat? Should we go somewhere?" Father asked her when they broke apart.

"Afterwards, Arthur. Can we go to mass right now? We need to pray for Maureen's soul."

I didn't know how she could continue to ask for God's help. God never listened. My eyes burned as I remembered Maureen's pouty lips and curly brown hair. Then they blurred so I could hardly see.

We stepped into the church and sat in the pew at the very back. An organ played and the melody lulled. Father knelt immediately. I saw his lips move. *Don't let my brother die*, I imagined his words. I was almost afraid to ask for God's help for Uncle Charlie.

In my head I tried to picture my mother, Colleen, and Baby Maureen together. I didn't think angels really had wings and halos, but I did see them sitting on clouds and they looked happy. I knelt then too. "God, let them be together. Mum can look after the babies. She would love that."

After mass, I asked Father if I could look in on Blue and Beauty. He nodded. That left him and Mrs. Gale time to be sad together and it gave me time to put my new plan in place. Another life those flies had to pay for, after all. I found a shovel hanging against the stable wall and talked to Beauty as I opened her stall door and scooped some of her manure. No, this was too fresh, I realized. I had to scoop some from Father's older pile. It needed to have maggots in it already if the flies were going to hatch in time.

I went round to the back of the stable. There I dug from the sides of the pile where white wormy maggots already wriggled.

Now where to put it so it would go undisturbed? I looked around. It should sit somewhere close, and yet somewhere no one looked. In front of the stable a well-attended, green lawn grew, with flowerbeds edging it closer to the manor; that meant the gardener would notice a pile of manure. I looked in back of the stable toward the small garbage shed. Between the manor and the shed the house help would likely travel at least once a day to empty the trash. Behind the shed. Yes, that was the only possibility. I carried the shovel around behind the shed and dumped the contents, banging the edge against the ground to shake it all loose. Back and forth I scooped, carried, and dumped the manure, thinking all the while about Baby Maureen and Colleen and Mum and now perhaps Uncle Charlie. When the manure lay across the length of the shed, I stopped, taking deep breaths to keep myself from crying.

And then a wonderful thing happened. The flies began shifting from the garbage to the manure. I had to resist the urge to bang at them all with the shovel. I didn't want to harm the babies already there. Instead, I watched and wondered just how long it would take till I had a new generation to kill for the competition.

"Will, Will?" a girl's voice called.

"Ginny?" I answered back.

"Will?" Her voice sounded closer now. "What are you doing back there?"

I wiped the tears from my eyes quickly.

"What's wrong?" she asked

I explained about Maureen and she hugged me tightly. Then I told her about my plan to grow and kill baby flies.

"Brilliant!" she gasped. "You kill their children because they killed ours." She stared at the aisle of horse dung behind the shed. "And maybe you'll beat Fred Leckie in the bargain."

"Exactly," I said. "But we'll need to borrow some screen from your brother tomorrow.

"That should be fine. Can we go for a walk?" She smiled at me.

"I'd like that. Let me just wash up a bit." We strode back to the stable where Ginny pumped the water for me. I hoped I didn't smell again but if I did Ginny didn't seem to notice or care. "Where are Bea and Ian?"

"Sunday, my mum doesn't work so she can look after them." She began walking and I followed along. "Do you want to go to the lake?"

"Yes. I've never been."

"Well," she flicked a braid, "you haven't lived in Hamilton that long."

I had no idea even which direction the lake was so I just followed her down the hill, through Gore Park, and even farther along King Street. Sweat poured off of my forehead. When we turned onto a street called Ferguson, I peered ahead, hoping for a glimpse of blue. No such luck. Just some sheds and in the distance a railway.

As we crossed the tracks, Ginny explained how her father had just gotten a job working on building the harbor. Things were going to be wonderful for her family from now on.

Unless someone gets sick, I thought to myself. Things had always gone well for our family till Colleen had taken that fever.

It was as if Ginny heard my thoughts. "I had a baby brother who died last summer. The illness came on sudden-like and there was nothing anyone could do."

"Do you think it was the flies?" I asked. I still couldn't see the lake but I could certainly smell something foul.

She shrugged her shoulders. "We didn't have enough to eat. My ma was too tired to feed him right."

"But you're helping me catch flies," I said as we passed

more houses and a grocery store. At the end of the street the stench became stronger. On the corner was a large brick building with the words *Sewage Disposal Works* over the front door.

"Killing bugs can't hurt, can it? Especially if you were to beat Fred Leckie. Just once it would be nice if the rich didn't beat us."

Finally, we arrived at the water. In the far distance, I could make out the shape of buildings on another shore. Another town? The air felt cooler even though the odor of sewage and seaweed hung heavy in it. The lake appeared two shades bluer than the cloudless sky and the water lapped gently along the wooden posts holding up the pier. We walked onto it.

"That's the boathouse," Ginny told me as she pointed to the large wooden building at the end of the pier. Ahead, white sailboats danced across the blue.

A young couple stood near the edge of the pier. The man wore a black-and-white striped undershirt—at least that's what it looked like—along with some tight black shorts that ended just above his knee. The young woman, wearing dark tights and a short dress styled to look like a sailor's uniform, giggled and held his hand. I couldn't help staring.

"Haven't you ever seen anyone in a bathing suit?" Ginny asked me. "My aunt has one. The latest thing."

I looked at the costume again. "We didn't bring anything to change into."

"Who cares?" Ginny took off her boots and then her dress. She dove over the side wearing nothing but her slip.

Dare I strip too? I took off my shirt and shoes, but didn't have the courage to show Ginny my underwear. I jumped into the water. It didn't smell fresh but it was cool, and splashing in it felt wonderful. Ginny swam like a frog but I just floated on my back, forgetting everything to stare up at the sky.

Afterwards we found a dead fish along the shore. "Quick, get something out of the bin so we can get the flies," Ginny said.

I rifled in the big round tin of garbage and found a piece of wood and a can. Together we smacked against the creatures buzzing along the scales. We managed to scoop another hundred dead flies that afternoon when we hadn't even set out looking. Too late for Colleen, too late for Mum, too late for Maureen. I only prayed it was soon enough for Uncle Charlie.

Chapter 22

The next day we visited the market stables again, this time the third building. In between tending the horses, even Tom joined in as we worked steadily to smack and swat in the heat. It was comforting to have Ginny, Bea, and Ian along side of me—a hint of what it might have been like if Mum had lived and had more children.

Five hours later, my arms ached and the odor of rot stuck in my nostrils. We had filled both pails and a potato sack. Tom also gave me a bolt of screen for my new fly trap. From the market we made the short walk across the street to City Hall. It was later than usual, a quarter to five, but that worked in our favor. The line had dwindled down. We didn't need to wait long at all before we could pile our catch on the table.

We hadn't seen Fred Leckie or heard his final count.

Dr. Roberts grouped the flies into tens and swished them into a bushel basket as usual, marking lines and crossing them through as he always did. When all the flies were cleared away, he spent a few minutes counting the marks on his page. He frowned and re-tallied. Then finally he looked up and smiled. "Congratulations. That's the record. For today and the whole contest. You've brought in 22,000."

Ginny and Bea jumped in the air, cheering. Ian slapped me on the back and I hugged Ginny and Bea as they jumped. Victory tasted as sweet as that orange we had shared back in Gore Park.

The hall was fairly empty as we left and I found myself looking around. Where was Rebecca? I wanted to share this moment with her too, but couldn't see her anywhere.

The Malones and I walked up the hill together again and, as usual, when we reached Hunter Street, they headed down to Corktown while I headed back to the Blink Bonnie. I arrived in the kitchen just as tea was being served and sat down at the bench behind the table. Father sat there with the parlor maid, the cook, and the butler, chatting and laughing, but it all sounded like birdsong in the distance. As I ate my chicken and potatoes and carrots, I felt my eyelids growing heavy. I would be glad when the contest was over—everything ached, I was so tired of chasing flies. My head nodded down twice. Then I felt someone shaking my arm.

"Will, Will. You have a visitor," Mrs. Swanson told me.

"What? Who?" I rose. As I turned toward the door, I saw Rebecca standing just inside of it. She was wearing a lavender-colored shirtwaist and skirt today, her hair held back with matching ribbons. I found myself blinking hard to make sure I wasn't dreaming. I quickly opened the door and guided her outside so we could be alone.

"I couldn't come today," she told me. "Instead, I brought you a present." She held out a large box.

"I won the count," I told her.

"Oh, Will! That's wonderful." She hugged me with the gift between us.

I took the box hesitantly. I hoped it wasn't some expensive trinket that would make me feel awkward. I lifted the lid and grinned at the pile of dried black bodies. "But, but...you told Fred you didn't want to catch flies."

"Nor did I. But it seemed the only thing I could do for you."

For a wealthy girl she sure understood me well. "We're going to beat him, Rebecca. I know we are."

"If anyone can, it shall be you." She smiled and lifted her chin.

There was a moment in which I wanted to hug her, but in the time it took me to wonder if I should, the moment passed. "Would you like to see my latest fly trap?" I asked.

"Very much," Rebecca replied.

I took her elbow and led her back to the garbage shed. "You must hold your nose." I walked around behind it and she followed. I had weighted down the corners of the screen with other garbage. Flies continued to buzz over it.

"Ugh, what an awful stink." She winced and fanned her hand in front of her face.

"It's horse manure. Of course it smells." I coughed myself at the heavy odor. "I waited till all the flies laid their eggs. Can you make out the slivers of white through the screen, there?" I didn't wait for her answer. "And I trapped other flies birthing even more when I laid down the screen. Once they grow into insects, I will just dump water on them and kill them all. An effortless catch. Should be good for thousands."

"But you're not catching flies here, Will."

I heard criticism in her voice and stepped back. "Certainly! Every one of those fly babies will be trapped, I assure you."

"Yes, I mean you are *catching* them...but you're keeping the manure here for them to feed."

"Brilliant, eh?" I looked at her face and saw her blue eyes widen, large as the lake. Only they had widened in horror— not in delight. Why? What was wrong with her? I thought she understood. "Rebecca, today I found out another baby died. The daughter of a good friend."

She shook her head at me.

"Don't you see, Rebecca. I must get even. They've killed two children that I know. Ginny's brother died too. And now, in return, I am killing their babies."

"But Will, if you're breeding the flies, you're no longer

saving any babies. You're raising them for slaughter."

My mouth dropped. I didn't think I'd ever felt as angry with anyone before. I wanted to yell out at her about her being rich and not understanding. My fingers curled into fists. I forced them open again and slapped the wall of the garbage shed. "I can win. You said it yourself."

"But you'll be no better than Fred Leckie. You've even used the Malone girl and her family...Fred stops at nothing to get his victory. And neither do you!"

"I've never used anyone! Not the way Fred Leckie does. Ginny wanted to help. Just as you did." At this moment, pride told me I should return her gift, but then I remembered my earlier victory. How sweet it had felt. I longed for another win, the big win. So instead, I turned from Rebecca and walked back toward the house.

"Will?" she called.

"What would you have me do?" I moaned. I stopped and looked back at her.

"Nothing. You're doing a wonderful job of killing thousands of flies. You don't need to raise more to kill."

"We need the prize money to buy a home."

"I've told you before, Will. None of the boys like writing and you're good at it. You know you are."

I rolled my eyes at her. "You want me to enter the essay contest."

"The prize isn't as great, I know. But if you really want to save children, you can give your winnings to the Babies' Dispensary Guild. The pure milk they provide keeps children healthy."

I shook my head. Her family could probably afford to buy milk for all the poor in Hamilton. She really didn't understand me at all.

I strode back inside the house to the room Father and I shared and threw myself onto the bed, bone-achingly exhausted.

Pure milk, pure milk, the words tumbled around my head until suddenly I had a picture of another time floating in my head. Far away and yet coming closer. In London. My sister and I are alone in a large yellow room, our flat. Mum and Father must be at work. Colleen pats my shoulder with a plump hand, cooing like a dove, her velvety head heavy against my neck. Then, suddenly, she is fussing, the way babies do, and I know I have to give her a bottle. I heat it in a pan of water on the stove but in a blink the bottle becomes too hot. I stand it on the counter. Colleen screams, waving at the milk, and I bounce her on my hip till I can't stand it anymore. I reach for the bottle. A fly sits on the nipple, rubbing its front legs together. Huge. I brush against its hairy body as I swish it away. *Wash the nipple. Wash the nipple,* I think to myself, but instead I put the bottle straight to Colleen's mouth. *No, no!*

My mind cries out, but it is as though I am frozen. She sucks at it immediately and is soothed into a blissful sleep. Quiet relief. Too much quiet. Time speeds ahead and a different scene plays in my mind.

Colleen is no longer crying. She's on fire—limp, not bouncing or waving—the scene speeds ahead again, and this time she lies still and gray in my mum's arms.

"William, love, can ye pry the poor babe from her?" Mrs. Gale's words. She holds the burial shroud ready for my sister. A white-veiled bag to send her to her grave.

"Mum, Mum, let me have her. I know what to do," I lie to my mother. My father has already failed to pull my sister away.

She smiles at me, trusting, and hands over her baby. Colleen is no longer limp. She's stiff, and her skin is cold, tinged with blue. *Forgive me, Mum.* I give my sister's body to Mrs. Gale and she slips her into the bag.

I awoke the next morning feeling as heavy and sad as the day I stole my sister from my mum. What could I do? There was no returning to sleep even though it was still early. Rebecca's words still played in my mind, but different ones this time: *None of the boys like writing and you're good at it.* I grabbed the pen and some paper from the bureau. I opened the jar of ink, dipped my pen, and began writing:

Why We Must Kill the Fly

In the autumn, when baby Colleen was born, I didn't know what to make of her. She was tiny and slept much of the time, but on the rare occasion she would stare into my eyes till I believed I was someone important, her big brother. By spring, she liked to stand on my lap and bounce, bending her dimpled knees and pushing off from her tiny feet. I would hold her tight so she would never fall. I was always going to protect her.

By summer, the flies were plentiful but no one thought anything of it. Colleen even seemed to like them. When one landed on her hand, she only laughed, and didn't her laughter sound like the bells on horses on Christmas Day.

When she fell sick, no food stayed in her. Every limb fell slack, her skin turned hot and her eyes glazed. Within the week, summer complaint killed her. The flies continued to buzz. In the fall my mother started coughing. The flies went to sleep, but it was too late. By the winter Mum was spitting up blood. By spring, she was dead too.

Father and I didn't know that germs traveled on these insects' feet till we arrived in Canada and Dr. Roberts came and talked to my class. For every fly killed at the beginning of summer, five hundred remain unborn. Perhaps *if I had killed just one fly, Colleen would still be alive and Mother would not have started coughing. You know now, too, about the germs on these deadly creatures' legs. You can save your own family. That is why you must kill the fly.*

I bawled right through the writing and had to wipe my sleeve across my face several times so that my tears would not soak the paper. Father awoke to the sight and, rubbing his own eyes, squinted at me.

"What are you writing, lad?"

"It's for a contest. You don't want to see it."

"Of course I do." He smiled and took the paper from me. As his eyes moved over the page, his breath grew heavy. He wiped at his eyes too. "It was not your fault, Will. Never. We were just too poor." He shook his head and stared at the essay again. "Today, I will deliver this to the *Hamilton Spectator* for you." He sighed heavily, clapped his hand on my shoulder and then kissed my cheek.

Chapter 23

"Tom said he had to order some boys away from the stable this morning. Fred Leckie has his friends as well as his dad's employees all out catching." Ginny seemed to be avoiding my question as we headed toward City Hall for the Tuesday count-in. Finnigan, Bea, and Ian scampered ahead.

"I didn't ask you about what Fred was doing," I insisted. "I asked you if you thought I was raising flies with my manure pile traps."

"Of course you are! And so what? You have to take every advantage. You have to win, Will. We're so close now!"

"Rebecca says I'm not saving any babies from dying. She says I've become just like Fred."

"What does she know, anyway?" Ginny threw one arm open wide. The other held up a bag of dead flies. "Fred is rich. You want to be rich, don't you, William Alton?"

I remembered what Mr. Moodie had predicted the day I confessed about vacuuming flies from the stable: "You're going to be a wealthy man someday." It would be nice to have enough money for a fine house like Mr. Moodie's. Imagine Fred's power over all of our classmates, all because his father had money. I wanted to take that power away from him, to have that power myself. Ginny was right. Winning was the important thing right now.

We had stayed extra late at the stable to maximize our kill. As a result we arrived at the health department a moment shy of five o'clock. Dr. Roberts was taking off his gloves for the day. He sighed. "Why don't you children just come back tomorrow? That way you'll have an even greater number to record."

Ginny dug her fists into her hips.

"Sir, please. Would you count them now? They are so many to carry and tomorrow we hope to have more," I pleaded.

Dr. Roberts sighed again as he slipped his gloves back on.

I emptied the first pail on the table. Dr. Roberts counted and counted. Ian hoisted up the second pail and Ginny dumped her bag. The speed at which the health officer lined up the creatures, marked them off and swept them into the bushel bucket was astonishing. Still it took him a good three quarters of an hour. Finally, he spoke: "Twenty-two thousand one hundred."

"And?" Ginny asked him.

"And what?" Dr. Roberts returned.

"Was that the highest score today, sir?" I asked.

"No, I believe Mr. Leckie had thirty thousand."

Ian whistled. Finnigan barked. Bea moaned. All that work, the whole day through, and we still hadn't beat Fred.

"You have four days," Dr. Roberts offered kindly as he removed his gloves again. "Anything can happen by then." He winked at us.

And anything did happen.

When I arrived home that night, I found another box of flies from Rebecca with a note:

Sorry we disagree about your new method. I'm still on your side.

> *Never forget that.*

>> *With admiration,*
>> *Rebecca*

That word *admiration* made me want to rush to my manure piles and stomp all over the maggots. But I also knew from Ginny that the market was closed on Wednesdays. Tomorrow we couldn't possibly kill as many flies. I might need those babies under the screen.

Mercifully, I did not dream about anything that night. I slept like a dog, barely twitching when Father shook me awake for breakfast.

"You have a visitor," Mrs. Swanson told me before I could even sit down. She raised her eyebrows at me.

I turned to see Ginny at the door. "Can she come in, Mrs. Swanson? Could she have some breakfast?" I put my hands together as if begging her and smiled.

The cook rolled her eyes, but ladled out another bowl of porridge for Ginny.

I brought her in.

"Blimey, Will. I think I've died. Could you show me around after?" Ginny spooned even more sugar on her oatmeal.

"No. Absolutely not. We can't wander the mansion."

"Just a little tour, no one has to know," she whispered.

I shook my head.

"Please, Will."

"No!" I snapped.

But after Father left for the stable I guided her through the kitchen, showed her the storage room with the Hoover O in it, our room, and the dumbwaiter. "Now we better go before the master catches us."

Ginny began climbing the stairs.

"Not that way! Ginny!"

She put her finger to her lips and, just to keep her out of further trouble, I followed her up. Luckily, none of the family was about and I dragged her through the hall as quickly as possible. The walls were papered with swirls of flowers and ivy, the dark oak floor carpeted with a deep red and gold tapestry.

"Ah, Will, to be wealthy like this," she said when she saw the drawing room with the fireplace and mirror. A large chandelier shimmered rainbows of sunlight everywhere.

"Let's just leave. Please. Or my Father won't have a job and we'll be even poorer."

I breathed fast and heavy when we finally made it outside. My heart hammered at my chest.

Finnigan yapped at me from the post where he was tied up. Ginny untied him and he leaped up happily on her and then me.

"Where's your brother and sister today?"

"Sorry, Will, they're fed up. Tom's taking them to the beach today."

"Of course. I'm fed up too. They've been marvelous to work so hard for so long for me." I frowned, missing the rest of my newfound family.

"Let's do the trash bins today, shall we?" Ginny suggested brightly.

"Yes, but we can start with our stable and garbage shed first."

In my own backyard, I found an almost empty bottle of tomato sauce with a couple of flies struggling in it. "We'll have to leave that and see if we can catch more. Then I'll smash it to get them out," I told Ginny.

We took along a rolled newspaper and a fly bat and walked

through the back alleys. By lunchtime we'd barely filled a pail. Still, Finnigan was happy with all the table scraps we'd turned up in the trash.

We tried the shops on King. I visited Mr. Souter and he let me use his vacuum cleaner along the window corners.

"Blimey, isn't that the most marvelous thing," Ginny said.

I told her how I'd used Mr. Moodie's Hoover O in the stable out back and how I had confessed when Fred threatened to tell.

"And you promised Mr. Moodie you wouldn't use it again? You didn't even cross your fingers. *Psht*," she said in disgust.

"He seems like a very nice man, Ginny. I couldn't use it again even if I had crossed them."

By the end of the day, we had a pail and three quarters. Sixteen thousand was all it amounted to.

"Nobody caught too many," the other health officer on duty explained. "I think the city is finally running out of flies. Isn't it wonderful?"

"Wonderful," I grumbled, knowing I shouldn't feel unhappy about the shortage. Didn't it mean children were safer, after all? "What did Fred Leckie catch?" I asked.

The officer scanned his papers. "Fourteen thousand."

I grinned as we left. "Two more days of it, Ginny. If we go full out, I know we can win."

Friday it rained for the first time since Father and I had arrived in Canada. A steady stream *shush-shushed* down, making the flies in the market stable dozier and easier to catch. Ian and Bea came back to help and Finnigan was in fine form.

"He's gets a little too lively when he can't run around outside," Ginny explained as Finnigan leaped up a wall for a fly.

I just laughed. On the way out, we walked closer to the building so we could stay dry. The rain cooled the air a little and I felt relaxed. I wasn't paying attention to what Bea and Ian were doing. They had been warned of pinching anything before they stepped inside the market and I trusted them. They walked by the baskets of fruit and vegetables without touching anything.

Suddenly, Finnigan bolted.

"It's a rat!" Bea called out.

Sure enough. A gray animal as big as Father's hand leaped ahead of the dog by a tail's length.

"Finnigan, stop!" Ginny called as she ran after him. The dog didn't even slow down. I followed with Bea and Ian.

The rat scrambled up and into a basket of potatoes. Finn scrambled after it, his hind legs sending spuds spraying across a chicken crate. The rat scurried down as Finn knocked into the crate. Chickens squawked and feathers floated out of it.

At least the chickens didn't get loose, I thought as the farmers yelled after them.

Still, carrots, lettuce, and leaves of all shapes spilled as the hunt continued.

As the rat tore across a pigpen, its back legs suddenly dropped through the slats. Its front legs held onto a rung for a second before they gave out and it dropped onto the pig's back.

The pig squealed as if it were being butchered. Finnigan leaped into hysterics, his paws scraping madly at the door of the wooden cage. Somehow his strength and persistence opened the door and the pig escaped too.

The farmer chased after the pig, I dove for Finnigan.

Perhaps I should have let the dog keep running, because that's how the cops finally caught up with us.

Chapter 24

Off in a little room in the market building, I answered the police constable's question. "I paid for that orange. That was two days ago! Yes, we bargained the price down but the man agreed. We would have returned the fruit if he hadn't." The constable was the same one who had caught us in the water fountain the other day.

"We never stole nothin'," Bea huffed in agreement.

The policeman raised his eyebrows at the orange vendor sitting across from them. He was the person who had sent the cops after us over Finn's rat hunt. Strangely, not the man whose pig was still on the loose out there.

"True enough. But why are they carrying those disgusting dead flies through a food market? And how can they let a vicious dog run loose like that?"

"Sir, these flies were caught in the market. We're doing the farmers a great service, getting rid of all those germ carriers," I explained. "And, frankly, sir, we were disgusted to discover a rat on the premises."

"If you ask me you should be giving Finnigan a reward for getting rid of it," Ginny said.

"He likes a nice pork hock," Ian suggested helpfully.

The constable slapped his hand on the table for silence. He looked around at all of us. "Here's what we're going to do. You children are going to promise not to come to the market anymore."

"Aw, that would be too bad. I was planning to buy a whole bushel of oranges this week once my father got paid," Ginny said.

The constable raised his eyebrows at her now.

"We promise," I answered for everyone. Ian repeated the promise. Bea and Ginny mumbled after him.

"And in return," the policeman faced the vendor now, "you're going to let the charges drop. No harm done, eh? Someone could put the health officer on to checking if you have a rat infestation, maybe."

"I'll drop the charges," the orange vendor said and stood from the table. "If you'll excuse me, I must return to my stand. I have my customers to attend to."

We shuffled out of the room too, the coppers leading the way.

"No more trouble out of you kids, eh?" the constable said as he followed us away from the market.

"Count on it," I promised as I sighed with relief.

But the interview with the policeman made us even later for the official Friday fly catch count-in. As we stepped inside the building, Dr. Roberts had already gone and the only health officer left was grabbing his umbrella to head out himself.

"Sorry, children. We're finished for today. You're not the only ones who didn't make it in this rain. Come back tomorrow. We're opening for an extra hour so we can count everyone's catch."

I frowned down at my soggy flies.

Finnigan gave a little half growl that ended on a whine. He made me smile again and I bent down to pat him.

His tail wagged and he licked at my face. Finally, I straightened and we all trudged out of the building into the pouring rain. "I don't know how we're going to come in with a win tomorrow. We're not even allowed near the market."

"What about your manure flies? The rain would have killed them for you today. All you have to do is collect those," Ginny said. "Can you get gloves somewhere?"

"I don't think so." Being rained on did nothing to make me feel more optimistic about the competition. When I arrived at home, I locked up my flies in the stable cupboard just to be sure. Then I swatted some more.

"Are you in there?" Rebecca's voice floated to me like music in a dream. She stepped into the stable.

"Hello," I called. She wore a plain brown dress and bonnet, but on her brown looked rich, like melted chocolate.

"I bet your horses are glad they aren't plagued by those awful creatures," she said as she looked at my evening catch.

"I suppose." I told her all about the rat race in the market.

"But that's terrible," she said. "Rats carry the black plague, you know. Well, the little fleas on their backs do."

"Perhaps the *Spectator* should have a rat-catching contest next."

"Or a flea-catching competition." She smiled and I thought I could feel the clouds leaving the sky. "Another can of flies for you." She handed it to me.

"Do you think I will win tomorrow?" I asked her.

She shrugged her shoulders. "Either way, it doesn't change how I feel about you." She reached over and kissed me on the cheek. "See you tomorrow. Make sure you don't let the little dog waylay you again."

"I won't." For one long moment, I didn't care about who won the contest either. I touched my cheek where it still felt warm, smiled as I stowed my latest catch in the cupboard, and then headed back to the house. I was starving and thought it might be supper time.

Next morning, with a clothes peg on my nose, garden gloves on my hands, and tweezers between my thumb and forefinger, I went to collect my manure flies.

First, I removed the garbage weights and then I peeled the screen back. I smiled. The manure was covered in blue and black bodies. Most lay still on their sides but some lay on their backs, their threadlike legs still twitching. They would make a fine catch, the winning one. As I plucked the flies from the manure, I thought about Father's criticism when I had told him this plan: "Don't fool yourself. This has nothing to do with avenging anybody's death anymore. This is strictly about winning, about beating that fellow you don't like."

Father was probably right, but he simply didn't know how awful Fred was. "One hundred and two, one hundred and three." I counted the bodies as I plucked them from the dung and dropped them into the bag, concentrating so I wouldn't throw up. As I cleared off each mound, I shoveled the heap back into the larger pile that would be taken away Tuesday.

I *did* want to beat Fred Leckie, to show him he couldn't just use people and treat them like the manure under his feet.

"William!" Father called from the house. "Come in now for breakfast and mind that you wash your hands."

As I pumped the cold water over first one hand and then the other, I thought about how I would finally prove myself to Fred. He would know that I wasn't just some poor boy living in a borrowed room. I was somebody to be reckoned with.

Ginny showed up in time for oatmeal. "I figured I'd leave

Finn with the kids back at home. Seeing as he caused so much trouble yesterday."

I told her about my painfully early morning fly harvest, which netted 2,310 flies.

"You know they just round up or down to the nearest hundred, right?"

"Yes. Are you ready? Today will make the difference between winning and losing."

"I know. Here's our catch from the outhouse near us." Ginny handed me a large can full of flies. "The toilet had overflowed so the pickings were good."

I winced. "Thank you. Thank you for all your help."

"It was the least we could do after I stole your flies for Fred. You're better than he is, *you* deserve to win."

Better than Fred. I savored the thought. It sounded much nicer than "No better than Fred," which was what Rebecca had said when I'd told her about the manure pile. Our target, we decided, would be every garbage bin, outhouse, horse livery, and fish market we came to. We would aim for three large cans full or stop at three o'clock, whichever came first. With that catch we would return to Blink Bonnie, pick up the stowed manure flies and assorted cans from yesterday, and head for the health department. We certainly didn't want to miss the deadline today.

First, I smashed the tomato-sauce bottle in the Moodie garbage bin for the ten flies I had trapped with it. We swatted for a bit there and then walked down the hill to King Street. As we neared the first fish market, Mr. Souter waved to us from his store.

"I heard you are a high contender in the fly-catching competition," he said. "I want to loan you something. Wait here." He ran to the back and wheeled out a wagon. On it sat his Hoover O. Taped around the Hoover was a sign that read "Souter's Amazing Fly-Catching Machine."

Ginny's eyes about popped out of her head.

"Now all I ask is that you bring the wagon to the health department today. I hear there will be all manner of dignitaries there and the *Hamilton Spectator* will be taking photos."

I grinned at Ginny. What a stroke of luck! We were certain to win the contest now.

Chapter 25

Ginny and I took turns with the Hoover O. A disadvantage of the machine was that we couldn't tell how many flies we caught as we went along. As she vacuumed, I continued to swat. One pail was full by lunch time.

We walked to Corktown to eat lunch with her brother and sister. It was the first time I had visited Ginny's home, and I was shocked. Their building was more worn and blistered than Madame Depieu's rooming house. We climbed to the fourth floor to the room that all six of the Malones lived in. It was only slightly larger than the one I shared with Father.

No flies buzzed around the pot of soup on the stove. Bea and Ian had caught every last one in the building for me today. I dumped their small bag into the second can. It would all help.

I didn't think I could refuse a bowl of the potato soup Ginny heated up for them. Ginny didn't finish hers. She offered what was left to Finnigan.

Then we headed off together again up the back alleys where the garbage drew tons of flies. No way to connect the Hoover here. Finnigan was in great form, though. Ginny had trained him to spit the flies directly into our tin on the wagon.

At two thirty, we emptied the flies from the vacuum cleaner into the can. We had two full cans now. "Is it enough?" I wondered out loud.

"Surely with your manure flies it will be," Ginny offered.

Bea and Ian agreed, but I knew they were just exhausted. And so was I. After today, I never wanted to see another fly in my life.

We pulled the wagon to Blink Bonnie and filled it with the containers from the cupboard in the stable. I hesitated over the bag containing my home-raised manure flies, frowning at it. Things changed somehow knowing that both Rebecca and Father disapproved. Something about these flies didn't feel right.

"Let's go, Will," Bea pleaded. "I heard they're going to take our picture for the paper."

I owed it to the Malones, now, didn't I? To do everything in my power to win? With a grimace, I squeezed the bag in behind the Hoover O.

Back down the hill we went.

Even though the lineup was the longest ever, there was a party-like feeling in the air. Everyone talked and laughed. Many of the parents had come down to City Hall.

There were new faces in line too.

"I've never seen you here before, have I?" I asked a girl ahead of me.

"No, I'm Edna Almas. Everyone who enters gets a prize, even if it's their first day. My aunt told me, that's why I'm here." She held up a can of flies for me to see. I looked at my own wagon full of cans and bags. I looked at Bea and Ian and then up to Ginny. They'd all be earning a prize if they hadn't contributed their dead flies to my catch. By the whooping and hollering, I could hear when Fred Leckie arrived with his gang of hired fly killers. His friends carried a bushel barrel each.

"Ready to lose, William Alton!" Fred hollered as he stepped up to me in line.

"As ready as you are," I answered.

"Say, little girl," Fred addressed Edna. "I'll give you five cents if you let me cut in."

Edna grinned and held out her hand.

Next thing I knew, I was standing one person away from my worst enemy. The line made a great shuffle forward so that everyone was inside the building.

"Listen, boys and girls," a gentleman with a camera said. "I'm with the *Hamilton Spectator* and I want all of you to stay for the awarding of the prizes. Afterwards I'm going to take you outside and arrange you on the stairs of the building for a picture. Only the registered participants, though."

Edna cheered along with the Malone children. But Ian, Bea, and Ginny wouldn't be registered, I thought. They wouldn't be in the newspaper. I remembered them all singing "Molly Malone" alongside me in the stable, hot and sweaty, swatting and killing.

The line moved ahead again. No numbers were called out. If the health officers didn't announce them, maybe they just weren't significant. Edna stepped forward again. The small counts of the last-minute entrants were making everything move quickly. I scanned the great hall. So many adults stood around, laughing and talking. Parents and relatives of all the participants? They would all be listening for the final winner's name. My heart pounded against my ribs in excitement. What if it were my name?

My eyes shifted and, suddenly, my heart stopped. Father stood chatting with Mrs. Gale and another taller man. Father had said he would try to get his work done early so he could be here for the final count. But it was the man next to him that made my head feel like it was floating. Could it be? I squinted to make sure. His hair was mostly gray with only a faded patch of rust-color at the top. He looked a lot paler and thinner than I remembered but it was Uncle Charlie, no doubt about it.

When Mrs. Gale saw me looking, she waved and smiled. She whispered something into Father's ear and then walked toward me.

From out of nowhere, a cluster of flies swirled to a nearby window. Finnigan barked sharply and then gave chase. He leaped for the flies. Once, twice, three times. Was he swallowing them? He continued to leap straight up in the air, jaws snapping.

All at once, Fred Leckie and his friends ran toward Finnigan.

Fred dropped down and grabbed the dog around the shoulders. He dug his fingers into the corners of Finnigan's mouth.

"Leave him be!" Ginny cried.

The dog held his jaws shut firmly.

I felt heat boil up inside me. "I can't hit him, I promised," I told myself out loud. But then I ran forward. "LEAVE HIM BE!" I yelled at Fred, who continued to pry at Finnigan's mouth.

Ian threw himself onto Fred and they both tumbled over, which gave me a chance to scoop Finnigan away. Ginny held her hand under his muzzle, and he hacked and spat up five flies.

We returned to the line, huffing and puffing. The strain of not hitting Fred had sent sweat pouring down from my forehead.

"You're a brave lad, standing up to that hooligan," Mrs. Gale told me gently.

"Not me. Ian was the one who threw him over." I looked at her face and, just for a moment, confused it with Mum's. I had to blink hard to clear my eyes.

"But your father has told me all about your exploits with him. How hard and honorably you've fought."

Honorably. I glanced back at the bag of manure flies sitting on the wagon.

"Perhaps if they'd had a fly-catching contest in London, my Maureen would still be alive."

I blinked even harder. Perhaps Mum and Colleen would still be alive too.

"I want to wish you good luck, young man. Your mother is so proud of you, never doubt." Mrs. Gale kissed me on my cheek. Then she returned to Father's side.

Would Mum be proud of me though? I remembered Rebecca and Father's disapproval of my manure-raising grounds. *You're not saving babies. You're raising flies for slaughter.*

Mum wouldn't like it either, I decided, and ran up to the head of the line. "May I have three cans from your bin, please?"

"Certainly." The health officer handed me some that had just been emptied.

I ran back to my space in line, opened the bag of manure flies, and poured them from the bag into the cans. "Here you go, Ian. For you, Bea. And Ginny, you deserve so much more."

"Have you come down with a fever?" Ginny asked.

"I want you to enter yourselves. You can all have your mugs in the paper and take a prize home. And I can have a clean... well, a cleaner conscience."

Ginny shook her head.

Finally, it was Fred Leckie's turn. Dr. Roberts took a full half hour to count his flies but he didn't announce his count.

"He's making sure we all stay to hear the winners," Ginny whispered.

I counted along as the doctor tallied Edna's. She had a full six hundred. Not a bad number for a beginner. She grinned as she turned and skipped to the side.

Then the three Malones registered and had my manure flies counted. Ginny had 1,200. Ian had 1,100 and Bea had 800.

"Not bad, little girl. Imagine if you had been catching since the beginning," Dr. Roberts told her.

And then it was my turn. I dumped one can and Dr. Roberts gestured for me to dump the rest. He shook his head and took a deep breath.

"Just think how many babies you've saved," Dr. Roberts told me.

Not enough, I thought.

"Well done, Will!" Father called from the side.

"Hurray, Will!" Uncle Charlie added. Having him here was almost too good to be true.

I grinned at him, finding it impossible to watch the counting now. Instead, I headed over and threw my arms around the one member of our family who had managed to survive a disease. *Thank you, God.*

"Boys and girls!" Dr. Roberts stood up and raised his hands in the air. "Congratulations to all. If our numbers are right, you have rid the city of Hamilton of about a million and a half pests."

The crowd roared.

"Which would have multiplied into at least 20 million before the season was over!"

A woman gasped. More cheers rose up.

"Keep up the good work and continue to swat."

Adults and children alike cheered and applauded.

"And now the winners. Everyone is to collect their prize after the photograph. In first place with 279,800...Fred Leckie! Fifty dollars."

Fred's friends whooped and hollered. Loud noise, but it came from only a few boys—the ones he had paid. No adults ran to throw their arms around him or shake his hand. Neither his mother nor father had turned up for the event.

"Second place...William Alton, with 278,100. A prize of twenty-five dollars." My face burned with disappointment even as applause thundered through the room. But then the cheering continued. Children leaped and screamed. Finnigan barked. Were all those people really clapping and cheering for me?

"Bloody hell," Ginny hissed at me. "You would have won if you hadn't made us take those flies!"

The flies that I raised myself from the manure. I shrugged my shoulders. My face grew cooler again, the disappointment leaking away.

From out of nowhere Rebecca appeared and gave me a hug. "I saw that you gave a few cans of flies away."

"The ones from the manure," I told her.

She nodded and smiled.

Dr. Roberts raised his hand for quiet and continued. "Remember to collect your prizes after the photo." He continued down the line announcing numbers.

I was too stunned to listen until I heard Ginny's name. She and her brother and sister each had earned two dollars.

I found my voice again to shout and cheer.

"Before we go outside, I would also like to congratulate the two essay winners. Rebecca Edwards for 'Germs on the Fly' and William Alton for the aptly titled 'Why We Must Kill the Fly.' Each earns five dollars and will have their essays published in the *Hamilton Spectator.*"

Father let out a loud yell. Uncle Charlie whistled. Mrs. Gale applauded wildly, her face flushing with the effort.

Hearing their reaction made me enjoy this victory more than I could have imagined. Definitely, Mum would be more excited over this win.

I took a deep breath and let it out slowly. The work was all over for me. I could collect my winnings, have my photograph taken, and spend the rest of the summer helping Father or visiting the beach with Ginny.

"You're rich now, Will. What are you going to do with all that money?" Bea asked as we headed outside to the stairs.

I glanced over to where Fred Leckie stood apart, snickering with his paid mates. I saw the look he gave Rebecca Edwards, longing and admiration that she did not return.

You're going to be a wealthy man someday. Mr. Moodie's words came back to me. Like Fred? With nobody slapping his back or pumping his arm, no one hugging him?

I shook my head and then answered Bea. "Well, I'm going to take you and Ian and your sister to the show." Then I turned to Rebecca. "And I'm going to give two dollars to the Babies' Dispensary Guild."

Rebecca smiled.

"You're daft. Let the wealthy help the poor," Ginny complained on the other side of me.

"Ah, but that donation will make me *feel* wealthy." I grinned at Rebecca. She had made me feel rich from the moment I had first watched her read, with those huge blue eyes and ribbons. "The rest will go to my Father so he can put it toward a new home."

"You there, stand over toward the back," the photographer told me. He organized all the children, little ones on the bottom step, girls to one side, boys to the other. Ginny stood grinning with her sisters. It had been worth it to give her the flies.

I stood on the top stair. The photographer didn't want Finnigan in the shot—he kept growling at Fred Leckie—so Father offered to take him until we were done.

We had to keep perfectly still for a long time and then, finally, there was a bright flash.

In that bright flash, I saw a future true and clear. I could study hard and become a doctor, like Rebecca's dad, so that I could help the sick. Or I could do research to find out why so many people were catching diseases. I might become a businessman like Mr. Moodie and donate my money to help the poor stay well. Or maybe I would write—even for this very same newspaper taking my photo—and my words could change the world instead. I smiled. So much possibility.

Acknowledgments

Thank you to the Canada Council for supporting this creative reach backwards in time. Stepping back into the early summer of 1912 was an exciting but daunting task. I could not have done it without the help of many people: writers, researchers, archivists, and historians Derek Grout, Anne Renaud, David Saint Pierre, Marsha Skrypuch, Nick Richbell, MLIS (Canadian Pacific Archive), John Alkma (Hamilton Educational Archives, Heritage Centre), and Marnie Birgess. The librarians at Hamilton Public Library's Local History and Archives Department and Burlington Public Library were also an enormous help. A lot of details were derived from the archives of one of my favorite newspapers, the *Hamilton Spectator*. Any errors or omissions are mine and mine alone.

Many real people from the past walked through these pages: Dr. Roberts was indeed the health officer of Hamilton, Ontario; William Morton was the principal of Central Public School; Mr. Moodie lived in the Blink Bonnie, but his stable was fictitious; and A.M. Souter did think the vacuum cleaner was a great way of catching flies. The *Hamilton Spectator* Fly-Swatting Contest was real, as were the amazing number of flies killed, but the boys and girls competing in this story are invented, along with Madame Depieu and her rooming house, of course. I could not have made up the courage of the extraordinary people who immigrated to Canada in search of opportunity. I salute them all.

DILEMMAS OF LIFE AND DEATH

DILEMMAS OF LIFE AND DEATH

Hindu Ethics in North American Context

S. CROMWELL CRAWFORD

State University
of New York
Press

Published by
State University of New York Press, Albany

© 1995   State University of New York

For information, address State University of New York Press,
State University Plaza, Albany, N.Y., 12246

Production by Susan Geraghty
Marketing by Dana Yanulavich

Library of Congress Cataloging-in-Publication Data

Crawford, S. Cromwell.
   Dilemmas of life and dath : Hindu ethics in North American
context / by S. Cromwell Crawford.
      p.   cm.
   Includes bibliographical references and index.
   ISBN 0–7914–21651X (acid free paper). — ISBN 0–7914–2166–X (pbk.)
   Hindu ethics.   2.   Hinduism—Social aspects—North American.
   I. Title.
   294.5'48697   1995
   291.4'2—dc20   93–50087
                                                          CIP

10 9 8 7 6 5 4 3 2 1

For Roberta,
here today and
here tomorrow

CONTENTS

ACKNOWLEDGMENTS

This book could not have been written without the tireless and meticulous collaboration of professors Lee Siegel, Ramanath Sharma, and David Kalupahana whose respective specialties in Indology, Sanskrit, and philosophy gave insight to my research.

Very special gratitude also goes to Roberta Mau who helped me collect and keep up with the daily flow of articles published through the popular news media on the issues covered in the book.

The editors of SUNY Press should be singled out for creating form where there was chaos, through their keen eyes and active pens.

The sources on which I depended much include the following: *Harper's Dictionary of Hinduism,* ed. Margaret and James Stutley; *Hindu Ethics: Purity, Abortion, and Euthanasia,* ed. Howard G. Coward, Julius J. Lipner, Katherine K. Young; *Hymns from the Vedas,* ed. A. C. Bose; the *Encyclopedia of Bioethics,* gen. ed. W. T. Reich; *Suicide over the Life Cycle: Risk Factors, Assessment, and Treatment of Suicidal Patients,* ed. Susan J. Blumenthal and David J. Kupfer; Edward Schneidman, *Definitions of Suicide; Encyclopaedia of Religion and Ethics,* ed. James Hastings; *New Introductory Essays in Moral Philosophy: Matters of Life and Death,* ed. Tom Regan; *Moral Issues and Christian Response,* ed. Paul T. Jersild and Dale Johnson; *History of Dharmasastra,* ed. P. V. Kane; Basil F. Herring, *Jewish Ethics and Halakah for Our Time;* Derek Humphry, *Final Exit; Active Euthanasia, Religion, and the Public Debate,* ed. Ron Hamel; Surendranath Dasgupta, *A History of Indian Philosophy;* Raghavan Iyer, *The Moral and Political Thought of Mahatama Gandhi; The Hindu Survey of the Environment,* ed. R. N. Ravi; Al Gore, *Earth in the Balance: Ecology and the Human Spirit;* the *Honolulu Star-Bulletin; Time* magazine.

The professional assistance of David J. Wethington with computer services was critical in times of need.

Finally, I thank my daughter Christine for her good cheer and inspiration, which sustained me in the completion of this project.

INTRODUCTION

THE CURRENT PROBLEM

"Most ethics become important when the roof falls in." So said TV Producer Fred Friendly as he began the timely task of making a PBS series aimed at examining "the tangled state of American ethics."[1] Indeed, beginning with Watergate, which did for the cause of ethics what Sputnik did for mathematics, we have become increasingly aware that wide sections of the nation's ethical roofing are perched perilously, "from the White House to churches, schools, industries, medical centers, law firms and stock brokerages—pressing down on the institutions and enterprises that make up the body and blood of America."[2]

Nowhere is this crisis more pressing than in respect to *life and death issues*, the subject of this book. As we survey the scene, we find "a widespread sense of moral disarray," to cite Church historian Martin Marty. Joseph O'Hare, president of Fordham University, adds, "We've had a traditional set of standards that have been challenged and found wanting or no longer fashionable. Now there don't seem to be any moral landmarks at all."[3]

The prospects for repairing the damage, and for America rebuilding a firmer structure of values than we have had in the past, are not immediately apparent. The situation is complex. But a major reason for apprehension is that with the breakdown of the traditional consensus, which was partly based on biblical sources, there is no more debate. Instead, activist groups, determined to preserve their partisan interests and ideologies, have taken to legislatures and lobbying, and we are now witnessing the *politicization of this nation's moral problems*.

The role of the media in shaping this turn of events is pivotal. Questions of life and death are fundamentally matters of religion, philosophy, and ethics, and are only secondarily connected with law and politics; but this fact has been obscured by the national media, which have presented these issues as political stories. Polit-

1

ical stories, like sports stories, always have a final score with a winner and loser. Clear resolutions are much easier to write about and make for catchier headlines than the ambiguities that hide behind the headlines. And so the basic questions go unanswered:

When does life begin?

Whose right shall prevail—the mother's or the fetus's?

Does an individual have the right to end his or her life when it becomes permanently meaningless and painful?

Do animals exist as means to human ends?

Must economic survival take priority over environmental survival?

The politicizing of abortion, suicide, euthanasia, and other life-and-death matters highlights the paralysis both of the press and of the public. There is a pervasive failure to come to grips with the dilemmas that divide us. As a result, in the place of open debate, moral issues have become the litmus test for political appointments, all the way to the Supreme Court. The full fury of "abortion politics" was felt at the nomination of Judge Clarence Thomas to the position of Supreme Court justice and also during the 1992 presidential campaigns, in which the Republican party tried desperately to put the focus on "preserving family values" instead of confronting the greater threat of economic loss.

In earlier times, when America was more homogeneous, we could look for answers to our moral questions within the Judeo-Christian tradition, and today, a self-proclaimed "Moral Majority" would nostalgically wish to keep it that way. Founder Reverend Jerry Falwell has stated how the New Right movement is "contributing to bringing America back to moral sanity." Their methods include "mobilizing millions of previously 'inactive' Americans," lobbying intensively in Congress to defeat any legislation that would further erode our constitutionally guaranteed freedom," "informing all Americans about the voting records of their representatives," and "organizing and training millions of Americans who can become moral activists."[4]

Moral Majority, Inc., is now dead as an organization, but its spirit is very much alive. As a salute to the members of the Moral Majority, Catholic theologian Father Robert Burns, C.S.P., writes that they "believe in fighting for the basic moral values on which this nation was built and upon which its strength rests. They are determined to prevent materialists, secular-humanists, and non-believers from destroying these values by replacing them with a value-less, amoral society."[5]

Some Roman Catholic prelates are turning excommunication into a political weapon. When John F. Kennedy ran for the presidency, he quelled the fears of voters by promising that he would resign if his Roman Catholicism ever intruded upon his political duties; but that stance of nonalignment was overturned recently when New York's John Cardinal O'Connor declared that Kennedy was wrong, and that Catholic officeholders must fight, not quit. In a twelve-page statement the cardinal pointed out that Catholic officeholders were obligated to support their church's moral teachings, or face excommunication. The most prominent target was New York's governor, Mario Cuomo, who called the statement "profoundly disconcerting." For his part, Cuomo, a devout Roman Catholic, accepts his church's stance on abortion, but has argued that it would be imprudent to politicize his position by imposing his personal views on the state.[6]

Auxiliary Bishop Austin Vaughan of New York has warned Governor Cuomo that unless he becomes more forthright in respect to his Catholic beliefs, he "is in danger of going to hell if he dies tonight." Disinterested citizens may find all of this inquisitorial rhetoric about excommunication and damnation medieval, with specters of penitent royalty shivering in the cold at Canossa. But America cannot "walk backward into the future." The tides that are washing across the country are moving society toward *pluralistic ways of thinking.* The New Right perceives this as a problem; instead, *it could become the wave of the future.*

Indeed, there is a new wave of internationalism that is now affecting the way we think in politics, business and industry. Social scientists are agreed that global interdependence and interaction constitute the common challenge facing mankind in the final decade of the twentieth century, and beyond.

THE ASIAN PERSPECTIVE

This book is a response to that challenge. It is presented to the reader in the spirit of East-West dialogue. It addresses the moral dilemmas Americans face from an Asian perspective. The justifications for this move in terms of comparative ethics are many and varied.

First is the basic matter of demographics. A headline reads: "Asian wave is changing U.S. scene." The new 1990 census shows that Asians are the nations fastest-growing minority group (up 80 percent since 1980, to 7 million), that their median household income is highest of any group (including whites), and that they are the best educated (40 percent are college graduates, compared with less than 25 percent of whites). Says economist Louis Winnick, author of *New People in Old Neighborhoods*, "Their impact will be far greater than their numbers."[7]

Second, as a result of this dynamic Asian presence, the concept of multiculturalism has evolved. *Multiculturalism* is "a new concept of American culture as a commingling of many distinctive strands, each equitably accepted within the fabric of our national life and all part of the rich interweaving of cultures that will be part of our emerging twenty-first-century civilization."[8]

Here in Hawaii, the "rainbow state," it has always been natural to think of ourselves as a "melting pot." However, according to *The Chronicle of Higher Education* (6/19/91), "melting pot" is now passé as a metaphor for cultural diversity, and has been replaced by "salad bowl" because "though the salad is an entity," its various parts can be distinguished. The special Hawaiian setting might better suggest the metaphor of "stir-fry" because there is a singular, identifiable flavoring that saturates all elements without submerging or subduing the identity of any.

Third, exposure to Asian spirituality has launched many Westerners on journeys of self-discovery through interreligious dialogue. Ewert Cousins of Fordham University observes, "In an unprecedented way, the religions of the world are meeting one another in an atmosphere of trust and understanding. The members of the different traditions not only wish to understand the others, but to be enriched by them."[9]

Fourth, Christian ethicists on the cutting edge of the discipline are becoming aware of the need to reconsider their positions as a result of encounters with Asian thinkers. John B. Cobb, Jr., a leader in the Buddhist-Christian Dialogue movement, states in the introduction of his book, *Matters of Life and Death*:

> We Westerners have inherited a way of thinking that holds that there is a radical gulf between human life and all other forms of

life. This can express itself in the idea that humans have both the right to live and the right to kill other animals with no compunctions at all. This drastic difference between human beings and animals of other species has been challenged and extensively debated in recent decades. The awareness that acting on the dualism of humanity and nature has done enormous damage for which human beings must pay a high price is forcing this reconsideration.[10]

Fifth, from the side of higher education in America, scholars are making a strong case for putting Asia in the core curriculum so that students can be exposed to the diversity of Asian culture and the richness within each culture. John B. Buescher believes that,

> Asia provides places where we can stand and look at our own culture with a new and comprehensive perspective. . . . We can study these cultures to illuminate our understanding of human culture. We can see what other human beings have accomplished and thereby what we, too, are capable of achieving.
>
> Asian cultures offer the West a treasure house of alternatives in everything from clothing, music, medicine, language, and art, to religion, ethics, politics, economics, and social organization.[11]

This is precisely what we wish to accomplish in this book. We view Asian culture as "a treasure house of alternatives," and seek to employ these resources "to illuminate our understanding" of the moral dilemmas confronting American society.

The Asian locus from which we wish to look at our own culture with a "new and comprehensive perspective" is the ancient tradition of Hinduism. This vast body of religious experience is a singular blend of spirituality and practicality, propelled by ideas and ideals that are pluralistic and progressive, and that embrace the well-being of humans and of all creatures alike. One verse sums up its entire body of ethical wisdom: "May all be at ease; may all be sinless; may all experience happiness; may none experience suffering."

RATIONALE FOR A HINDU APPROACH

The following chapters provide a detailed rationale for selecting Hinduism as the ethical vehicle for rebuilding public morality in the North American context. Here, we briefly outline the unique orientation of Hindu ethics to show its appropriateness to the present project.

Hindu ethics is a moral system which acknowledges genuine moral dilemmas. We encounter a dilemma when values to which we are equally committed are brought into conflict, so that the honoring of one value necessitates the violation of the other.

The Hindu position is to be distinguished both from the religious fundamentalist, who views dilemmas in the light of revelation, and the secular rationalist, who views them as problems to be solved by the use of reason. For the one, the problem is the need for better faith; for the other, it is the need for superior knowledge. In either case, there are no genuine dilemmas.

In Hinduism dilemmas are not denied. Its scriptures strain with the tension of irreconcilable alternatives. The best examples are found in the epic literature. The Mahābhārata and the Rāmāyana are not just works of antiquity but embody the social sinew which connects past with present and makes the epics dateless, deathless treasuries of true dilemmas.

The Bhagavadgītā opens with a moral dilemma tugging at the heart and mind of Arjuna, as this lonesome warrior faces the choice of having to kill or be killed by his own kinsmen. Bimal K. Matilal in his *Moral Dilemmas in the Mahābhārata* transports us to another episode in the life of Arjuna in which he confronts the difficult claims of promise keeping versus fratricide.

> On the very day of final encounter between Karṇa and Arjuna Yudhiṣṭhira fled the battlefield after being painfully humiliated by Karṇa in an armed engagement. When Arjuna came to the camp to pay visit to him and asked what really had happened, Yudhiṣṭhira flared up in anger and told Arjuna that all his boastfulness about being the finest archer in the world was a lot of nonsense, because the war was dragging on. He reminded Arjuna that the latter claimed to be capable of conquering everybody and thus end the war within a few days. In a rage, he not only insulted Arjuna but also slighted the "Gāṇḍiva bow," the most precious possession of this valiant warrior. The bow was a gift to Arjuna from Agni, the fire-god. He held it so dear to his heart that he had promised to kill anyone who would ever speak ill of "Gāṇḍiva."[12]

Yudhiṣṭhira's vehemence put Arjuna in a tight corner where he would either have to kill his elder brother or break his promise.

"When his Kṣatriya duty (*dharma*) made him choose the first alternative, Kṛṣṇa (his alter ego) appeared. On being asked, Arjuna explained: he was obliged to commit fratricide in order to fulfil his obligation to keep his promise."[13] His strong sense of duty made Arjuna reduce the situation to a moral conflict in which duty must prevail. To be sure, the duty of promise keeping was inviolable—the moral equivalent of protecting the truth (*satya-rakṣā*). Matilal observes that the scenario resonates with Kantian ethics, which also gives highest priority to truth telling.[14]

But Kṛṣṇa was no Kant. He argued with Arjuna that "promise-keeping or even truth-telling cannot be an unconditional obligation when it is in conflict with the avoidance of grossly unjust and criminal acts such as patricide or fratricide. Saving an innocent life is also a strong obligation; saving his elder brother would naturally be an equally strong obligation, if not stronger. Hence, in fact, according to Kṛṣṇa, two almost equally strong obligations or duties are in conflict here."[15]

In all such conflicts, the dharmic thing to do is to be guided by the demands of the situation. There is no question about the need to maintain the consistency of an ethical system; but sometimes the infraction of these virtues is permitted to achieve noble ends. This does not reduce ethics to opportunism; but neither is it made the captive of absolutism.

The point is illustrated by Kṛṣṇa's story about Kauśika, a hermit who had taken a vow always to speak the truth. One day, while seated at a crossroad, this holy man was begged by a band of fleeing travelers not to divulge their escape route to bandits in hot pursuit, with intentions to take their lives. Kauśika did not reply. When the bandits arrived at the scene, knowing fully well that the hermit could not tell a lie, they asked about the travelers, and Kauśika told them the truth. The travelers were caught and killed. Kauśika's fate was equally sad. Though he had punctiliously practiced virtue in order to reach heaven, he failed to achieve his goal because, in this instance, truth telling was a violent act which emptied his store of merit. Clearly, the demand of the situation was the overriding duty to save precious lives, even though to effect this meant recourse to dissimulation. But Kauśika was an absolutist who could not see that truth telling ceased being an unconditional obligation when weighed in the balance with the need for preserving lives.[16]

The Mahābhārata recounts numerous other instances illus-
trating the relativity of moral conduct in the context of "duties in
distress." A Brāhmaṇa in distress is allowed to perform sacrifice
even for an unworthy person, and may eat prohibited food. A
Kṣatriya, unable to subsist by his caste duties when his own avo-
cation is destroyed, is allowed to engage in the duties of a Vaiśya,
taking to agriculture and cattle rearing. The Śāntiparvan declares
it is *not sinful* to drink for medical purposes, to accede to a pre-
ceptor's wish to cohabit with his wife for the purpose of raising
progeny, to steal in a time of emergency, to tell lies to robbers,
and so on.[17]

Similar exceptions are permitted by Manu, the greatest expo-
nent of orthodox morality. Personal survival is deemed higher
than the stealing of property, making it justifiable for a hungry
person to steal food when all other measures fail.[18] Following
Manu, other Dharmaśāstra writers permit perjury to save life as
an act of *dharma*.

However, notwithstanding the dharmic justification of lying
and other such acts in situations of moral conflict, Hindu ethics
strictly enjoins the maintenance of its integrity in keeping with the
puruṣārthas or values of life. These values are integrated and progressive, culminating in the *summum bonum* of liberation.

In other words, the internal flexibility of Hindu ethics gives it
a certain advantage over two extreme positions on the current
social spectrum dealing with life-and-death issues.

First there is the position of *Authoritarianism*. It surfaces in
different degrees in the moral stance of religious groups such as
the Roman Catholic church, Protestant fundamentalists, Mor-
mons, and activists such as Operation Rescue. They base their
truth claims on holy books in which they find objectively valid
norms of conduct. They see human reason as flawed, and therefore rely on revelation for the truth, the whole truth, and nothing
but the truth. This makes them tend to see moral issues in terms
of black and white, and therefore to have little tolerance for
exceptional cases.

At the opposite end of the spectrum is the position of *Relativism*. Relativists argue that value judgments and ethical norms
are reducible to matters of subjective preference, and therefore
questions of life and death are considered private issues to be
answered by each individual. They, too, minimize the capacity of

reason. With hedonic overtones, Relativists make the individual's own experience of happiness the standard of value, worthy of protection by the American constitution.

Hindu ethics is distinguished from both extremes by the importance it gives to rational authority. This claim may be questioned because of the part played by revelation within its own system. However, Hinduism's recognition of revelation as a conduit of knowledge does not depreciate the role of reason. The Hindu *śāstras* make liberal use of reason in support of the positions they take. Only the final validity of reason is questioned in matters which lie beyond its purview, such as the survival of the soul after death. Thus the admission of revelation does not prejudice reason, for there is continuity between the two. Whereas in Western thought revelation is conceived as an external mode of testimony, in Hinduism revelation is an internal activity, similar to intuition. "It begins, no doubt, as an external opinion inasmuch as we appropriate it from our guru. But we do not merely acquiesce in it. We are under an obligation to intuit it and make it our own, when it will cease to be external and become inwardly as clear to us as it is to our teacher."[19]

Through reason and intuition, Hinduism finds the source of ethics in the nature of the human being. It agrees with the Relativists that the claims of Authoritarianism to finding absolute values is illusory and pretentious because social morality is inevitably the construct of subjective, historical forces that reflect the accidents of time and place; but this admission of subjectivity is not tantamount to saying that all of our choices between life and death are merely the products of subjective preferences. To the contrary, we can arrive at objectively valid norms based on our knowledge of *positive human capacities* for life, for love, for freedom, for integrity. Our *cultural formulations* of these objective values will always be relative, constantly to be refined over the long haul of human experience—which is to acknowledge that objectivity is not absolute or unconditional. The notion of absolutism is alien to Hindu ethics because it is a concept of transcendental revelation that is removed from an appreciative understanding of human nature and human history.

The fundamental operative term of Hindu ethics is *dharma*. This is not a static notion, standing only for the values of India in a bygone time with little relevance for other peoples and other places. *Dharma* is natural law. But the characteristics which define this law are movement, change, dynamism, and adaptability.[20]

SUMMARY

We start with the observation that American society is passing through a time of moral disarray. Until not so long ago, "there was a traditional language of public discourse, based partly on biblical sources and partly on republican sources," as Bryn Mawr political scientist Stephen Salkever attests.[21] Now, that language has fallen into desuetude, leaving Americans with no moral *lingua franca*.

With the breakdown of the Christian consensus, creative public discourse on moral issues, particularly those dealing with sensitive matters of life and death, have ceased, and, instead, contending groups are relying on legislators and laws to preserve or promote their points of view. Many of these battles are being fought in the public media where talk about abortion, euthanasia, and so on are fairly well politicized.

However, it is not all gridlock. At a time when America must rebuild a structure of values, the tide of multiculturalism is rising. In many interesting sectors of life, East and West are meeting, to mutual advantage. The argument of this book is that we can reevaluate the basis of public morality and rebuild the edifice with guidelines found in the ancient wisdom of Hinduism. This is not to claim that Hinduism has all of the answers to America's moral problems, but only that Hinduism does possess resources which could prove constructive.

What commends Hindu ethics is that it affirms universal values empirically grounded in human nature, but at the same time it is sensitive to the individual and the particular. Although Hindu ethics subscribes to the reality of cardinal virtues such as truth telling, it takes into account the conditionality of circumstances and makes its judgment for the good of each particular case. Human good is conceived in both empirical and spiritual terms, as befits human nature, the highest consideration being ultimate liberation of the individual.

CHAPTER 1

The Ethics of Abortion

INTRODUCTION

The battle over abortion was the political fight of the 1980s, and it continues as the most divisive issue confronting American society since the days of slavery. In its cover story, *Time* magazine reports, "The language of the debate is so passionate and polemical, and the conflicting, irreconcilable values so deeply felt, that the issue could well test the foundations of a pluralistic system designed to accommodate deep-rooted moral differences."[1]

The contest is between the advocates of "life" and "choice." The "right to life" movement has emerged as "the most powerful single-issue force in American politics,"[2] with a following of several million members drawn from New Right groups, and a coalition of fundamentalist Protestants and Roman Catholics. They brand legalized abortion as genocide and murder. In the long run they campaign for a "Human Life Amendment" to the Constitution that would safeguard the life of the unborn from the moment of conception. In the short run they seek legislation that would cut off funds for abortion both on the local level and on the federal level through Medicaid.

Leading the "pro-choice" group is the nation's oldest and largest family-planning organization, Planned Parenthood. Through 177 affiliates and 850 clinics in forty-six states, it annually serves over 3 million people with prenatal care and infertility counseling.[3] For fourteen years Planned Parenthood was led by Faye Wattleton. Her position was always "If we can't preserve the privacy of our right to procreate, I can't imagine what rights we will be able to protect."[4] Following 1992, Pamela Maraldo has assumed the leadership of Planned Parenthood. She is currently eager to present her ideas to the Clinton administration. Although she has no plans to relax the pro-choice emphasis of her predecessor, she recognizes that a single issue does not serve an organization well. Therefore under Maraldo's presidency we can expect Planned Parenthood to create a broader health and social policy agenda, giving priority to health care reform in addition to guarding a woman's reproductive freedom.

On both sides of the issue passions are high because abortion raises questions that touch on life, liberty, and the connections between religion, morality, and law. In the absence of open debate on the levels of religion and morality, the issues are reduced to questions of law.

The current battle over abortion is being fought in the political arena. At issue is what interest the government has in a woman's decision to terminate her pregnancy, whether abortion should be criminalized, and whether funds should be made available to poor women wanting abortions. Legislators debating these hot issues find themselves plunged into "the middle of a war zone."

THE CONSTITUTIONAL ISSUE

These were the sort of issues which the Supreme Court tried to settle in its controversial decision in the abortion case *Roe v. Wade*, 410 U.S. 113 (1973). As noted by Lawrence M. Friedman of Stanford Law School, the decision "sent shock waves through the country, affecting every aspect of political life."[5] "In one bold, cataclysmic move the Court undid about a century of legislative action. It swept away every abortion law in the country. . . . "[6]

The Supreme Court is the final arbiter in cases involving interpretation of provisions in the U.S. Constitution. It would be instructive, therefore, to analyze *Roe v. Wade* in some detail to determine precisely what the Court held and the grounds for its holding.

Jane Roe (a pseudonym) was an unmarried pregnant woman who wished to terminate her pregnancy by abortion. She brought an action in the U.S. District Court for the Northern District of Texas seeking, among other things, a declaratory judgment that the Texas criminal abortion statute was unconstitutional.

The Texas law made abortion a crime except when done "for the purpose of saving the life of the mother." A three-judge district court held that the statute was unconstitutional. On a direct appeal, the U.S. Supreme Court affirmed in a 7 to 2 decision (Justices Byron R. White and William H. Rehnquist dissenting).

The majority opinion, written by Justice Harry A. Blackmun, starts by acknowledging the Court's awareness of the sensitive and emotional nature of the abortion controversy.[7] It reviews at some length the historic, medical, and legal background. Particularly, it notes that restrictive abortion laws, such as that in Texas, are not of ancient origin nor even part of the English common law that was received in this country.[8] Rather they came about by legislative enactments mostly in the latter half of the nineteenth century.

The Court then proceeds to the constitutional question. It starts by noting that the right of privacy is not explicitly mentioned in the Constitution. However, in a long line of cases, the Court has recognized as implicit in various provisions in the Constitution the existence of a right of personal privacy or zones of privacy, protected against state intrusion. These are personal rights that can be deemed "fundamental" or "implicit in the concept of ordered liberty." They have been extended to activities relating to marriage, procreation, contraception, family relationships, and child rearing and education.

The Court finds in the Fourteenth Amendment's[9] concept of personal liberty and restrictions upon state action a right of privacy that "is broad enough to encompass a woman's decision whether or not to terminate her pregnancy."

> The detriment that the State would impose upon the pregnant woman by denying this choice altogether is apparent. Specific and direct harm medically diagnosable even in early pregnancy may be involved. Maternity, or additional offspring, may force the woman a distressful life and future. Psychological harm may be imminent. Mental and physical health may be taxed by child care. There is also the distress, for all concerned, associated with the unwanted child, and there is the problem of bringing a child into a family already unable, psychologically and otherwise, to care for it. In other cases, as in this one, the additional difficulties and continuing stigma of unwed motherhood may be involved. All these are factors the woman and her responsible physician necessarily will consider in consultation.[10]

Where "fundamental rights" are involved the Court had previously established in a number of cases that a state regulation limiting such a right may be justified only by a "compelling state interest." The Court then proceeded to consider whether the Texas statute met this test.

Texas had argued that life begins at conception and is present throughout pregnancy and that therefore the state has a compelling interest in protecting that life from and after conception. The Court responded that it need not resolve the question of when life begins. "When those trained in the respective disciplines of medicine, philosophy and theology are unable to arrive at any consensus, the judiciary, at this point in the development of man's knowledge, is not in a position to speculate as to the answer."[11]

> It should be sufficient to note briefly the wide divergence of thinking on this most sensitive and difficult question. There has always been strong support for the view that life does not begin until birth. This was the belief of the Stoics. It appears to be the predominant, though not unanimous, attitude of the Jewish faith. It may be taken to represent also the position of a large segment of the Protestant community, insofar as that can be ascertained; organized groups that have taken a formal position on the abortion issue have generally regarded abortion as a matter for the conscience of the individual and her family. As we have noted, the common law found greater significance in quickening. Physicians and their scientific colleagues have regarded that event with less interest and have tended to focus either upon conception, upon live birth, or upon the interim point at which the fetus becomes "viable," that is, potentially able to live outside the mother's womb, albeit with artificial aid. Viability is usually placed at about seven months (28 weeks) but may occur earlier, even at 24 weeks. The Aristotelian theory of "mediate animation," that held sway throughout the Middle Ages and the Renaissance in Europe, continued to be the official Roman Catholic dogma until the 19th century, despite opposition to this "ensoulment" theory from those in the Church who would recognize the existence of life from the moment of conception. The latter is now, of course, the official belief of the Catholic Church. As one of the briefs amicus discloses, this is a view strongly held by many non-Catholics as well, and by many physicians. Substantial problems for precise definition of this view are posed, however, by new embryological data that purport to indicate that conception is a "process" over time, rather than an event, and by new medical techniques such as menstrual extraction, the "morning-after" pill, implantation of embryos, artificial insemination, and even artificial wombs.[12]

The Court also noted that the law has traditionally been reluctant to recognize the unborn as "persons in the whole sense."

In view of all these considerations, the Court held that Texas, by adopting one theory of the commencement of life, could not override the right of the pregnant woman to decide whether or not to abort.

However, that right is not absolute. The state still has "an important and legitimate interest in protecting the health of the pregnant woman" and in "protecting the potentiality of human life." These are separate interests, and each "grows in substantiality as the woman approaches term and, at a point during pregnancy, each becomes 'compelling.'"[13]

With respect to the state's interest in the woman's health, the "compelling point" is at the end of the first trimester. This is based on the medical evidence that until that point mortality in abortion may be less than in normal childbirth. After the first trimester, the state may regulate the abortion procedure covering matters relevant to maternal health, such as the qualifications of the person who is to perform the abortion and the type of facility in which the procedure is to be performed. Prior to this "compelling point" the woman in consultation with her physician is free to determine whether her pregnancy is to be terminated, free of interference by the state.

With respect to the state's "important and legitimate interest in potential life," the compelling point is at viability: "This is so because the fetus then presumably has the capability of meaningful life outside the mother's womb."[14] After viability, the state may even proscribe abortion except when it is necessary to preserve the life or health of the mother.

Thus, the law of the land, as established in *Roe v. Wade*, is the following:

(a) During the first trimester, the abortion decision and its effectuation must be left to the medical judgment of the woman's attending physician, free of state interference.

(b) After the first trimester, the state may regulate the abortion procedure in ways that are reasonably related to maternal health.

(c) After viability the state may regulate, and even proscribe, abortion except where necessary to preserve the life or health of the mother.[15]

This 1973 legislation legalizing abortion almost suffered a reversal on July 3, 1989, when in a series of votes, many of them 5 to 4, the justices of the High Court restored key provisions of a Missouri law that a lower court had invalidated for unduly interfering with the constitutional right to abortion. Significantly, the Court appeared to invite further challenges to its 1973 decision, prompting an angry dissent from its author, Justice Harry A. Blackmun, but exultation from antiabortion activists. The Associated Press reported the following: "In his dissenting opinion, Blackmun said: 'For today, at least, the law of abortion stands undisturbed. For today, the women of this nation will retain the liberty to control their destinies. But the signs are evident and very ominous, and a chill wind blows.'"[16]

Two key points stand out in the Court's 78-page decision on abortion. States may:

(a) ban any public employee—doctor, nurse, or other health care provider—from performing or assisting an abortion not necessary to save a woman's life;

(b) ban the use of any public hospital or other facility for performing abortions not necessary to save life.[17]

Essentially, *Roe v. Wade* survived, though weakened. The new situation was reflected in the reactions of opposition leaders to the Supreme Court decision. Molly Yard, president of the National Organization for Women said, "Pretty soon nothing much will be left for a woman in controlling her reproductive life." John Wilke, president of the National Right to Life Committee, was jubilant: "We are smiling. We are thumbs up all the way."[18]

The mood on both sides changed sharply when the U.S. Supreme Court took up the challenge to Pennsylvania's restrictive abortion laws. On June 29, 1992, by a 5 to 4 vote, the Court barred states from flatly outlawing abortion, but upheld limits in a Pennsylvania law that gives states sweeping new power to make it more difficult for women to terminate their pregnancies. The majority decision was controlled by three conservative justices: Sandra Day O'Connor, Anthony M. Kennedy, and David H. Souter. In surprising language, the three wrote the following:

Men and women of good conscience can disagree . . . about the profound moral and spiritual implications of terminating a pregnancy. . . . Some of us as individuals find abortion offensive to our most basic principles of morality, but that cannot control our decision. Our obligation is to define the liberty of all, not to mandate our own moral code.[19]

With that declaration, the three justices got to the crux of the matter: a woman's right to reproductive freedom. In general principle, the framers of the Constitution spoke of the right to "the pursuit of happiness." The justices upheld that right of individual freedom in this uplifting way:

At the heart of liberty is the right to define one's own concept of existence, of meaning, of the universe, and of the mystery of human life. . . . The destiny of the woman must be shaped to a large extent on her own conception of her spiritual imperatives and her place in society.[20]

Justice Harry A. Blackmun said of the ruling: "Now, just when so many expected the darkness to fall, the flame has grown bright."

However, it was not all brightness and joy for the supporters of *Roe*. Although the Court did strike down Pennsylvania's requirement that married women tell their husbands about their plans for an abortion, it upheld the following restrictions in the Pennsylvania law:

- Women seeking abortions must be told about fetal development and abortion alternatives.
- Women must wait at least 24 hours after receiving that information to have an abortion.
- Doctors are required to keep detailed records, subject to public disclosure, on each abortion.
- Unmarried girls under eighteen and not supporting themselves are required to get parental consent or the permission of the judge.[21]

Following the Pennsylvania case, the Supreme Court refused to hear the Guam case. This does not mean that the abortion rights issue will vanish from American national politics, but only that it will now be fought out in state capitals as opponents of abortion rights attempt to legislate restrictions that will conform to the standard set by the Pennsylvania ruling.

The election of President Bill Clinton promises to change the lineup of the Supreme Court justices. He has declared that he intends to appoint justices who share his view on abortion rights. On the twentieth anniversary of *Roe*, Clinton overturned a series of abortion restrictions imposed by his Republican predecessors. Stating that "we must free science and medicine from the grasp of politics,"the president signed orders on January 22, 1993 that did the following:

- Lifted the tight restrictions on abortion counseling at federally supported clinics
- Overturned prohibitions against research using fetal tissues from abortion
- Ended a ban on abortions at military hospitals and funding for overseas population control programs
- Ordered a review of the ban on imports of RU-486, the French abortion pill.[22]

THE MORAL ISSUE

Although the constitutional question has thus been determined, the question of the morality of abortion still remains. Essentially, in *Wade* the Court was determining the extent to which the state could exercise its power to regulate abortion under the Fourteenth Amendment, not its morality.[23] The pregnant woman who is considering abortion, or any other person pondering the question, must make a personal judgment on whether or not abortion is morally justifiable.

As noted by the Court, there is a wide divergence of views on the nature of fetal life and when life begins. One's view on these questions to a large extent determines one's judgment about the morality of abortion. These indeed are matters of life and death, and yet there is a certain sadness to the present situation because the complexity of the issues place in stark relief the emotional simplicity of the responses made by the contestants and crusaders in this battle royal. Jonathan Glover sums it well:

> Emotionalism and simplification lead to implausible claims on both sides. Some take it to be an obvious fact that an abortion is just something done to a woman's body, comparable to the removal of an appendix. Others take it to be an obvious fact that a newly fertilized egg is as much a person as any teen-ager or adult. Opponents on either side are accused of supporting either the oppression of women or murder. It is sad that the

debate is like this, since its outcome will affect even larger issues than the ones now seen to be at stake.[24]

THE HINDU PERSPECTIVES

The present study will attempt to shed new light on aspects of the abortion issue from the perspective of the Hindu tradition. It is basically a religio-philosophical exploration based on classical texts, with no pretensions to any sociological claims.

The most important texts for our purpose are the medical manuals of Caraka and Suśruta which date from the beginning of the Christian era. The medical science they represent was known as *Āyurveda*, which has had a new lease on life in our own day. Semantically the word is significant for our study because the first term (*āyur*) defines the purpose of classical Indian medicine as the *prolongation* and *preservation* of life, and second term (*veda*) anchors the science within the religious tradition of the Hindus. Āyurveda was designated as a secondary science (*upānga*) linked to the Atharvaveda. This means that it looks upon science as collaborative with religion so that the cultivation of a sound body and mind is seen as ensuring the welfare of the soul.

From ancient times, the tradition out of which the medical manuals speak placed the highest premium on life in the womb. Feticide was killing. Correspondigly, there developed a system of supportive values, buttressed by rewards and punishments in this life and the next. Pregnant women were subjects of solicitude and were treated with kindness and care.

Before we examine the tradition, we shall be spared some confusion by noting, as Julius Lipner points out in his seminal article on abortion, "the distinction implied in the Sanskrit between the terms for abortion (*garbha-, bhrūṇa-: hatyā, vadha*) and those for (involuntary) miscarriage. The former terms assume that a morally reprehensible killing (*hatyā*) has taken place, rather than an ethically neutral evacuation, dislodging, or excision, for example, while . . . the standard Sanskrit words for miscarriage refer simply to a falling or emission (of the embryo)."[25]

The Śruti Literature

The earliest Vedic literature provides us with an attitudinal framework, plus certain specific injunctions, that give us definite clues to Vedic views on abortion.

The Āyurvedic ideal of longevity is a predominant value of Āryan society. The Vedic sages want people to escape the pitfalls of premature death and to live to the optimum period of life, set at one hundred years. A vibrant "will to life" is resounded in numerous prayers. Although there is the recognition that men are mortal, there is hope through the "gift to men" of biological immortality—"life succeeding life."[26] A father prays: "May I be immortal through my children."[27] Since Āryan society was patriarchal, it is to be expected that genealogical continuity was sought through the birth of many sons,[28] though it would be incorrect to limit all references to progeny to apply only to sons. "As in the Veda *putra* means "a male child" as well as "a child" (e.g., *putra* for the child in the womb), one has to refer to the context to find out which of the two meanings is intended. (Śayana represents the attitude of later ages in interpreting *putra* in every context as a "male child.")"[29]

This quest for earthly immortality is reflected in positive attitudes toward women, marriage, and parenthood. The poet brings it all together in "The Wedding" hymn:

Behold the comely forms of Sūryā!
    her border-cloth and her headwear,
and her garment triply parted,
    these the priest has sanctified.

I take thy hand for good fortune, that thou
    mayst attain old age with me thy husband. Devas—
Bhaga, Aryaman, Savitri, Purandhi—
    have given thee to be my house-hold's mistress.

Pushan, arouse her, the most blissful one;
    through whom a new generation will spring to life.
She, in the ardour of her love, will meet me,
    and I, ardently loving, will meet her.

For thee at first they escorted
    Sūryā with her bridal train;
Give the wife, Agni, to the husband
    and also give her progeny.

Agni has given him the wife
    with long life and brilliance;
long-lived be he who is her husband,
    may he live a hundred autumns.

Soma gave her to the Gandharva,
   the Gandharva gave her to Agni,
And Agni has given her to me
   granting me wealth and sons.[30]

In the Yajurveda the womb is mystically exalted as the place
in which *Purusha* (the Supreme Being) takes birth:

He is the Deity who pervades all regions,
   born at first, he is also within the womb.
Verily, he who is born and is to be born,
   meets his offspring facing him on all sides.[31]

The womb is here a metaphor of creation, denoting the manifestation of Deity as a continuous process, repeated from birth to
birth, and encompassing the past, present, and the future. The
womb is hallowed as the creative center of the universe and as the
point of intersection of divine-human activity which unites all
creatures with the "Lord of life."[32]

A unique feature of the Vedic hymns is their natural blending
of spiritual and moral values with physical well-being—a note
that is fully orchestrated in later Āyurveda. Longevity is not simply valued in terms of duration, but by the quality of life. The
Vedic code of life does not tolerate distinctions based on spirit
and matter, as in later periods, but displays the groundwork of a
vision of life in which full biological growth—from womb to
tomb—is a spiritual quest. Vigor, virility, valor and virtue are
parts of a single mosaic. The ideal of brave warriors living for a
hundred years has embryonic beginnings in fine offspring, and it
is for such progeny that the seers pray.

Earth, Ether, Sky!
   May we be proud possessors of fine children,
proud possessors of fine heroes,
   and be well nourished by fine food.[33]

The above verse is one of many which illustrates the biological
purpose of marriage in which Prajāpati (Lord of Creation) brings
forth children through the coupling of husband and wife.[34]

We now move from the three earlier Vedas to the fourth Veda
within the orthodox corpus, called the Atharvaveda (Veda of

knowledge of magic formulas). It dates from 900 to 600 B.C. and is closely associated with the science of Āyurveda.

A. C. Bose rightly observes that in the address of the bride-groom to the bride—"I am song, thou art verse, I am Heaven, thou art Earth, we two together shall live here becoming parents of children"[35]—is a sacred formula that lifts "the biology of human reproduction to a spiritual plane."[36] Indeed, the formula was continued in later literature.

The Āyurvedic connection is systemically apparent in the Atharvaveda's preoccupation with the preservation and prolongation of human life. The sage sings:

> For a hundred autumns, may we see,
> For a hundred autumns, may we live,
> For a hundred autumns, may we know,
> For a hundred autumns, may we rise,
> For a hundred autumns, may we thrive,
> For a hundred autumns, may we be,
> For a hundred autumns, may we become,
> Aye, and even more than a hundred autumns.[37]

To preserve and prolong life, the union of body and spirit is the sine qua non of health—"May all my limbs be uninjured and my soul remain unconquered."[38] A healthy couple marries, and the "good fortune" of "ten sons" is sought from "bounteous Indra."[39] "Bearing sons," the wife becomes "queen of the home."[40]

Certain charms prevent miscarriage: that the "embryo be held fast, to produce a child after pregnancy!"[41] Defensive charms are employed against fiends of disease that produce abortions, such as Kanva, "the blood-sucking demon," "the devourer of our off-spring."[42] There are charms also for easy parturition: that "the gods who created the embryo" may "open her, that she shall bring forth!"[43]

Given the values of the Atharvaveda, where life is construed as longevity, happiness as health, and boys as bounty, it follows that abortion is to be treated as a heinous crime, bearing the greatest guilt. In two hymns Pushan is invoked to wipe off "the misdeeds upon him that practiseth abortion!"[44] As the commentator explains, in a pyramid of evil, abortion is deemed the basest crime.[45]

Abortion as a crime is repeated in the Brāhmaṇas (1000–700 B.C.), which constitute the second major body of Vedic literature. The Brāhmaṇas are mainly ritual texts. The priests show little interest in questions of right and wrong, their imagination having run riot with the theory and practice of ritualism. The allusions to abortion are therefore significant.

In the Śatapatha Brāhmaṇa abortion is used as a criminal yardstick to illustrate the despicable character of ritualistc sins and their punitive consequences. One passage conjures up the fate of an abortionist in order to evoke the hell awaiting a person who has violated the sacred prohibition against eating the flesh of an ox or a cow. "Such a one indeed would be likely to be born (again) as a strange being, (as one of whom there is) evil report, such as 'he has expelled an embryo from a woman,' 'he has committed a sin'; let him therefore not eat (the flesh) of the cow and the ox."[46]

Another passage, aimed at enforcing the carrying of the sacred fire around the neck of the sacrificer during the time of his initiation, warns: "Surely, he who kills a human embryo, is despised, how much more then he who kills him (Agni), for he is a god: 'Let no one become an officiating priest for an (Agni) who has not been carried about for a year,' said Vatsya, 'lest he should be a participator in the killing of this, a god's seed!'"[47]

More important than the textual evidence is the emergence, during the period of the Brāhmaṇas, of a new set of ethical values which make a permanent contribution to Hinduism's attitude toward the procreation and preservation of progeny. The need arose in Āryan society to strengthen the community and to safeguard its cultural heritage. The response was the introduction of the concept of *obligation* in the doctine of *ṛṇa* (indebtedness). It was held that all Āryans were born with three binding duties: to the gods, to the sages, and to the ancestors. The first duty was discharged by the performance of sacrifices; the second, through the study of the Vedas; and the third, which interests us here, by producing sons, and thus ensuring the survival of the family. In time it was deemed a sin to seek liberation before the fulfilment of these values.

The Upaniṣads (700–500 B.C.) shed Vedic ceremonialism for the supreme quest of self-realization. *Brahman*, ultimate Reality, objectively perceived, is none other than *Ātman* in the depths of the self. *Tat tvam asi:* "That art thou." Liberation is the discovery of one's identity with the Supreme. To be sure, the Upaniṣads subscribe to a variety of metaphysical views, but the dominant belief in the unity of life has profound bearing on the status of the unborn and the taking of life. Given the monistic outlook of some Upaniṣads, it is a natural corollary that abortion is regarded as gravely evil.

This attitude is evident in two passages. The Bṛihadāraṇyaka Upaniṣad, describing the soul in the trance state—a state of deep, dreamless sleep—points out that the state is so much out of this world that deepest distinctions are erased, so that "the destroyer of an embryo becomes not the destroyer of an embryo," just as a father is not a father, and a mother is not a mother.[48] In the Kaushītaki Upaniṣad we learn that the liberated soul, having realized his unity with the Ātman, is freed from his good and evil deeds because these deeds belong to the individual existence, now seen as illusory. In the following passage, Indra, declaring that knowledge of him is the greatest boon to men, says: "So he who understands me—by no deed whatsoever of his is his world injured, not by stealing, not by killing an embryo, not by the murder of his mother, not by the murder of his father; if he has done any evil (*pāpa*), the dark color departs from his face."[49] In both passages, the Upaniṣads assume that abortion is among the most deplorable evils, subject to consequences that karmically affect both this life and the next, and that only through enlightenment is one delivered from its malevolent force.

The Smṛti Literature

We now examine the data from the Sūtra and epic periods found in the *smṛti* literature (that which is remembered), covering the period 500 B.C. to A.D. 300. *Smṛti* incorporates all authoritative texts outside the Vedas. The most important works for our purpose are the Dharma Sūtras, Dharma Śāstras, and the two epics.

The Dharma Sūtras are aphoristic codes (*sūtras*, threads) that impart general principles of moral law (*dharma*). Their sanctions for ethical behavior are religious, not judicial. The treatment of law is not systematic, and their teachings on civil and criminal law are scarce. The most significant of these early lawbooks are the Dharma Sūtras of Gautama, Baudhāyana, Vasiṣṭha, and

Āpastamba. They date approximately from the sixth to the second centuries B.C.

The Dharma Śāstras date later than the Dharma Sūtras and are more precise and complete. Like the early lawbooks, the Dharma Śāstras are not as concerned with legal distinctions and technical definitions as with moral duties. The most authoritative text on the subject of *dharma*, professing divine origin, is the Laws of Manu. It is claimed: "What Manu says is medicine." The date of its composition is sometime between the first century B.C. and the second century A.D.

The Mahābhārata and Rāmāyaṇa are the two most cherished works of popular Hinduism. The epics are splendid illustrations of the evolutionary character of Hindu thought, having undergone successive accretions and transformations over a period of four to five centuries.

The general picture that emerges from this vast literature is that life begins at conception, feticide is a major sin, progeny is a great good, women are worthy of respect and care, and pregnant women are especially to be protected and granted concessions.

Yājñavalkya presents a view of embryology in which the soul takes form at conception and is progressively invested with all elements for human development.[50]

According to Manu, the process of hominization begins at conception, whereby, through the act of impregnation, the husband takes birth as the fetus in the womb of his wife. The wife is therefore called *Jāyā*, "inasmuch as the husband is again born in her."[51]

The assiduous protection that is enjoined for the wife does not appear to be so much for the woman's sake as for the purity of progeny, because, as stated above, it is the man who has impregnated her that is reborn. This seems to suggest that in the act of conception there is the implantation of the seeds of personhood.[52] From day one, pregnancy is a particular man in the making. Gestation is the development of a specific human who enters the womb at conception.

This view of what takes place in the moment of conception is reflected in the fixing of the dates for the *saṁskāras* (sacraments) by counting from the time of conception, and *not from the day of birth*. For instance, Yājñavalkya decrees that the Upanayanam ceremony of a Brahmin must be in the eighth year, calculated from conception.[53]

The belief that fetal existence is elementally human provides the basis for branding the "killing of an embryo" as mortal sin, to be redressed by severe penances and punishments. It is classifed as one of the five *mahāpātakas* or atrocious acts. Several authorities aver that the procurer of abortions is a *mahāpātakin*. Gautama equates abortion with Brahmanicide, punishable by the "deprivation of the rights and privileges of a Brahmana, and a degraded status in the next world."[54] Similarly, Vasiṣṭha categorizes the *bhrūnahan* as the slayer of a learned Brahmin or a destroyer of an embryo.[55] Such a comparison can only mean the personalization of the embryo. Manu enjoins the same expiatory penance, even when a fetus is *unwillingly* killed, as for the sin of "Brāhmaṇa-killing."[56] Yājñavalkya places "destruction of the fetus" on par with a woman's slaying her husband, and therefore subject to identical ostracism.[57] The personal factor that makes feticide a *mahāpātaka* similarly accounts for the celebration of progeny as a great good.

A father is expected to give his daughter in marriage upon attainment of puberty in order that she may be fruitful. Should the girl menstruate before she marries, the father is guilty of the sin of abortion and becomes degraded.[58] Vasiṣṭha endorses this teaching of Vyāsa and adds: "As often as are the menstrual courses of a maiden, who is desirous of, and is solicited in marriage by, a qualified bridegroom of the same caste, so often her father and mother are guilty of [the crime of] killing an embryo: such is the sacred law."[59] Vishṇu goes one step further and permits a maiden who has "passed three monthly courses" to "choose a husband on the expiry of her third menstrual period." Otherwise she lives in disgrace. He also states that a suitor "commits no sin, by carrying her away (from the custody of her guardians)."[60]

Once married, procreation is paramount. "He who does not visit his wife on the day of her menstrual ablution becomes certainly guilty of the dreadful sin of faeticide [sic]."[61]

Given its patriarchal structure, the procreation of sons is especially coveted, partly for economic and social reasons, but mostly for religious reasons. The *śrāddha* ceremony is a religious rite performed for deceased ancestors. It is believed to have the power to avert the sins of omission and commission of the parents which are visited upon their family. The rite also assists the admission of the deceased father into the company of the forefathers. It follows that a father not having a son to effectuate his passage into the assembly of the *pitṛ*, through *śrāddha* offerings, is indeed cursed.

This need for many sons accounts for the old Hindu law's recognition of twelve kinds of sons. Yājñavalkya describes one type of offspring (*kshetraja*) of a wife by a kinsman duly appointed to raise up issue to the husband.[62]

Because of their vital role in bringing sons into the world, pregnant women are accorded care and concessions. Yājñavalkya urges all indulgence: "By not giving what a woman, in pregnancy, wishes for, the embryo meets with some shortcomings, either [in the shape of] disfigurement or death. Therefore what is liked by [a pregnant] woman must be gratified."[63] Likewise Vishṇu exempts pregnant women from having to pay toll;[64] and Manu enjoins that the needs of the pregnant woman in the home must take precedence over those of the *atithis* (chance guests).[65] Again, the reason for Manu's insistence that the wife should be "assiduously protected" is that the husband takes birth within her womb, and "for the purity of his progeny. . . . "[66]

Female protection does not seem to be based on caste. Life is at stake, and hence all women have a right to protection. Yājñavalkya enjoins punishment upon one "who destroys the embryo of a female servant."[67] Killing any woman in her menses or who is pregnant is "equal to that of killing a Brahmana."[68]

From the time of conception, and thereafter as the child develops and grows, certain Vedic rites are called for to purify the individual both in this life and the next. Manu: "By means of the Vedic rites of consecration of the womb, post-natal purification, tonsure, and initiation with the thread, the sin of the twice-born ones, pertaining to the seed and womb (of their parents) is absolved."[69] Likewise, Yājñavalkya states that with the performance of the prescribed rites "the sin begotten of semen and blood, is dissipated. . . . "[70] This expiatory function of prenatal rites attributes a personal character to the unborn; otherwise it would make no sense to claim the mystical removal of sin.

The common themes of the legal literature—identifying abortion as a heinous sin, rejoicing in many sons, deference to pregnant women, and the practice of *niyoga* (levirate marriage)—are all present in the Mahābhārata and need not be repeated. They collectively affirm the ancient view that life in the womb is not tissue of the mother's body, but a separate life bearing the essential marks of humanity from the time of conception.

The value that cradles this view of the unborn is *ahiṃsā* (nonviolence). It is present in the rules of hospitality, gentleness, care for the young and aged, and kindness to the land, birds, insects, animals; above all, it is the birthright of that most vulnerable form of all existence—a child in the womb. And so it is that Kṛṣṇa informs Arjuna that among the endowments of those who are born with the divine nature, the first is nonviolence.[71]

The Āyurveda

Āyurveda (the science of life) is a branch of the Vedas. Over the centuries, it has shaped the ancient ideas along the lines of medical, scientific, and rational investigation. It treats the person as a psychosomatic unity, with due regard for constitutional differences among individuals. It is a natural system that promotes a total style of life aimed at happiness and longevity. In the context of this study, Āyurveda is concerned with the promotion of fertility and the preservation of progeny. From among the numerous collections, the best-known texts that have come down to us are those of Caraka, Suśruta, and Vāgbhaṭa. The first has known the greatest popularity, and has been commented upon by notable scholars.

We now explore the various concepts and theories in the Caraka Saṃhitā to ascertain its line of thinking on the subject of abortion. The relevant section is Śarīrasthānam (study of the human body).

We start with the concepts of *person* and *nature*. Both the human individual and the natural world are seen as manifestations of the eternal Brahman. The person and nature are constituted of six elements—earth, water, fire, air, ether, and the spirit or self in the person and Brahman in the universe. Thus "person is equal to the universe."[72] Man is a microcosmos of the macrocosmos, which means that spirit and matter are not alien or opposite, but parts of an integral whole.

In addition to the five *mahābhūtas* (gross elements) and the *ātman* (self), the individual is invested with *buddhi* (intelligence) and *ahaṅkāra* (ego).[73] The ego is separable from the body and is made up of action, the fruit of action, reincarnation, and memory.[74] Conscious perception is brought about in the individual by the agency of the *Puruṣa* (transcendent self) which integrates the *ātman*, mind, senses, and sense objects.[75]

> There cannot be light, darkness, truth, falsehood, scripture, auspicious and inauspicious actions if there be not the active and intelligent person. There would be no substratum (body), happiness, misery, going and coming, speech, understanding, treatises, life and death, knowledge and emancipation if the person were not there. That is why the person is recognised as the cause by the experts in (theory) of causation. If there be no self, light, etc., would be causeless; they cannot be perceived nor can they serve any purpose.[76]

Thus according to Caraka's theory of causality, the agent behind all happenings, including birth and death, the continuity of life, pleasure and pain, knowledge and ignorance, morality and immorality, is the everlasting, all-pervading, and changeless *Puruṣa*.

Life comes into being by the "conjunction" of body, mind, senses, and the self (*ātman*). Caraka uses the figure of the "tripod" to illustrate the vital combination of the body, mind, and the self.[77] Life vanishes when any one part is missing.

Turning to the subject of the development of the fetus, Caraka delineates the factors from which the embryo is originated, the definition of the embryo, the factors producing the embryo, and the order of its development.

> Embryo is originated by the aggregate of these entities—mother, father, self, suitability, nutrition and psyche. . . .
>
> The combination of sperm, ovum and life-principle implanted in the womb is known as embryo.
>
> Embryo is the product of *ākāśa, vāyu, tejas, ap* and *pṛthvī* being the seat of consciousness. Thus, embryo is the aggregate of the five mahabhutas being the seat of the consciousness which is regarded as the sixth constituent of embryo.
>
> Now the order in which the embryo is formed is explained. After the accumulated menstrual blood is discharged and the new one is situated, the woman having cleanly bathed and with undamaged genital passage, ovum and uterus is called as having opportune period. When the man having undamaged sperms cohabits with such a woman, his semen, the essence of all the śarīradhātus, is extracted from the whole body impelled by orgasm. Thus being impelled by the self in the form of orgasm and also seated by him, the semen having potentiality of a seed,

is ejaculated from the man's body and through the proper track enters into the uterus and combines with the ovum.[78]

Thus conception occurs when the male semen (sperm cell) and the female ovum (germ cell), having come together in the act of intercourse, are united with the spirit which, in association with the mind, "descends into the zygote situated in the uterus," and "the embryo is formed."[79] "The entire process of receiving the qualities (of mahābhūtas by uniting with them) is completed within a subtle measure of time."[80]

It is important to note that the spirit is an original and necessary constituent of embyronic existence. It abides as the embodied soul, and provides the unborn life with spiritual continuity. The embryo is called "the self" precisely because it is the spirit that has entered the uterus, and having combined with the sperm and ovum, produces itself in the form of the embryo.[81]

Caraka has many interesting observations pertaining to heredity and embryonic growth, but significant for our purpose is the notion that it is the past karma of the individual, carried into the present embodiment, that imparts to the newborn child its special features, in addition to the contributions made by its parents.[82]

By virtue of its karmic inheritance, the unborn is invested with moral qualities, and as such is the object of medical care and protection. Similar care is extended to the mother. "The pregnant woman has to be managed very cautiously like one carrying a vessel full of oil without agitating it."[83]

On the basis of the evidence before us, Caraka Saṁhitā is allied with the earlier tradition found in the Śruti and Smṛti texts in opposing abortion as morally evil. It does so on the assumption that spirit is present in matter from the moment of conception, and is the causal agent in its progressive development. This creative manifestation of the spirit in the microcosmos is similar to the process of creation in the macrocosmos. On the human side, the moral character of the individual is also given in conception. Karma is carried over from one life to the next. Together, the spiritual and moral constituents of the individual make for the production of a person through a continuous process that is developmental but not disjunctive. It is therefore pointless to discriminate between different degrees of human potentiality in terms of "ensoulment," "viability," and "brain waves." The new life is an intimate, inseparable blending of human and physical-biological existence.

The upshot of Caraka's view is that at no time within embryonic development is there a state of pure matter in which the termination of that life is morally justified.

CARAKA AND THE WEST

We have seen that the current abortion debate in the West is irreconcilably split between two camps: pro-life and pro-choice. One group stands for the inviolable right to life of the fetus as a full human person, and is therefore antiabortion. The other group upholds the woman's right to control her own body and its reproductive processes, and therefore stands for abortion-on-request. The Hindu position, represented by Caraka in particular, assumes a mediating position. It affirms the arguments of each camp while differing from both.

Along with the pro-life people, Hinduism believes in the spiritual creation of nascent life, which invests it with inviolable dignity and sanctity. The womb can be called an "incubator," but it is not for the woman's handiwork but for the Creator's. The embryo or fetus is more than tissue in the mother; it has a separate, individual life of its own. Just as there is no such thing as being "a little pregnant," gestation—from the first mitosis of the fertilized ovum-cell to birth—is one continuous process. To say that termination of the process is morally permissible at one stage but not at another is to truncate the untruncatable. Termination at an early stage may be easier and safer, but it is no less the termination of a person-in-being. The anguish of a pregnant woman may be real, but it is seldom commensurable with the fetus's life that is being taken.

At the same time, Hinduism breaks rank with Roman Catholic and Protestant fundamentalist representatives of the pro-life group on the grounds that the right to life of the fetus ought not to be absolutized. In place of absolute rights, Hinduism advocates addressing competing rights and values. Ethical dilemmas arise in cases of rape and incest and when the mother runs the risk of grave injury or death. Each situation is unique, with its own moral tragedy. The best we can do in such situations is evil, but then it boils down to a question of degree.

In a pregnancy where the mother's life is in a balance, Hindu ethics places greater weight on maternal rights than on fetal rights. The adult human being, having arrived at a karmic state in which there is much more at stake for her spiritual destiny, and in which there are existing obligations to be performed for family and society, is in a position to be favored over an equal human being whose evolution in this life is by comparison rudimentary, and who has not yet established a social network of relationships and responsibilities.

The Suśruta Saṁhitā, which comes to us from the beginning of the Christian era, recommends abortion in difficult cases where the fetus is irreparably damaged or defective and the chances for a normal birth are nil. In such instances the surgeon should not wait for nature to take its course but should intervene by performing craniotomic operations for the surgical removal of the fetus.[84]

The quality that Hinduism calls upon in tragic situations involving the necessary destruction of the fetus is *dayā* or compassion. Legislatively, this was the clear intent of the Medical Termination of Pregnancy Act of 1971 passed by the government of India. The bill states two indications for terminating pregnancy: "(1) The continuance of the pregnancy would involve a risk to the life of the pregnant woman or grave injury to her physical or mental health; or (2) there is substantial risk that, if the child were born, it would suffer from such physical or mental abnormalities as to be seriously handicapped." Two appendices follow:

Explanation 1—"Where any pregnancy is alleged by the pregnant woman to have been caused by rape, the anguish caused by such pregnancy shall be presumed to constitute a grave injury to the mental health of the pregnant woman."

Explanation 2—"Where any pregnancy occurs as a result of failure of any device used by any married woman or her husband for the purpose of limiting the number of children, the anguish caused by such unwanted pregnancy may be presumed to constitute a grave injury to the mental health of the pregnant woman."[85]

The quality of *dayā* lies at the heart of this Pregnancy Bill and is manifest in its humanitarian achievements. The legalization of abortion has removed the practice from unsanitized back rooms and the butchery of unscrupulous opportunists, and has placed it in government hospitals and clinics run by qualified medical personnel.

However, science is only as good as its practitioners, and today we witness the invocation of *dayā* through a convoluted ethic that attempts to hallow professional greed and public prejudice. Indian newspapers carry the familiar advertisement: "Boy or Girl—know the sex of the unborn child." The "boy-girl test" is determined by a scientific procedure known as amniocentesis. The *medical intent* of this test is to detect congenital deformities by sampling amniotic fluid which is withdrawn from the womb by a hypodermic needle during the sixteenth week of pregnancy. The fetus which is enveloped in the fluid casts off cells containing chromosomes which can be tested for birth defects; but the procedure also reveals the sex of the unborn. The test takes three weeks, costs Rs. 3000, and is totally accurate.

A second sex test is ultrasound. A machine takes a sonar picture of the fetus when the mother is sixteen weeks pregnant, and this picture shows what the fetus's sex is. The cost is about Rs. 300, and its accuracy is 90 percent.

Either way, should the test indicate that the fetus is female, the chances are high that the family will request the attending physician to perform an abortion, and this because the prejudice against females is old and deep. This medical practice is now a growth industry. Physicians who profit from this business do so on claims of compassion. The sugar-coated prescription of morality reads like this: "It is better to abort a female fetus than to subject an unwanted child to a life of suffering. People are willing to keep producing children until they get a son. Is it not better to let them have a choice so that they don't have six daughters before they have a son? The test, in fact, is helping the population control program of the government."[86]

If *dayā* is to be regulated by such specious logic, then the doctors should help round up all social outcasts—the poor, the sick, the aged—and mercifully kill them off, rather than allow them to be victimized by a heartless society. The population control program of the government should be helped even more!

Similar ethical reasoning was heard during the debate surrounding the Indian government's move to pass legislation that would ban sex-determination tests. The bill was drafted by the Health Ministry as a new amendment to the Medical Termination of Pregnancy Act of 1971, introduced in the Lok Sabha in December 1990. The bill was crafted to overcome the shortcomings of a similar law passed in Maharashtra in May 1988. Journalist Arvind Kala asks his readers to compare two scenarios: one allowing tests, the other not. Scenario 1: A couple having one female child is now trying for a boy, to complete a family of two children. A problem arises when the next child is also a girl. The wife then has a choice. "She can have an abortion and try for a boy again and again and again, each time terminating her pregnancy until she conceives a son."[87] Scenario 2: With tests banned, the wife delivers her second child, who again happens to be a girl. The cycle may be repeated. "Ultimately, a couple may be saddled with one, two, or three daughters they don't want. Is that fair?At this point the writer interjects the question of ethics. "Our law allows abortions. To curb the population, the government encourages them. So can you question the motive—not wanting a girl—which leads to abortions?" Kala concludes: "Once sex-determnination tests are banned countrywide, the government's position will be this: couples can decide the number of children they want, not their sex. Won't this affect family planning? Will couples not end up having more children than they want? Is it fair to bring into the world children the parents do not want?"[88] With such moral arguments to satiate families that might have qualms of conscience, the "boy-girl test" goes on, and baby girls die. Between 1978 to 1983, 78,000 female fetuses were aborted.[89]

The situation is clearly barbaric. No civilized society can condone the horrifying practice of female feticide. There is no accommodation here to the principles of Hindu ethics. What is needed is some legislation banning amniocentesis, except to determine genetic deformities. But the law must be enforceable. This means that when the procedure is used to determine the sex of the fetus, with the anticipation of aborting a female fetus, punishment should be meted out to all parties involved—doctors and clients—following the *sati* act model. The law should also shut down clinics in which these techniques are practised.

The Maharashtra experience demonstrates that reliance should not be placed on law alone. Illegal operations have a way of springing up, which then charge high fees, and only the poor are penalized. In addition to law, social education is needed to end the age-old prejudice against women. Cultural accretions have created attitudes in the Hindu family which make blessings of boys and burdens of girls. The practice of dowry, outlawed in 1961 but still prevalent, is now exacerbated in a developing consumer society where the stakes are raised to include TVs, refrigerators, cars, and houses. These marital economics have ignited the ultimate evil of "bride burning" whereby young wives meet with convenient "accidents" around kerosene kitchen stoves, contrived by greedy husbands and in-laws. At least two women die such fiery deaths each day in the nation's capital. Social education and public awareness are essential parts of a solution. Where standards of literacy are high, dowry deaths do not take place, as in the state of Kerala.

Finally, it all boils down to the role of the physician who performs the "boy-girl test." Clinic advertisements meant to grab people's attention read: "Better to spend Rs. 500 now than Rs. 5000 later." The message is that the small sum spent now on aborting a female fetus will save the parents the huge price of a dowry down the road. This is exploitation at its worst because it elevates materiality above life, and destroys in the guise of good.

Doctors should be made to face these dilemmas at the time of their medical training. At the present time, Indian doctors are schooled in Western science but are ignorant of the medical ethics of their own culture. This may be due partly to the effort to distance themselves from Āyurvedic medicine, in which the ethical codes are found. But values have universal applicability, regardless of the mode of practice, Western or traditional; and the patients are the same people. The Caraka Saṁhitā is a rich repository of ethical codes pertaining to the training, duties, and privileges of the physician. While it regards the desire for success, wealth, and fame on the part of the doctor as proper and normal, it balances ambition with obligations to patients and to society. Caraka states: "When you join the medical profession and wish success in work, earnings of wealth, fame . . . , you should always think of the welfare of all living beings. . . . You should make effort to provide health to the patients by all means."[90] The passage is especially sensitive to the mental, physical, and social position of females. In no way must she be violated. The very thought of a young woman having to endure the pain of abortion with her only solace being the sparing of her unborn daughter the wrath of an angry family, would be utterly and unequivocally abhorrent to the medical codes of ancient India.

CHAPTER 2

The Ethics of Suicide

SUICIDE PROFILE

During the past thirty years, a major American health riddle has risen out of the fact that, in the midst of a promising scenario of improvements in the general health of Americans, there lies masked the tragedy of suicide. Long a taboo subject, suicide is today recognized as "a public health concern."[1]

The figures tell their own story. In the last one hundred years, the national rate has averaged 12.5 per 100,000. The highest rate was registered at 17.4 in the Depression of 1932; the lowest was recorded in 1957 at 9.8.[2] Today the national U.S. suicide rate per 100,000 population stands at 12.4, slightly below the 1987 figure of 12.7. It is the eighth leading cause of death. An average of 1 person self-destructs every 17.3 minutes, or 83.1 per day, for an annual total of 30,796.[3]

The group at greatest risk is white males, especially those 80 to 84 years old. Their suicide death rate is twice that of their younger counterparts, four times the rate for black males of the same age, and nine times that of comparable women.[4] In all age groups, men are more likely to commit suicide than women (3.8 male completions for each female completion).[5] Men resort to more lethal methods, such as guns, hanging, and jumping, whereas women choose nonviolent means of drug overdose.[6]

In the past decade, "by far the most profound and disturbing trend" has been the increase of suicide among young adults by "epidemic proportions."[7] "From 1970 to 1980, suicide rates for young males (ages 15 to 24) increased by 50%, from 13.5 to 20.2 suicides per 100,000 population (U.S. Department of Health and Human Services, 1986)."[8] Suicide is the third leading cause of death among young people generally, and second among college students.[9] In 1988 an average of one young person committed suicide every 1 hour and 47 minutes. Compared with males, young females are more prone (by four to eight times) to attempt suicide, but are less likely to succeed.[10]

Caucasians commit suicide twice as often as nonwhites. The incidence is lowest for adolescents and highest for those 75 years of age.[11] Parents of large families are at minimal risk for suicide, compared with individuals who are single, divorced, or widowed. "The loss of a spouse increases risk, the risk being greater during the first year after the loss, and extending for 4 years thereafter."[12] Religious affiliation is also a demographic factor, even though death certificates seldom include it. Protestants have a higher incidence of suicide than do Catholics and Jews.[13] Geography is a variable in the distribution of suicide. The mountain states are most vulnerable (19.0), with Nevada ranking first (26.0), and the Middle Atlantic states are lowest (8.6), with New York ranking last (6.7).[14] Among professionals, psychiatrists stand out with the highest suicide rate. Finally, there is the seasonal factor. Contrary to the popular notion that most suicides occur during the Christmas and New Year seasons, the lethal periods are actually summer and fall.[15]

Along with the completers of suicide are the attempters. Attempted suicides may be treated as "cries for help." Estimates are that there are between 240,000 and 600,000 annual attempts in the United States. For the nation, there are 8 to 20 attempts for every completion. Approximately 5 million living Americans have attempted to kill themselves (3 female attempts for each male attempt).[16]

Statistics are incomplete without mention of the survivors, that is, family and friends of those who have taken their lives. We may estimate that for each suicide, 6 other persons are intimately touched. This means that if there is a suicide every 17 minutes, then there are 6 new survivors also for that time. Based on the number of suicides from 1970 to 1990, it is estimated that the number of survivors of suicides is 3.5 million, or 1 of every 71 Americans in 1990.[17]

Grim though this profile of suicide is in the United States, the figures do not accurately represent the enormity of the problem. Reportage is flawed because the medical examiners tend to classify a suicide as a homicide or an accident because of pressure from families anxious to eliminate the stigma of death by suicide.[18]

All of the above statistics speak for themselves. They point to the recognition of suicide as a public health problem, and to the need for its understanding and prevention. The problem of suicide is as complex as it is tragic. To understand the problem we shall investigate several approaches that have been adopted in the Western tradition. These explorations will yield diverse definitions of suicide, reflecting attitudes of the predominant culture. Then we will examine the Hindu tradition. Thus our approach will be multidisciplinary and multicultural. The understanding of suicide which emerges from this study should provide the basis for developing strategies to prevent it. These strategies will also be multifaceted, incorporating health education, information, and programs of intervention. Throughout this study our primary focus will be religious and ethical.

THE WESTERN TRADITION

Historically there have been many Western approaches to the problem of suicide. The main streams of thought are psychiatric, psychological, sociological, philosophical, and theological.[19]

The Psychiatric Approach

Western tradition has characteristically attempted to understand and evaluate acts of self-destruction in moral terms. The psychiatric approach reverses that trend with the knowledge that suicide is invariably a medical problem. As we probe into the mysteries of the human mind, we are discovering that, in numerous cases, suicide is preceded by some form of mental malady that destroys the instinct of self-preservation. The data show that 94 percent of patients who go on to kill themselves suffer from a major treatable psychiatric illness. Approximately 45 to 70 percent of these individuals are diagnosed as suffering from an affective disorder such as major depression or bipolar illness, alcholism, schizophrenia, personality disorders, and neurosis.[20]

Among specific psychiatric disorders, depression carries the highest risk for suicide. "Estimates of the lifetime prevalence of major affective disorder in the general population range from 6.1% to 9.5%. . . . Studies that have followed cohorts of depressed patients over time have shown that 15% of depressed patients kill themselves. . . . "[21]

Next to depression, alcoholism supplies the highest risk for suicide. It is estimated that approximately 10 percent of the population is afflicted with alcoholism, which increases the risk for a number of medical problems, not the least of which is depression. Together, alcoholism and depression elevate the figures of persons who kill themselves while suffering from uncomplicated affective illness from 64 to 75 percent.[22] Alcoholism raises the rate of suicide prevalent in the general population 75 to 85 times.

Alcoholics at maximum risk are males at mean age of 47 and those who are recently discharged from hospital treatment, weighed by personality difficulties, socially isolated, unmarried or divorced, and struggling with personal loss.[23] It takes about twenty years of drinking before the patient ends his life.

Schizophrenia accounts for some 10 percent of sufferers who take their lives. Unlike major affective psychoses, schizophrenia occurs among young persons, generally males who are unmarried, who are of better than average education, and who become ill at the beginning of a career. The dashing of their hopes and dreams by the dire prospects of their illness drives them to despair.[24] They take the plunge when they are caught in states of depression, rather than in intensely psychotic states. Often they are victims of antipsychotic medications that produce side-effects of involuntary movements that incapacitate them. These decompensations necessitate frequent hospitalizations, which in turn produce other personal losses and exacerbate feelings of hopelessness. Not surprisingly, the fateful decision is often made following one of the frequent trips to the hospital. As in the general population, males are prone to kill themselves by violent means, such as shooting, jumping, and stabbing, whereas females resort to less violent means, including drug overdoses.[25]

The Psychodynamic/Psychological Approach

Sigmund Freud pioneered the psychological understanding of suicide. He isolated the unconscious mind as the repository of suicidal activity. "The major psychoanalytical position on suicide was that it represented unconscious hostility directed toward the introjected (ambivalently viewed) love object. Psychodynamically, suicide was seen as murder in the 180th degree."[26] Other thinkers developed their own theories of the psychodynamics of suicide. In his book *Man Against Himself*, Karl Meninger amplifies the psychodynamics of hostility and identifies three wishes within the suicidal drive: the wish to kill, to be killed, and to die. Gregory Zilboorg expanded the causal theory of unconscious hostility as a factor in suicide to include the deprivation of the capacity to love within the agent. Robert Litman carried the psychodynamics of suicide beyond hostility to encompass a cauldron of destructive emotions such as rage, guilt, anxiety, and dependency, along with a predisposition to failure and hopelessness.[27]

Edwin Schneidman follows a psychological approach which is distinguished from the psychodynamic one in that it does not posit a universal unconscious scenario. Instead, he emphasizes four psychological features which are present in most acts of suicide:

> (1) acute *perturbation*, that is, an increase in the individual's state of general upsetment; (2) heightened *inimicality*, an increase in self-abnegation, self-hate, shame, guilt, self-blame, and overtly in behaviors which are against one's own best interests; (3) a sharp and almost sudden increase of *constriction* of intellectual focus, a tunneling of thought processes, a narrowing of the mind's content, a truncating of the capacity to see viable options which would ordinarily occur to the mind; and (4) the idea of *cessation*, the insight that it is possible to put an end to suffering by stopping the unbearable flow of consciousness. This last is the igniting element that explodes the mixture of the previous components.[28]

The last feature is important because it defines suicide primarily as a flight from unbearable emotion, and not so much as the embracing of death.

The Sociological Approach

The sociological approach is indelibly associated with the work of Emile Durkheim. In his groundbreaking book, *Le Suicide* (1897), he traces the roots of suicide to the relationship of the individual to his society. Depending on the extent of society's control of the individual, Durkheim formulated four types of suicide. *Altruistic* suicide is brought about when the individual is dominated by his culture, and finds no other exit from his predicament than to take his own life. The examples of hara-kiri in Japan and *satī* in India are given to illustrate the power of society to dictate death as the only honorable act under certain socially defined circumstances. *Egoistic* suicide occurs in the opposite situation, when the tentacles of the group upon the individual are few and feeble. Here the individual is isolated from the community, and in the absence of any bonding between himself and any friends and loved ones, considers his lonely life of no larger value. *Anomic* suicide is triggered by the sudden severance of the individual's relation to society through the loss of his livelihood, his life's earnings, fame, or friends. *Fatalistic* suicide arises from feelings of utter despair, as in the case of a married woman who is doomed to childlessness.

In summary, Durkheim states: "The term suicide is applied to all cases of death resulting directly or indirectly from a positive or negative act of the victim which he knows will produce this result."[29] Durkheim's definition served as the basis for subsequent sociological thinking in this field. In 1967, Jack D. Douglas presented a thoroughgoing critique of Durkheim's work in *The Social Meaning of Suicide*, where he postulates six basic dimensions of meaning in the definitions of suicide.

The Philosophical Approach

The currents set in motion by the scientific inquiries of the nineteenth century became waves in the first half of the twentieth century. Suicide was alternately viewed as a result of individual psychopathology and as a symptom of pernicious socioeconomics. In either case, the traditional religio-philosophical view that suicide was a rational, deliberate, and voluntary act of the individual was severely undermined. Questions pertaining to the morality of suicide were seen as irrelevant. After all, what has morality to do with a problem that is agitated either by a disordered individual or a disordered society?

The impact of these scientific waves upon the moral concerns of philosophy and religion was also felt in public policy. If, for example, a patient had proven suicidal tendencies, it was required by law to employ all coercive means to provide him with the medical services he was incapable of summoning himself because of his mental incompetence. Under these circumstances, it was quite possible for an individual to be hospitalized against his will because, in the judgment of the public policy assessment of the situation, it was the will of the person which was precisely the problem, and therefore he was in need of public guardianship. This sort of situation, in which an individual involuntarily falls into the grasp of a caretaker institution, was dramatized in the film

One Flew over the Cuckoo's Nest.

Since the sixties, countercurrents to the dominance of the scientific perspective have been released. The new situation is the product of recent developments, such as the artificial prolongation of life through medical technology, the view of the patient as a person who possesses rights and reason, and discoveries into the larger meanings of life and death. The momentum of these new waves of thinking is now displacing the barriers to autonomy erected by the older medical models and is opening channels for the moral discussion of suicide through the disciplines of philosophy and religion.

Western philosophers have debated the issues of suicide from the time of the ancient Greeks and Romans. The earliest literary citation of suicide in Greek legend is Jocasta's unwitting marriage with her son, Oedipus, the shameful discovery of which drives her to hang herself from a noose in the house of Hades. The characters in the poems of Homer choose suicide for heroic reasons, preferring death to worthless existence. Life itself is deemed good compared with the sunless realm of Hades. Suicide is therefore only fitting and natural in the face of overwhelming sorrow, bereavement, or the duty to uphold some high purpose. However, pessimism about life creeps into the post-Homeric period. For example, Hesiod finds the Golden Age in the past, the present being an inferior age of iron. The logic of this pessimistic view of life is that we are justified to end that which we cannot mend.

Among the philosophers, the Pythagoreans opposed suicide on the grounds that God had sentenced the soul to penitential discipline within the body as the result of prior sins. To attempt to escape this sentence through suicide is therefore deemed an act of rebellion against God, who alone has the right and authority to release the soul from its prison house.

Antisuicide arguments are also found in Plato's *Phaedo* and *Laws*. Plato admits with Hesiod that life indeed can be filled with sorrow, but he does not consider this a legitimate reason for taking it within one's own hands and ending it. To do so would be an act of usurpation against the sovereignty of God, whose possessions we are. At the same time, Plato harbored some of the sentiments of Homer, and therefore occupied a median position on the question of suicide. In the *Laws* (9. 873) he argues that suicide is licit when required by the state in the form of the death penalty, and also in compelling circumstances (*anagke*). Socrates agreed that men are possessions of the gods and that life is a prison from which one must not escape. Even so, he drank the cup of hemlock when he felt the gods had put upon him the *necessity* to do so.

Plato's disciple, Aristotle, is an early representative of the conservative attitude toward suicide. He argued against it chiefly on social and ethical grounds. Suicide is an offense against the state because the citizen thereby robs the state of his obligatory services. It is an act of injustice against fellow Athenians, who are all mutually dependent upon one another. Against the notion that suicide can be noble and heroic, Aristotle contended that the individual who kills himself in order to escape poverty, disappointment in love, or bodily and mental anguish is "a coward rather than a brave man."

Liberal attitudes toward suicide were represented by the Stoics. Indifferent to the merits of life and death, they did not think suicide was a question to be dictated by morality or virtue, but rather by force of circumstance. The Stoic ideal was to live in accordance with nature, but when circumstances made this ideal impossible, it was appropriate to end it all.

Suicide for great causes was socially accepted in the early history of Rome. Heroic suicide in terms of self-sacrifice for the fatherland (exemplified by the Decii) and suicide to escape unbearable dishonor (illustrated by Lucretia) were lauded as marks of robust character. As with the Greeks, suicide by hanging was despised and would be punished posthumously. Thus, suicide for great causes was accommodated within the piety of Republican Rome.

Under the Empire, due to the loosening of earlier religious constraints, and due to the influence of certain strains of Greek philosophy, suicide became more popular. Stoicism provided one form of appeal. So did Platonism, after undergoing a subtle change. The external "necessity" or call of God for which Plato was prepared to make exceptions as grounds for suicide was now internalized and became the voluntary act of an autonomous agent who wished to be freed from an oppressive environment. "Whereas to Plato suicide had seemed permissible only . . . under compulsion . . . of an external nature, this compulsion is now so interpreted that suicide becomes in fact not so much the involuntary act of the unwilling victim of circumstances as the voluntary assertion by the individual of his freedom."[30] The change meant that the individual who could no longer live according to the law of his nature was "to perceive precisely in this fact an intimation from God that it is time to depart from life."[31]

Further, the tension described by Plato between the need for going through the trials and tribulations of mortal existence without precipitating its end, and the attraction of a future life with God, is now dissipated by the sense of the bankruptcy of life—a conviction which served as an added motive to suicide. The only remaining restraint was for the individual to be certain that "God gives the signal for him to depart."[32] Though the emphasis was upon suicide as an individual act, it was not to be impulsive but the result of rational deliberation. Pros and cons were to be evaluated contextually, depending on the situation of the person. It was recognized that individuals differ with time and place, and therefore what might be deemed justifiable grounds for suicide for one person in a particular set of circumstances might not be appropriate for another person in a different context. In keeping with the doctrine of propriety, Stoicism required that "a man's death must be in consonance with his life."[33]

The importance attributed by these ancient Greeks and Romans to the subject of suicide was kept alive through the Renaissance and the Enlightenment, and is of focal interest today. Camus declared in the beginning of *The Myth of Sisyphus* that suicide constitutes the basic problem of all philosophy.

Contemporary philosophy exhibits a wide spectrum of views on suicide. Since it is not possible to do justice to individual thinkers in this field, we shall summarize the standard definitions. In an insightful essay, Tom L. Beauchamp categorizes three popular types of definitions.[34] The prevailing definition promoted by moral philosophers such as R. B. Brandt and Eike-Henner Kluge says that "suicide occurs if and only if there is an intentional termination of one's own life."[35] The second definition, derived from Durkheim, is broader. In the place of intention it emphasizes knowledge. "The term suicide is applied to all cases of death resulting directly or indirectly from a positive or negative act of the victim himself, which he knows will produce this result."[36] The third definition is broadest, and is appropriately referred to as the "omnibus definition." In the words of Ronald Maris, "suicide occurs when an individual engages in a life-style that he knows might kill him (other than living another day)—and it does [kill him]. This is an omnibus definition of suicide, which includes various forms of self-destruction, such as risk-taking and many so-called 'accidents.'"[37]

Beauchamp dismisses the third definition because it would radically alter the concept of suicide as it is generally understood. "Those who engage in waterfall rafting, hang gliding, police bomb-squad work, mountain diving (into oceans), and space exploration of an adventuresome sort—and who die as a result of these activities—would be suicides if this definition is accepted."[38]

The first two definitions are also rejected by Beauchamp for several reasons, including the fact that "they omit all mention of the precise nature of the intention (motivation) or knowledge involved in a suicide."[39] He finds that some of their inadequacies are compensated for in the following definition proposed by philosopher Joseph Margolis:

> A man may knowingly, and willingly, go to his death, be rationally capable of avoiding death, deliberately not act to save his life, and yet not count as a suicide. In this sense, we usually exclude the man who sacrifices his life to save another's, the religious martyr who will violate his faith, the patriot who intentionally lays down his life for a cause. Not that men in such circumstances may not be suiciding; only that they *cannot be said to be suiciding solely for those reasons.* Some seem to have thought otherwise [such as] Durkheim. . . . [40]

Beauchamp accepts this narrower (compared with Brandt's and Durkheim's) definition of Margolis as correct but proceeds to construct a more satisfactory definition of his own. He concludes: "An act is a suicide if a person intentionally brings about his or her own death in circumstances where others do not coerce him or her to the action, except in those cases where death is caused by conditions not specifically arranged by the agent for the purpose of bringing about his or her own death."[41] Thus according to Beauchamp, a person commits an act of suicide when he or she *intentionally* brings about self-destruction, free from external coercion, and when death is caused by conditions planned by the person himself for the express purpose of terminating his life.

The Theological Approach

The prevailing views of Western civilization toward suicide have been molded by Christianity. In turn, Christian views have been shaped by both the Greco-Roman and Hebraic traditions. The thoughts of Plato, Aristotle, and the Stoics are baptized in Christian form; this is particularly true of Jewish thinking on suicide as it appears in the Old Testament.

The Old Testament provides little basis for the later denunciation of suicide in the Jewish tradition. The stories of Abimelech (Judg. 9:52–54), of Saul (1 Sam. 31:4), of Ahitophel (2 Sam. 17:23), of Zimri (1 Kings 16:18), and most famous, of Samson (Judg. 16:28–31) appear as instances of heroic suicide to rescue honor. The Sixth Commandment (Exod. 20:13, "You shall not kill") is opposed to murder. However, notwithstanding this limitation of textual support, from postexile times Judaism did develop a theology which sternly condemned suicide. This was a logical development from the doctrine that Yahweh is the sole Creator and possessor of human life, and that only he who gives life has the sovereign authority to take it away. The Sixth Commandment, prohibiting unjustified homicide, was then read in the light of the above theology.

The rabbinical tradition is clearly opposed to suicide, but its attitude toward those who take their lives is tempered by clinical considerations and allowances for conditions of duress, especially during persecutions, when the Jews had to remain true to their faith. The mass suicide at Masada in A.D. 74 is looked upon as a heroic sacrifice in the face of Roman oppression. Periodically, Jewish communities in medieval Europe and England found themselves trapped is such tragic situations, and at all times they preferred mass suicide to apostasy.

Christianity inherited the Jewish repudiation of suicide, along with the fundamental notion of God as the sovereign Lord of Life. The New Testament describes the betrayal of Jesus by Judas as an act of such heinous proportions that the taking of his own life in suicide is reckoned a fitting sign of repentance (Matt. 27:3–5).

Christian theologians began formulating their views about suicide in the context of the persecution of the early Church by the Romans. The Patristic writings joyously embrace martyrdom as the supreme means of witnessing to the faith, and celebrate such sacrifice as an open door to Paradise. Soon martyrdom was valued as a second baptism (Tertullian, *On Baptism*, 16) that renewed holiness, and martyrs were accorded saints' privileges and the veneration of their relics. The numbers of those who deliberately sought the martyr's crown rapidly multiplied until

Church Fathers, such as Clement of Alexandria, had to remind the flock of the difference between martyrdom as a self-regarding act and martyrdom as witness to the faith.

By the time of the fourth century, the fanatic zealotry of Christians and the decimation of their numbers through martyrdom reached a fever pitch. That tide was stemmed through the theological intervention of St. Augustine (354–430). Augustine pronounced suicide as a crime and a sin, and thereby formulated Western society's stance on suicide for the next one thousand years.

Augustine's arguments against suicide are chiefly found in *The City of God* (A.D. 428). Taking his stand on God's Commandments, he says: "It is significant that in Holy Scripture no passage can be found enjoining or permitting suicide either in order to hasten our entry into immortality or to void or avoid temporal evils. God's command, 'Thou shalt not kill,' is to be taken as forbidding self-destruction. . . . "[42] At the same time, he explains that the same divine law which forbids killing of a human being allows exceptions. This applies in general law when the state's authority puts criminals to death or authorizes war for a just cause. It also applies when God "gives an explicit commission to an individual for a limited time," exemplified by Samson, who "crushed himself and his enemies to death beneath the ruins of a building."[43] To kill oneself at God's command is not suicide, but Augustine warns one should be absolutely certain about the divine command.

Outside these instances of special commission, Augustine refuses to make room for special cases. For instance, he does not find suicide as the Christian way of dealing with rape. He reasons: "So long as the will remains unyielding," no crime "perpetrated on the body or in the body, lays any guilt on the soul."[44] Along the same lines, the gist of Chapters 17 to 18 of Book 1 reads: "Because chastity is not identical with bodily integrity but is a virtue of the soul, no woman need lose her chastity through violation. Moreover, suicide is not a proper means to use in protecting one's chastity."[45] Suicide as a means of avoiding a sin is in fact the perpetration of a greater sin to avoid a lesser. Finally, suicide is one crime for which a person cannot repent.

Augustine's dictum that suicide is the worst of sins found expression in the laws of church and state, which were as barbarous as they were popular. In 693 the Council of Toledo

ordered that a person guilty of attempting suicide be excummuni-
cated from the Church.

Thomas Aquinas (1227–1274) restored the Greek intellectu-
alism which gave primacy to the intellect. He blended Church
dogma with Aristotelian science, newly brought from Spain. He
considered the preservation of life as a universal instinct, in conformity with natural law and sound reason:

> Since . . . good has the nature of an end, and evil, the nature of a
> contrary, hence it is that all those things to which man has a
> natural inclination are naturally apprehended by reason as
> being good, and consequently as objects of pursuit, and their
> contraries as evil, and objects of avoidance. Therefore the order
> of the precepts of the natural law is according to the order of
> natural inclination. Because in man there is first of all an incli-
> nation to good in accordance with the nature which he has in
> common with all substances; that is, every substance seeks the
> preservation of its own being according to its nature. And by
> reason of this inclination, whatever is a means of preserving
> human life and warding off its obstacles belongs to the natural
> law.[46]

Further, Aquinas understood the Decalogue, with its command against murder, through an interpretative key in which the
individual, social, and divine elements were seen as organically
bound. By this logic, to respect the life of another human being,
we must first have respect for our own life, and this self-respect
comes through a loving relationship with God. It follows that
self-destruction cuts one off from obligations to one's fellows and
from our obligations to God, who is the giver and owner of life.
Aquinas understood all the precepts of the "Old Law" as serving
a single end, namely, the love commandment of the Gospels. Thus
suicide was not just the violation of one of the Ten Commandments, but cut to the very heart of the Christian Gospel of love to
self, to others, and to God. In this way Aquinas employs the arguments of biology derived from the instinct of survival manifest in
all forms of sentient existence, and also the arguments of sociol-
ogy earlier advanced by Aristotle, to supplement his theological
position that suicide ultimately violates love to God.[47]

As a result of the teachings of such giants as Augustine and
Aquinas, the Church adopted a position of absolute condemnation
of suicide throughout the Middle Ages, banning it as mortal sin,

and civil law made it a crime. These popular notions are grue-
somely exemplified in Dante's *Divine Comedy*, in which those who
tried to "escape scorn by death" are consigned to the seventh circle
of hell where "the foul Harpies make their nests."[48] This attitude
prevailed through the centuries that witnessed the rise of the
Renaissance and the Protestant Reformation. At the same time, the
revival of classical learning in the Renaissance introduced the old
Stoic attitudes toward suicide in terms of toleration and rational
choice. And the Reformation promoted individual inquiry into
established ideas and institutions. By the end of the seventeenth
century, these developments had the effect of making the intellectual classes a little more tolerant of suicide along with relaxing the
laws a little. Even so, the law continued to confiscate the property
of those who had committed suicide, and their bodies were bru-
tally desecrated, often being buried at crossroads with stakes driven into their hearts to prevent their ghosts from doing mischief.

The classical notion, expostulated by Plato and the Stoics,
that in extreme cases suicide could be regarded as a "summons
from God," was revived by the Anglican clergyman John Donne,
in his *Biathanatos* (1608). He questioned the Augustinian assertion that suicide is one sin for which the sinner cannot repent, and
charged that the completely hopeless attitude taken toward suicide limited the wonder of God's grace.

More representative of the times was the stand taken by the
Westminster Assembly, a synod (1643–1648) which formulated
the Westminster Standards, embodying the doctrines of Puri-
tanism. One of the documents it produced was the Shorter Cate-
chism which upheld the Augustinian opposition to suicide in its
dictum: "The sixth commandment forbiddeth the taking away of
our own life, or the life of our neighbor unjustly, or whatsoever
tendeth thereunto."[49] This position of the Westminster Assembly
was accepted by Presbyterian churches in America, by Congrega-
tional American churches, and by the Philadelphia Confession of
the Baptists.

The contemporary hold of the Augustinian position on Christian conscience is demonstrated in the testimony of Lutheran theologian Dietrich Bonhoeffer, who was in the forefront of German
resistance to Hitler, a crime for which he paid with his life. Bonhoeffer argues that the freedom in which a person possesses his or
her body requires him to look beyond bodily existence and to

"regard the life of his body as a gift that is to be preserved and as a sacrifice that is to be offered."[50] The counterpart to the right to live is the freedom to give one's life in sacrifice. In sacrifice a person has the right to death, but only to the extent that it is not the destruction of his life, but sacrifice for some cause. This liberty to die heroically is a unique power given to humans which can easily be abused. "Man can indeed by its means become the master of his earthly destiny, for he can by his own free decision seek death in order to avoid defeat and he may thus rob fate of its victory. . . . Suicide is a man's attempt to give final meaning to a life which has become humanly meaningless."[51] Suicidal victory over the cruelties of fate are often courageous acts, greeted with praise. Nevertheless, if suicide is to be declared wrongful, it is to be arraigned solely before the forum of God, and not of humans. God is the Maker and Master of life; therefore the person who takes his life is guilty only before God. Suicide is a sin because it demonstrates a lack of faith in the living God. "God has reserved to Himself the right to determine the end of life, because He alone knows the goal to which it is His will to lead it. It is for Him alone to justify a life or to cast it away. Before God self-justification is quite simply sin, and suicide is therefore also sin. There is no other cogent reason for the wrongfulness of suicide, but only the fact that over men there is a God. Suicide implies denial of this fact."[52]

Summary of the Western Tradition

The traditional Christian opinion generally held by today's Roman Catholics and Protestants maintains that suicide is a grave sin when it is undertaken deliberately for any self-regarding motive. It is a sin against God, who is Creator, Redeemer, and the Lord of Life. It is a sin against ourselves, made in God's image. It is a violation against God's command, having no possibility of repentance. It is a sin against family, friends, and society, denying them the contribution of our life, as well as the opportunity to minister to our needs.

The Current Western Dilemma

The ethos fashioned by our Judeo-Christian tradition for the preservation of life is reflected in our current laws and in the principles and practices of medical associations. Today our venerable assumptions, in concert with their legal and medical ramifications, are being questioned. There is a growing interest in the morality of suicide. Beauchamp observes:

> First, biomedical technology has made it possible for ill and seriously injured persons to prolong their lives beyond a point at which, in former times, they would have died. Many of these patients are seriously ill and in considerable agony. The suicide rate is remarkably high in some of these populations, and numerous people have come to think not only that suicide is justified in such cases but even that those who are incapacitated should be assisted in their acts of suicide. Slogans such as "the right to die" and "death with dignity" have grown up around such cases. Second, although suicide laws have been repealed recently in many jurisdistions in the United States, repeal is a matter of present debate in others. It is clear that this debate turns more on moral considerations than on legal ones.[53]

Several societies have developed in Europe and America that are working toward the liberalization of traditional attitudes, practices, and laws, such as the Hemlock Society. As a result, we can observe new trends toward double suicide and murder suicide.

Prior to 1980, there were only three documented cases of double suicides, the most celebrated being that of Elizabeth and Henry Pitney Van Dusen. Dr. Van Dusen, 77, was a Presbyterian minister and had served as president of the Union Theological Seminary in New York. The couple signed a suicide pact and took an overdose of sleeping pills. Elizabeth, 80, explained:

> We have both had very full and satisfying lives. . . . But since Pitney had his stroke five years ago, we have not been able to do any of the things we want to do . . . and my arthritis is much worse. There are also many helpless old people who without modern medical care would have died, and we feel God would have allowed them to die when their time had come. Nowadays it is difficult to die. We feel that this way we are taking will become more usual and acceptable as the years pass. We are both increasingly weak and unwell, and who would want to die in a nursing home? . . . "O Lamb of God that takest away the sins of the world, grant us thy peace."[54]

Norman Cousins wrote of this Christian couple's deaths: "Death is not the greatest loss in life. The greatest loss is what dies inside us when we live. The unbearable tragedy is to live without either dignity or sensitivity."[55]

From 1981 to 1988, the number of documented cases of double suicides rose to thirty-one. "In half the cases, both spouses were either chronically or terminally ill; in one out of three, only the wife was ailing, although the husband . . . was often in frail health."[56]

The dramatic increase of double suicides is being matched by a spate of murder suicides where one spouse kills the other, and then himself or herself. Between 1950 and 1980, there were three cases. From 1981 to 1988 the number rose to sixty-six. "Both partners were ill in one-third of the marriages; only the wife was ill in another one-third. Of the remaining cases, either the husband was the sole sufferer, or both spouses were very old. . . . In 20 percent of the marriages, either the wife was institutionalized for Alzheimer's disease or had been in and out of nursing homes or hospitals for physical ailments. Where the wife was institutionalized, the husband shot her on the premises before turning the gun on himself."[57]

Proponents who advocate the acceptance of suicide as a "rational choice" plead the support of the Fifth and Fourteenth Amendments of the United States Constitution. Although most jurisdictions have decriminalized suicide, assisting suicide is considered homicide. These proponents are trying to change that.

The battlelines are clearly drawn. The states have a duty to prevent suicide, and the legitimacy of this concern has been upheld in the number of cases involving termination of treatment. "Society has always praised the state's efforts to assert this interest in order to prevent citizens from self-harm. Civil law has recognized a similar interest in its citizens by allowing them to interfere to prevent a potential suicide. Such interference is not classified by the law as a breach of the suicide's privacy, nor is it an unlawful restraint or tort such as assault and battery."[58]

The American public is clearly strained between the traditional attitudes and the new forces for "self-deliverance." It is in this dilemma that we turn to the Hindu tradition for whatever light it may be able to shed on our problems.

THE HINDU TRADITION

P. V. Kane declares that in India "the practice of religious suicide has a very respectable antiquity."[59] He cites the case reported by Megasthenes, of Kalanos, the Indian gymnosophist from Taxila who had accompanied Alexander the Great from India. At the age of 73 he burnt himself alive on a funeral pyre at Sousa, being "afflicted with a malady that made life more and more burdensome."[60] This incident took place in the fourth century B.C., but it is more than a safe inference that the practice of religious suicide was in vogue long before that time. What follows is an attempt to trace the development of the whole phenomenon of suicide through an investigation of the Hindu śāstras. In addition to the textual evidence, we shall be interested in finding clues from the broader climate in which the scriptures take shape.

The Śruti Literature

Through the hymns they composed when they settled down in the region of the upper Indus and its tributaries, the Āryan tribes give us a clear and consistent picture of how they understood their lives in the new territories they had conquered. We shall explore these hymns for those elements that have a bearing on suicide.

First of all, religion played a primary and positive role in the life of the Āryans. They perceived the most important distinctions between themselves and the Dasas as being religious, referring to the aborigines as "not sacrificing," "devoid of rites," "god-hating," and "without devotion." Each epithet tells a tale. The soma ritual, connected with an exhilarating libation extracted from the soma plant, reached back to the Indo-Iranian period. It made the time of sacrifice a happy hour. Through their sacrifices the Āryans induced the gods to descend with gifts of victory and wealth. The gods are deifications of natural phenomena, gloriously conceived. Indra, the national god, was imaged as strong, young, and brilliant. No demons could survive his thunderbolt. Varuṇa, the noblest one, maintained the universe in order and righteousness, and made the world safe and secure.

The Āryans did not feel like strangers in their new land, but as sons of the soil. The family unit nurtured the young, old, and infirm with equal care. Devotion was to life and its multiple pleasures. The values of spiritual and physical balance were actively cultivated. The hymns resound with a vital will to live, along with the hope of escaping the traps of premature death, and the dream to live a "hundred autumns."[61] The many prayers can be reduced to a single supplication: "May all my limbs be uninjured and my soul remain unconquered."[62]

It must be admitted that there is enough superstition in the Ṛgveda to make one depressed; yet, as Farquhar observes, "the black arts are held in check, and human sacrifices, cruel rites, eroticism, and other horrors are noticeably absent. The religion is, on the whole, a healthy, happy system. Neither asceticism nor austerity, neither pessimism nor philosophy, disturbs the sunshine of the early day."[63]

There appears to be some doubts about the practice of *sati* in the Vedic period. The literature suggests that during this time *sati* was a "mimetic ceremony."[64] The Atharvaveda declares: "Get up, O Woman, to the world of the living; thou liest by this one who is deceased; come! to him who grasps thy hand, thy second spouse, thou hast now entered into the relation of wife to husband."[65] Both here and in the Ṛgveda,[66] the widow ascends the funeral pyre of her dead husband as part of her "ancient duty," but although she lies by the corpse of her dead husband, she is told to rise and go forth with her new spouse to a life of "progeny and property." Once she departs, the pyre is set ablaze. Thus the Vedic Indians ceremonialized an earlier custom enjoining widows to cremate themselves along with their dead husbands.

Turning to the Brāhmaṇas, Keith is of the opinion that there is no trace of the custom of religious suicide in these sacrifical texts, "unless we accept the suggestion of Hillebrandt . . . that the consecration ceremony (*dīkṣā*), which is an essential preliminary to the most important rites, is in reality a faded form of the older practice of suicide by fire."[67] Keith gives reasons why he thinks this is not the case. However, he does acknowledge that the Brāhmaṇas do propound two doctrines which prepare the way for the approval of religious suicide. The first is that the ideal sacrifice is that of the sacrificer himself, and that all other sacrifices are as shadow to substance. Second, in the Śatapatha Brāhmaṇa (13.6.1ff.), "the closing act of both the *puruṣamedha* and the *sarvamedha*, the human and universal sacrifices, is the giving away by the performer of the whole of his possessions, including in the latter case even the land, and his wandering into the forest, doubtless as a preliminary to an early death."[68]

An important development in the Brāhmaṇas that is saliently related to suicide is the conception of man's duties, known as the "triad of obligations," or *ṛnatraya*. The ideal of *ṛnatraya* is comprehensive, involving not only a man's duty to the gods through sacrifice but also his obligation to the perpetuation of the family and the cultural heritage which it embodies. This sense of social obligation infused by *ṛnatraya* is a powerful deterrent against the idea of taking one's own life.

Also, the Brāhmaṇas mark the beginnings of the scheme of *āśramas*. The *Brahmacarya* and *Gārhasthya* stages of life have taken form, but the *Vānaprasthya* and *Saṁnyāsa* stages must await the period of the later Upaniṣads for their formation. The *āśrama* notion that human needs and aspirations must change through time makes for an ethic of relativism with developmental values of life and death.

Turning to the Upaniṣads, we find the Indian sage finally completing his long quest after unity—a quest which discards all mythology and becomes truly philosophical. Here Vedic ceremonialism and caste duties give way to a new spiritual quest which turns inward for the purpose of understanding Ultimate Reality. The sage prays:

> From the unreal [*asat*] lead me to the real [*sat*]!
> From darkness lead me to light!
> From death lead me to immortality![69]

The motivation behind this introspective search is the fundamental idea, running through the early Upaniṣads, that underlying the exterior world of change is an unchangeable reality which is identical to that which underlies the essence of the person. "Verily, he is the great, unborn Soul, who is this [person] consisting of knowledge among the senses. In the space within the heart lies the ruler of all, the lord of all, the king of all. He does not become greater by good action nor inferior by bad action."[70]

The logic of this Upaniṣadic teaching could suggest that everyday existence is insignificant compared with the experience of mystical union which carries one beyond this ephemeral world, and the thirst for such knowledge could persuade one to leave all and enter the forest. In later works such as the Jābāla and Kanthaśruti Upaniṣads, this logic indeed turns on life, and the enlightened *sannyāsin* is instructed to make the great journey or to choose voluntary death in some heroic manner.[71]

However, in fairness to the ethical ethos of the Upaniṣads, life, not logic, prevailed. Elsewhere I have explained:

For all their emphasis on renunciation, the Upaniṣads never mini-mize the importance of the family. The departing student is instructed by his teacher: "cut not off the line of progeny." [Taitt. Up.1.11.1] A man is incomplete and unfulfilled without a wife, children, and earthly possessions. [Bṛh. Up.1.4.17] All aspects of the householder's life are ethically regulated. He must especially be hospitable to guests; otherwise, "hope and expectation, inter-course and pleasantness, sacrifices and meritorious deeds, sons and cattle"—all of these will be snatched away from him for the niggard shows himself to be "a man of little understanding." [Kaṭha Up.1.8] Before he can understand *Brahman* the house-holder must propitiate the gods and gratify his father. [Kaṭha Up. 1.10–13] In order to share, the householder must first possess; he therefore prays for all the good things in this life: wealth, cattle, clothes, food, drink, and longevity. A typical prayer: "May I become glorious among men! May I be better than the very rich! Hail!" [Taitt. Up.1.4.3] The speaker, here, is a teacher. All the teachers of major Upaniṣads, like Yājñavalkya, were *gṛhasthas*.[72]

The Chāndogya Upaniṣad provides an allegorical interpreta-tion of life as a great soma festival.[73] We have here a miniature ethical system built around the notion of sacrifice to be performed *in spirit*, without recourse to physical rites, and certainly not the act of self-destruction. The *dīkṣā* or initiatory rite is allegorized as privation. Gifts to the priests are in the form of "austerity, alms-giving, uprightness, nonviolence, truthfulness."[74] It should be pointed out that here is the sole reference to *ahiṃsā* in the Upaniṣads.

In addition, it should be noted that, notwithstanding the doc-trine of *jīvanmukti*, the Upaniṣads are realistic enough to recog-nize that only a few reach to the sublime level of existence in this life.[75] This keeps one bound to the full living of this life and to the cultivation of reason, virtue, and faith for attaining strength (*vīrya, bala*).

Until the higher self is realized, the individual is ruled by the lower self. Though it is the higher self which is the basic reality of the lower self, it is the latter, the phenomenal self, which under-goes birth and death. The wheel of births and deaths around which most lives revolve is known as *saṃsāra* (transmigration).[76] Later, this doctrine of *saṃsāra*, and deliverance therefrom, pro-vided the rationale and motivation for those seeking a religious basis for suicide.

The Smṛti Literature

In this section we witness the formulation of certain representative approaches to suicide, as we trace their progress through the Sūtra period (500–200 B.C.), the epic period (200 B.C.–A.D. 300), and through the Puraṇic age (A.D. 300–750). As a result of the interaction of scripture and tradition, norms with ancient roots are developed in respect to the morality of suicide. Some of these ideals survive the passage of time through the medieval and modern periods.

The movement from the Sūtra to the epic period heralds the expansion of Brāhmaṇism into Hinduism. The main features of the latter constitute the matrix in which the discussion of suicide takes place. These features, as they exist to the present day, are Vedic authority; sacrifice; the laws of karma and *saṁsāra*; the four stages of life; the four ends of life; the three obligations; and faith in pilgrimages to holy shrines, rivers, cities and mountains.

Generally speaking, the Dharmaśāstra writers consider suicide, or the attempt to consider suicide, a major sin. This sentiment is understandable within a cultural environment in which nonviolence is one of the cardinal virtues. For instance, if the king is to attain Indra's heaven, he must see to it that no form of murder is perpetrated in his kingdom, and suicide, according to the law, was a form of murder.

Several authorities lay down that law. The Parāśara Saṁhitā states:

> The fate, which a man or woman comes by after having committed suicide by hanging, either out of inordinate pride, uncurable love, or excessive fright or anger, will be presently described.
>
> For a period of sixty thousand years, the spirit of a suicide is consigned to the darkness of a hell, which is full of blood and fetid pus.
>
> No period of uncleanness should be observed in respect of such a violent death. The rite of cremation is denied to the corpse of a suicide; no tears should be shed for, nor any libation of water should be offered unto, the (spirit) of a suicide.
>
> Carriers and cremators of the corpse of a suicide, dead by hanging, as well as the cutters of the noose (round his neck) should regain their personal cleanness by practicing a *Tapta Krichchha Vratam*. This has been enjoined by Prajāpati.
>
> Brāhmaṇas who touch, carry or commit to flames the

corpse of a suicide dead by hanging . . . should recover the natural cleanness of their persons by each practicing a Tapta Krichchha Vratam and by feeding the Brāhmaṇas as well, by way of atonement.[77]

In similar vein, Vasiṣṭha invokes the law forbidding *sapiṇḍa* (blood relations) to perform the funeral rites "for him who committing suicide becomes an *Abhisasta*."[78] A suicide is defined as one who destroys himself by means of wood, water, clods of earth, stones, weapons, poison, or a rope. Quoting an ancient authority, Vasiṣṭha enjoins that in the case of a twice-born man being sentimentally moved to perform the last rites for a suicide, the penalty is to perform a Kāndrāyaṇa penance (a three-day fast for resolving to die by one's own hand). The penalty for one who survives an attempt of suicide is to perform a *Krikkhra* penance during twelve days. Following that "he shall fast for three (days and) nights, being dressed constantly in a garment smeared (with clarified butter), and suppressing his breath, he shall thrice recite the *Aghamarshana*."[79]

Kauṭilya's *Arthaśāstra* (ca. A.D. 320–480), essentially a work on the science of polity, differs from the Dharmaśāstras in that it demonstrates a more realistic attitude to life and deals with matters that are of interest particularly to political authority. It is therefore significant to note that on the subject of suicide it more or less accepts the omnibus views and sanctions of the religious law books. Kauṭilya states:

> If a man or woman under the infatuation of love, anger or other sinful passions commits or causes to commit suicide by means of ropes, arms, or poison, he or she shall be dragged by means of a rope along the public road by the hands of a *candala*. For such murderers as the above, neither cremation rites nor any obsequies usually performed by relatives shall be observed. Any relative who performs funeral rites to such wretches, shall either himself be deprived of his own funerals or be abandoned by his kith or kin.[80]

The indignities hurled upon the corpse of a suicide are intended to desecrate the dead and to deter the living. Lecky reminds us of similar practices of the church in medieval Europe: He records that no religious rites were to be celebrated at the tomb of the "culprit," and that masses should not be said for his soul. Instead, "gross and various outrages" were to be heaped upon the corpse. "It was dragged upon a hurdle through the streets, hung up with the head downwards and at last thrown into the public sewer or burnt or buried in the sand below high water-mark or transfixed by a stake on the public highway."[81]

Thus the general attitude of the Dharmaśāstra writers is that suicide is a major sin. To kill oneself is the moral equivalent of killing another person.[82] A passionate, foolhardy act, impelled by selfish, shortsighted considerations, suicide forfeits blissful worlds beyond.[83] It is so heinous that, even to contemplate it in thought or to attempt it is a major evil. Those who aid and abet, among family and friends, are deserving of punishment.

"In spite of this general attitude," according to Kane, "exceptions were made in the smṛtis, the epics and purāṇas."[84] Perhaps the word *exceptions* is not the most appropriate in the Hindu context because it fails to do justice to the positive attitudes toward religious suicide. After all, in this context, suicide is not simply counted as the absence of guilt but as the acquisition of merit. This positive assessment made suicide a common practice that was engaged in by people of all classes in India. The deeds were proudly commemorated on tablets of stone or metal, many of which are preserved to this day.

The peculiar circumstances of the hermit in the forest made suicide quite natural for an individual in such an austere physical environment, heightened by the acute focus of the mind and spirit. In order to attain his goal of complete union with the supreme Soul, the hermit had to observe extreme bodily severities and had to immerse his mind in the sacred texts contained in the Upaniṣads. At an advanced stage, the option was given for another path toward his goal. After describing the conventional path to final liberation, Manu adds: "Or let him walk, fully determined and going straight on, in a north-easterly direction, subsisting on water and air, until his body sinks to rest. A Brāhmaṇa, having got rid of his body by one of those modes practised by the great sages, is exalted in the world of Brahman, free from sorrow and fear."[85] This came to be known as the Great Journey (*mahāprasthāna*). This option was deemed especially appropriate for the forest hermit afflicted with some incurable disease, unable to perform the duties of his order, and having a sense that his end is near. Taking the lead from Manu and Yājñavalkya, other texts recommend a more precipitous option with the exhortation that "a forest hermit may resort to the distant journey or may enter water or fire or may throw himself from a precipice."[86]

At the opposite end from the suicide of saints through *mahāprasthāna* was the suicide of sinners because of *mahāpātakas*. The "great sins" included murder of Brahmins, imbibing of *surā*, theft of gold belonging to Brahmins, and incest. The criminal was given the option to make suicide into a penitential act that would secure the expiation of his offenses. The text reads: "Or let him, of his own free will, become (in a battle) the target of archers who know (his purpose); or he may thrice throw himself headlong into a blazing fire. . . ."[87] Likewise, a twice-born man who has been deluded into drinking the spiritous liquor called *surā*, expiates his sin by swallowing that liquor "boiling hot," and when his insides are "completely scalded," he is "freed from his guilt."[88] As one might expect, this form of suicidal penance, involving cruel death, was condemned by some lawmakers such as Hārīta.[89]

In addition to the reasons we have mentioned for the resort to suicide, both by those who had adopted the life of renunciation and wished to eliminate future possibilities for sin, and those who wished to atone for some heinous sin, there were many other reasons for which people killed themselves. Some felt that life no longer held any purpose. They had lived by the values of *dharma*, *kāma*, and *artha*, but now that type of life no longer had any appeal, and they longed only for release from the weary cycle of birth and death. If the burden of old age or the bane of disease were added to ennui, they wished quickly to put an end to it all.

In select cases, the purpose of suicide among certain sects of sādhus was connected with the rite of *trāga*. If the sādhus were being oppressed or cheated out of a fundamental right, a member took it upon himself to rectify the wrong by focusing his thoughts upon the oppressor, and then he either killed himself or was ceremonially killed in sacrifice "so that the guilt of killing a sādhu would fall upon that person's head."[90]

As a similar strategy, certain sādhus and bardic clans of Rajputana employed suicide as a protest against some injustice, with the intention that the evil of the protestor's death would be heaped upon the head of the guilty party.[91]

Another select form of suicide was by fire. The tradition of burning oneself to death was long and common, especially among yogis. It was elemental and reverential, being associated with the perennial theme of sacrifice. Royalty in the south of India were known to practice the "great sacrifice" (mahām-makha). This meant that when a king was enthroned in the Pandya, Chola, and Tamil regions, about a hundred of his compatriots expressed their solidarity by participating in a sacramental meal, and promised to take their own lives by fire, upon the king's demise. "This terrible vow of suicide was known as māmakham . . . and was witnessed by the entire population of the city."[92]

Suicide by drowning was commended, especially at an auspicious place such as Prayāga, where the holy Gaṅgā and Yamunā come together with the invisible Sarasvatī. It is known as tīrtharāja. To drown oneself at the samgama is to enter mokṣa, which ordinarily is only open to the yogin who achieves this highest puruṣārtha through a lifetime of discipline and learning. This promise of the Purāṇas was received joyously not only by common folk, but also by sages such as Kālidāsa. Kings and rulers such as Yasah-karnadeva, Candella Dhangadev, and Chālukya Someśvara chose to die at Prayāga. A famous historical case is that of King Gangeya, who committed suicide at the sacred banyan tree of Prayāga, accompanied by one hundred of his wives. So great is the fame of Prayāga that the Purāṇas assure the pilgrims that even if they die along the way, they will accrue great blessings for having remembered Prayāga. In the words of the Matsyapurāṇa: "A man whether in his own country or house or after leaving his country dies in a forest, while remembering Prayāga, he still secures the world of Brahma. . . . "[93]

A more benign though highly meritorious form of suicide was through fasting (prāyopaveśa). The Anuśāsanaparva of the Mahābhārata claims: "A man knowing the Vedānta and understanding the ephemeral nature of life abandons life in the holy Himalayas by fasting, would reach the world of Brahma."[94] This method became popular among the Jains (sallekanā). Chandragupta Maurya is the most famous of those who ended their lives through starvation.

Suicide by leaping from a tower, cliff, or precipice was regarded as an act of courageous abnegation, worthy of much merit. The Matsyapurāṇa has high words of praise for the peaks of Amarakantaka, for whoever throws himself down from those heights never returns to saṁsāra.[95] Similar blessings are said to come to one who jumps from the rock called Bhairavajap, near Girnar onto the rocks below.

By virtue of their final journey to the Himalayas, the Pāndavas are said to have been the progenitors of a form of suicide which involved a ceaseless pilgrimage from one holy site to another, until the pilgrims dropped dead of exhaustion.

Sometimes suicide took the form of a vow which involved the promise of a boon from a chosen deity, in return for which the devotee sacrificed his or her life.

The greatest human toll was the suicide of widows by self-immolation. The practice of *satī* was not a phenomenon peculiar to Hindus but was known to people of Mesopotamia, the ancient Chinese, and early Indo-Europeans. The funeral hymn in the Rgveda clearly shows that at this time the "immolation" of the widow was ritualistically enacted in mimetic form, because, after lying down beside the corpse of her husband, the wife is then called to return to the land of the living, and to a new relationship with a second spouse. It is quite apparent that the ceremony thus performed has ancient roots in a time when the widow was actually burnt alongside her husband as "her ancient duty."

Later, the "ancient duty" was revived by Brahmins anxious to secure control over the widow's property. To give religious legitimacy to their sanctions, the passage in the Rgveda (10.8.7) which instructed the widow to ascend from the pyre of her deceased husband and to "go forth in front" (*agre*) was altered to read, "go into the fire" (*agneh*). As a consequence, wherever Brahminic authority prevailed, the custom of *satī* began to spread, especially in the regions of the Ganges Valley, Bengal, Oudh, and Rajputana. We know from the accounts of historians accompanying Alexander in his conquest of India that *satī* was practiced in the Punjab as early as the fourth century B.C. The early Smrti literature permits *satī* but does not popularize it. Two occurrences are recorded in the epics. Commenting on the Garudapurāna, Kane states:

> The Garudapurāna here (11.91–100) waxes eloquent over the immolation of a wife on her husband's pyre, over the miraculous power of a *pativratā*, and states that a brāhmana woman should not burn herself apart from her husband's body (or after he is cremated), but that ksatriya and other women may do so, that the practice of *satī* is common to all women even including chāndāla women, but pregnant women or those that have young children should not do so and that a woman does not

become free from the liability to be born again and again as a woman until she becomes a *Satī*.[96]

The Nāradapurāṇa repeats the restrictions on the conditions of the woman qualified for *satī*, adding that she should have attained puberty, and that she must not be menstruating at the time.[97]

A mass form of *satī* is represented in the rite of *jauhar*. It became common among the wives of Rajput warriors, who preferred to burn themselves by entire tribes rather than suffer the degradations consequent upon their defeat in battle. Though of early origin, *jauhar* became a respected rite during the medieval period.

Keith notes, "A new aspect of suicide appears in deities which is characteristic of Hinduism, for suicide now means not so much absorption to an impersonal absolute as union with a very personal deity."[98] An illustration of this is the narrative of Mīrā Bāī, Lord Kṛṣṇa's devotee who, while engaged in worship, is said to have suddenly vanished into a fissure formed in his image.

A second aspect of suicide relative to devotion to sectarian deities is connected with the worship of Viṣṇu as Jagannātha at Purī. During the Rath Jatra festival, Vaishnava deities were transported to their country home. Stories have long circulated of frenzied devotees throwing themselves under the huge wheels of the cars and being crushed to death. These older reports were greatly exaggerated. Many pilgrims did die, but as a result of being accidentally trampled by the teeming throngs caught up in great excitement. Others collapsed through heat exhaustion while hauling the heavy cars. "The few suicides that did occur were for the most part cases of diseased and miserable objects who took this means to put themselves out of pain."[99] Actually, self-destruction is hostile to the spirit of Viṣṇu worship. Should a death occur within the confines of the temple, even by accident, it is regarded as polluting and offensive to the deity, making it necessary for the whole ritual to be brought to a halt.

The custom of suicide under Brahmanical auspices flourished in various forms into the nineteenth century. Though it was official policy of the British government not to interfere in religious matters of the natives, it often felt forced to intervene on humanitarian grounds. In 1802 the legislature put an end to the practice of suicide on the island of Sagar, where devotees fulfilled their vows by voluntarily throwing themselves into the waters, to be devoured by sharks.

The most momentous intervention by the government was in connection with the practice of *sati*. This is a complicated subject with diverse strands. During the Moghul period, the custom was "frowned upon," but it was never completely prohibited for fear of alienating the Hindu subjects. As Muslim power declined, the practice was revived. By the time of the British era the custom became popular in the Bengal presidency. Almost 60 percent of all *satis* between 1815 and 1826 occurred in Calcutta and the neighboring districts. The reason for this upswing in localities affected by the British impact was the fact that the British provided new opportunities for upward social mobility. These opportunities were seized by urbanites who became rich by the system, but in the pursuit of Mammon they lost a good deal of their traditional virtues and social standing. *Sati* provided the nouveaux riches with a means of demonstrating their allegiance to the older norms from which life in the city had seduced them.

In addition to the socioreligious motives, economics played a part. Property rules gave wives and mothers a certain stake in the distribution of property. In competitive times there was a high possibility that a widow would inherit considerable property which she could use for bargaining purposes. These privileges were deemed dangerous. The safest and most sanctimonious way of avoiding this danger was to persuade wives to blaze a path of virtue.

The government of Warren Hastings, on the advice of Brahmin pandits that *sati* was a religious institution, adopted a policy of noninterference, but this brought the administration into a collision course with the Evangelicals, both in England and in India. In 1813 rules were formulated by the government based on the principle that *sati* be permitted whenever it is countenanced by Hindu religion and law, and that it be prevented when prohibited by the same authorities. The prohibitions included cases in which the widow was (1) unwilling; (2)under sixteen years of age; (3) pregnant; (4) drugged or intoxicated; or (5) mother of a child under three years of age, unless legal guardianship were secured on behalf of the child.

Further clarification of the legal disabilities preventing a widow from ending her life involved the practice of widow burying by the *jogi* sect of East Bengal. The Hindu law officers of the Provincial Court of Appeals for Dacca gave the opinion that in conformity with the customs of the *jogis* (though not founded on scriptures), it was lawful for a widow to be buried alive with her dead husband. On the issue of tying the widow to the funeral pile, or pressing her down with green bamboos to avoid escape, the pandits of the Sadar Diwani Adalat opined that no scriptural authorities permitted the use of restraints.

British policy of noninterference in religious matters did not change throughout the ruling terms of Hastings and Amherst, but during this time foundations were laid on which William Bentinck could later take his stand. Two figures played pivotal parts: Mrityunjay Vidyalankar, chief pandit of the Supreme Court, ranking Hindu scholar, and formidable advocate of Hindu orthodoxy; and Ram Mohan Roy (1772–1833), social reformer, and Vedāntin scholar.

Commissioned by the chief judge of the Sadar Diwani Adalat to determine the precise measure in which *satī* is supported by the *śāstras*, Vidyalankar produced some surprising findings. He stated that scriptural injunctions apply only to those who feel the pain of disease or separation or who act voluntarily, and that the "act of dying is not enjoined, but merely the mode of it. If you are bent on suicide, say the scriptures, 'put an end to yourself by such and such means' . . . "[100] For his part, Vidyalankar recommended "a life of abstinence and chastity" as more "highly excellent" than the woman burning herself.[101]

Vidyalankar's opinions reinforced the thinking of Ram Mohan Roy. In 1818 he published a Bengali tract entitled *A Conference between an Advocate for, and an Opponent of the Practice of Burning Widows Alive.* First, the "Advocate" of concremation and postcremation (*anumaran*) of widows lists several sacred lawgivers enjoining *satī.* The "Opponent" accepts these injunctions but points out that whereas the scriptures are written on different levels to cater to the moral development of diverse individuals, we must finally evaluate the lesser moral injunctions by the higher ones. Manu is the most unimpeachable witness of moral law. Therefore the commands of lesser authorities must be judged in the light of Manu. And on the authority of the great lawgiver, widows are enjoined to pass their days cheerfully by living a life of simplicity and virtue.

Furthermore, every act is qualified by its motivation. The driving force behind concremation is always some form of sensual gratification. Such virtue has its own reward; but being the product of selfish desire, it sooner or later is dissipated. Rites, dutifully performed, may bring one to the celestial abode of the gods, but when merit is exhausted, one is subjected again to birth, disease, and death. Therefore, instead of seeking the pleasures of transient heaven, one should have faith in the Supreme Being, which leads to absorption, and from which there is no returning to this life of suffering. Such is the testimony of the Upaniṣads.

Having been routed on the grounds of scripture, the "Advocate" takes shelter in tradition. The "Opponent" dislodges him from here, too, first by showing that the custom of *satī* is not sanctioned by the most ancient Hindu sources, and that though the practice is long, that is no justification that it should be prolonged.

Displaced from scripture and tradition, the "Advocate" assumes the role of a moral pragmatist. If women are allowed to survive their husbands, these weak creatures may go astray and bring disgrace to their husbands. The "Opponent" replies that the possibility of infidelity is present also when the husband is alive, especially when he resides for a long time in a distant place, and that in order to avoid the danger of social disgrace, the enforcers of *satī* are committing the greater sin of female murder.[102] Fourteen months later, Ram Mohan produced a *Second Conference* in which he argued for women's rights and demolished the premise on which *satī* was practiced, namely, that women are constitutionally weaker than men.

Roy's campaign for the abolition of *satī* was unrelenting. Through his literary works and newspaper publications he condemned *satī* on moral grounds and on the basis of those very scriptures which were held sacred by his opponents. Thus, taking the position that true Hinduism is both moral and rational, he was able to move with the winds of liberalism which were blowing from the West.

In 1828 Lord William Bentinck, a protégé of Jeremy Bentham, was appointed governor-general. In 1829 Bentinck acted where others had called for reports and abolished *satī* by Regulation XVII of 1829. Ram Mohan helped Bentinck in forming his decision by breaking the moral deadlock which had stymied earlier administrators—the deadlock between the principle of liberty and the principle of life.

Roy convincingly demonstrated to the governor-general that the custom they had pledged themselves to protect in the name of religious liberty was "nowhere enjoined as a duty; and that a life of piety and self-abnegation was considered more virtuous."[103] On the practical side Roy also gave convincing testimony that the motives behind the proponents of *sati* were often less inspired by creed than by greed. The poor, defenseless creature upon the funeral pyre might have been prayed for, but in truth she was preyed upon.

Thus, on the grounds of scripture and morality Ram Mohan Roy showed the governor-general that the elimination of *sati* could not amount to an infringement of religious freedom. The only remaining issue was the right to life. Both these considerations are reflected in Bentinck's Preamble to the *sati* Regulation of December 4, 1829.[104]

Summary of the Hindu Tradition

The Hindu view of suicide has a core and a periphery. The core centers around those scriptures and traditions which look to the Upaniṣads as their fountainhead. The philosophic goal of the center is the attainment of the highest human value, namely, liberation from *saṁsāra*, or the round of rebirths. The moral values which facilitate this goal are those which preserve and promote a quality of life commensurate with spiritual aspiration.

Within this philosophic framework, Hinduism condemns suicide as evil when it is a direct and deliberate act with the intention voluntarily to kill oneself for self-regarding motives. Subjectively, the evil resides in the act as the product of ignorance and passion; objectively, the evil encompasses the karmic consequences of the act which impede the progress of liberation. It is in this context that the Dharmasūtras vehemently prohibit suicide.

On the other hand, Hinduism permits selective recourse to suicide when it is religiously motivated. The ideal which is meant to guide us in this very intricate terrain is that of the enlightened person who has renounced all and now lives in the forest.

Manu clearly distinguishes between courses that are ordinary and extraordinary for the *sannyāsin*—the individual in the fourth and final stage of life. He points out the normal path to be followed: "He should sleep on raised ground (*sthandila*), should feel no concern if he suffers from an illness, he should neither welcome death nor should he feel joy for continuing to live, but he should patiently wait till the time of death, as a servant waits till the time he is hired expires."[105]

These instructions of Manu are in accord with the teachings and spirit of the Upaniṣads, which elevate the knowledge of *ātman* and *Brahman* to the highest place and ascribe greater value to study and meditation than to the performance of sacrifices and self-immolation. And so the sage prays:

> From the unreal [*asat*] lead me to the real [*sat*]!
> From darkness led me to light!
> From death lead me to immortality![106]

By uniting with *Brahman*, the *ātman* transcends all such vicissitudes of mortal existence as hunger and thirst, sorrow and confusion, old age and death. "As the sun, the eye of the Universe, remains far off and unaffected by all sickness that meets the eye, so also the One, the *Ātman*, who dwells in all creatures, dwells afar and untouched by the sorrows of the world."[107] Thus no state can possibly excel the state of realizing one's identity with *Brahman*.

Further, the bliss of *Brahman* is not just an eschatological possibility, but an empirical reality. You do not have to die to reach Brahma-realization. That union can be had here and now and is known as *jīvanmukti*. The Kaṭha Upaniṣad affirms: "when all the desires the heart harbors are gone, man becomes immortal and reaches *Brahman* here."[108] Finally, the Upaniṣads teach that liberation is not acquired from without, by some extraneous act, but is realized from within. And so the *mokṣa* doctrine supplies the basis for moral optimism in that the capacity of the present life to achieve perfection is fully realized.

In this light the Upaniṣads deplore the person who kills his soul by remaining in ignorance of the true self:

> Joyless are those worlds called,
> Covered with blind darkness.
> To them after death go those
> People that have not knowledge, that are not awakened.[109]

Such demands for knowledge to attain *mokṣa* clearly contravene the later developments in the magical and meritorious efficacy of dying in holy places such as Benares or Prayāga, or by daredevil acts such as jumping from cliffs or slitting one's throat before an idol. The fact is that to the extent the influence of the Upaniṣads prevailed, some of the Dharmaśāstras, such as Gautama, declared their opposition to those who wilfully died "by starving themselves to death, by weapons, fire, poison, or water, by hanging themselves, or by jumping (from a precipice)."[110] In the same spirit, deadly penitential deaths, such as allowing oneself to become a target in battle to expiate the guilt of murdering a Brahmin, is condemned by Hārīta and others.[111]

Upaniṣadic reason and sensitivity was also vindicated at the height of the medieval season of suicide in that "gradually there was a revulsion of feeling against suicide at Prayāga or Kāśī or starting on the Great Journey."[112] Kane observes that some of the later medieval writers try very hard to combat the view that suicide is approved in the smṛtis. He says, "It is refreshing to find Nārāyaṇabhaṭṭa perhaps the most learned and renowned Pandit of his age steeped in all the lore of ancient India, make, in spite of the overwhelming weight of sastric authority in favor of suicide at Prayāga, exceptions that surely appeal to reason, sentiment and common sense. Nārāyaṇabhaṭṭa probably followed traditions several hundred years older than his times."[113]

The "revulsion" also carried over to the populace at large. Alberuni, reporting on India in A.D. 1030, says about suicides inspired by religion: "It was resorted to by those who are tired of life, who are distressed over some incurable disease, some irremovable bodily defect or old age or infirmity. This however no man of distinction does, but only vaiśyas and śūdras. Burning oneself is forbidden to brāhmaṇas and kṣatriyas by a special law. Therefore these if they want to kill themselves do so at the time of an eclipse in some other manner or they hire somebody to drown themselves in the Ganges."[114]

After excising the vast number of suicides performed in the name of religion but actually accountable for in terms of socioeconomic pressures, and for selfish desires both for this world and the next, the question still remains as to the religious legitimation of suicide in Hinduism. The answer is far from plain, or always consistent, but given the Upaniṣadic norm with which we began this discussion, the following outlines emerge.

Though empirical existence is the vale of unreality, ignorance, and mortality, it is also the place of soul making. This polarity creates a lively tension between making the most of the world while at the same time renouncing it. On the one hand we must look upon the world as home and not be overanxious, even for dire reasons, to make a hasty exit. On the other hand, should we reach the point when through disability, age, or disease the body is no longer capable of keeping pace with the spirit, then the body may be respectfully left behind. *Life must not be allowed to come in the way of Life.* Our essential existence, as the bearer of *mokṣa*, must ultimately prevail over empirical existence, the bearer of *saṁsāra*. The whole of Hindu discipline is an exercise in progressive renunciation, and continuous with that, *suicide is the supreme act of renunciation.* For the sage, it is the death of death.

Although Hinduism keeps the door open, only those who have met their obligations to society, who have been enlightened, who act with knowledge, and who are not driven by pressures from without or passions from within may pass through the doors, provided impelling circumstances make this necessary.

Our sketch incorporates the teachings of the early and later Upaniṣads, such as the Jābāla and Kaṇṭhaśruti, which expressly lay down that the *sannyāsin*, upon acquiring full insight, "may enter upon the great journey," and also the exfoliation of the tradition in those writings which Kane describes as appealing to "reason, sentiment and common sense."

THE APPLICATION OF HINDU PRINCIPLES

Hinduism and the Right to Die

Contemporary American society is facing a mounting opposition to its traditional position in which suicide is condemned both by Christian and Jewish authorities, by a legal system which forbids it in most jurisdictions, and by the medical establishment, which finds it in opposition to its professional ethics.

The strongest signal yet of the "right to die" movement is the phenomenal popularity of a book recently (1991) published, *Final Exit*, by Derek Humphry. It rapidly surged to No. 1 on the *New York Times* best-seller list for nonfiction. Its early sales were described as a "publishing phenomenon."

Printed in large type, the 192-page manual explains how patients undergoing "unbearable suffering" can peacefully die with lethal drug doses and by following specific tips and instructions. The chapter titles include "How Do You Get the Magic Pills?" "Self-Deliverance via the Plastic Bag," and, for husbands and wives, "Going Together."

A clue to why thousands of people are buying this book may be found in the foreword by television journalist Betty Rollin, who has admitted to assisting her mother commit suicide. Ms. Rollins quotes her mother, terminally sick with ovarian cancer: "I'm not afraid to die, but I am afraid of this illness, what it's doing to me." Issues surrounding the right to die are becoming strident in American society precisely for this reason: because advances in medical technology have left some people more afraid of dying than of death itself.

One reporter, shocked as to how a book that instructs the terminally ill to kill themselves should shoot to the top of the sales charts, makes the following commentary:

> Bookstore owners have reportedly said many of the buyers are older people in good health and humor. . . . But perhaps they are also people who have gone to doctors and who know that when you become a patient, often you cease to be an actor and become an acted upon.
>
> They are people who know from experience that certain illnesses leave the sick stripped of everything they think makes life worth living, prisoners of pain and indignity.
>
> Perhaps they are men and women approaching old age who have visited nursing homes and seen people who are husks, tied in wheelchairs, saved from death by any means possible, saved for something that is as much like life as a stone is like an egg, a twig like a finger.[115]

Response from the American Medical Association has been as expected. Dr. Lonnie R. Bristow, a board member of the AMA in San Pablo, California, calls the message of *Final Exit* "repugnant" because it goes against the medical profession's ethics. "It strikes at the very foundation of what makes the profession noble," and there is "no reason in this day and age for a patient to have unbearable sufferings." If it became legal for doctors to assist in suicide, Bristow argues, the mutual trust between doctor and patient would be destroyed.[116]

Approximately twenty-five states have laws forbidding suicide assistance, and medical society rules in all states bar doctors'
involvement. Yet polls on the West Coast and Pennsylvania indicate that two-thirds of those surveyed think "doctors should be
allowed by law to help terminally ill patients end their lives pain-
lessly."[117]

Despite AMA opposition, it appears doctors are beginning to
appreciate and act upon the patient's right to die. "Thirty percent
of U.S. primary-care physicians say there are circumstances in
which a doctor is justified in deliberately causing a patient's
death," according to a poll published in July 1991 by Physicians's
Management Magazine.[118] The poll states that "one in five doctors said patients have asked for information about how to end
their lives. Nearly one in 10 said they have deliberately taken
direct actions to cause a patient's death."[119]

The publishing success of *Final Exit* clearly typifies a struggle
of values in American society. On the one hand we consider it the
mark of our national character to uphold independence, personal
autonomy, and the taking of responsibility for our own lives. Yet,
when it comes to *the most crucial articulation of these values in
terms of making critical choices as to how and when we should
die*, the law steps in and makes personal decisions in our stead.
This creates a situation in which people are fearful of having to
eke out a costly, vegetative existence, bereft of any worthwhile
human qualities and capacities, especially the power to control
one's own dying process. And so it is that when a "how-to" book
comes along, people rush out and buy it for some future time
when, struck by terminal illness, they may feel so drained of sta-
mina, purpose, and the will to live that they may want to know
"How Do You Get the Magic Pills?" As a best-seller, *Final Exit*
clearly underscores the need for the sort of information it con-
tains, and is therefore a strong indictment of our social, legal,
medical, and religious establishments.

In this setting, what are the implications of the Hindu attitude
toward suicide in respect to the issue of the right to die? First, we
must clearly distinguish suicide from those acts of self-destruction
which do not belong to that category. In Hinduism, the word for
suicide, *ātma-ghata*, has the elements of intentionality. It is self-
killing for a high end. The individual engages in an act which he
knows will terminate in his own death. Further, the act is that of a

free, rational agent, not coerced by social conditions from without or by psychiatric compulsions from within. Finally, death is caused by the arrangement of that individual for the express purpose of bringing about his or her own death. Thus, the principle in Hinduism is that for an act to qualify as a suicide it must involve a process of rationally weighing all of the options, deciding upon one that is most appropriate, and then assuming full responsibility for having brought about one's own death.

Ātma-hatyā or *ātma-ghata* in Hinduism is therefore an act of self-killing which is different from other acts which result in the death of the agent but do not qualify as suicide. For example, the bystander who rushes into a burning building to rescue the trapped occupants does not commit suicide because his intention is not to die but to save. Similarly, a soldier who throws himself upon a live grenade lobbed into the trench is not committing suicide but protecting his buddies against death. Both of these are acts of sacrifice performed in order to relieve others, whereas in the case of suicide the intention is to relieve oneself.

Judged by the criterion of *intention*, it is doubtful if all of the historic cases of *jauhar* and *satī* could qualify as suicides. It is possible that some of the Rajput ladies who killed themselves en masse when attacked by Muslim invaders did so under the frenzied spell of their leaders or were overcome by hysteria and paranoia. Similarly, it is possible that the young women who committed *satī* were merely acting out the dictates of their greedy elders. This would correspond with Durkheim's "altruistic" type of suicide wherein the victim is too weak to defy the expectations of obtrusive customs. That was precisely the conclusion of Roy. That is why he insisted that the pyre be lit before the widow ascended the heap, and that it be forbidden for her to be held down by attendants pressing on her body with green bamboos. Roy wanted to make sure that the widow was doing what she wanted to do, rather than acting out the plans of designing relatives.

Hinduism's emphasis upon defining suicide as the intentional termination of life is in keeping with our common linguistic usage. Durkheim rejected intentional definitions because they were not easily verifiable. In the case of a person falling to death from a tall building, it would be difficult to verify what that person's intentions were, apart from being sure that the individual wished to die. Therefore, Durkheim substituted knowledge for intention in his definition.

Actually, the Hindu definition includes both intention and knowledge because in the Indian context they both go together. But Hinduism operates on a completely different level of concern than that of Durkheim and others. Social scientists, insurance companies, and coroners insist on knowledge because they must be able to demonstrate that this particular act was an act of suicide. Hinduism' primary concern is not with the objective, verifiable aspect of behavior, but with its subjective mechanisms. To understand these mechanisms, we must understand Hinduism's view of the self-body relationship.

The body to which the self is attached is of three kinds: physical, subtle, and causal. In suicide, it is only the physical body that is destroyed. Death constitutes the dissolution of the physical body into the five elements out of which it originates. The subtle body is of interest to us. It embodies the vital, mental, and intellectual functions as a whole. It provides the mechanism through which the inexorable law of karma functions, and therefore is instrumentaly connected with the transmigration of the self from one body to another. In other words, although suicide brings about death, it is only the end of corporeality, not of individuality. Individuality only ceases in the moment of enlightenment, when the individual realizes union with the Supreme Reality. Death is therefore that point of intersection where the essential self changes bodies, and perhaps, direction, depending on the store of moral consequences reposed in the subtle body.

One advantage of the karma doctrine is that it removes the need for us to project our moral judgments against suicide onto the actions of an angry God who adds punishment to injury by consigning the suicide to a fiery hell. Aside from the actual future fate of the suicide, this type of theological thinking is exceedingly harmful to the mental state of the one who has attempted suicide and failed, cutting the individual off from possible sources of spiritual support; and it is also a blight on the peace of mind of loved ones left behind. The karma doctrine satisfies our moral need for accountability of our actions without perpetuating the image of God as the Great Avenger. Even civil law no longer punishes the unfortunate individual who has tried to take his or her life. Our image of God ought to supersede that level of human compassion.

Next, in what way and to what extent does the above definition of suicide in Hinduism help create a right to suicide? Summarily stated, life is a hierarchy of values, broadly four in number. The highest value, dictated by the essential nature of the self, is spiritual enlightenment. The three other values proceed from the nature of the empirical self and express themselves in terms of instinctual and aesthetic needs, the wish for material prosperity and social recognition, and aspirations for moral ends. In an integrated personality, all four ends are correlated and regulated by the ultimate end of liberation. Accordingly, Hindu medicine is concerned that a person be physically and mentally sound because good health is the prerequisite for all other human pursuits, including the life of the spirit.[120] However, when the physical base is impaired, it is detrimental to living on that level of life in which our peculiar human qualities have the opportunity to flourish. When that situation becomes intolerable and irreversible, a rational, autonomous individual, eager to hold on to what makes one truly human, has the right and the duty to determine the rest of the course of his or her earthly journey.

This is the philosophical support in Hinduism for the right to suicide in terms of the principles of personal autonomy and rational choice. However, it should be pointed out that *this right is a limited right; it is only a religious option, permitted in the pursuit of higher goals, and therefore to be undertaken with much gravity.*

As we have shown above, Hindu tradition is preeminently on the side of the principle of the sanctity of all life, most especially human life. The normal path is to endure bravely the sorrow and suffering that is our human lot. It is an accepted fact of life: *saṁsāra* is suffering. It is also recognized that the average individual is bound within a social nexus by certain obligations which it is his duty to uphold. When the sense of the sacred is forgotten, when one becomes cowardly in the battle of life, when one shirks responsibility for family and friends—in a word, when one allows the needs of the ego to dominate one's life—then suicide is a major sin.

Thus Hinduism resonates to both sides of the current debate without being caught in either camp. While affirming the cardinal principle of the sanctity of life, it is not absolutist in its ethical thinking, and allows for the right to suicide on the basis of rational choice and personal autonomy.

Hinduism and Suicide Prevention

The twofold stance of Hinduism in respect to suicide enables it to do justice to two moral principles that are presently in conflict within our society. On one side is the Principle of Autonomy which affirms the right to commit suicide. Hinduism recognizes the exercise of free choice as the mark of human dignity, especially when that dignity is directed toward the individual's outreach to his or her higher self. Consistent with this view, it would be wrongful, amounting to a breach of privacy, for an individual or the state to interfere with a person's right to commit suicide.

On the other side is the Principle of Human Worth, which affirms that people count, and that individuals and the state are obligated to intervene when a person is doing harm to himself or herself. Hinduism inculcates a strong sense of responsibility within the family and to the segments of society to which we belong. Consistent with this view, suicide prevention is a strong arm of its beneficent concerns.

The Principle of Autonomy and the Principle of Human Worth are in bitter contention both in America and the rest of the Western world. Traditionally, Western societies have favored the latter principle, historically for religious reasons; more recently, secular reasons have also come into play. But the momentum of the Principle of Autonomy is gaining ground with all sorts of implications for suicide prevention.

Hindu ethics tackles the problem on two levels. First, it is justifiable to intervene in the case of nonautonomous suicides. We have already seen that a great many people who commit suicide are victims of mental and chemical disorders which irrationally drive them to acts of self-destruction. There are very young people who act impulsively out of ignorance, immaturity, and addiction to drugs and alcohol. There are old people who cannot come to terms with the sudden loss of a loved one, or a job, or health. Some vulnerable souls are coerced by exploiters, often in the name of chastity, honor, loyalty, or reunion with a loved one. All of these individuals can be removed from their temporary crises through the intervention of appropriate medical or social agencies. Often it is a matter of simply showing them their options. This reflects the fact that a large number of suicides are actually cries for help. Under these circumstances, suicide intervention is an act of humanity, and is the preferred moral alternative than to do nothing in the name of autonomy.

The real difficulties lie on the second level, involving autonomous cases of suicide. Is it valid to interfere with the plans of persons capable of autonomous choice? The response of the Church and all medical and state agencies is to invoke the Paternalistic Principle. The principle of paternalism "asserts that limiting people's liberty is justified if through their own actions they would produce serious harm to themselves or would fail to secure important benefits."[121] Justification in the case of suicide is that there is less loss to the individual as a result of the intervention than follows from his deed, that is, death.

Hindu ethics is in principle opposed to paternalism, when considered in the context of personal choices affecting one's spiritual destiny. It allows for concerned parties to intervene to find out what the situation is and to be prepared to remedy it, or to prevent any harm that might accrue to others. But beyond moral dissuasion and remonstrating with the individual, there should be no efforts to coerce or control. Instead, there is the respectful acceptance of an individual's wish for a peaceful and ennobling death, having renounced all earthly attachments and all desires, including desires for the avoidance of suffering and the hope of happiness in some future existence. Because this state of mind and spirit is possible only for the few who have led a disciplined life, it is assumed that the person who is fully capable of making this awesome decision must be a sage or ascetic. For such a perfected one, suicide is eternal release from the wheel of rebirth (*saṁsāra*) and awakening to the Soul. And so the sages ask:

> If a person knew the Soul (*Ātman*),
> With the thought "I am he!"
> With what desire, for love of what
> Would he cling unto the body? (Bṛihadāraṇyaka Up. 4.4.12)

CHAPTER 3

The Ethics of Euthanasia

INTRODUCTION

In its annual survey of historical highpoints of 1991, *U.S. News and World Report* addressed the following question to noted medical ethicist Daniel Callahan: "Why did 'assisted suicide' become such a hot topic this year?" Callahan gave this reply:

> People began to get the idea that it's not easy to die well in our society, and hence the issue of euthanasia and assisted suicide began to attract more attention. Opinions actually began to change more than 10 years ago. There were a number of court cases on right-to-die issues, beginning with the Karen Anne Quinlan case in 1976. Simultaneously a number of states were debating living wills and the like.
>
> Then along came Jack Kevorkian, Timothy Quill [who helped a terminal patient end her life] and Derek Humphry [author of the bestselling suicide book, "Final Exit"], all within a short period. They attracted a lot of attention to the issues, in great part by taking the stance of radicals trying to break through on this issue.
>
> I think all three probably felt that the times were going to be more congenial for their cause. If you look at public-opinion surveys, you might get the impression that those promoting the right to die will find an easy victory. But the evidence from the effort in California three years ago and the recent Washington State vote rejecting the right-to-die bill is that when people think twice about this issue they are likely to be less enthusiastic than at first.[1]

Callahan is correct that the idea that "it's not easy to die well" has taken root in the psyche of the American people, but perhaps he underestimates the power of its momentum.

As medical technology becomes more capable of prolonging life past its natural span, and as the population grows older and

79

falls prey to the diseases and infirmities of advanced age, fears of a painful, prolonged death become predictable realities. The secret fear of the unknown "perils of the soul" threaten people's constitutional need for some degree of control over their manner of dying. Life, not death, is the true specter when existence is reduced to the level of biology, sustained by "miracle machines" that, once turned on, are difficult to turn off. "To be or not to be" is not a philosophic conundrum anymore, but an existential dilemma faced by a growing number of persons for whom a quick and merciful death at the hands of a medical professional is to be preferred to a mindless existence racked by pain. This was the moral dilemma faced by the mother of journalist Betty Rollin who, while dying of ovarian cancer, felt she needed to take charge of how, when, and where she should end her life. She reflects and resolves:

> I've had a wonderful life, but now it's over, or it should be. I'm not afraid to die, but I am afraid of this illness, what it's doing to me. . . . There's never any relief from it now. Nothing but nausea and this pain. . . . There won't be any more chemotherapy. There's no treatment anymore. So what happens to me now? I know what happens. I'll die slowly. . . . I don't want that. . . . Who does it benefit if I die slowly? If it benefits my children I'd be willing. But it's not going to do you any good. . . . There is no point in a slow death, none. I've never liked doing things with no point. I've got to end this.[2]

The case for active voluntary euthanasia, or direct killing, has developed into a major social issue, more potent than Callahan is prepared to admit. There are no empirical data to support his claim that voters rejected the right-to-die bills in California and Washington because, in spite of their initial popularity, when people gave it careful thought, they changed their minds. To the contrary, Parachini demonstrates that the reason why the California Humane and Dignified Death Initiative lost was that "too little attention was paid to the organizational details of such a precedential enterprise and the measure's advocates took too much comfort in public opinion polls—both their own and others."[3]

Regardless of the reasons why the initiatives lost in California and Washington, the mere fact that the euthanasia tide had come so far should be sufficient reason to recognize it as a pressing issue in our society. And the chances are that the tide is bound to rise even higher. McCormick appears to anticipate this augmentation, albeit with Catholic trepidation. Citing a 1991 poll conducted by the *Boston Globe* and the Harvard School of Public Health, he observes that most Americans (64 percent of those questioned) approve of physician-assisted suicide. Therefore,

> it was somewhat surprising . . . that an initiative to legalize it was defeated in Washington State on November 5. The American Medical Association opposed Initiative 119, and its senior vice-president of medical education and science, M. Roy Schwarz, stated that the profession would not soon change its position. "Maybe in five or ten years, but not soon." Five or ten decades would be too soon, in my judgment. But Schwarz's prediction may be close to the mark. The medical profession is usually, and often enough properly, conservative on these matters, but one wonders how long it will hold out against proposals like Initiative 119, especially if these represent shifts in public opinion. Not long, I fear.[4]

According to Andrew Greeley, the growth of the euthanasia movement points to "a dramatic social change in a brief period of time."[5] Data from the National Opinion Research Center's annual General Social Survey record that "Americans' support for 'the right to die' increased significantly during the 1980s."[6] Initiative 119 must therefore not be seen as a rationally vacuous bubble that burst, but as the point of eruption of several social concerns which have been building up over the past decade. McCormick cites "five cultural trends" that came together in the promotion of the initiative: patient autonomy; the separation of medical practice from its moral roots; the inadequate management of pain; the issue of whether nutrition and hydration are required for persons in a persistent vegetative state; and the great pressure of health care costs, especially upon the debilitated elderly and chronically ill.[7]

The defeat of Initiative 119 in Washington should not give the wrong signal that these cultural trends have been dissipated, for unless these concerns of the American public are satisfactorily addressed, we shall soon witness clones of Initiative 119 both in Washington and the rest of the states. The media have understood that euthanasia is still a "hot topic" with the public and keep stoking the fire with the latest incidents and growing statistics.

It is common knowledge that 80 percent of Americans will die in hospitals, with 50 percent of that number being connected to some life-support system. If one is not cured, the only way to be unplugged from these machines without any legal or moral hassle, is to be registered as "brain dead." The fate of others will be less certain, depending on whether they are "terminal," "comatose," or "vegetative." It costs more than $1,000 per day to maintain a terminal or comatose patient, and approximately $300 a day for the ten thousand Americans who are presently in vegetative states.

The grim statistics demand a closer look at the dilemmas of life and death confronting the American public, and also our medical and judicial systems. We begin by investigating the historical dynamics of the ideas that have shaped Western thinking on euthanasia, going back to antiquity.

HISTORICAL PERSPECTIVES

The Greco-Roman Tradition

The English word *euthanasia* was first used in 1646. Its etymology indicates its Greek derivation (*eu thanatos*; "a quiet and easy death"). Hence we start our survey with the Greek tradition. It appears that the ancient Greeks commonly practiced infanticide in the case of defective children. Plutarch tells us that this was state policy in Sparta.

> Nor was it in the power of the father to dispose of the child as he thought fit; for he was obliged to carry it before certain triers at a place called Lesche; these were some of the elders of the tribe to which the child belonged; their business it was carefully to view the infant, and, if they found it stout and well made, they gave order for its rearing, and allotted it to one of the thousand shares of land above mentioned for its maintenance, but, if they found it puny and ill-shaped, ordered it to be taken to what was called the Apothetae, a sort of chasm under Taygetus; as thinking it neither for the good of the child itself, nor for the public interest that it should be brought up, if it did not, from the outset, appear made to be healthy and vigorous.[8]

Spartan ideas in respect to the elimination of weaklings within the ideal state reappear in the political writings of Plato and Aristotle. The *Republic* states: "The proper officers will take the offspring of the good parents to the pen or fold, and there they will deposit them with certain nurses who dwell in a separate quarter;

but the offspring of the inferior, or of the better when they chance to be deformed, will be put away in some mysterious, unknown place, as they should be."[9] Similar eugenically inspired ideas are found in Aristotle's delineation of the ideal state.[10] Later, the practice of exposing maimed children met with heated opposition by Musonios in the first century.[11]

Though his religious assumptions made Plato generally oppose the practice of suicide, he was more sympathetically disposed to euthanasia, considering it appropriate when a person was afflicted with an incurable disease which rendered him unfit for service to the state, and argued that it was not the duty of a physician to employ extraordinary means in medically hopeless cases. He derided Herodicus for utilizing his medical and athletic training for "torturing first and chiefly himself, and secondly the rest of the world." How? "By the invention of lingering death; for he had a mortal disease which he perpetually tended, and as recovery was out of the question, he passed his entire life as a valetudinarian; he could do nothing but attend upon himself, and he was in constant torment whenever he departed in anything from his usual regimen, and so dying hard, by the help of science he struggled on to old age."[12]

Defining the boundaries of the medical art and the role of the physician, Plato argued that care and cure must be determined by their profitability to the state. When that line was crossed, the aggressive treatment of an individual could no longer be justified. He declared:

> Asclepius may be supposed to have exhibited the power of his art only to persons who, being generally of healthy constitution and habits of life, had a definite ailment; such as these he cured by purges and operations, and bade them live as usual, herein consulting the interests of the state; but bodies which disease had penetrated through and through he would not have attempted to cure by gradual processes of evacuation and infusion: he did not want to lengthen out good-for-nothing lives, or to have weak fathers begetting weaker sons—if a man was not able to live in the ordinary way he had no business to cure him; for such a cure would have been of no use either to himself, or to the state.[13]

Aristotle differed from Plato on the question of euthanasia. He considered the taking of human life a loss to the state. He condemned the individual as a despairing coward, "conspicuous for his excess of fear in painful situations."[14]

The most quoted legacy of the Greek tradition is the Hippocratic Oath, specifically the clause which says: "I will give no deadly medicine to any one if asked, nor suggest any such counsel; and in like manner I will not give to a woman a pessary to produce abortion."[15] Our knowledge of the historical Hippocrates comes from Plato in the *Protagoras* and *Phaedrus*. These works place him as a contemporary of Socrates and as a teacher and practitioner of medicine who believed that a true knowledge of the body depends on a knowledge of the whole person. But this native of Cos soon became the legendary "Father of Medicine," which means that the writings attributed to him (including the Oath) belong to a later time. In the opinion of some scholars, the "Hippocratic Oath" is not representative of the medical thought and practice of classical Greek antiquity, but only of a sect that was probably schooled in Pythagoreanism. Philosophers of the Pythagorean school taught that the vicissitudes of mortal existence, including the traumas of painful death, were divine recompense for past sins. Therefore resort to euthanasia was considered a violation of divine law because it cut short the appointed time of the soul's captivity within the body. It is worth noting that though the values of the "Hippocratic Oath" were revived in modern times, in its own time and place it only represented a minority position.

By contrast, the majority position in classical Greece held that attempts to prolong the life of an individual who was beyond recovery were medically unethical. It was considered acceptable practice for a physician to engage in active euthanasia by administering poison or other deadly potions, and doctors were even eulogized for concocting swift and painless means of death.

Among the Romans, Stoic philosophers were eager to embrace euthanasia whenever they lost their zest for living. Infanticide was commonly practiced on weak and deformed children. Their attitude toward euthanasia was shaped by the Stoics' fundamental philosophy: *zen kata physin*—"to live according to Nature." This meant cultivating a life of indifference (*apatheia*) toward all the ups and downs of mortal life—sickness and pain, fortune and misfortune, life and death. Only morality counted. The possession of human dignity was prized more highly than life itself. In the words of Lucius Annaeus Seneca (the Younger; 4 B.C.–A.D. 65): "Living is not the good, but living well. The wise man therefore lives as long as he should, not as long as he can. He will think of life in terms of quality, not quantity. . . . Dying early or late is of no relevance, dying well or ill is. To die well is to escape the danger of living well. . . . Nothing is less worthy of honor than an old man who has no other evidence of having lived long except his age."[16] Seneca preferred euthanasia to a prolonged and painful existence.

> I will not relinquish old age if it leaves my better part intact. But if it begins to shake my mind, if it destroys my faculties one by one, if it leaves me no life but breath, I will depart from the putrid or the tottering edifice. If I know that I must suffer without hope of relief I will depart not through fear of the pain itself but because it prevents all for which I would live.[17]

Seneca's words are reminiscent of those most famous lines from Epictetus: "If the room is smoky, if only moderately, I will stay; if there is too much smoke I will go. Remember this, keep a firm hold on it, the door is always open."[18]

It should be clarified that there is an important distinction between our current meaning of the word *euthanasia* and the meaning it had for the ancient Greeks and Romans. In the classical tradition, *euthanasia* referred to the manner of dying, a "good death" signifying the control and composure one might possess in the fleeting days and hours of life on this earth. To possess this equanimity justified the shortening of one's final days. The contemporary meaning of euthanasia is much more constricted and act oriented. It refers to the means and method of precipitating death.

Summing up, Greek and Roman physicians felt no need heroically to prolong the life of an individual who appeared to be acting rationally and courageously in the request for active voluntary euthanasia. "The average Greco-Roman physician was trained to assist the forces of nature in finding a natural resolution of patient discomfort and disease. Because the body possessed its own biological rhythms and curative powers, the physician's task was to discover how these forces worked and then do nothing that would impede nature in its normal course. Death represented a natural resolution to the human suffering generated by certain forms of disease."[19] In cases where medications failed to restore the curative rhythms of the body, the physican submitted to nature's cycle of life and death, for to do otherwise would have amounted to an act of *hubris*.

The Jewish Tradition

The Greek notion of letting nature take its course appealed marginally for the Jews, who saw the workings of God principally in history. Medical intervention to save lives and promote health was counted, not as social service, but divine obligation. "During the Middle Ages even those traditional figures, such as Solomon ben Adreth of Barcelona, who banned philosophy and natural sciences, excluded medicine from their bans."[20] The ideal scholar combined religious knowledge with medical skill. The most brilliant in this long line of luminaries was Maimonides (1135–1204), who was born in Spain and settled in Egypt, where he acquired great fame as a physician and as a philosopher.

The Jewish tradition differs from the Hippocratic tradition in terms of both sources (Torah and Talmud) and authoritative interpreters. "Whereas professional medical groups have tended to turn to the profession itself to interpret moral imperatives, Judaism turns to rabbinical authorities and Jewish councils."[21] The Jewish medical ethics derived from its scriptures and commentaries also differs from Hippocratic ethics in regard to moral norms. "In particular there is a rigorous commitment to the sacredness of life and the duty to preserve it, a duty that is much more emphatic than in Hippocratic, Christian, or secular traditions."[22]

The talmudic commentary on the creation of Adam illustrates the point that "in Jewish law and moral teaching, the value of human life is supreme and takes precedence over virtually all other considerations."[23] The passage reads:

> Therefore only a single human being was created in the world, to teach that if any person has caused a single soul of Israel to perish, Scripture regards him as if he had caused an entire world to perish; and if any human being saves a single soul of Israel, Scripture regards him as if he had saved an entire world.[24]

The preciousness of life in Judaism is *sui generis*. Its goodness is not contingent upon its being the bearer of other good qualities; it is good by virtue of itself. Therefore "the obligation to preserve life is commensurately all-encompassing."[25]

Whereas the Stoic sage viewed life and death with indifference (*adiaphora*), as being morally neither good or bad and therefore simply a matter of circumstantial preference if one chose to live or die, the Jewish sage always counted life as an absolute, intrinsic good. Life was better in spite of suffering, rather than destroyed because of it.

As part of the created order, the human being does not possess ultimate rights over his life. As a steward, he has a God-given duty to preserve that which he has been privileged to receive. "Never is he called upon to determine whether life is worth living—this is a question over which God remains the sole arbiter."[26] The Jewish physician is mandated to render the best possible service to a deformed child or to a person who has only moments to live, even if the saving of that human life incurs the violation of holy laws.

These theological assumptions of Judaism have direct bearing on the issues of euthanasia. Pivotal to the discussion is Judaism's hatred of suicide, based on Genesis 9:5—"For your lifeblood I will surely require a reckoning." Suicide is prohibited because life belongs to its Creator. Since death is regarded as a punishment, the loss of life in death is normally rewarded with some degree of forgiveness to the sinner. But when a person brings about his own death, there can be no reason for divine forgiveness.

Biblical and talmudic stories are sometimes cited as exceptions to the ban on suicide, as in the case of the suicide of King Saul (1 Sam. 31:1–10) and the four hundred children who jumped into the sea to avoid the wickedness of their abductors. These instances are not counted as ordinary suicides by the tradition. They are viewed permissively on the grounds that the victims were defending their faith, just like martyrs.

Can this permissive attitude be extended to euthanasia under special circumstances, as when a doctor is requested by a patient to bring his misery to an end?

> The Beraita in Semahot 1:4 (B) states unequivocally that one who so much as moves the limb of a dying man in such a way as to shorten his life by a few moments is a murderer. So too the Mishnah in Shabbat 151b (C) brands such an act as homicide. The reason is clearly as the opening words of Semahot indicate: Until the precise moment of death the dying person has every claim on life and the living. This principle is codified verbatim by Maimonides in Hilkhot Avel 4:5 (K).[27]

We have previously seen that the Greco-Roman tradition laid great store by patient autonomy, and that the physician was required to accede to the patient's wishes in matters of dying. In the Jewish tradition the case is entirely different because the patient does not own his "own" body; how then can he request a doctor to do away with something that is not his to dispose of? Moreover, in Jewish law the physician derives his authority directly from the Torah, and its only commandment is to heal, nothing more. In Bava Kamma 85a, the Gemara interprets an injunction in Exodus 21:19 ("and shall have him thoroughly healed") as the Torah's sanction for the physician to heal. Beyond this point, when therapy fails, the physician is not authorized to precipitate the death of his patient. "Having made the patient as comfortable as possible, he must recognize the limitation of his calling."[28]

Thus the verdict of Jewish law on the question of active euthanasia as administered by a physician is categorically negative. One must not engage in any intervention that would even slightly hasten a person's death, such as closing the eyes of a dying person (goses).[29] A sputtering candle is easily extinguished upon the faintest touch. Rema (R. Moses Isserles, d. 1572) on Yoreh Deiah 339:1 illustrates that this applies not only to direct acts but also to indirect acts. "It is forbidden to cause the dying to die quickly, such as one who is moribund over a long time and who cannot die, it is forbidden to remove the pillow from under him on the assumption that certain birdfeathers prevent his death. So too one cannot remove the keys of the synagogue from beneath his head, or move him that he may die."[30]

Next, what is the position of Jewish law on passive euthanasia? Does it permit the physician to withdraw all life-sustaining treatment in the face of imminent death, and allow the inevitable to take its toll? The rabbis sharply differed in their interpretations of legal precedent, and those divisions persist today.

Contemporary opponents of passive euthanasia emphasize the need for hope, believing that even a divine decree of death can be altered, as with King Hezekiah (Isa. 38); and like Job (Job 13:15), one must never despair. Medically, a fatal prognosis could be based on incorrect information; statistically, there are survivors among victims of fatal diseases; finally, there is always the possibility of remission. So no matter what the quality or brevity of a life may be, the physician must never give up.

Supporters of passive euthanasia also cite the tradition. One passage often quoted is the following.

> They took R. Haninah b. Tradyon and wrapped a Torah scroll around him, and encompassed him with faggots of vine branches, to which they set fire. They brought woolen tufts, soaked them with water, and laid them on his heart, so that his soul should not depart quickly. . . . His disciples said to him: "Open your mouth that the fire may penetrate." He replied: "Better is it that He who gave the soul should take it, and that a man should do himself no injury." Then the executioner said to him: "Master, if I increase the flame and remove the woolen tufts from off thy heart, will you bring me to the life of the world-to-come?" "Yes," said Haninah. "Swear it," demanded the executioner. Haninah took the oath. Forthwith the officer increased the flame and removed the woolen tufts from over Haninah's heart, and his soul departed quickly.[31]

Another passage that is often invoked is taken from Rema, whom we have already referred to as forbidding any action that causes the dying to perish quickly. The rabbi introduces an exception to this rule, saying, "But if there is something that delays his death, such as a nearby woodchopper making a noise, or there is salt on his tongue, and these prevent his speedy death, one can remove them, for this does not involve any action at all, but rather the removal of the preventive agent."[32]

The object of the above citations is to demonstrate that the tradition does not support the maintenance of the life of a person who is terminally ill, and whose life is only being prolonged by artificial means. Rabbi Haninah b. Tradyon consented to having the woolen tufts removed, and Rema approved the removal of the wood-choppers. In both cases there is no interference with the natural forces, but only the removal of the extraneous, unnatural factors responsible for prolonging the patient's life. These authorities certify that the modern physician is not obligated to prolong the life of a terminal patient by artificial means, beyond food and water. As nature takes its course, the will of God is done. According to Rabbi Immanuel Jakobovits, some authorities even go further, "holding that there is no obligation to maintain the life of a patient in a permanent coma, and with no prospect of recovery, by medical treatment or the provision of food."[33]

On the basis of our brief survey, we conclude with Herring that whereas contemporary Jewish opinion shares something of a

consensus on the matter of active euthanasia, because of its biblical beliefs systematized in the responses of the rabbis, the same
consensus does not apply to the issues of passive euthanasia. "The
variety of sources and the possibility of varying interpretations by
later authorities lead to a Halakah that is responsive and
dynamic, yet also critical and conservative in maintaining traditional values."[34]

The Christian Traditions

Christianity represents the coming together of the two streams of
Greek and Jewish thought. Its biblical inheritance invests it with
an uncompromising belief in the sanctity of innocent life, based
on the doctrine of creation as the handiwork of a personal god. Its
biblical faith made Christianity an early opponent of active
euthanasia. This meant that as Christianity grew in strength and
influence by the end of the Roman Empire, the tolerance which
was earlier accorded to active euthanasia in the face of chronic or
terminal illness was summarily brought to an end.

The effect of Greek thought was mainly felt by Christianity in
the area of passive euthanasia, giving rise to a diversity of opinions. The Hippocratic tradition was easily assimilated into Christianity's life-affirming stance. Thus, whereas the influence of
Hebraic thought imparted unity to Christian thinking in its rejection of active euthanasia, the Greek heritage made for heterogene-
ity in attitudes toward passive euthanasia. That situation has been
carried over to our day.

Let us now mention certain beliefs peculiar to Christianity
which helped mold its early attitudes toward euthanasia. The
gospel of Jesus can be summed up in two themes: divine sonship
and heavenly citizenship. Sonship was the basic assumption of the
the good life. God is the father; Christ is the only begotten Son;
and believers enter the divine family by becoming as little children—implicitly trusting in the goodness of the Father. Jesus
urges a quiet faith in the wisdom, goodness, and guidance of the
Father, who provides for the grass, the fowls of the air, and the
lilies of the field. The second great theme of the gospel was the
Kingdom of God. Kingdom means the reign of God within each
soul living under the divine sovereignty.

It is easy to see how for the early Christians the gospel message rendered the taking of life in active euthanasia a violation of

the sovereign right of God, who alone can give life or take it away. What mattered at the end was not peace or dignity, but being in the will of God. Thus the gospel emptied the notion of a "good death" of its Greek and Roman aspirations, and substituted classical humanism with Hebraic theocentricism.

In addition to the teachings of Jesus, the outlook of the early Christians on euthanasia was shaped by historic circumstances which sometimes made virtues out of necessities. A major political condition was the persecution of Christians at the hands of their Roman masters, a bloody affair which was only ended by Constantine in 311. Christians believed that the "blood of the martyrs was the seed of the Church"; but, for this belief to prevail (and it did), it meant the transvaluation of suffering. The first seed had already been sown by the Master himself, who did not allow suffering and death to come in the way of doing God's will. Christians saw in Jesus the fulfilment of the prophecy of the "Suffering Servant" announced by Isaiah. The proclamation "by his stripes we are healed" elicited the realization that suffering must be accepted as a providential opportunity to transform evil into good and pain into power. So Peter exhorts believers who must endure pain, "Christ also suffered for you, leaving you an example that you should follow in his steps. . . . Since Christ suffered in the flesh arm yourselves with the same thought" (Peter 2:21, 4:1).

The Christian transmutation of suffering meant that there could be no justification for the killing of a person who was dying in pain. In place of a "merciful death," Christians were extended consolation that they may be conformed to Christ, and crucified with him in the sure and blessed hope of resurrection from the dead.

Augustine systematizes the Church's opposition to "mercy killing" by arguing against suicide and by eulogizing the saving power of suffering. Citing the Old and New Testaments, he expands his contention that physical loss can be turned to spiritual gain.[35] At no time does he blithely or moralistically romanticize suffering. To the contrary: "These ills must be very real indeed if they can subdue the very instinct of nature that struggles in every possible way to put death off; overwhelm it so utterly that death, once shunned, is now desired, sought, and, when all else fails, is self-inflicted."[36] In this respect, he finds the Stoic philosophers, with their talk about "the happy life," blatantly naive. Suffering has the power to "turn courage into a killer." At the same time, Augustine believes that Christians need never succumb to suffering because of the hope that is in them. "When virtues are genuine virtues—and that is possible only when men believe in God—they make no pretense of protecting their possessors from unhappiness, for that would be a false promise; but they do claim that human life, now compelled to feel the misery of so many grievous ills on earth, can, by the hope of heaven, be made both happy and secure."[37]

During the thousand-year period called the Middle Ages, the religious pressures against active euthanasia came from a belief in miracles through veneration of saints and relics, and through pilgrimages to wonder-working shrines. This period also witnessed the beginnings of clerical medicine, in which the practitioner was seen as servant of the "The Great Physician" himself. The most potent pressure was exerted by Thomas Aquinas in the thirteenth century. He denounced euthanasia as a heinous sin because it violated both divine and natural law. It robbed the individual of the opportunity to make peace with God, and the community of a productive member.[38]

Thomistic thinking became the basis of the opposition to active euthanasia by the Roman Catholic Church throughout the Middle Ages. It also found no merit in efforts to prolong life when these means became more of a burden than a blessing to the patient.

The current position of the **Roman Catholic Church** is stated in its *Declaration on Euthanasia* (1980):

> Human life is the basis of all goods, and is the necessary source and condition of every human activity and of all society. Most people regard life as something sacred and hold that no one may dispose of it at will, but believers see in life something greater, namely a gift of God's love, which they are called upon to preserve and make fruitful. And it is this latter consideration that gives rise to the following consequences:
>
> 1. No one can make an attempt on the life of an innocent person without opposing God's love for that person, without violating a fundamental right, and therefore without committing a crime of the utmost gravity.
>
> 2. Everyone has the duty to lead his or her life in accordance with God's plan. That life is entrusted to the individual as a good that must bear fruit already here on earth, but that finds its full perfection only in eternal life.

3. Intentionally causing one's own death, or suicide, is therefore equally as wrong as murder; such an action on the part of a person is to be considered as a rejection of God's sovereignty and loving plan. Furthermore, suicide is also often a refusal of love for self, the denial of the natural instinct to live, a flight from the duties of justice and charity owed to one's neighbor, to various communities, or to the whole of society—although, as is generally recognized, at times there are psychological factors present that can diminish responsibility or even completely remove it.

. . . .

By euthanasia is understood an action or an omission which of itself or by intention causes death, in order that all suffering may in this way be eliminated. Euthanasia's terms of reference, therefore, are to be found in the intention of the will and in the methods used.

It is necessary to state firmly once more that nothing and no one can in any way permit the killing of an innocent human being, whether a fetus or an embyro, or an infant or an adult, an old person, or one suffering from an incurable disease, or a person who is dying. Furthermore, no one is permitted to ask for this act of killing, either for himself or herself or for another person entrusted to his or her care, nor can he or she consent to it, either explicitly or implicitly. Nor can any authority legitimately recommend or permit such an action. For it is a question of the violation of the divine law, an offense against the dignity of the human person, a crime against life, and an attack on humanity.[39]

In respect to the cessation of treatment, the document recommends that where it is established that the therapeutic means are disproportionate to their benefits to the patient, with the consent of the patient and the family, and upon advice of the doctors, the treatment may be terminated. This refusal to continue with extraordinary medical means is not tantamount to suicide, but is an acceptance of the human condition, and an unwillingness to utilize precious resources that are of little good to the patient facing imminent death.

Next, we turn to the positions of the various Protestant denominations on euthanasia.

Seventh-Day Adventists view personal life as a precious gift of God. On active euthanasia, ethicist Jack Provensha states, "The patient has the right to do what we may think is wrong but not the right to have others violate their moral standards in assisting her. Self-destruction is wrong, whether assisted or not and whether compassionate or not. Compassion should be directed toward supportive care and pain control."[40] On passive euthanasia (allowing to die), David Larson of Loma Linda University refers to "an informal consensus" among Seventh-Day Adventist clinicians and theologians, permitting it in certain cases. "The religious rationale is that it is both pointless and cruel to prolong the process of dying for no justifiable reasons."[41]

The Christian Life Commission of the **Southern Baptist Convention** asserts that human life is sacred, "from fertilization until natural death." Therefore, it is committed to "oppose infanticide and active euthanasia, including efforts to discourage any designation of food and/or water as 'extraordinary' medical care for some patients."[42]

The **General Association of General Baptists** is more explicit. It charges that since "life and death belong in the hands of God," no matter how dire the circumstances, a person must know that his life is given by God, for which he is held accountable. "The deliberate termination of life is a serious concern, whether it be done by the person himself, a friend, or the physician. We oppose euthanasia, sometimes referred to as mercy killing."[43]

The **American Baptist Churches of the U.S.A.** discuss issues of passive euthanasia in their 1989 statement, "Death and Dying: Responsibilities and Choices." They approve of the termination of treatment "if no reasonable expectation exists for recovery," and recommends the use of living wills.

The **Christian Church (Disciples of Christ)** classifies active euthanasia as nothing short of murder. The *Gospel Advocate* presents the biblical attitude toward suffering as a positive alternate to the "materialist view" which champions euthanasia as an easy way out of a profound human experience.

> James in the fifth Chapter suggests that Christians ask for healing of those who suffer. However, we certainly realize that healing is not automatic. Jesus prayed to be relieved of the cup of suffering (Matt.26:39).But was this prayer answered? No! Jesus had to suffer. Non-Christians find suffering to be repulsive. With their materialistic view they cannot appreciate God compensating suffering when the new heaven and new earth happens.

Temporary healing does occur today when Christians pray faithfully according to the will of God. No man has the power to lay on hands and heal. It is the prayer of faith that saves the sick (James 5:15). Therefore all the more reason to cling to life rather than promote death.[44]

Christian Science approaches the question of euthanasia from its foundational premise of spiritual healing. Believing that Jesus cured many diseases that were deemed incurable, his followers are expected to extend his healing ministry to those struggling with pain and disease. In such a curative system, euthanasia can never be an option. "A Christian Scientist does not consider any disease beyond the power of God to heal. For this reason, he would not be an advocate of euthanasia."[45]

The **Episcopal Church** is favorably disposed to the termination of extraordinary means of keeping a patient alive, but rejects the legalization of active euthanasia on any account. The 1952 General Convention declares that the "Church believes that as God gives life so only through the operation of the laws of nature can life rightly be taken from human beings."[46]

Jehovah's Witnesses call active euthanasia murder. They base their position on the biblical principles of the sanctity of life (Exod. 20:13) and on obedience to the laws of the land (Rom. 13:1). However, they cautiously approve of passive euthanasia where death is clearly imminent and unavoidable.[47]

The **Latter-day Saints (Mormon Church)** hold to the policy that "a person who participates in euthanasia—deliberately putting to death a person suffering from incurable conditions or diseases—violates the commandments of God."[48] In cases where death is inevitable, the admonition is to look upon death as "a purposeful part of eternal existence," and therefore the family and medical advisors should "not feel obligated to extend mortal life by means that are unreasonable."[49]

The **Lutheran Church (Missouri Synod)** published a study, the *Report on Euthanasia with Guiding Principles* (1979), in which it defined active euthanasia as "taking direct steps to end the life of persons who are not necessarily dying, but who, in the opinion of some, are better off dead" and as "the deliberate easing into death of a patient suffering from a painful and fatal disease."[50] The study argued that the term *passive*, or *negative euthanasia* does not correctly serve to describe the withholding of extraordinary means of prolongation when prospects of recovery are nil; instead, the term more properly describes "the refusal . . . to use ordinary life-sustaining medical treatment," and is therefore tantamount to "unjustified killing." The study then condemns both active and passive euthanasia on moral and theological grounds, stating that "euthanasia, in its proper sense, is a synonym for mercy killing, which involves suicide and/or murder. It is, therefore, contrary to God's Law."[51]

The **United Methodist Church** issued a statement in 1980, "Death with Dignity," which asserts "the right of every person to die in dignity, with loving personal care and without efforts to prolong terminal illnesses merely because the technology is available to do so."[52] Interestingly, in contrast with most other denominations, Methodists maintain that in certain situations active euthanasia "might be an ethically permissible action."[53]

The **Reformed Presbyterian Church** appears to share similar sentiments as the Methodists on active euthanasia. It has issued a "Form or Declaration under the Voluntary Euthanasia Act of 1969" in which the option of active euthanasia is not necessarily considered contradictory to the biblical notions of the sanctity of life. The first clause of the Declaration reads:

> 1. If I should at any time suffer from a serious physical illness or impairment reasonably thought in my case to be incurable and expected to cause me severe distress or render me incapable of rational existence, I request the administration of euthanasia at a time or in circumstances to be indicated or specified by me or, if it is apparent that I have become incapable of giving directions, at the discretion of the physician in charge of my case.[54]

The tentative leanings of the Methodists and Presbyterians toward active euthanasia are forthrightly affirmed by the **Unitarian Universalist Association**, which calls for its enactment in public policy. The church's 1988 statement on "The Right to Die with Dignity" asserts that, recognizing that the inherent dignity of human life "may be compromised when life is extended beyond the will or ability of a person to sustain that dignity," and being aware that legal, religious, and moral barriers exist against the voluntary request for aid in dying, members are called upon to "support legislation that will create legal protection for the right to die with dignity, in accordance with one's own choice."[55]

Secular Traditions

The Middle Ages witnessed the complete dominance of the Church in matters pertaining to life and death. In 1516 an early voice of dissent was raised by Sir Thomas More in his *Utopia*. Through the eyes of imagination, he peers into the perfect community:

> When any is taken with a torturing and lingering pain, so that there is no hope either of cure or ease, the priests and magistrates come and exhort them, that, since they are now unable to go on with the business of life, are become a burden to themselves and all about them, and they have really outlived themselves, they should no longer nourish such a rooted distemper, but choose rather to die since they cannot live but in such misery.[56]

The Renaissance (1341–1626) marked the unparalleled blossoming of the human spirit. Its humanistic orientation had a direct bearing on euthanasia. Humanistic scholars such as Luigi Cornaro (1467–1566) took the classical idea of "easy dying" and baptized it in Christian values. The old physiological theory had held that each individual is endowed at birth with an animating principle which, if drawn upon with restraint, would lead to a long life and "natural" death. But if this vital substance were expended in a profligate manner, the outcome would be sure to result in disease and an early and agonized death. The Renaissance humanists gave these ideas Christian content, making "natural death" into something more sublime. The keynote was temperance. Cornaro, a Venetian nobleman, advocated temperance in diet. Following several bouts of illness, he gave up reliance on medicine and regained his health by attending to his own dietary needs. He subsequently published his findings in *Discorsi della vita sobria* (1558), a collection of treatises on the physiological advantages of the temperate life. He lived up to the ripe old age of 120, and then passed away through a "natural," "holy" death.

Francis Bacon (1521–1626), English philosopher and statesman, shared Luigi's humanistic values of dignity and well-being. He utilized the skills of science to promote long life, free of the maladies of old age, and when death intervened, to free it from mortal pain. He employed the word *euthanasia* to refer to the act of hastening a person's death for medical reasons, and advocated this procedure on the grounds that the relief of pain and suffering was essential in the care of the dying. He described the task of the physician as "not only to restore the health, but to mitigate pain and dolours; and not only when such mitigation may conduce to recovery, but when it may serve to make a fair and easy passage."[57]

Gerald J. Gruman explains how Cornaro's humanistic approach in regard to the "temperate" life and "natural" death serves as precedent for the present practice of passive euthanasia and "letting die." He says, "This standpoint persists in countries where the customs and judicial codes show traditional reverence for natural law. Omission of extraordinary measures continues to summon an imagery of natural death by 'exhaustion' that seems preferable to the comparatively 'unnatural' procedures of active euthanasia, connoting violent 'extinction' and something of the illicit."[58] So too, Bacon's approach, employing science to control the bodily processes for humanistic ends, serves as an antecedent for active euthanasia, "using nature's secrets to attain, for the moribund patient, a more *human* death. ('Exhaustion' and 'extinction' are Aristotelian terms.)"[59]

The phenomenon of "thrift euthanasia" arose in the ethos of scarcity economics between the fifteenth and seventeenth centures, in a period when mercantilism and the social contract set the stage for civic and ecclesiastical policy. The concept of "thrift euthanasia," as Gruman describes it,

> would permit the community to close off, by one means or another, lives requiring "undue" expenditure of inherently limited resources. The quantification of the life-and-death questions was remarkably parallel to the managerial accounting in economic and political matters. The body thus has a fixed sum of vital force: enough, e.g., for "x" number of heartbeats or hours of work. Authorities, including the individual's own conscience, must vigilantly prevent any waste of vital powers (on loan from God and nature) in sexual indulgence, luxury, or even illness. In the contractual imagery of that era, death is a veritable *debt*, payable at threescore years and ten, if not sooner.[60]

Thus, by the calculus of scarcity economics, it is counted reasonable, profitable, and socially beneficial to allot medical resources to prolong the life of a sick individual who yet retains the capacity for productivity, scientifically determined, but in the case of one whose condition denies such prospects, considerations for euthanasia come into play.

More's *Utopia* romanticizes the concept of "thrift euthanasia." Here, a panel of priests and magistrates legislate as to whether a terminal patient should live or die—a fateful decision which is intended to elicit a heroic response on the part of the individual, believing that it is indeed "the will of God." The utopian thinking of Thomas More is not that far-fetched. "One may note analogous present-day interest in social strategies of selective implementation of birth control and suicide prevention while simultaneously withholding costly therapies, except in patients of unusual social 'worth.'"[61] The danger of "thrift euthanasia" arises whenever economics becomes a determinant for social policy, such as in times of war, depression, and other instances of scarcity.

As a physician and as a philosopher, John Locke, whose *Treatise on Government* (1690) belongs to this era, warns against the usurpation of power by tyrants, and the gullibility of people to sacrifice their right to life. It is an inalienable right that can neither be given or taken away. Locke held to the opinion that the individual who relinquished his life, as in suicide or euthanasia, had to be "alienated," meaning not in full possession of his faculties.[62]

Kant (1724–1804) and Hegel (1770–1831) are prominent among eighteenth-century philosophers who held that morality must be based on reason and individual conscience, and not on religious commands. However, as Rachels points out, though they maintained that moral insights are apprehended by reason alone, "when they exercised their reason on such matters as suicide and euthanasia they discovered that the Church had been right all along."[63]

British philosopher David Hume (1711–1776) was much more consistent in his secular approach. In his essay *On Suicide* (1777), he demolished the old theological arguments opposing suicide and euthanasia, and boiled down the ethical issues to one: If through euthanasia we violate the domain of Providence by shortening life, through medical science we do the same by lengthening it.

British Utilitarians, such as Jeremy Bentham, lent their support to the option of justifiable homicide in select cases. Consistent with his moral philosophy, on his deathbed Bentham requested his physician to "minimize pain."

Generally, euthanasia was not widely discussed during the Enlightenment (1687–1804). Instead, faith in progress supplied the stimulus for a "heroic approach" in medicine with the view to achieving "prolongevity." Heroic medicine in the Enlightenment involved the employment of life-affirming power over the forces of nature. Benjamin Franklin declared senility a disease that could be medically treated with the prospects of extending life to one thousand years![64]

Recent Cases of Euthanasia

Transition to the present discussion of euthanasia has been effected by medical innovations in sophisticated means of life support. Until the last world war, a patient was pronounced dead when his heart stopped, his breathing ceased, the body became rigid, temperature fell to ambient, and the blood settled. But with respirators, heart-lung machines, organ transplants, and other mechanical marvels, patients who would have normally died can now be kept alive (technically) for indefinite periods. Technology has advanced to the point that no one has to die; therefore difficult ethical choices must be made.

Ethical dilemmas have been somewhat eased by the definition of "brain death," introduced by researchers at the Harvard Medical School (1968) and subsequently refined. The basic criteria are the absence of brain waves on an electroencephalogram for 24 hours, in conjunction with a lack of spontaneous breathing, fixed and dilated pupils, and no response to external stimulation.

In the case of Karen Ann Quinlan, there was probable damage within four critical brain areas: the midbrain, controlling alertness; the cerebral cortex, controlling reasoning and memory; the basal ganglia, controlling motor activities; and the thalamus, a relay center for sensations. In spite of this damage, Karen was not in any technical sense already dead. The condition into which she lapsed in the early morning hours of April 15, 1975, after drinking a few gin-and-tonics, was a permanent vegetative state—having no awareness, no consciousness.

Joseph T. Quinlan, Karen's father, asked to be made her guardian in order to have her removed from the respirator, and be allowed to die. He explained: "I didn't want her to die. I just wanted to put her back in her natural state, and leave her to the

Lord. If the Lord wants her to live, she'll live. If He wants her to die, she'll die."[65] Quinlan was supported in his request by his parish priest, who declared that the moral teaching of the Roman Catholic Church does not obligate one to resort to "extraordinary means" in a hopeless case.

The case of Karen Quinlan brought into public debate a set of new issues. With the right to live, is there, sometimes, a right to die? Is there any real difference between "active" and "passive" euthanasia? Should such moral dilemmas be dragged into courts of law for resolution?

The Quinlan case signaled a new legal chapter in the practice of medicine, and a new ethical awareness for the need to respect all conditions of life. First, doctors were made to think twice about their practices for fear of criminal liability. Second, there was the ethical concern about the difference in killing and "letting die." Those opposed to withdrawing life-support systems in hopeless cases pointed to the origins of the euthanasia policy of Nazi Germany in respect to those written off as socially useless. Ethicist Richard A. McCormick defended the Catholic position on the removal of mechanical supports for such patients as Karen Quinlan. He testified: "There is a moral difference between killing and allowing to die. When you cease extraordinary effort, it is the disease that kills, not the withdrawal."[66]

Finally, when Karen was removed from her respirator, the withdrawal of life supports was considered "passive euthanasia." Physicians are less wary of being slapped with a malpractice suit for deciding not to initiate treatment in cases that are already doomed. For example, should a patient in a coma with an inoperable brain tumor suffer a heart attack, no special efforts are made to resuscitate. Legal problems arise once treatment is initiated and then the decision is made to withdraw.

Removed from the respirator, medics projected that Karen would not live long, but, to the surprise of many, she continued to live in a comatose state for another nine years, sustained by food and water. The case of Karen Ann Quinlan created a flurry of activity in state courts to formulate rules to determine when medical treatment, life support, and even nutrition and hydration could be withdrawn from a still-living patient. Since 1976, a general legal consensus took shape, with at least twenty-eight state courts allowing a right to die for patients who were irreversibly terminal. These court rulings were diversely based on the authority of state constitutions; the "right to privacy," presumably guaranteed by the U.S. Constitution; and the "common-law principle" that medical treatment must have the approval of the patient involved.

While the states were developing their laws, the Supreme Court remained silent. It admitted several judicial rulings that upheld a "right to die," but it issued no opinion as to whether these rulings were grounded in the U.S. Constitution. The silence of the Supreme Court was ended by developments that took place in the Nancy Cruzan case.

Nancy Cruzan was a 25-year-old woman whose nightmare began on January 11, 1983, when the car she was driving on an icy and deserted Missouri road crashed, landing her face down in a ditch. Medical aid arrived soon, but not fast enough to save her oxygen-deprived brain from losing consciousness. Nancy lay in a permanently vegetative state at the Missouri Rehabilitation Center at Mount Vernon. Her body stiff and contracted, her knees and arms in a fetal position, her fingers dug into her wrists, Nancy was kept alive by a feeding tube implanted in her stomach on February 5, 1983. Medical costs amounted to $130,000 per year.

The Cruzan family took legal steps to end the life-sustaining treatment. On July 27, 1988, Probate Judge Charles Teel issued a judgment that Ms. Cruzan's parents could request withholding food and water from their daughter. On November 16, 1988, the state supreme court overturned Teel's ruling. The Cruzans took the case to the U.S. Supreme Court, and on December 6, 1989, for the first time it heard arguments in a right-to-die case.

On June 25, 1990, the Court ruled against the Cruzans, saying that the parents of the comatose woman do not have an automatic right under the U.S. Constitution to insist that the hospital stop feeding her, and that the state could keep a patient on life support in the absence of "clear and convincing" evidence that the patient would want to die. Such evidence was lacking in Cruzan's case. Chief Justice William H. Rehnquist, writing for the Court, said: "In sum, we conclude that a state may apply a clear and convincing evidence standard in proceedings where a guardian seeks to discontinue nutrition and hydration of a person diagnosed to be in a persistent vegetative state."[67]

Thus, in the ruling of the High Court, a conscious patient has a right to refuse all medical treatment, but in situations where the patient cannot speak for herself, members of her family cannot automatically invoke that right. In that instance a state is empowered to require the family to provide the necessary proof that the patient would wish to die.

On November 1, 1990, a second hearing before Judge Teel was held, in which former coworkers recalled Ms. Cruzan as saying she never wanted to live "like a vegetable" on medical machines. The attending physician also testified that the patient should be allowed to die. On December 5, 1990, the Court-appointed guardians recommended that the feeding tube be removed, on December 14, 1990, Teel so ordered, and on December 26, 1990, Nancy Cruzan died.

Cruzan's death, like the last three years of her life, was not without moral polemics and legal skirmishes. David O'Steen of the antiabortion National Right to Life Committee said her death "diminishes hope for thousands of medically dependent people nationwide." And Ed Grant of Americans United for Life considered the ruling as "a move toward passive euthanasia."[68]

One benefit of Nancy Cruzan's "right-to-die" legal odyssey was that it made Americans aware of the need to write a living will, spelling out precisely what medical decisions they want made should they become unable to make those wishes known, and also the need to draft a durable power of attorney for health designating a specific person or persons to make such decisions. Such consciousness raising comes none too soon because, according to the American Medical Association, some 70 percent of Americans at some time will be forced to decide whether to provide life-sustaining medical care for themselves or a loved one.

The Cruzan ruling was reinforced by passage of the federal Patient Self-Determination Act, which took effect on December 1, 1991. It is now the law that when persons check into a hospital, nursing home, or other care facility, they will be informed of two crucial rights: the right to make medical decisions about their medical care (including the right to refuse it), and the right to prepare advance directives—written instructions whether they want life-sustaining medical treatments if they should become incapacitated.

The debate over the patient's right to die with dignity and the ethics of assisting with such deaths was reignited by the shocking case of Janet Adkins and Dr. Jack Kevorkian, inventor of a suicide machine. Janet Adkins of Portland, Oregon, was a 54-year-old, happily married wife, and mother of three adult sons. For one year she struggled with the diagnosis of having Alzheimer's disease. Physically and intellectually an active person, Adkins could not endure the prospects of existing while her brain degenerated. So, having tried all medical solutions, she decided to end her life before the mild symptoms of fading memory became acute. She first sought the assistance of three neighborhood doctors to help her die, but they refused because she was not their patient, and were afraid of criminal charges. According to the family therapist, a week before she died, "both Mrs. Adkins and the rest of the family were at peace with her decision to die at the time of her choosing."[69] She also made her peace with God, and informed her Unitarian minister of her plans.

Janet Adkins's fatal contact with Dr. Kevorkian came via television when she heard him offer the peaceful and dignified exit for which she was hoping. She contacted him in Michigan, where the legality of assisted suicide was murky, and prepared to make the 2,000-mile trip. Her husband bought her a round-trip ticket just in case she should change her mind, and accompanied her on her journey of death.

Following a videotaped interview, at which time the doctor was convinced that his client was rational, it was decided that the suicide would take place in Kevorkian's 1968 Volkswagen van at a campsite in Grovelands. Adkins forbade her husband to join them.

In the van was a machine which Kevorkian had constructed. Three inverted bottles hung from an aluminium frame, the first containing a saline solution, the second sodium pentothal, and the third a solution of potassium chloride and succinylcholine. A toy electric motor drove the intravenous lines. She took four steps to her death:

1. Mrs. Adkins was hooked up intravenously to the harmless saline solution.

2. Her heart was monitored by cardiograph electrodes on her arms and legs.

3. When Mrs. Adkins was ready to die, she pushed a button that caused a valve to shut off the saline solution and open

the adjoining line of pentothal (thiopental). This drug put her to sleep within about 30 seconds.

4. A timing device connected to the line between the second and third containers triggered after one minute. The potassium chloride and the succinylcholine (a muscle relaxant) began to flow into the arm of the now unconscious woman. Death occurred within six minutes.[70]

By Kevorkian's account: "She was anxious and didn't want to delay. But she was the calm—the calmest one involved with the procedure. I can tell you from experience it was rough. . . . Her last words to me were something like, 'Thank you, thank you very much.' I wished her a good trip, and as I leaned over her, she seemed like she was rising to meet me, perhaps to give me a kiss of gratitude."[71] Dr. Kevorkian reported to Mr. Adkins, to the office of the medical examiner, and then told his story to the *New York Times*, which blew open the debate over the boundaries of mercy killing.

Legally, the murder charges brought against Kevorkian for Mrs. Adkins's suicide were dismissed in December, 1990, because the state of Michigan had no law against physician-assisted suicide. In Adkins's home state of Oregon, providing the means to commit suicide is a felony. In a large number of states, aiding and abetting suicide is unlawful.

Politically, the case gave a boost to the Washington State initiative to pass an assisted-suicide law in November 1991, but as we have already noted, in the end the attempt failed.

Medically, Alzheimer specialists had indicated that Adkins could have been incorrectly diagnosed, and that even if the diagnosis were correct, at age 54 she still had some good years ahead of her. Dr. Robert Butler, head of geriatrics at Manhattan's Mt. Sinai Hospital, said: "It's very demoralizing to hear of a 54-year-old giving up life when you're in your 80s and have heart disease and arthritis and some dementia and are still surviving, maybe working and taking care of your spouse."[72] There was also the fear expressed over the damage that would be done if doctors were routinely placed in the role of executioners. Said Dr. Nancy Dickey, a trustee of the American Medical Association, "The doctor-patient relationship is based on mutual trust. Our patients should not be concerned that we are going to make a value judgment that their lives are no longer worth living."[73]

Morally, the case drew attention to the sharp line between the prolongation of life by artificial means and overt intervention to bring about death. According to medical ethicist Leon Kass, "There's a world of difference between ceasing treatment and acts of deliberate killing."[74]

Religiously, Dr. Kevorkian was anathematized by every church group but the Unitarians. A representative of the Archdiocese of Detroit said, "Any such thing as a suicide machine is a moral abomination. God alone is the author of life, from beginning to end."[75]

Four years after the Adkins/Kevorkian saga, Janet Adkins has emerged as the symbol of the thousands of persons who are ravaged by a horrible disease and who are resolved to meet death with dignity. Dr. Jack Kevorkian is still the standard-bearer for a patient's right to commit suicide and a doctor's right to help. Yet neither the patient nor the doctor is the best symbol in the euthanasia debate, because Adkins was still at a point in her life where she could enjoy romance with her husband and beat her 32-year-old son at a tennis match, and Kevorkian is too much of a maverick. Though approving of Kevorkian's action to help Mrs. Adkins die, the Hemlock Society opined: "But it is hardly death with dignity to have to travel 2,000 miles and die in the back of a van in a campsite lot."[76]

Though atypical, Kevorkian's crusading role symbolizes the gain in public support for assisted suicide. Since 1990 he has attended nineteen deaths. In November 1993 he was ordered to jail by Michigan Judge Thomas Jackson, but, for the present, the sentencing only serves to dramatize the issues. Among the professionals, prestigious medical journals are now debating euthanasia, and legal opinion increasingly favors the administration of lethal injections to end the life of patients who ask for it. Similarly, Adkins's resolve to act according to her circumstances and conscience symbolizes the rising rate of suicide among the elderly. Older people are fearful that they will end their days on a machine, powerless to determine how they would wish to die. They worry about becoming physical and financial burdens upon their children should they become victims of Alzheimer's disease. Older white males, who have been used to more money, privilege, and status than their female counterparts, are also four times

more liable to kill themselves because of their "relative deprivation." Some of these seniors may seek death because they are dis-
oriented through depression, yet many are perfectly rational, and
Adkins symbolizes the need to help such people in ways that are
safe and ethical. In the final analysis her case is a cry for humaniz-
ing existing laws so that a compassionate doctor can help a person in her circumstances in a home or in a hospital, and not in
some rusty van two thousand miles from friends and family.

Our historical survey has highlighted the issues involved in
the euthanasia debate, and our examination of recent cases provides agonizing evidence that these dilemmas of life and death
remain unresolved for the American public. The greatest difference of opinion is around the subject of active voluntary euthanasia. Is active euthanasia ever morally justified for terminally ill
patients who ask for their lives to be ended? We now turn to Hinduism for whatever light it can shed on this question.

HINDU APPROACHES TO EUTHANASIA

Active Voluntary Euthanasia

Hindu ethics finds itself facing two groups which think that they
have the correct answer to the question of the moral justifiability
of active voluntary euthanasia.

Pro-lifers condemn active euthanasia. The churches are solidly
on this side. Their voice of protest is strengthened by a quasi-reli-
gious tradition which believes in the sanctity of individual life.
They are joined by the American Medical Association, which has
declared: "The intentional termination of the life of one human
being by another—mercy killing—is contrary to that for which
the medical profession stands and is contrary to the policy of the
American Medical Association."[77]

Pro-life advocates fear that the efforts to legalize euthanasia
on the grounds of constitutional right to privacy might be on a
"slippery slope" which they compare with Nazi Germany's
eugenics experiment. As an alternative to euthanasia, pro-life
groups advocate the hospice option for the patient who is terminally ill and failing. The purpose of the hospice is to provide loving care, along with the management of pain.

On the other side is the movement toward physician-assisted

suicide for patients with terminal illness. With grass-roots vigor, it is rapidly gaining ground. Factors accelerating its momentum include the recruitment of the elderly, who fear a prolonged, painful death, and rising medical costs; the end of a long legacy of paternalism in medicine; the legal acceptance of withholding or withdrawing extraordinary medical treatment; the emergence of a new treatment philosophy that sets the alleviation of pain above the aggressive prolongation of life; and a rediscovery of the classical values of autonomy, dignity, and the quality of life.

Hindu ethics does not cast its vote on active euthanasia, either with those who are opposed, on the grounds of the sanctity of life, or with those who are in favor, on the grounds of the quality of life. Its unitive philosophy and consequent reverence for life invest it with a prima facie bias on the side of protecting and preserving life in all circumstances. As such, it condemns all acts that destroy life. At the same time, Hindu ethics displays a certain tolerance and flexibility in the context of individual intentions, motives, and circumstances.

This bipolar approach of Hindu ethics is evident in its treatment of suicide. In the previous chapter we have seen that there is philosophical support for the right to suicide in terms of the principles of autonomy and rational choice, but this is only a limited right—a religious option, permitted in the pursuit of higher goals. The case for euthanasia in the Hindu tradition flows from its acceptance of suicide on religious grounds.

In our study of Hindu suicide we noted that the authorized *modus operandi* for taking one's life included immolation, drowning, poisoning, falling, and fasting. The point to note in the present context is that most of these forms, with the exception of fasting, require the direct participation of another individual(s) acting upon the request of the person who wishes to die. We can well imagine a friend or family member helping the person to the water's edge, carrying him up to the peak of the precipice, lighting a brisk pyre, or preparing a lethal potion. Once the preparations are made, the old, infirmed, or incapacitated person takes the final leap, or drinks the cup of hemlock like Socrates of old. What we are looking at is the picture of assisted suicide.

On the basis of its ancient practice of assisted suicide, we can make a moral argument for active voluntary euthanasia in Hindu ethics because the two practices are essentially one. The only difference between assisted suicide and active voluntary euthanasia is that in the case of the latter the decisive deed is performed by another. On the level of intention, attitude, and outcome, both forms of participation are virtually the same. In a modern setting, there appears to be no real difference between someone putting a lethal pill in the mouth of a quadriplegic, and that person performing that final physical act himself, had he the capacity and wish to do so. In principle, assisted suicide as practiced by the ancient Indians and active euthanasia are only instrumentally different, but are one in terms of ends and consequences.

Before we introduce some of the philosophic concepts in Hinduism that have important implications for the euthanasia debate, we must pause to hear two objections from within the Hindu tradition itself to the interpretation we have given above which endorses some aspects of active euthanasia as being the extension of assisted suicide.

By active euthanasia we mean the intentional ending of the life of a terminally ill or dying person who is enduring intractable pain and who wishes a merciful end to life. Two main objections advanced against any such endorsement of this practice are based on the doctrines of karma and *ahimsā*.

First we will consider objections to active euthanasia from considerations of karma. In the fall of 1988, *Hinduism Today* published a three-part series on euthanasia featuring "The Swamis' View" in Part 2. A few extracts should suffice to convey the general message of these religious leaders that "only God should take a human life."[78]

According to Swami Bhasyananda of the Vivekananda Vedānta Society, "Life has been brought to this world by God, and this life should naturally go, but not by artificial means. We should try to minimize the suffering. Apart from this, nothing should be done. Life does not end at the body's death. Just because a law [to give lethal injection] is passed in the USA, that doesn't make it right. A Hindu doctor should not do it."

Swami Satchidananda of the Integral Yoga Institute thinks it is "not advisable for anybody to request a lethal injection" because "it is a form of suicide which will affect their next life." He believes patients die "in the natural way," and the fact that they continue to live is "due to certain karma" which they must "purge." If the body is terminated before its karma is completely burnt, patients miss the opportunity to destroy that karma in the present life. "So then they have to continue to purge somewhere, even in the next life, because karma has to be purged." "To me, no doctor should [give a lethal injection], even if they make a law. Man-made laws are different from God-made laws."

Sivaya Subramuniyaswami of Saiva Siddhanta opposes active euthanasia on the grounds that "a lethal injection severs the astral 'silver cord' connecting the astral body to the physical. Those involved then take on remaining karmas of the patient." The swami is of the opinion that the wishes of patients to be relieved of sufferings should not be granted because the suffering which they are undergoing can be "healing" and "cleansing." He thinks that the request for mercy killing ought to be taken as "a sign of weakness and ignored." "Every soul must be encouraged to live in the physical body as long as it naturally lasts, so as to experience all karmas, good, bad and mixed, so that these karmas will not be carried into the next incarnation."

Finally, Swami Bhaskarananda of the Vedānta Society states, "A person has to work out his or her prarabdha karma [karma allotted for this lifetime]. If the life is suddenly cut short, the after-effect is bad, as it is for a person committing suicide and some-times in accidental death. Our scriptures very clearly say that this must not be done, because after death that person goes through a lot of suffering."

A fundamental flaw in the reasoning of these religious leaders is their association of karma with fatalism. This is an old confusion. The theory of karma became confused with fatality in the Indian mind when it grew weak and uninspired to do its best. Certain scriptures suggest this association, such as Krishna's declaration to Arjuna that his resolve not to fight is vain and that his own nature will drive him into battle, for he himself has created the karma that binds him and is now helpless in its power. But the scriptures are more complicated. They also affirm human freedom and hold out the hope that persons can change the world in which they find themselves.

Traditionally, two types of karma have been distinguished: anārabdha-karma, and prārabdha-karma. The first type refers to karma that has not begun to bear fruit; and the second type refers to karma that has already come to fruition. The latent karma of the first type (anārabdha) could either refer to our accumulated karma from past lives (*sañcita*), or the karma generated in the present (*vartamāna*-karma). The tradition also states that only interested activity arising from selfish motives produces karma. Disinterested actions performed in the present (*vartāmana*-karma) not only are free of binding consequences but can help to dissipate the karma of our past and present life which has not yet begun to bear fruit. Only the results of the karma (*prārabdha*) that has begun to exfoliate cannot be avoided, and must be endured until fully depleted. Thus, even within this *traditional* view of karma, there is room for action which can undo the effects both of the past and the present. The Hindu does not have to grit his teeth and helplessly submit to a doomed future. With the proper motives, he has it in his power to turn back the past and transform the present.

In addition, a fatalistic reading of the law of karma is disastrous when it comes to the performance of social service. On its deterministic logic, one ought not to render service to some sufferer, for by our actions we might be interfering with the just deserts the individual is receiving for some past or present deeds. But surely this would be a pious shirking of moral responsibility. If Hinduism correctly teaches that God dwells in all beings, then to help those in distress is to serve God. True, the sufferer might be reaping what he has sown, but to fail to come to his aid would be to incur sin, for one would thereby be refusing to serve God who is immanent in that suffering being.

The best rebuttal to the pious position that active euthanasia is forbidden by the scriptures on the grounds that it terminates a life before its karma is exhausted is the philosophy of Āyurveda. It might be objected that the speculations of the medical schools should not be discussed alongside the orthodox philosophic systems, but the fact is that medical science was the premier physical science studied in ancient India; it was closely tied with the physics of Sāṁkhya and Vaiśeṣika, and was probably the inspiration behind the logical speculations later codifed in the Nyāya-sūtras.[79]

Caraka does not attribute immutability to the laws of karma. He allows room for human efforts to curtail the effects of ordinary nonmoral actions by the use of intelligence, wisdom, balanced conduct, and recourse to medicine. Only the fruits of immensely good or bad moral actions cannot be averted by these means. Caraka's position lies somewhere between the idealistic thinking of the *pauruṣa-vādins*, such as the followers of the *Yoga-vāsiṣṭha* school, and the view dealt with in Patañjali's Yoga-sūtra. The first group of scholars argues that all our karmic ties to the past can be severed by the power of the will, whereas the second view holds that our deeds are our destiny, fixing the nature of our birth, its life span, and the forms of our pleasures and pain. Caraka avoids these extremes, grounding his position on karma theory in the science of medicine.

Dasgupta describes Caraka's position as a "common-sense eclecticism" which is unique in Indian philosophy. He explains that ordinarily a person is said to reap the fruit of actions performed in a previous lifetime, along with the consequences of deeds that are excessively good or bad, and that the ripened fruit of deeds performed in the present existence sets the pattern of future birth, its duration, and types of experiences. However, in Caraka, only the fruit of extreme evil cannot be arrested by good deeds. Dasgupta explains:

> The fruits of all ordinary actions can be arrested by normal physical ways of well-balanced conduct, the administration of proper medicines and the like. This implies that our ordinary non-moral actions in the proper care of health, taking proper tonics, medicines and the like, can modify or arrest the ordinary course of the fruition of our *karma*. Thus, according to the effects of my ordinary *karma* I may have fallen ill; but, if I take due care I may avoid such effects and may still be in good health. According to other theories the law of *karma* is immutable. Only the fruits of unripe *karma* can be destroyed by true knowledge. The fruit of ripe *karma* have to be experienced in any case, even if true knowledge is attained. The peculiar features of Caraka's theory consist in this that he does not introduce this *immutability* of ripe *karmas*. The effects of all *karmas*, excepting those which are extremely strong, can be modified by an apparently non-moral course of conduct, involving the observance of the ordinary daily duties of life.[80]

Within the theoretical framework of the immutability of the law of karma, if the days of our lives are already numbered, then not only are our ordinary efforts futile in the face of predestined calamities, but there is no scope for medical science to work its cures. Caraka finds such fatalism contrary to the purpose of medicine, which is precisely interventionist.

In common-sense ways of belief one refers to "fate" or "destiny" only when the best efforts fail, and one thinks that, unless there is an absolute fatality, properly directed efforts are bound to succeed. Caraka's theory seems to embody such a common-sense view. But the question arises how, if this is so, can the immutability of the law of *karma* be preserved? Caraka thinks that it is only the extremely good or bad deeds that have this immutable character. All other effects of ordinary actions can be modified or combated by our efforts. Virtue and vice are not vague and mysterious principles in Caraka, and the separation that appears elsewhere between the moral and the physical sides of an action is not found in his teaching.[81]

Our examination of the functioning of the law of karma has shown that, within the traditional schools, it is granted that enlightened actions have no good or bad effects in one's life, and that indeed they eliminate the accumulated karmas, both of the past and the present, which have not yet come to fruition . Also, our study of the Āyurvedic philosophy of Caraka has shown that by the intervention of medical science the effects of *all* karmas can be set aside, with some exceptions.

This evidence undercuts the fear expressed in connection with active euthanasia, that unless a person's karmas are allowed to terminate with natural death, they will have to be purged in the next life, "because karma has to be purged." We are saying that, in keeping with the ancient tradition which allowed for an enlightened person to choose the precise time of his death, it is morally permissible for him to do so with medical aid should he find himself terminally ill and in great pain. He knows that today his mind can control his body, but tomorrow his body will control his mind. Excruciating suffering will then rob him of the equanimity he so cherishes for his final moments of life. Euthanasia ensures a merciful death because he can leave this life with consciousness unclouded by the stupor of drugs, and without fear that some unexhausted karmas will plunge him back into mortal existence.

Before we leave this subject, it is worth pointing out that the declarations of the Hindu religious leaders on the effects of karma in the case of active euthanasia are strikingly similar to Christian remonstrances about the dangers of "playing God." A common objection in America to active euthanasia is that the persons involved in the decision making are playing God, for it is only

God's prerogative to end life. God is our Creator, and to take a life before one's time is to violate the property rights of God over human life.

The source of this objection is a sort of biologistic Christian "karma." God's will is biologically revealed in the process of nature, so that the date and time he has predestined unfolds with the collapse of biological nature. The phrase "to let nature take its course," is the secular equivalent of letting God's will be done. Medical intervention to accelerate death is seen as a presumptuous effort to take the matter out of the hands of God—a sin of pride. Here we recall the words of Swami Satchidananda: "You don't have to keep the body alive by hooking this and that. At the same time, you don't have to kill the body either. If you cannot treat them, leave it; they will die in the natural way. It is due to certain karma. They are purging out this karma."[82]

One problem with the protest not to "play God" or to "let nature take its course" is that all of technological existence is an interference with things as they are. If to shorten life is to frustrate the will of God, identified with nature, to lengthen life must also be unnatural, and equally opposed to God's will. Regardless of their outcomes, both are forms of interference. It is a fitting reminder that the centerpiece of Āyurvedic medicine is its revitalization therapy, scientifically developed to turn back the hands of time.[83] Clearly, the objection not to play God, in either the Christian or the Hindu version, is at root a form of natural determinism, and yet neither of these religions teaches that humans are pawns of the earth's forces.

The second objection to active euthanasia from within the Hindu tradition states that it is a violation of *ahiṃsā* or nonviolence. Most Hindu cults revere *ahiṃsā* as a cardinal virtue. In the Upaniṣads, *ahiṃsā* is associated with "austerity, alms-giving, uprightness . . . truthfulness" as one's "gifts for the priests."[84] *Ahiṃsā* is the key concept for understanding Hinduism's view of the sacredness of life. With such an entrenched virtue, how can one morally justify the taking of a life, even when that is done upon the request of the individual?

To answer this objection, we can do no better than to go to the man who has made *ahiṃsā* synonymous with Hinduism. Gandhi incurred the wrath of his countrymen when he promoted the eradication of pests, the killing of a rabid dog instead of allowing it a slow demise, and particularly the killing of a sick calf. Gandhi's response to his critics was that there is a distinction between *ahiṃsā* and nonkilling. He explains:

> Let us now examine the root of *ahiṃsā*. It is uttermost selfless-ness. Selflessness means complete freedom from a regard for one's body. If man desired to realize himself, i.e. Truth, he could do so only by being completely detached from the body, i.e. by making all other beings feel safe from him. That is the way of *ahiṃsā*.
>
> *Ahiṃsā* does not simply mean non-killing. *Hiṃsā* means causing pain to or killing any life out of anger, or from a selfish purpose, or with the intention of injuring it. Refraining from so doing is a*hiṃsā*.[85]

Gandhi taught that violence will be violence for all time, and that all violence is sinful. However, violence that is inevitable is not to be *regarded* as a sin. The actual sin of *hiṃsā* lies not in merely taking life, but in doing so in the interests of one's perishable body. "But the destruction of bodies of tortured creatures being for their own peace cannot be regarded as *hiṃsā*, or the unavoidable destruction caused for the purpose of protecting one's wards cannot be regarded as *hiṃsā*." He elucidates:

1. It is impossible to sustain one's body without the destruction of other bodies to some extent.
2. All have to destroy some life, (a) for sustaining their own bodies, (b) for protecting those under their care, or (c) sometimes for the sake of those whose life is taken.
3. (a) and (b) in "2" mean *hiṃsā* to a greater or less extent. (c) means no *hiṃsā* and is therefore *ahiṃsā*. *Hiṃsā* in (a) and (b) is unavoidable.
4. A progressive *ahiṃsā*-ist will, therefore, commit the *hiṃsā* contained in (a) and (b) as little as possible, only when it is unavoidable, and after full and mature deliberation and having exhausted all remedies to avoid it.

Taking life may be a duty. We do destroy as much life as we think necessary for sustaining our body. Thus for food we take life, vegetable and other, and for health we destroy mosquitoes and the like by the use of disinfectants etc. and we do not think that we are guilty of irreligion in doing so . . . for the benefit of the species, we kill carnivorous beasts. . . . Even man-slaughter may be necessary in certain cases. Suppose a man runs amuck and goes furiously about sword in hand, and killing anyone that comes in his way, and no one dares to capture him alive. Anyone who despatches the lunatic, will earn the gratitude of the community and be regarded as a benevolent man.[86]

The next passage is most pertinent for our subject:

I see that there is an instinctive horror of killing living beings under any circumstances whatever. For instance, an alternative has been suggested in the shape of confining even rabid dogs in a certain place and allowing them to die a slow death. Now my idea of compassion makes this thing impossible for me. I cannot for a moment bear to see a dog, or for that matter any other living being, helplessly suffering the torture of a slow death. I do not kill a human being thus circumstanced, because I have more hopeful remedies. I should kill a dog similarly situated, because in its case I am without a remedy. Should my child be attacked with rabies and there was no helpful remedy to relieve his agony, I should consider it my duty to take his life. Fatalism has its limits. We leave things to Fate after exhausting all remedies. One of the remedies and the final one to relieve the agony of a tortured child is to take his life.[87]

Raghavan Iyer comments on Gandhi's view of *ahiṃsā*:

There is more *himsa*, he [Gandhi] said, in the slow torture of men and animals, the starvation and exploitation to which they are subjected out of selfish greed, the wanton humiliation and oppression of the weak and the killing of their self-respect, than in the mere benevolent taking of life. . . . Although *ahimsa* was a comprehensive concept for Gandhi, he felt that in view of the unavoidability of some *himsa*, it was necessary to put first things first and not to reduce *ahimsa* merely to a doctrine of *jivadaya* or kindness to animals or to an emotional loathing of every form of violence.[88]

Thus, by Gandhi's analysis, we do not violate the principle of *ahiṃsā* in the context of the benevolent taking of life, where the well-being of the victim is our sole motivating force. Most people would agree with this commonsensical stance of the Mahatama. The question then arises: Why should we be able to end the suffering of pets, yet not that of a loved one?

Having answered two main objections to active euthanasia from within the Hindu tradition, we now examine arguments supporting the morality of active voluntary euthanasia in Hindu ethics.

Arguments from the Meaning of Death   Attitudes toward euthanasia are ultimately decided by the meanings we attribute to death and to life. In this section we look at death. How does the Hindu understand "a good death"?

In Vedic times, life in this world was seen as good: to be lived vigorously, and to be lived long. In time the goal of longevity was institutionalized, incorporating four cycles regulated toward the achievement of diverse human needs and values. The concern for an abundant life prior to death is celebrated in Hindu mythology, where the magical restoration of youth is conceived through various means. With the popularization of the notion of karma, the evils encountered in life were counted as retribution for past deeds, spreading a veneer of fatalism over the earlier exuberance for life and living. Together, these elements shaped the Hindu's concepts of human destiny beyond death.

In Vedic and Brāhmanic times, foundations were laid for giving the deceased an ancestral role, through the mediation of elaborate funerary rites and rituals. When the notion of a universal cosmic law (*ṛta*) caught the Vedic imagination, the belief developed that by conformity with the physical, mental, and moral rhythms of *ṛta* the best of the present life could be recreated beyond death. The Brāhmanas propound another theory of restoration, based on the notion that there is a correspondence between the immortal elements of man and the universe which can be sacrificially united after death.

Popular Hinduism has placed less faith in good works and in rituals, and has preferred to rely on the grace of chosen deities— Śiva, Vishnu, or the Goddess. It also relies on the attainment of celestial bliss by concentrating on a religious thought at the moment of death; and the most auspicious death is one that takes place in the holy city of Benares, where the ashes of one's mortal remains can be hallowed by the waters of the Ganges. Throughout their long history, Indians have drawn on these beliefs in the hope of a heavenly destiny and the avoidance of suffering in some hellish afterlife.

At the same time, Indians have cherished another tradition, rooted in the Upaniṣads, which sees the vale of human existence as devoid of ultimate meaning and as the scene of suffering. To be sure, it is possible to attain to some heavenly realm by virtue of good deeds or the proper performance of sacrifice, but after one's fund of merits has been depleted, there is a return to worldly existence, and this cycle goes on and on.

The cause of these rebirths is ontological ignorance, which obscures the reality of the soul (*ātman*) that is entrapped within the body. But hope abides that by enlightenment a person can discover the true self, and thereby bring the cycle of rebirths to a final halt. True bliss is therefore discovery of oneness with the One. That is the life of Life and the death of Death. A momentary glimmer of this bliss is caught in the passage of death. Frank Reynolds states:

> During the past 2,500 years, the most authoritative and esteemed sages and thinkers of classical India have viewed death . . . as the pervasive fact of the cosmic existence in which men are imprisoned. But these same sages and thinkers have also insisted that death, when it is viewed from a slightly different point of view, may serve as a paradigm for a truly soteriological experience of Release; it is at the point of death, they noted, that the soul which has been dragged into the cycle of transmigration gains, for a very brief moment, a certain separation from the grosser elements of psyche and body that hold it in bondage. Thus, at this most profound level of Indian thought, death comes to serve as a prefiguration and model for various meditations and disciplines (classical yoga, devotional disciplines, tantra, etc.) through which the ties that bind man's self or soul to cosmic impermanence can be completely broken, and through which the ultimate soteriological goals of immortality and freedom can be finally and definitely attained.[89]

What insights may we draw from these Hindu views of death in respect to active euthanasia?

Whereas in the Christian tradition "Adam, the first man, enjoyed immortality" but, striving to make his own life apart from God, "chose death," in the Hindu tradition, death is not a punishment handed down from God. Here, karma takes the place of God and acts as the regulating principle which neutrally fixes our place in an appropriate existence. The tradition says that we must assume responsibility for our own death, and that heaven and hell are worlds of our own creation. We are our own creators who, through ignorance, perpetuate our being through many lifetimes, until the whole process is seen for what it is. The bubble then bursts. Therefore, death is not the opposite of life but the opposite of birth. The expectation of numerous rebirths metaphysically diminishes the tragedy of death for the Hindu. What is tragic is premature death.

But one who has lived a long and fruitful life is more concerned about the quality of life than the inevitability of death. That especially applies to life's end. A "good death" is a spiritual death. The individual is in a psychologically balanced state of mind, composed and in control. His heart and mind are free—without the wish either to live or to die. To ensure such a death, Hindu ethics permits the purposive shortening of a person's life.

Arguments from the Meaning of Life   Paradoxically, a direct route toward understanding the meaning of life in the Hindu tradition is to examine what it has to say on the subject of renunciation. Here is where its soteriological drama takes place, and this is the ground of its highest moral values. Our chief sources are the Saṃnyāsa Upaniṣads.

The status of the individual in the early Vedic period was marginal. Brāhmaṇical dharma defined the individual in terms of his sacrificial and social duties. He hardly had a life which he could call his own. To overcome death, he sought immortality through his offspring.

All that changed as the result of socioeconomic changes in sixth-century India which made possible the ascetic challenge to the Brāhmaṇical definition of the meaning of human life. Autonomy constituted the core of that meaning. It was facilitated by the individualistic mentality of kings and the merchant class, which lived in urban areas. The new urban environment made it possible for individuals and groups to exercise their freedom to choose on the religious level in the same manner that kings and merchants exercised their individual initiatives on the political and economic levels. As a result we witness the emergence of voluntary organizations such as the Buddhist and Jain monastic orders, which individuals joined because of their personal preferences, and not because they were following "a set pattern for correct living ritualized in life-cycle ceremonies."[90]

The theology of the new ascetic groups is summed up in three key concepts: *saṃsāra, karma,* and *mokṣa*. We need not pursue the details but shall emphasize those components which have bearing on our subject.

Life is understood as a series of births, fraught with suffering. W. McNeill and R. Gombrich suggest a link between the ideology of suffering and vast epidemics which decimated early urban populations residing along the Ganges valley in the sixth century B.C. Whatever the catalyst for considering life as suffering, the notion early entered the Indian mind that life, as is normally lived, is one of alienation, quite unlike the view of the creator god of Genesis, who says it is "very good." Karma, in its ritual and moral aspects, is the principle by which *saṁsāra* is regulated, and thereby contributes to human bondage and suffering. *Mokṣa* is release from the cycle of rebirths—a liberating experience brought about by the acquisition of proper knowledge, along with self-control of our intentions and actions.

Ascetic ideology had an impact on life-style. Whereas the old sacrificial ideology elevated the householder, who found corporate meaning in and through marriage and children, the ascetic ideology promoted the celibate as "the paragon of the religious life," being complete in himself to find liberation. Unlike the householder, whose life is marked by attachment, the ascetic follows the pathway of detachment to liberation.

> Verily, he is the great, unborn Soul, who is this [person] consisting of knowledge among the senses. In the space within the heart lies the ruler of all, the lord of all, the king of all. He does not become greater by good action nor inferior by bad action. He is the lord of all, the overlord of beings, the protector of beings. He is the separating dam for keeping these worlds apart.
>
> Such a one the Brahmans desire to know by repetition of the Vedas, by sacrifice, by offerings, by penance, by fasting. On knowing him, in truth, one becomes an ascetic (*muni*). Desiring him only as their home, mendicants wander forth.
>
> Verily, because they know this, the ancients desired not offspring, saying: "What shall we do with offspring, we whose is this Soul, this world?" They, verily, rising above the desire for sons and the desire for wealth and the desire for worlds, lived the life of a mendicant. For the desire for sons is the desire for wealth, and the desire for wealth is a desire for worlds; for both these are desires.
>
> That Soul (*Ātman*) is not this, it is not that (*neti, neti*). It is unseizable, for it cannot be seized. It is indestructible, for it cannot be destroyed. It is unattached, for it does not attach itself. It is unbound. It does not tremble. It is not injured.
>
> Him [who knows this] these two do not overcome—neither the thought "Hence I did wrong," nor the thought "Hence I did right." Verily, he overcomes both. What he has done and what he has not done do not affect him.[91]

This passage makes it plain that the acquisition of *gnosis* in the new theology of the Upaniṣads is essentially the experience of freedom through the realization of one's true self, and this experience transcends not only the concerns and questions of ritual but also of ethics. Liberation is metaritual and metaethics.[92]

In time, the two contending worlds of religious life compromised and coalesced within the doctrine of *āśramas*. The ascetic ideals were seen as the crowning point of a Hindu's earthly pilgrimage, and defined its ultimate goals.

Within the *āśrama* theory of existence, renunciation or *saṃnyāsa* signifies the abandonment of ritual activity. Instead of having to rely on priests and sacrifices, a man's renunciation becomes the perfection of ritual through a process of internalization. The Kaṭhaśruti Upaniṣad declares: "What he eats in the evening becomes his evening sacrifice. What he eats in the morning becomes his morning sacrifice."[93] The renouncer's whole life is viewed as one continuous sacrifice, for with each breath he takes, he kindles the internal fires, making his body into a veritable altar. The renouncer's independence of external rituals is the hallmark, within that culture, of complete individualization. It is also the perfection of ritual life in terms of erasing both the renouncer's sins and those of his family. The Śātyāyanīya Upaniṣad states:

> Now, my dear, after receiving this final *dharma* of the self, this Vaisnava state, he who lives without violating it becomes a master of himself. . . . He attains the highest Brahman, the Lord, and he rescues from this existence his forefathers, relatives by marriage, blood relations, companions and friends.[94]

The last lines are an important corrective to the common notion that the renouncer is lost to his family, when in fact he is their greatest beneficiary.

The chief characteristic of the renouncer is detachment. His life is so internally self-sufficient that he does not have to attach himself to anyone or anything—on earth or in heaven—to know permanent bliss. This is the state of *vairāgya*. "Only when indifference toward all things has arisen in their minds do they seek renunciation."[95]

Vairāgya is chiefly directed to the body. The body must be seen for what it actually is: not a corporeal castle of pleasure and permanence, but a tottering house beset by disease and misery. "It has beams of bones tied with tendons. It is plastered with flesh and blood and thatched with skin. . . . Covered with dust and harassed by pain, it is the abode of disease."[96] In the final analysis, the body must be viewed as a corpse . . . dust to dust, ashes to ashes. For something so impermanent, detachment is the only rational attitude.

Detachment is not an end, but only a means toward a larger end. That final goal is liberation, *mokṣa*.

> My nature is replete in all.
>   I am being, consciousness and bliss.
> I am the essence of all sacred bathing spots.
>   I am the Supreme Self.
>   I am Siva!

> I am beyond the visible and the invisible.
>   I am the essence that perishes not.
> I am beyond the measurer, the measure,
>   and the measured.
>   I am Siva!

> I am free from the six changes.
>   I am without the six sheaths.
> I am free from the six enemies.
>   I am nearer than the heart.[97]

The six changes referred to are existence, birth, growth, maturity, decay, and death; the six sheaths are skin, blood, flesh, fat, marrow, and bones; and the six enemies are desire, hatred, greed, delusion, pride, and envy.[98] The person who has reached this state is deemed out of this world. He is physically alive, but ritually he is a dead person.

We have followed this single thread of renunciation in the fabric of Hinduism to unravel its meaning of life. Its applications to euthanasia are many, but we mention only the most salient.

First, there is the problem of suffering. The Hindu would agree that physical suffering can surely drive a person to the point of asking that life be ended; but of greater concern than physical suffering is existential suffering, which keeps one fettered to many such lives. Yet physical suffering can impede the self-possession that makes deliverance from the cycle of rebirths possible. Intractable pain destroys self-control and disintegrates personality. In the event this may arise, a self-realized being, who has already stopped the wheel, may mercifully have someone break the momentum of its milling moments. Spiritually, he has left this world and is ritually dead. The physical deed only brings down the curtain on a magic show that is already over.

Second, the overwhelming emphasis that Hinduism places on spirituality makes it diametrically opposed to a purely vitalistic doctrine of what it means to be human. The question the tradition asks in the context of active euthanasia is: Is *human* life adequately represented by mere biological functioning, or is something else needed to qualify as human life? It is a question of *personhood*. Who is a person? And can someone relinquish personhood while still being alive? The answer that Hinduism gives to this question is that *living* is more than being alive. This places Hinduism squarely on the side of those who would argue for active euthanasia on the grounds of the quality of life over the claims of vital existence. In Āyurveda, health itself is spiritually defined. The term used to describe a healthy person is *svastha*. It is a compound word meaning self (*sva*), and (*stha*) to "establish," "stand," or "maintain." A healthy person is therefore one who is established, in his self, the soul.

Third, in the Hindu tradition the person who has conquered all attachments and who has thereby acquired liberating knowledge is eulogized as the highest type of renouncer. Detachment is the necessary condition for renunciation, especially detachment from the body. There are numerous passages that appear to loathe the body as "produced by sexual intercourse," "devoid of consciousness," "filled with feces, urine, wind, bile, phlegm, marrow, fat, serum, and many other kinds of filth."[99] The heaping of this verbal defecation is not so much against the body, conceived as evil, but the evil of *attachment* to the body. As the composite of matter, the body is impermanent, and therefore to relate to it as permanent is gross ignorance.

In this light, Hinduism sees the state of crisis in American medicine as a crisis of faith and theology. It arises from a compulsive need to make gods of the body, of health, and of life. A positivist style of heroic medicine finds itself technologically difficult to detach itself from the delusions of immortality. Attachment to a regimen of tenacious maintenance of life makes it hard to distinguish between the prolongation of living and the prolongation of dying. Hinduism says that agonizing situations sometimes arise when the drive for self-preservation must halt, and even *ahiṃsā* must yield to the request to end it all.

The Argument from the Golden Rule   Hinduism's strong sense of the sacredness of life expresses itself in diverse forms, including the Golden Rule. There are various instances in the epic literature. The Mahābhārata first exhorts the norm of self-similitude: "Good people do not injure living beings; in joy and sorrow, pleasure and pain, one should act toward others as one would have them act toward oneself."[100] And then, more broadly: "Whatever one would wish for oneself, that let one plan for another."[101] The basic idea behind the Golden Rule, as Kant expostulated, is that a person should act only on those rules he or she is willing to have universally applied. "Act only according to that maxim by which you can at the same time will that it should become a universal law."[102] Of course, Kant was only giving a philosophic definition to a value that is fundamental to the Judeo-Christian tradition, and indeed, a value that is found in all religions.

It is a matter of some irony that whereas the Christian ethos of Immanuel Kant made him an opponent of active euthanasia, his philosophic argument lends it support. Philosopher James Rachels explains the application of the Golden Rule to euthanasia.

> Each of us is going to die someday, although most of us do not know when and how. But suppose you were told that you would die in one of two ways, and you were asked to choose between them. First, you could die quietly, and without pain, from a fatal injection. Or second, you could choose to die of an affliction so painful that for several days before death you would be reduced to howling like a dog, with your family standing by helplessly, trying to comfort you, but going through its own psychological hell. It is hard to believe that any sane person, when confronted by these possibilities, would choose to have a rule applied that would force upon him or her the second option. And if we would not want such a rule, which would exclude euthanasia, applied to us, then we should not apply such a rule to others.[103]

We turn now from a hypothetical situation involving two choices, to a true case in which active euthanasia is the only option. R. M. Hare cites this example to illustrate that mercy killing need not always be wrong, and that, indeed, it could be the enactment of the Golden Rule.

> The driver of a petrol lorry was in an accident in which his tanker overturned and immediately caught fire. He himself was trapped in the cab and could not be freed. He therefore besought the bystanders to kill him by hitting him on the head, so that he would not roast to death. I think that somebody did this but I do not know what happened in the court afterwards.
>
> Now will you please all ask yourselves, as I have many times asked myself, what you wish that men should do to you if you were in the situation of that driver. I cannot believe that anybody who considered the matter seriously, as if he himself were going to be in that situation and had now to give instructions as to what rule the bystanders should follow, would say that the rule should be one ruling out euthanasia absolutely.[104]

The ethical principle on which Kant and company are making their argument is the principle of "universalizability." In Hindu ethics this principle is embodied in the quality of *dayā* or compassion, mythologically personified as a daughter of Dakṣa and the wife of Dharma. Compassion does indeed supply a moral motive, but that does not necessarily justify some of its outcomes. Robin Hood was a compassionate man, but that did not justify his behavior of robbing from the rich to feed the poor. In Hinduism the justification of compassion comes not from its nobility as a virtue but from its universalizing source, which finds identity with the whole human race. If we want the rule of euthanasia, in dire circumstances, to apply to us, then it ontologically follows that we must want the same rule to apply to others.

Other Forms of Euthanasia

The question of a person's right to active voluntary euthanasia and the question of whether consensual homicide should be made legal represent the most controversial aspects of the euthanasia debate. We now move on to other divisions of the subject in which the issues are somewhat less contentious.

Most ethicists would repudiate *involuntary euthanasia*. This involves the taking of the life of an individual, supposedly in his own interests, but either against his wishes or without the benefit of consultation. Hindu ethics rules out involuntary euthanasia because it flatly contradicts its principle of autonomy and is fraught with ominous side-effects.

Passive euthanasia is often identified with the stopping of treatment which is no longer beneficial to the patient, but this meaning is a source of confusion. In its clear form, passive euthanasia means the intentional ending of life by refusing treatment that is beneficial and not burdensome. It is synonymous with passive suicide. In normal circumstances, Hindu ethics would find passive euthanasia in violation of our obligation to employ all reasonable means to preserve life.

Though passive euthanasia is commonly confused with terminating treatment, the latter is technically not a form of euthanasia. Take the case of a patient who is kept alive by mechanical and artificial means. His condition gradually deteriorates, and sooner or later he will die, but there is no certainty as to how and when. With full knowledge that his condition is irreversible, the patient requests that he be removed from the respirator and the feeding tubes, and that in the event of cardiac or respiratory arrest he be allowed to die.

This is not a case of euthanasia because the treatment is of no benefit to the patient; instead it is seriously burdensome. It is not life that is being prolonged, but only the process of dying. As long as the individual has a fighting chance to regain health, Hindu ethics would acknowledge the obligation to preserve life, but where such prospects are nil, that obligation diminishes along with the decline of the vital signs of the individual.

Āyurvedic medicine recognizes that there are limits to our responsibility for preserving life. The charge "Do not resusitate" was applied in early times to diseases that were typed as curable and incurable. In part, the admonition to terminate treatment was professionally self-serving, as we shall see, but it was also with consideration of the overall costs to both the physician and patient. According to Caraka,

> The physician, who knows the classification of curable and incurable diseases and proceeds with treatment in time after thorough knowledge certainly succeeds.
>
> On the other hand, the physician, treating an incurable disease certainly suffers from the loss of wealth, learning and reputation and from censure and unpopularity.
>
> Curable diseases are of two types—easily curable and hardly curable. In curable ones are also two types—palliable and unmanageable. In curable diseases too there are three grades—low, medium and high; but as regards incurable ones,

there is not any gradation. . . . the rejectable (incurable) disease is caused by three dosas, not amenable to any therapy, involving all the passages, producing anxiety, uneasiness, and disorders of consciousness, destroying the (function of) the sense organs, quite advanced, having developed fatal signs particularly in weak patients.

Thus a wise physician should first examine the specific characters of diseases and then take up the treatment only in case of curable diseases.[105]

Caraka advises withholding medications from a dying patient, but should the family insist, some nutrition is allowed.[106]

Lastly, there is the *nonvoluntary* form of euthanasia. It involves the taking of a person's life, supposedly in the patient's interests, but under conditions in which he is incapable of formulating a preference, or being able to communicate it. "Non-voluntary euthanasia is an issue for doctors, because there are people whom we think may have lives worse than death, but who are not in a position to express any decision of their own on this."[107] Falling into this category are babies with terrible abnormalities, the senile, the totally paralyzed, and the comatose.

Let us take the case of the infant born with abnormalities which threaten its life. Hindu ethics would first attend to quality-of-life considerations. According to Dr. Siva Subramanian, describing current Indian practice,

the quality-of-life decision may include, in addition to medical factors, the family make-up, the family's ability to obtain further care, and cost considerations. Also considered are limited resources that could be utilized more beneficially on another patient with the potential for an outcome described as a "good" quality of life. The definition of quality of life is left to the individual physician and the family.[108]

In the event that the physician comes up with a poor prognosis, he has the following alternatives: to take extraordinary steps to save the child, to do the ordinary, to do nothing, or to take positive steps to end its life.

The first two steps may be dismissed if the gains fail to exceed the losses. The third alternative of doing nothing may be the best course if the baby's health is rapidly failing and death appears imminent. The infant should then be allowed to be taken home where friends and family can extend mutual comfort before and after it dies. However, if the infant is undergoing considerable pain, if death is not imminent, and if its case is still hopeless, the fourth alternative may, unfortunately, be the most appropriate. This could be accomplished by administering a lethal dose of morphine. It might be said that the intent is not to kill, but to relieve pain. We are not convinced by arguments that make this distinction, for the practical outcome is the same. Hindu ethics would respect this reluctance to kill and would be quick to cultivate that sentiment because it is our best defense against slipping into progressive forms of legalized killing. But having acknowledged that, Hindu ethics would concur with Gandhi that there is more *hiṃsā* in the slow and pointless torture of this child than in the "benevolent" taking of its life by corporate decision. Legality aside, this is what is often done.

Nonvoluntary euthanasia is a difficult issue for doctors and patients alike, precisely because the latter are not in a condition to articulate decisions of their own. The nightmare of ever finding oneself in such a situation is now mitigated by the passage of the Patient Self-Determination Act on December 1, 1991. The federal law mandates that all health care institutions that receive Medicare and Medicaid funds provide patients who are checking into hospitals details of their right to die. Patients are required to make out a Living Will—a directive to cease life-sustaining measures if there is no chance for recovery. The document gives doctors the legal authority not to connect life-support systems if one is hopelessly and terminally ill, or, if one is already connected, to "pull the plug." The Living Will is only a request, not an order. It provides the doctor with valuable information for taking care of a person's dying; it also shields him from possible litigation.

For more powerful legal protection, one should draw up a Durable Power of Attorney for Health Care, which must be signed, dated, and witnessed to be valid. The document is a health care proxy. Individuals name another person to make medical decisions in their behalf if they are in an incapacitated state. Without this protection, "a court could name someone you would never have selected to manage your health care—someone who might insist on treatment you oppose," says Charles Sabatino, assistant director of the American Bar Association's Commission on Legal Problems of the Elderly.[109]

Provision for the Durable Power of Attorney for Health Care, ensued from the Nancy Cruzan case (1990) to give "clear and convincing evidence" of one's health care directives. However, this document and the Patient Self-Determination Act only apply in cases of the termination of treatment ("passive euthanasia"), but not in cases of "helping to die" (active euthanasia).

CONCLUSION

The contribution of Hindu ethics to the euthanasia debate lies in its attempt to do justice to the concerns of contending parties. We have seen the normative role of renunciation in the life of the Hindu, which essentially involves the renunciation of all forms of killing. *Ahiṃsā* therefore serves as a general principle within this system. At the same time, the pro-life principle in Hinduism is not absolute. It is qualified by the admission of the unavoidability of *hiṃsā*. This stance is stronger than the alternate position, which starts with the justification of killing. In Gandhi's view,

> The man who starts justifying the use of force will become addicted to it, while the man who renounces it from the start may find that he has to come to terms with the practical limitations of nonviolence, but he ceaselessly tries to reduce *himsa* and replace it by *ahimsa*. The difference between a belief in *ahimsa* and a belief in *himsa* is the difference between north and south, life and death.[110]

Hindu ethics is not passive in the face of suffering. It has more to say to the patient suffering the torments of cancer, AIDS, or Alzheimer's disease than: "Sorry, but you are reaping, as you should, the fruit of your own action." Karma does not give us the right to keep such people alive and in pain when all they want is a peaceful death. Their karma is our dharma. We have a duty to our fellow human beings. If they are suffering because of some sin, it is no less a sin to let them suffer. Mahatama Gandhi had said, "God comes to a hungry man in the form of a slice of bread." In what form does God come to a person begging to die?

CHAPTER 4

The Ethics of the Environment

INTRODUCTION

The most distinguishing feature of the twentieth century is that a single species, humanity, has become the creator of its own future. Through the mastery of science and its applications, humans possess the ability to change the environment of Planet Earth, and can do so within the lifetime of a single species member.

From its genesis as a chunk of molten rock and gas some 4.5 billion years ago, the earth's climate or topology has undergone successive upheavals and extinctions. Ice and fire have sculpted the shape of the planet from age to age as mountains have risen from the deep and continents have sunk to the ocean floor. This struggle of life and death is spectacularly illustrated by the demise of the great dinosaurs during the Cretaceous period, some 136 to 65 million years ago.[1] There is much speculation as to the specific cause of their death, though there is little doubt it was brought about by some sudden shift in the environment. The most plausible theory is that a mammoth meteorite crashed on the earth, sending up billows of dust which blocked out the sun, thus destroying the plants on which the dinosaurs survived.

The shocking fact is that similar waves of extinction are breaking out all over the globe at this very time, but in the present instance the destroyer is not some visitor from outer space or some balancing act of nature, but humans themselves. Twentieth-century *Homo sapiens* has become a force of nature, and like the sun, the moon, the wind, and water, people exercise a power over nature which can reduce it to the fate of the dinosaur.

WESTERN VIEWS OF THE ENVIRONMENT

The environmental crisis in the United States arises out of the dilemmas of prosperity. In his study of America in the mid-nineteenth century, Alexis de Tocqueville observed: "Their ancestors gave them the love of equality and of freedom; but God Himself gave them the means of remaining equal and free by placing them upon a boundless continent."[2] Indeed, the natural abundance of this country has made it a "promised land" of biblical proportions—a cornucopia of riches which have, no doubt, helped shape the national character of its people. In the words of a recent president, "The breadth and variety and beauty of our land, the richness of our mines and soil and forests and water, the favorable nature of our climate—all of these natural factors have provided a setting in which the optimism, the ingenuity and drive of the American people thrive and grow and are rewarded."[3]

The price of plenty has also meant that it has been impossible for Americans to imagine a time when its "spacious skies" could be polluted, and its "alabaster cities" be reduced to asphalt jungles. Since these problems were not anticipated, neither were we prepared to prevent them. "Even as we are heirs to the products of our forefathers' genius, so our generation has also inherited the results of past carelessness."[4]

Actually, the problem is one of more than "carelessness." It is a defect which arises out of the strengths of American society—its science, democracy, individuality, and prosperity. Broadly, it is a flaw of our civilization; and that ultimately boils down to how we, as Westerners, perceive ourselves in relation to nature.

This chapter addresses the challenge coming out of America's abuse of the environment: its failure to respect the delicate web we share with other forms of life, and its neglect of humane design in manufactured artifacts, most conspicuously in the area of urban planning. Our purpose is not to indulge in doom and gloom, but to go beyond mere survival to finding new ways of bringing quality into our lives and restoring the balance of nature.

We begin by isolating the main agent of environmental destruction. The picture is much more complicated, but if we are to narrow the field to a single cause it would have to be technology, or better stated, our handling of technology.

Modern technology is the special child of Western culture; that is to say, it required a particular ethos and ideology in which to take birth and flourish. Western philosophy set the stage with a built-in dualism between spirit and matter reaching back to Plato and earlier to the Orphic mysteries. This strain of classical thinking was passed on to the modern West through René Descartes (1596–1650), French philosopher and scientist. In his scientific investigations, he followed the methods laid down by Francis Bacon. His philosophy was almost completely dualistic. His view of the physical world was that of a machine, wholly different from the mind. Only through the intervention of God were the world and mind brought together. As the "father of modern philosophy," Descartes had an immense impact on the development of European thought, especially through the Cartesian philosophers, who chiefly studied the problem of the relation of body and soul, of mind and matter.

During the Enlightenment, the mechanistic interpretation of the world was symbolized by the workings of a watch. Watches came in diverse forms and shapes, but their movements were all predetermined. Once God, conceived as the heavenly Watchmaker, had created it, the machine was able to run as determined. The sharp metaphysical line between humans and their environment was continued in the thinking of Berkeley, Kant, Hegel, and Sartre. None of these philosophers conceived of the subhuman world in terms that would entitle it to fundamental human concern.

Western religion has followed a similar path. The three major Western religions—Christianity, Judaism, and Islam—teach that the universe is the creation of God, who has given human beings a special place in that creation. The book of Genesis (1:28–30) describes the position of persons in relation to the rest of creation:

> And God said to them, "Be fruitful and multiply, and fill the earth and subdue it; and have dominion over the fish of the sea and over the birds of the air and over every living thing that moves upon the earth."
>
> And God said, "Behold, I have given you every plant yielding seed which is upon the face of all the earth, and every tree with seed in its fruit; you shall have them for food.
>
> And to every beast of the earth, and to every bird of the air, and to everything that creeps on the earth, everything that has the breath of life, I have given every green plant for food."

The story of Creation is followed by the story of the Fall. Later a wholesale purge of wickedness became necessary, and God sent the Flood, which exterminated not only the majority of the human population but innocent subhuman species as well. God then made a covenant with his servant Noah in which man's earlier dominance was reaffirmed, and he was also permitted the liberty of a carnivorous diet. Genesis 9:1–3 states:

> And God blessed Noah and his sons, and said to them, "Be fruitful and multiply, and fill the earth. The fear of you and the dread of you shall be upon every beast of the earth, and upon every bird of the air, upon everything that creeps on the ground and all the fish of the sea; into your hand they are delivered. Every moving thing that lives shall be food for you; and as I gave you the green plants, I give you everything.

The pattern of Western philosophy and religion to distinguish sharply between humans and nature, and thereby to objectify nature so that it is seen from the outside, was extended by Western science. The separation became the attitudinal basis for an ever-increasing knowledge of nature by science. In Western thought, nature was desacralized, and therefore considered an object fit to be studied by separating part from part, limb from limb. "This superlatively effective way of discovering solidly verifiable truths tends, precisely because it is sharply focused, to ignore whatever lies outside its periphery of attention."[5]

This phenomenon goes a long way toward explaining why Western culture has dominated the field of science for four hundred years. This has worked both as an asset for Western culture and also as a liability. "Because our strength is derived from the fragmented mode of our knowledge and our action, we are relatively helpless when we try to deal intelligently with such unities as a city, an estuary's ecology, or 'the quality of life.'"[6]

To the extent that the goal of science is knowledge, it must be freed of any direct blame for the environmental crisis. On the other hand, technology, which is oriented to action, derives its power from science and applies it in its projects. According to Max Ways, "Although its categories are not the same as those of science, technology in its own way is also highly specialized, directed toward narrowly defined aims. As its power rises, technology's 'side effects,' the consequences lying outside its tunneled field of purpose, proliferate with disastrous consequences to the environment—among other unintended victims."[7]

To conclude this train of thought, our argument is that technology is the central agent behind the destruction of the environment, and that the West's innovations in this field derive from attitudes which have been shaped by the dominant religio-philosophical currents of Western culture. The principle of separation or differentiation has produced much scientific discovery and advance, but its very virtue—progress through isolation, individuation, and fragmentation—has also been its weakness in that its tunnel vision has proven myopic in viewing the environment as a whole.

There is one danger in tracing the roots of the environmental crisis to its cultural roots in religion. In his celebrated essay, "The Historic Roots of our Ecologic Crisis," Lynn White asserts that "what people do about ecology depends on what they think about themselves in relation to things around them. Human ecology is deeply conditioned by beliefs about our nature and our destiny—that is, by religion."[8] The danger in this sort of claim is that it makes religion the primary conditioner of human interaction with the environment.

The model which White proposes has three progressive steps: (1) Judeo-Christian tradition, (2) science and technology, and (3) environmental degradation. The picture is more complicated. Certainly religion has a basic role to play, since it accounts for the way we perceive ourselves, our fellows, and the world around us. But Western civilization has also been conditioned by the institutions of democratization and capitalism, aided by science and technology. These political and economic forces have produced wealth, individual ownership, urbanization, and population increase. Each one of these sources has taken more from the environment than it has put in, and thereby has been responsible for degrading it. The principle of separation, the method used by science to separate one aspect of nature from another for the purpose of study, has equally been at work in the operations of our political and economic institutions, and this has only provided us with short-term, piecemeal approaches to our environmental problems.

We now turn to the major problems which make up the environmental crisis.

ECOLOGICAL PROBLEMS

In a rare departure from its tradition of naming a "Man of the Year," *Time* magazine designated Endangered Earth as Planet of the Year for 1988. Like God warning Noah of the coming flood, this was the year that Planet Earth spoke with tremors which were heard around the globe.

In the United States drought stalked the land from California to the Deep South, depleting the grain harvest by 31 percent, and killing thousands of cattle. The combined effects of heat waves and lack of rain ignited forest fires, with the largest conflagration in Yellowstone National Park. Beaches were fouled with garbage, raw sewage, and medical wastes, showing the limited capacity of the ocean to absorb pollution.

Similar despoliation of the oceans occurred in areas of the Mediterranean, the North Sea, and the English Channel, making beaches unfit for recreation. Killer hurricanes roared through the islands of the Caribbean and sent thousands in Bangladesh to a watery grave. In Soviet Armenia, 55,000 persons perished in a gigantic earthquake. There were grave warnings of the further depletion of the ozone layer, and all the while tropical forests, which house half the earth's plant and animal species, were being destroyed at the speed of one football field per second.

> Most of these evils had been going on for a long time, and some of the worst disasters apparently had nothing to do with human behavior. Yet this year's [1988] bout of freakish weather and environmental horror stories seemed to act as a powerful catalyst for worldwide public opinion. Everyone suddenly sensed that this gyrating globe, this precious repository of all the life that we know of, was in danger. No single individual, no event, no movement captured imaginations or dominated headlines more than the clump of rock and soil and water and air that is our common home.[9]

With each passing year, threats to the survival of Planet Earth have increased with nothing less than mind-boggling rates. Following are the chief problem areas: biodiversity, global warming, pollution, waste, overpopulation, and the nuclear epidemic.

The Problem of Biodiversity

Mother Nature never puts all of her eggs in one basket: diversity is the key to survival. Variety is not just the spice of life, but its sum and substance. "Complex beyond understanding and valuable beyond measure, biological diversity is the total variety of life on earth."[10]

During the time when humans were hunters and gatherers,

their sustenance depended on biodiversity. This dependence changed when society looked for its livelihood, first to agriculture, and then to industry. Now, with the research knowledge that biological diversity is crucial for the environment which sustains life, people are being roused to ensure its conservation.

Our knowledge of the total count of life with which we share this planet is still shrouded in mystery, but what we do know is that biodiversity is vanishing at an incalculable speed. Eugene Linden tells a story of what is happening in Brazil, but which is actually a global phenomenon.

> Before Brazil's great land rush, the emerald rain forests of Rondonia state were an unspoiled showcase for the diversity of life. In this lush territory south of the Amazon, there was hardly a break in the canopy of 200-ft.-tall trees, and virtually every acre was alive with the cacophony of all kinds of insects, birds and monkeys. Then, beginning in the 1970s, came the swarms of settlers, slashing and burning huge swaths through the forest to create roads, towns and fields. They came to enjoy a promised land, but they have merely produced a network of devastation. The soil that supported a rich rain forest, is not well suited to corn and other crops, and most of the newcomers can eke out only an impoverished, disease-ridden existence. In the process, they are destroying an ecosystem and the millions of species of plants and animals that live in it. An estimated 20 percent of Rondonia's forest is gone, and at present rates of destruction it will be totally wiped out within 25 years.[11]

Like Brazil, India is also a land of rich diversity. Its geographic location makes it "one of the world's top twelve 'megadiversity nations.'"[12] But the subcontinent's biodiversity is being dangerously eroded.

One cause for India's loss is earlier British policy, which "drastically reoriented the resource-use pattern, largely exporting teak, tea, and indigo outside the locality. The prices were greatly depressed. After Independence this system of undervaluing biological resources was taken to extremes. Thus bamboo, of great utility to the rural people, has been made over to the paper industry at royalties of Rs. 1.50 a tonne, when the price for basket weavers was over Rs. 3000 a tonne."[13]

A second cause for the erosion of biodiversity in India is the scant attention paid to the quality of life among its rural and tribal peoples. "In pre-British India, vast tracts were available to fulfil the biomass needs of the local people. Parts of such lands were set aside as 'sacred groves' for total protection of biological communities, while others were treated as community woodlots from which regulated harvests were carried out."[14] A few of these systems survive today in remote areas such as Mizoram, but they were deliberately and effectively destroyed by the British, who granted no rights but only some privileges to the local communities over common lands. "As a consequence such lands became 'no man's lands' abused by all but protected by none. This situation has worsened after Independence. All this has affected the local people such as the tribals."[15] The stories of India's and Brazil's battles for biodiversity are sadly repeated all over the globe.

Biodiversity is analyzed in three ways: by ecosystems, species, and genetic diversity.[16] Ecosystems are the communities in which organisms live and move and have their being. They comprise forests, wetlands, mangroves, and reefs. Of these, tropical forests are of highest value. They cover only 7 percent of the earth's surface, but they are the habitat for 50 to 80 percent of its species. Tropical forests are now only half their original size. In 1990, deforestation reduced that aggregate further by an area the size of Washington State.

Of all nations, Brazil has the most extensive range of tropical forests, housing the highest number of species. By 1987, as a result of government action, economic shifts, and climatic changes, the massive deforestation of earlier years was brought under control. "Moreover, with nearly 90 percent of its groves still standing, by national or international standards the Brazilian Amazon is relatively untouched. Brazil's most endangered ecosytems are its unique coastal forests. Logging and agriculture and urban expansion have destroyed more than 95 percent of the once-vast coastal rain forests and the coniferous Araucaria forests of southern Brazil."[17] Given the fact that only 5 percent of the world's tropical forests are protected by their governments, "the stage is set for mass extinctions."[18]

Temperate rain forests are in even greater danger than the tropical forests. Half of the original 31 million hectares have fallen prey to logging. In the United States, only pockets of the old-growth rain forests survive in the Pacific Northwest.

In India, trees are among the most important of natural resources, but this has not lessened the pace of deforestation across the land. In Punjab forest cover declined from 120,000 hectares to 49,000 hectares between 1972 and 1982.[19] In Rajasthan some three hundred mines extracting marble, limestone, soapstone, silica, bauxite, and granite have suddenly brought an army of eight thousand laborers into the forests of Alwar district, with predictable damage.[20] Madhya Pradesh is undergoing rapid denudation of its forest cover "from the notional 35 percent of the area to 19 percent."[21] In Assam, deforestation is "the greatest threat to the environment in the region as a whole," producing lesser rainfall and severe floods caused by hillside erosion.[22] In Tripura, the Gumti dam project has ousted some 2,600 tribals from their homes, forcing them to seek livelihood in the upper catchment areas of the Gumti and to resort to the practice of *jhum* (slash-and-burn) agriculture, causing tremendous damage to the trees.[23]

Uttar Pradesh is high among the regions hardest hit by deforestation. "From time immemorial, the Himalayas have played a crucial role in maintaining the ecological balance, particularly in the North."[24] In literature and legend, these pristine heights have served for millennia as the playground of the Hindu gods, and their exquisite beauty has inspired generations of holy men to seek heaven on earth, but like the cedar groves of Lebanon, soon the only record of the Himalyan forests may be found in sacred texts.

Wetlands, like forests, are productive habitats for biodiversity. They are home to countless varieties of fish and waterfowl, and have natural mechanisms which control water flows and cleanse the system of sediments and pollution.

Among India's most picturesque lakes, Renuka, situated in Himachal Pradesh, is a crown jewel. But Lake Renuka is dying. In 1989 the Ministry of Environment and Forests designated it the state's only "natural wetland" and accorded it national status. But the state's rhetoric has fallen short of conservation efforts to save the lake from being choked by elephant grass and heavy siltation during monsoons.[25]

The greatest loss of wetlands, exceeding 90 percent, has occurred in New Zealand, Australia, and in California. The blights of heavy industry, urbanization, agricultural use, overgrazing, and logging are among its enemies. Canada has a quarter of the world's wetlands, which fare the best.

Among coastal wetlands, mangroves are most valuable. The complex ecosystems are good examples of how each part is dependent on the whole for survival. Until recently, no value has been placed on mangroves, and they have been considered destroyable wastelands. As such they have been subject to massive destruction in Asia and the Pacific, where forests are reduced to wood chips utilized by rayon and other industries.[26] India, Pakistan, and Thailand have lost three-fourths of their mangroves. Heavy losses are also recorded for Indonesia, New Guinea, Latin America, and West Africa.

Coral reefs are at greater risk than forests or wetlands. According to the latest global survey, reefs off 90 of 109 countries suffer heavy damage due to sedimentation, water pollution, and the effects of fishing and water sports.[27] A ten-year study by the government of the Philippines, where the most diverse reefs in the world are to be found, estimated that 71 percent of the nation's reefs were in "poor to fair" condition.[28] Along with mangroves, coral reefs are part of an interdependent ecosystem which protect coastal areas from the erosive power of the ocean. They can take the constant beating of the waves, but have little protection against pollution from sewage, fertilizers, and the spread of algae.

Next to ecosystems, species are a second aspect of biodiversity. Scientists say some 10 to 80 million species share the planet with humans. Of this population, 1.4 million species have been identified. But the numbers are fast disappearing. Harvard biologist Edward O. Wilson predicts that 50,000 invertebrate species occupying the tropical rain forests are doomed to die each year, their fate sealed by deforestation.[29] Extinctions take place in nature all the time as a necessary part of the evolutionary process, but man-made extinctions proceed at 1,000 times the rate that has held since prehistory. Peter Raven, director of the Missouri Botanical Gardens, projects that over the next thirty years humans will be responsible for the extinction of one hundred species per day. Forests, wetlands, and reefs are the nurseries for new forms of life, so when these are destroyed, the crisis that looms is the "death of birth."[30] This represents the gravest assault upon life on this planet, ever since its dawn 4 billion years ago. It would be tantamount to some maniac going from one hospital to another, blowing up the natal wards.

The invertebrates of the tropical forests are most numerous of species, and by that same calculation have the greatest toll of extinction. Freshwater fish have declined in major areas. In the former Soviet Union, over 90 percent of commercial fish species have been lost. Similar declines, over a twenty-year period, have been reported for the Atlantic cod and herring, South African pilchard, Pacific Ocean pirch, king crab, and Peruvian anchovies.[31] Amphibians have also declined. In India, the state of Maharashtra has suffered the decline of insect-eating frogs, which has resulted in pest damage to crops. The same circumstances in West Bengal have incurred the spread of malaria by mosquitoes, which otherwise would have been controlled by frogs.

The most fecund diversity of plants is also found in the tropics. Because only a fraction of these forests are safeguarded, researchers estimate that a minimum of 12 percent of the plants in Central and South America are headed for extinction, and therefore must be counted among the "living dead." Four- fifths of the plants that grow in southern Africa are to be found nowhere else; yet 13 percent of these (2,300 species) are threatened. In the United States, 3,000 species are in danger, with the likelihood that 700 of them, mostly native plants, will vanish over the next decade.[32]

The loss of every species is to be bemoaned because a species is unique and irreplaceable, the repository of millions of years of evolution, a source of scientific knowledge, a group of beautiful objects, and of self-interest to humans, whose well-being is interdependent with the lowliest of creatures. Even on a mundane level, humans reap "dividends from diversity" in several practical ways. Biodiversity has especially been beneficial and life-saving to humans in the area of medicine.

In every culture and every age, humans have looked to nature's medicine bag for cures to heal their ills. Queen Nefertiti of Egypt is known to have administered a pain killer in the form of mandrake to her husband. The ancient Egyptians also used onion to cure scurvy among the slaves who built the pyramids. The inhabitants of the Nile used aloe to ease intestinal troubles, and henbane as a sedative. Chinese physicians catalogued thousands of herbal cures in the pharmacopoeia *Pen-ts'ao Kang-mu.* Long recognized as a laxative, rhubarb was found growing in China by Marco Polo. Indian doctors calmed disturbed patients with the "medicine of sad men"—rauwolfia, the forerunner of modern tranquilizers. Ancient Greeks and Romans had a vast plant knowledge that included colchicum to treat gout, squill to stimulate the heart, tansy for worms, and fennel and senna for digestion; assassins poisoned their enemies with belladonna, which later provided the medicine atropine.[33] And in modern America phamacists have used the venom of the Brazilian pit viper to develop Capoten for high blood pressure, among hundreds of other such remedies. All of this is to say that there are very good reasons, involving human survival, to preserve and protect the survival of diversity in plant and animal species.

In addition to ecosystems and species, biodiversity must be viewed at the level of genetic diversity within the species. According to some scientific analyses, the loss of diversity within species poses the most formidable danger to human survival, particularly where food crops are concerned.

> Farmers have used and created genetic diversity for millenia to increase agricultural production; genetic engineering and other high-tech forms of crop breeding are equally dependent on it. Especially in developing nations, generations of farmers have developed a remarkable array of crops. The Ifugao people of the island of Luzon in the Philippines identify more than 200 varieties of sweet potato by name, while farmers in India have planted perhaps 30,000 different strains of rice over the past 50 years.[34]

Ryan senses imminent danger in the tendency in agriculture to concentrate research and production on high-yielding crop varieties because they boost food production at the expense of the many traditional strains that are adapted to local ecosystems and capable of being developed into higher-yielding, locally suitable crops. "At current planting rates, three quarters of India's rice fields may be sown in only 10 varieties by 2005. In Indonesia, 1,500 local varieties of rice have disappeared in the past 15 years, and nearly three fourths of the rice planted today descends from a single maternal plant."[35] The same situation prevails in the United States, where 71 percent of corn comes from a mere six varieties, and half the production of wheat from nine varieties. The lesson of the Irish potato famine of 1846, which sent waves of immigrants fleeing to the United States is that high levels of agricultural uniformity can suddenly collapse by onslaughts of pests and disease.

Genetic erosion affects the survival of wildlife as well as agriculture. In the United States and elsewhere, deliberate homogenization has led to the loss of internal diversity among many species, and that poses a threat to their collective survival.

In all of these instances of genetic engineering, humans are engaged in acts which formerly were the prerogatives of the Creator himself. Problems arise, ultimately threatening our own survival (for nothing survives separately), when we ignore nature's own agenda to conserve biological diversity.

The Problem of Global Warming

Atmospheric changes that used to take a century are now taking place in a decade. The two main foci of climatic change are ozone depletion and global warming. Though different, both are closely related.

Ozone is a form of oxygen having a molecular structure of three atoms instead of the normal two. Its peculiar structure enables ozone to absorb biologically hazardous ultraviolet 'B' radiation from the sun. The ozone layer is located some 10 to 30 miles in the earth's stratosphere. The vital gas thus serves as a life-support system for planet earth.

By 1972, early warnings were sounded that the nitric oxide produced by supersonic aircraft was damaging the ozone layer. Other causes were subsequently cited, the most formidable being the chlorofluorocarbons (CFCs) from aerosol sprays, refrigerants, and air-conditioning.

On their own, CFCs are inert, but as they rise, solar radiation dissociates them, releasing chlorine. The chlorine atoms invade the ozone, removing one of the three oxygen atoms and forming chlorine monoxide. The chlorine monoxide in turn synthesizes with another oxygen atom, forming a new oxygen molecule and a chlorine atom. Unlike the ozone molecule, these newly formed oxgen molecules are unable to screen the ultraviolet radiation which passes through to the surface of the earth.

Upon reaching the earth, the effects of ultraviolet light can be devastating. People who are exposed can develop cataracts in their eyes, wrinkling and cancer of the skin, and a breakdown of the immune system. Radiation can affect the growth of crops by interfering with photosynthesis, diminishing yields, and it can impact marine life by affecting the growth of phytoplankton, the chief link in the ocean food chain.

Since the early 1970s when they were commercialized, vast volumes of CFCs have been released into the atmosphere, the present annual level being some 7,00,000 tons. By 1992, it was estimated that 20 million tons of CFCs had been pumped into the atmosphere.[36] All countries produce these potent chemicals. India's production is at about 5,000 tons per year.[37] What is truly frightening is that once they have been emitted into the atmosphere, CFCs can last for one hundred years or more. This means that even if there were an immediate global ban on CFCs, their effects would still be felt by our great-grandchildren.

But the danger is not in some future; it is here and now. The damages cannot be escaped; the best that can be done is to stabilize ozone loss by the end of this century. Following the confirmation of the ozone hole over Antarctica in 1985 it was thought that Ground Zero was the South Pole. Now there is evidence that Ground Zero is not just the South Pole. A hole in the earth's protective shield could soon open above Russia, Scandinavia, Germany, Britain, Canada, and northern New England.[38]

Till only recently, there were many doubters of any serious ozone depletion, especially in the Reagan and Bush administrations. Their policies counseled caution until studies could come up with hard proofs. That changed in February of 1992 when the National Aeronautics and Space Administration announced startling findings from atmospheric studies done by a modified spy plane and an orbiting satellite.

As the two craft crossed the northern skies last month [Jan. 1992], they discovered record-high concentrations of chlorine monoxide (CIO), a chemical by-product of the chlorofluorocarbons (CFCs) known to be the chief agents of ozone destruction.... Previous studies had already shown that ozone levels have declined 4 percent to 8 percent over the northern hemisphere in the past decade. But the latest data imply that the ozone layer over some regions, including the northernmost parts of the U.S., Canada, Europe and Russia, could be temporarily depleted in the late winter and early spring by as much as 40 percent. That would be almost as bad as the 50 percent ozone loss recorded over Antarctica. If a huge northern ozone hole does not in fact open up in 1992, it could easily do so a year or two later. Says Michael Kurylo, NASA's manager of upper-atmosphere research: "Everybody should be alarmed about this. It's far worse than we thought."[39]

NASA's alarm made the earlier schedule set by the international community to clean up the ozone appear too leisurely. When it was confirmed in 1985 that there was a hole over Antarctica, several nations decided that the problem had to be jointly tackled. In 1987 they drew up the landmark Montreal Protocol, which set the goal of 50 percent reduction of CFCs by 1999. As new evidence of ozone loss augmented, another meeting was held in London in 1990, agreeing to a total ban of CFCs by the year 2000.

NASA's discovery has forced nations to pick up the pace. German Environment Minister Klaus Topfer has issued a call to other nations to match Germany's pledge to terminate CFC manufacture by 1995. In February 1992, the U.S. Senate, by a 96 to 0 vote, considered the situation so critical that they decided to accelerate the phaseout period set by earlier calculations of ozone depletion. The administrator of the Environmental Protection Agency announced that the phaseout could come about by 1996.

The lesson of ozone should be remembered by world leaders as they consider other environmental problems. Business interests are bound to come in the way of environmental priorities because, as the manufacturers of CFCs admit, they are going to entail considerable financial loss. Governments, with an eye to economics, are therefore slow to move in the interests of the people, especially when some of the people are beyond their national boundaries. The standard ploy in such circumstances is to study the subject to death for the declared purpose of learning the truth. Then Senator Al Gore had a point when he said, following NASA's announcement, "Now that there's the prospect of a hole over Kennebunkport, perhaps Bush will comply with the law." If governments always wait until there is metaphysical certitude that a hazard is on hand, it may be much too late to halt the hazard. A good example of bureaucratic foot dragging is the issue of the greenhouse effect, to which we next turn.

The greenhouse effect is a by-product of ozone depletion, but it is potentially more hazardous because it is far more difficult to control. It became a household word when, following the tepid congressional hearings conducted by Colorado Senator Timothy Wirth in the fall of 1987, the topic suddenly generated heat during the summer's disasters of 1988, sparked by the testimony of James Hansen, head of NASA's Goddard Institute for Space Studies: "It is time to stop waffling so much," he declared. "The evidence is pretty strong that the greenhouse effect is here." In point of fact, the summer's drought and record-high temperatures may have had nothing to do with the greenhouse effect and were caused, rather, by random, annual climatic variations, but the events did serve to demonstrate to the government and the American public the climatic calamities that can occur when greenhouse gases are released into the atmosphere.

The greenhouse effect which causes global warming began long before civilization. The natural occurrence of CO_2 gases created a heat-trapping blanket which made life on earth possible. Without this atmospheric shield, the average surface temperature of the planet would be a frigid 0° F instead of 59° F. The mechanics of the greenhouse effect are theoretically simple. The sun radiates energy in the form of lightwaves that are able to reach the surface of the earth because the CO_2 molecules in the atmosphere are transparent to visible light, in the same manner that glass panes of a greenhouse allow light to pass through. The heat of the lightwaves is absorbed by the land, water, and organisms. Excess heat is then released back into the atmosphere, not as visible light, but as infrared radiation. Infrared rays are longer and have less energy to escape the atmosphere easily. Some of the rays escape, but the rest are trapped by carbon dioxide and other gases in the troposphere, warming the earth. The amount of heat is correlated to the amount of CO_2 in the air.

The problem today is that the industrialized world is emitting vast quantities of its waste products into the atmosphere, including carbon dioxide, methane, nitrous oxide, and chlorofluorocarbons. These greenhouse gases prevent additional infrared radiation from escaping, and thus serve to thicken the atmospheric blanket, trapping more heat and warming up the earth even more.

Atmospheric scientists have long known that the earth follows a rhythm of warming and cooling. The present warming phase probably began some eighteen thousand years ago, following the peak of the last ice age. Scientists now believe that these climatic rhythms can be triggered by human activity. Says Stephen Schneider of the National Center for Atmospheric Research: "Humans are altering the earth's surface and changing the atmosphere at such a rate that we have become a competitor with natural forces that maintain our climate. What is new is the irreversibility of the changes that are now taking place."[40]

The consequences of rapid alterations in the atmosphere could be dire. Dramatic weather changes could shift the configurations of deserts and fertile regions, spark tropical storms, cause sea levels to rise as the result of the expansion of water caused by warming, and usher mass starvation and soaring food prices.

An example of these consequences is the plight of the fabled city of Venice. Built on an archipelago in a lagoon, it has long been perched on the edge of disaster. Experts believe that the city has now ceased sinking, but it faces an equally threatening development: the slow rise of the Adriatic, largely as a result of a global warming trend that is causing the world's oceans and seas to expand gradually. Other cities that are thought to be living on borrowed time, affecting some 500 million people, are Miami, New Orleans, Alexandria, Bangkok, Dhaka, Hamburg, Leningrad, London, Shanghai, Sydney, and Thessalonika. Closer home, Waikiki could well be the Venice of Hawaii. Other islands of the Pacific could face similar fates. The Marshall Islands are in particular danger, because many of them top off at 12 feet above sea level. Global warming could be sending nations, ancient cultures, and ecosystems to watery graves.

But the current data are insufficient to make specific predictions. Notwithstanding the high-level production of carbon dioxide over the past two hundred years of industrialization, it has not yet been fully proven that humans have triggered a process of global warming. It is easy to mistake short-term variations like droughts for long-term climatic change. The picture will only become clearer toward the end of the 1990s. The Earth has great capacities to adjust to changes. A warmer ocean could create more cloud cover that could cool the earth and thus offset the greenhouse effect. It is also possible that the ocean could absorb the carbon dioxide in the air.

There is much we do not know, but on the basis of what we do know, it would be imprudent to flirt with disaster on a global scale. There yet may be no conclusive evidence linking human actions to the greenhouse effect, but this does not mean that sometime in the future the problem is not going to materialize. Researchers may differ over the temperature effects of the carbon dioxide build-up, but no one disagrees about the carbon dioxide build-up itself. Besides, time is not on our side.

Even if the build-up of carbon diozide and other gases does

not produce significant temperature rise, researchers such as Harvard University's Fakhri Bazzaz are warning that the increase could disrupt farms and forests. The main culprit behind the greenhouse effect is the use of fossil fuels by industrial nations. It is too much to expect that any significant changes in the status quo will be ushered in before the middle of the next century, because there are high economic stakes, backed by the moghuls of the oil, coal, and auto industries.

The Problem of Pollution

In the spring of 1989 the *Exxon Valdez* ran aground on Bligh Reef, Alaska, and spilled 260,000 barrels of crude oil into one of the world's most pristine bodies of water. It cost Exxon a billion dollars for the cleanup, and the state of Alaska millions more to restore the beaches fouled with oil. But the cost to wildlife exceeds a dollar value: more than 34,000 birds and 984 sea otters fell prey to the slick, among other animals.

In the spring of 1991, Iraq's "scorched sand" tactic in Kuwait brought a brutal twist to the Gulf War. Saddam Hussein's retreating army set ablaze five hundred oil wells (roughly 50 percent of the nation's total). Thick streams of soot darkened the sky over more than a third of the Kuwaiti battlefield and beyond into Saudi Arabia. The desert was suddenly turned into a burning wasteland. One soldier said it all: "It's amazing. You look at Kuwait, at the whole area. It's just fire." In the light of the burning wells, and under the pall of black rain, there were fears of eco-calamity, but in the months that ensued, the scars of Saddam's scorched-earth policy against Kuwait proved terrible but not catastrophic.

These recent environmental disasters join the ranks of Love Canal, Chernobyl, and Bhopal to dramatize man-made environmental pollution that threatens the health, not of humans alone, but of birds, beasts, and beaches. Sometimes the threat is visible, but mostly it is silent, pervasive, deadly, and a growing menace to the health and safety of people everywhere. The soot generated over Kuwait had soon traveled across to Asia, so though we examine particular instances, we are also aware of their global impact.

Until recently it was thought that disease occurred spontaneously, but there is growing evidence that many diseases are environmentally induced. We shall try to identify that connection, confining our remarks to the connection between pollution and two medical problems: chronic respiratory disease and cancer.

Our data are derived from the Environmental Protection Agency's 1987 inventory of toxic chemicals emitted by U.S. industries.[41] The EPA's inventory is a result of a 1986 federal reporting law that covers a list of 328 hazardous chemicals and compounds. The Emergency Planning and Community-Right-to-Know Act mandates that large industries report their annual chemical use. The regulation followed on the heels of the chemical disaster in Bhopal, India, that killed and injured thousands of people.

The EPA's inventory reveals a gargantuan problem generated by industrial emissions of toxic pollutants. In 1987 industries spewed out 7 billion pounds of toxic chemicals, with 2.65 billion pounds being released into the air. Industries are making the skies into a garbage dump. Among the fifty states, Texas ranked first in the amount of toxic chemicals. Comfort, Texas, released 465 million pounds of toxic wastes; most of this was buried, but the numbers are not very comforting to the neighborhood. Hawaii ranked last, pumping 2.6 million pounds of toxic chemicals into the air, land, and water.

The EPA toxic inventory is a step in the right direction. For the first time, the public has some idea of the national pollution problem and knows that it has a "right to know." However, the inventory is marred by numerous limitations and loopholes. Only large plants processing 75,000 pounds of toxic chemicals per annum are required to report. The statistics do not cover car emissions, power plants, the military, municipal sewage, or small companies. We therefore are left in doubt about the toxic total. There is no doubt that whatever the true numbers are, environmental pollution is responsible for chronic respiratory disease, cancer, birth defects, mutations, and psycho-behavioral defects.[42] We take a closer view of chronic respiratory disease and cancer.

Large numbers of Americans suffer from bronchitis, asthma, and emphysema, which are caused by air pollution, especially from the sulfates found in auto emissions. Samuel S. Epstein states: "It has been estimated that failure to meet current sulfur dioxide standards, which are exceeded in most U.S. cities, is responsible for six thousand premature deaths annually, six to ten million avoidable asthma attacks, and twenty to thirty million days of exacerbated cardiovascular and respiratory disease."[43]

A host of other chemicals are hazardous to the lungs and contribute to chronic respiratory diseases, including ammonia, a colorless gas used as a refrigerant and in the manufacture of fertilizers, synthetic fibers, dyes, and explosives; chlorine, a heavy greenish-yellow gas used for water treatment, food processing, disinfectant production, and cleaners; and sulfuric acid, a colorless, odorless liquid or crystal used in soaps, auto batteries, animal feed, and polishes. Occupational dust is also a toxic agent which causes various forms of pneumoconioses. An estimated 125,000 coal miners are afflicted with this disease, which enfeebles the lungs and kills approximately 4,000 workers each year.[44] This debilitating disease takes other forms as well: asbestosis from asbestos dust; byssinosis from cotton dust; bagassosis from sugar cane dust; and silicosis from silica dust. Every year in the United States some 9,000 deaths can be traced to these dust-related occupational diseases.[45]

The Greeks called cancer *karkinos*, "the crab-like disease," because of its spreading growth. In its Latinized form, *cancer* is the most ominous word in our modern vocabulary because it is seen as a death sentence. Although cancer is second to cardiovascular disease as a cause of death, it is the most feared. Cancer afflicts 1 in 4 Americans now living, with approximately 800,000 new cases diagnosed each year.[46] One-third of those will survive to live out a normal span of life, but such statistics do not diminish the fears.

Cancer is not a single disease but a combination of different diseases identified by their unregulated cell growth. Therefore the causes, diagnoses, and treatments of cancer vary. In the past decade, the media have spotlighted the carcinogenic properties of household items such as saccharin, cyclamate, and methpyrilene (used in sleeping tablets), known from laboratory experiments on rodents. We do not yet know whether these chemicals cause cancer in humans, but research sheds new light on the role of chemicals in producing cancer. Until only a few years ago, it was thought that cancers were caused by hereditary factors, and perhaps viruses. Researchers are now examining the role of natural and synthetic chemicals in the production of the majority of human cancers.

The evidence for environmental sources comes from various directions. First, although different cancers are variously distributed in different parts of the world, cancers occurring in the families of immigrants to another country tend to take on the cancer pattern of the adopted homeland. Second, it is now documented that exposure to certain chemicals in the workplace causes cancer. For instance, the known carcinogen benzene is associated with leukemia. It is used in the manufacture of rubber, detergents, and dyes. Asbestos has been a much-discussed work hazard in recent years. A mineral found in rocks, it is a durable product found in construction and industrial work. The danger comes when the asbestos fibers break into microscopic dust that is inhaled by the workers, producing a condition known as mesothelioma, or cancer of the chest and abdominal membranes. The disease is incurable. Third, the most convincing data linking cancer to chemicals in the environment arise from the high mortality rate of lung cancer. During the first fifty years of this century, American males increased their smoking by 10 percent and their death rate from lung cancer rose 100 percent; the cycle has been repeated by American women since the end of World War II. In the words of one cancer researcher: "It is almost as if western societies had set out to conduct a vast and fairly well-controlled experiment in carcinogenesis bringing about several million deaths and using their own people as the experimental animals."[47]

There is growing consensus that, although viruses do produce cancers in laboratory situations, "they seem unlikely to be primarily responsible for causing any of the common human cancers." Although heredity does play a part in increasing the susceptibility to cancer, there is no hard evidence that common tumors are inherited.[48] The spotlight therefore shifts to environmental chemicals as the causes of cancer. These chemicals may be synthetic, produced in factories, natural chemicals found in homes (food contaminants), or chemicals produced by bacteria in the large intestines.

The pollution problem in the United States is replicated in the rest of the industrial world. History may yet prove that the real damage done to Eastern Europe was not political or economic, but environmental. Communist leaders were wont to proclaim that pollution was a by-product of capitalism, but it is now an ironic discovery that political systems that encouraged profits, like the United States, proved more resistant to environmental exploitation than systems that disavowed profits. Under the socialism of Karl Marx, natural resources were to be factored into the cost of production, so the present environmental holocaust should theoretically not have occurred. But there was a big gap between theory and practice. In practice, the individual was reduced to a cog in the political machinery. Any talk about the "right to know" would have been deemed subversive. People were prevented from protesting known catastrophies, and steps were taken to keep information on pollution, secret. The build-up of heavy manufacturing, begun by Josef Stalin after World War II, had no impetus to improve its technology in the absence of competition. The more outdated the technology, the greater its capacity to pollute. Similarly, the demands for more food were met by greater distribution of free fertilizers to farmers. The consequence: "contamination by cancer-causing nitrates that will take decades to cleanse from the water and soil."[49]

Now, with the lifting of the Iron Curtain, the world can see the extent of the deadly pollution in Eastern Europe. We concentrate on the area where Poland, Czechoslovakia, and East Germany meet, for these are "the planet's most polluted lands."

Czechoslovakia is the worst polluted. Seventy percent of rivers "cannot be used for drinking, fishing or swimming."[50] Only six rivers in Bulgaria are fit for human use. The Danube is blue only in song: "it flows brown and polluted at every point on its 2,000-mile journey to the Black Sea." Among the new "dead seas" are the Caspian, Baltic, Barents, Black, and White seas. Air pollution has defaced statuary and stone buildings, so there is no doubt what it has done to the health of people. Pollution, stemming from intense coal mining and burning, has produced acid rain that has replaced once lush forests with miles of dead trees.[51] Josef Vavrousek, head of Czechoslovakia's new environmental agency, could well be speaking for all of Eastern Europe: "We are an example to the world of how not to treat the environment."[52]

The same can be said of the former Soviet Union. In January of 1991, then President Mikhail Gorbachev said in a speech: "The time is ripe to set up an international mechanism for technological cooperation on environmental protection."[53] The need to reverse decades of pollution could hardly have been more urgent. Some 50 million Soviet citizens were living in environments where the pollution levels were ten times those prohibited by the West. The estimated costs for tackling the pollution problems over the next ten years was a hefty $40 billion annually.[54] The Chernobyl disaster defies all estimates.

In South America, the worst-case scenario of air pollution is Mexico City. Morning, noon, and night, 23 million souls breathe in the vortex of a toxic cloud. The winters of 1991 and 1992 were particularly severe. The people call it *nata*, or scum. It hangs like a brown, rotting mushroom over the megapolis, composed of carbon monoxide, sulfur dioxide, nitrogen dioxide, and ozone. It has produced a 16 to 20 percent rise in respiratory infections, nosebleeds, and emphysema. The high volume of noxious gases that is daily pumped into the air makes it impossible for the atmosphere to recuperate, creating a situation that is chronic. A full 7 percent of the city's industrial pollution was being caused by an oil refinery which spewed 88,000 tons of contaminants into the atmosphere every year. It had to be shut down, at great financial loss.[55]

The developing countries of Asia present new sources of pollution which could surpass those of the industrialized nations. Two opposite forces are simultaneously at work. On the one hand is the vertical thrust as the developing countries try to catch up with the more affluent West. To find their place in the sun, they are pushing their factories and farms to the limit. On the other hand, there is the horizontal counterforce of explosive populations. With more mouths to feed, they must push even harder, sacrificing health for economic gain. Pollution control is a luxury they can ill afford. In the bargain, the sun gets covered with smog, disease spreads, and the price of success often exceeds economic gain. It is a vicious circle, and even when it is medical knowledge that the health stakes are high, poverty makes industrial slaves.

An example is the Kesoram Rayon Factory at Tribeni, near Calcutta. A report states that, without warning, the factory emits an invisible poisonous gas which soon seeps into the homes of the fourteen villages in the immediate neighborhood. "Coughing, retching, the suffocated victims run futilely out of their homes in search of fresh air."[56] For twenty years the factory has been contaminating the air with sulphur dioxide, sulphur trioxide, and carbon disulphide gases. A spokesman for the villagers says, "We have been fighting against the Kesoram factory management since 1961 to prevent their gases from destroying our lives."[57]

In response to picketing of the factory, the management has made promises to improve things, but "typically, nothing was done." The environment minister was invited to study the situation. "The visit achieved nothing, nor has the state Environment Department been able to do anything. Curiously enough, the environment minister's son . . . has been given a job as a chemist in the factory."[58] The villagers have given up organizing committees to lead the agitation "because in the past, committee members have been silenced by being employed in the factory."[59]

There is no denial on the part of the factory management that they are emitting poisonous gases. "We have two sulphuric acid plants with a total capacity of 50 tonnes per day. During restarting, a huge quantity of sulphur dioxide gases escape as stack gas which are not only losses in production, but they also pollute the atmosphere of the neighbourhood."[60]

The health hazards of these gases are well known. Sulphur dioxide attacks the respiratory system, causing bronchitis and other complications such as gastritis, and eventually coronary diseases. Carbon disulphide is worse. It damages the nervous system, causing behavioral impairment, including the loss of the sex drive. The gases also destroy plant life, killing the bamboo and mango trees that otherwise thrive in the area.

The report ends on a tragically realistic note: "Understandably, despite everything, nobody wants the factory shut down. Says schoolteacher Meera Chakraborty: 'How can we demand the closure of the factory when the livelihood of so many depend on it?' Pollution control equipment could minimize the harmful effects of the gases, but it is expensive."

B. B. Sundaresan declares that the problem of industrial pollution is an all-India problem. "The rapid growth of industries, especially chemicals and allied products, has resulted in the production and use of substances some of which are health hazards. A significant amount of these compounds also get released into the environment, affecting the flora and fauna. A number of organic chemicals are being synthesized and their toxicity values are so profound that they are gradually threatening the environment."[61]

Asian countries that do make it to the top often find that they are victims of their own success. Taiwan is a country that is rich in cash, and also rich in pollution. It is now as cash rich as Japan, with $70 billion in foreign-exchange reserves. In the forty years since the Nationalist Chinese fled here from the mainland, Taiwan has burgeoned from a small backwater into a "major economic powerhouse." Heavy industry has been the strength of its economic muscle. But the price has been high. Rigorous development programs have spawned industries which are among the worst polluters in the business. Says K. L. Chang, professor of physics at the National Taiwan University, "When other countries were phasing out these industries in the 1960s, we welcomed them with open arms. Now we're stuck with the pollution."[62]

According to one environmental report, Taiwan is

> one of the dirtiest places in Asia. At least one third of the island's rivers and one eighth of its farmlands are contaminated. Air quality in parts of Taipei routinely surpasses the harmful level, and visitors to the city often develop a lingering cough. Exhaust fumes from cars, motorcycles and scooters leave a permanent haze over the capital. In the countryside, households and villages dispose of garbage and refuse by dumping it into a field or ravine. Asthma cases among Taiwanese children have quadrupled in the past 10 years. Cancer, Taiwan's leading cause of death, has doubled over the last 30 years. And although the Government has taken modest steps toward safeguarding the environment, state run enterprises and large corporations continue to pollute with impunity.[63]

As Edgar Lin, former president of the Taiwan chapter of Greenpeace, sees it: "There is no political will to change. The situation keeps getting worse. You can see it, feel it and breathe it."[64]

Japan reveals yet another side of the face of Asia. Japan leads the world in the manufacture of fuel-efficient automobiles. With China, it is one of the largest consumers of gasoline in Asia, and the fuel is largely lead free. Japan also has stringent specifications for sulphur in oil products in order to combat air pollution and acid rain.

By all accounts the engine which drives the Japanese economy is finely tuned, but within the mechanical complexity there are cultural components which must not be overlooked. The cultural elements show that Japan has a somewhat split personality in regard to the environment. Professor Stephen Kellert of Yale University explains that the Japanese "display a detached appreciation for the beauty of species that fall within their cultural and historical heritage and can be manipulated to fit within their stylized picture of what the natural world should be."[65] On the other hand, "nature in the raw" is often treated as an alien force to be overcome. In this role, Japan was recently criticized by *Newsweek* as a "whale-killing, forest-stripping bogeyman on the environmental stage."

Alan Miller, a specialist on Japanese environmental policy and executive director of the University of Maryland Center for Global Change, views this attitudinal schizophrenia contextually. By one report:

> He believes the Japanese people's split environmental personality stems from their island home's lack of significant natural resources and the absence of a wilderness tradition.
>
> For centuries, the predominantly agrarian Japanese society had to battle the elements to eke out a living. Being inhabitants of an island nation, the Japanese viewed marine life as a commodity to be exploited, not as anything possessing an intrinsic value of its own. The sea was a force to be feared, not revered.
>
> On top of all this, Japan made a decision that it had to industrialize in order to compete with the Western world.
>
> Economic growth became the secular religion, with environmental concerns not even worthy of an afterthought.
>
> This was reflected in modern Japan's environmentally insensitive overseas trade policies, particularly its participation in and encouragement of overharvesting of tropical forests for commercial gain.
>
> But even on the domestic front, where many of the Japanese government's pollution control efforts have been relatively effective, the remedial measures have tended to be localized and quite limited.
>
> The environmental movement in Japan remains embryonic. There is little if any public participation in environmental decision-making. No citizen environmental organizations of any consequence are around to badger authorities to act responsibly.
>
> Miller and other expert observers of Japan attribute this set of circumstances to the nation's ancient tradition of placing blind faith in established authority.[66]

At the same time there is hope for positive change because, on the same cultural note, it should be observed that Japan is sensitive about how it is being perceived by the world, especially at this time when it is developing a strategy for world leadership. The

West has the chance to influence Japan's environmental policies, and recently Japan has bowed to changes demanded by Greenpeace and other agencies.

The most lethal form of pollution derives from nuclear power. It is the stuff of doomsday books, summoning the fears of a meltdown at Three Mile Island, and the hellish explosion at Chernobyl, rocketing a cloud of radioactivity over the Ukraine and Europe.

Eduard Shevardnadze takes us back to that red-letter day, now become a watershed in environmental thinking.

> On that morning, the telephones jangled at an hour when they are normally silent. I postponed my usual Monday meeting to answer all the agitated questions. They all boiled down to one: What had happened? I had no answer. During those first morning hours I didn't yet know that an accident had occurred at one of our nuclear power stations. My efforts to extract news from the sources I could reach produced little. "Yes," they told me. "Something's happened in the Ukraine, but so far we can't get any clear information." Scraps of news trickled in, but did not give the full picture of what had happened.
>
> Gorbachev telephoned and asked me to come right over. By that time more than a dozen foreign ambassadors had requested emergency meetings with me or my deputies. Their governments had urgently ordered them to find out which radioactive elements were spewing into their countries' atmosphere, soil and water. Once they had ascertained that their own reactors were functioning normally, they had traced the leak to the Soviet Union. The affair was turning into a scandal![67]

The then foreign minister goes on to state that though he had been raised in a spirit of mystical veneration for the "top secret" stamp, in this instance, the principle of *glasnost* had to displace all ideological safeguards, and the whole truth had be told to the world.

> "Chernobyl Day," as I privately called April 26, 1986, marked a watershed in world history, a new criterion for foreign policy. We hadn't managed to pronounce this phrase yet and had not clarified the real dimensions of the catastrophe, but in one second, the explosion heralded an era when no ecological disaster caused by a breakdown in technology could be kept within rational borders. In the modern world, the boundaries and radius of various natural disasters were very conditional. There

was an unconditional need for outside international resistance to a threat no less than a thermonuclear war: the ecological collapse of a planet.[68]

Shevardnadze concludes his remarks on a new note. "'Chernobyl Day' tore the blindfold from our eyes and persuaded us that politics and morals could not diverge. We had to gauge our politics constantly by moral criteria."[69]

In spite of the new policy of *glasnost*, Soviet official secrecy prevailed. Now it is known that the true body count of that fateful day was as many as ten thousand dead by the explosion, and millions more afflicted by its radioactive fallout. Gorbachev marked the fifth anniversary with the warning that "humanity is just beginning to realize fully the global nature of social, medical and psychological problems created by the catastrophe."

Back home, the message of Chernobyl is being used by antinuclear groups, such as Greenpeace, to discontinue use of nuclear power for domestic energy. In 1992 the United States derived 21 percent of its electricity from nuclear power, as against 27 percent for Japan, 33 percent for Germany, 36 percent for Bulgaria, 60 percent for Belgium, and 75 percent for France.

On the credit side, whereas fuels (coal, oil, and gas) produce greenhouse gases and other pollutants in large quantities, nuclear energy is a power source that is clean. It is derived from plentiful uranium, and the new generation of reactors and waste disposal are increasingly safe. On the negative side, nuclear fuel and waste are highly radioactive. As a general comment: nuclear power is a vast energy source, immensely oversold at the beginning, but is now making a comeback.[70]

The Problem of Waste

The notion of the world as a global village is fast being replaced by the reality of the world as a global wasteland. Throwaway societies are befouling their land, air, and oceans. Believing that the planet has an infinite capacity to digest the volumes of waste we feed into it, no nation has ever thought this to be a problem. The common wisdom has always been: "Out of sight, out of mind." Now we are down in the dumps. The urgent global dilemma facing America and the rest of the world is: "how to reduce the gargantuan waste by-products of civilization without endangering human health or damaging the environment."[71]

A symbol of our civilization was the two-year odyssey of the freighter *Pelicano* which, like the legendary *Flying Dutchman*, seemed doomed to sail the seven seas endlessly, with no ports willing to receive her cargo. And with good reason. The ship was carrying 14,000 tons of toxic ash that was loaded in Philadelphia in September of 1986. In October 1988, the captain impudently dumped 4,000 pounds of its unwelcome cargo in Haitian waters. A month later he struck a deal with an unnamed country to accept the noxious load.[72]

As John Langone observes, the voyage of the *Pelicano* typifies the "environmental exploitation of poor countries by the rich," and also "the single most irresponsible and reckless way to get rid of the growing mountains of refuse, much of it poisonous, that now bloat the world's landfills. Indiscriminate dumping of any kind—in a new Jersey swamp, or a Haitian beach or in the Indian Ocean—simply shifts potentially hazardous waste from one place to another."[73] The common mentality behind this peculiar saga is the NIMBY mentality—the acronym for Not In My Back Yard.

The problem of waste is one that no one wishes to see, let alone smell. Yet the global wasteland covers all nations, rich and poor.

> From the festering industrial landfills of Bonn to the waste-choked sewage drains of Calcutta, the trashing goes on. A poisonous chemical soup, the product of coal mines and metal smelters, roils Polish waters in the Bay of Gdansk. Hong Kong, with 5.7 million people and 49,000 factories within its 400 sq. mi., dumps 1,000 tons of plastic a day—triple the amount thrown away in London. Stinking garbage and human excrement despoils Thailand's majestic River of Kings. Man's effluent is more than an assault on the senses. When common garbage is burned, it spews dangerous gases into the air. Dumped garbage and industrial waste can turn lethal when corrosive acids, long-lived organic materials and discarded metals leach out of landfills into groundwater supplies, contaminating drinking water and polluting farmland.[74]

America's affluence and industrial might also gives it a high place on the waste heap. We are familiar with the grim statistics of the nation's trash:

- We generate more than 160 million tons of solid waste a year—approximately 3.5 pounds a day per person, or 1 ton each year. "A convoy of ten-ton garbage trucks carrying the nation's annual waste would reach half way to the moon."[75]

- We create one ton of solid industrial waste every week for each citizen.

- We produce an average of 20 tons of CO_2 per year for each individual.

- We discard enough aluminum cans per annum to rebuild the whole U.S. commercial airline four times over.

- We cast off sufficient iron and steel every year to supply the total needs of GM, Ford, and Chrysler.

- We toss out each year enough writing paper to erect a 12-foot wall, reaching from Los Angeles to New York City.

- We throw away every two weeks the number of glass bottles and jars it would take to fill both Towers of the World Trade Centre.

Between 1960 to 1986, the volume of American garbage grew 80 percent. By the turn of the century the malodorous mound is expected to rise by 22 percent to a volume of 192.7 million tons.[76] Only the Australians come close to U.S. statistics, while the West Germans and the Japanese come in at half the figures.

Among Americans the most profligate offenders are Californians, who throw away an average of 2,555 pounds a year. Says one environmentalist: "In Los Angeles County we generate enough trash to fill the Dodger Stadium with garbage every nine days or so."[77]

But Dodger Stadium is not prepared to provide this service, and the number of other less prestigious facilities is fast diminishing. This is what is posing the present waste problem. Says Vice President Al Gore: "the volume of garbage is now so high that we are running out of places to put it. Out of the 20,000 landfills in the United States in 1979, more than 15,000 have since reached their permanent capacity and closed. Although the problem is more acute in older cities, especially in the Northeast, virtually every metropolitan area is either facing or will soon face the urgent need to find new landfills or dispose of their garbage by some other means."[78]

The epicenter of the crisis is New York City, which produces 44 million pounds of garbage every single day. Mountains have always served to inspire and elevate the human spirit. And then there is "Mount Trashmore" on Staten island, rising, load by solid load, toward a peak of 505 feet. Beyond that point there would be the jeopardy of a garbage avalanche. It will have to obtain a permit from the Federal Aviation Administration, posing danger to air traffic. Beside this "Everest" of paper, aluminum, tin, glass, motor oil and car batteries, other monuments are planned for heights of 450 feet and several at 300 feet. The mounds will be covered with clay and soil, making parts of the area into a park. Probably some entrepreneur will come along and change all that into a ski resort.

Eighty percent of the nation's waste is buried in landfills. In the public perception, landfills appear "natural" because we are told that the waste in them is biodegradable. Landfills are therefore viewed as huge compost piles. In fact, they should be seen as solid vaults which preserve the garbage because it is covered, compact, and shielded from sun and moisture. The slow decomposition that does take place is an efficient producer of methane gas that contributes to the greenhouse effect.

In 1991 the Environment Protection Agency set up new standards to ensure that the country's remaining six thousand landfills be guarded against hazardous leakages of gases and pollutants. This will add some 900 million dollars to the nation's waste costs, now calculated at $4 billion to $5 billion annually.[79]

There are a few alternative forms of garbage disposal. Incinceration reduces the weight by 70 percent, and produces heat that can be sold to generate electricity. Shipping wastes across state lines is commonly practiced, but southern states seem to be mobilizing against the invasion of Yankee garbage. Third World countries also resent the "garbage imperialism" of rich industrialized nations. Gore reports:

> On the West Coast, some municipal officials in California have been negotiating with the Marshall Islands in the South Pacific to receive regular shipments of solid waste. The residents of these islands, many of whom are suffering from the lingering effects of the U.S. government's atmospheric nuclear testing program in the 1950s, would not ordinarily consider receiving such an unsavory and even dangerous import, but their poverty forces them to do so. Meanwhile, Greenpeace recently disclosed that officials in Baltimore were negotiating with authorities in China for permission to dump tens of thousands of tons of

municipal solid waste in Tibet. Nothing could be more cynical. The Tibetan people are powerless to prevent Chinese officials from destroying the ecology of their homeland because of China's armed subjugation of Tibet for the last forty years. But the shipment has not taken place, and the United States has not yet become heavily involved in cross-border waste trafficking.[80]

The most environmentally sound way to tackle the waste problem is through recycling. Japan recycles 50 percent of its trash; Western Europe, 30 percent; but the U.S. only recycles 10 percent (16 million tons per year). Cities such as Seattle, Newark, San Francisco and San Jose are leaders in the field. What impedes the process is that the way goods are packaged for the market-place makes recycling expensive and complicated. Besides, there is lethargy on the part of the public. "Many Americans simply refuse to be bothered with sorting and separating garbage into recyclable and nonrecyclable parts."[81]

The waste problem is complex, but it should be plain that the element of culture has much to do with it. As the privileged citizens of a wealthy nation, we Americans have developed a throw-away, convenience culture which is responsible for this mess. Before we alter our production processes, and radically reduce the quantity of waste we produce, we must dump the cavalier way in which we think about waste.

The Problem of Overpopulation

Overpopulation is the ultimate environmental problem. Its sudden surge in our century defines and dramatizes all aspects of our ties to the earth. Each of the problems we have looked at can be reduced to the numbers of the people on this planet, at any given time and place, except that now time and place have vanished, and nations are scrambling for what remains of earth's precious resources.

To illustrate our point, let us examine a single resource: water. Whatever high principles the Gulf War of 1991 was fought over, it finally boiled down to oil. That era is ending. More vital environmental issues are now at stake. Future wars will be fought over water. The thought is not that far-fetched when one considers the claims and counterclaims to rivers and lakes being made by Israel and Jordan, Egypt and Ethiopia, and India and Bangladesh, among others. Fourteen countries depend on the Nile for their water supply, and all fourteen of them are bursting at the seams; yet the Nile has no more water than in the days of Moses. Similarly, the Tigris and the Euphrates and the river Jordan are no better than in biblical times, but their limited supplies are in demand by competing groups of growing populations. Professor Arnon Sofer, a geographer at the University of Haifa, sounds an alarm: "Wars over water might erupt in the Middle East in the '90s when the states try to control each other's supplies."[82]

Water is an issue because population growth and development have depleted and polluted the world's water supply, raising the risk of starvation, epidemics, and wars.

The problem of overpopulation is best told by the figures themselves. It took 3 million years for the world's population to reach the billion mark in 1830. A hundred years later, it hit 2 billion in 1931. Thirty years later it reached 3 billion in 1960. By 1974, in fourteen years, it jumped to 4 billion. In 1986 it was 5 billion. By 1996 it will be 6 billion. Demographers had been predicting that the world population would stabilize at 10 billion in the next century, but now that figure is revised to 14 billion. But statistics can be abstract. More concretely, every decade the world is adding one China to its population; every year one Mexico; and every month one New York City.

More disturbing is the fact that 90 percent of population growth is taking place in Third World countries. In Africa, the numbers will rise from 650 million to 900 million by the end of the century. In Latin America and the Caribbean, the figures will increase by 100 million to 540 million at the turn of the century. A rise in China's birth rate and an apparent halt to the decline of India's fertility rate are major factors in the accelerated growth of population. Together, China (1.087 billion) and India (816.8 million) make up 37 percent of the world population.

A contributing factor to the the world's population growth is improved life expectancy, now 63 years worldwide, up from 45 in 1950.

The figures are multiplying fastest in urban areas. Lee-Jay Cho, Director of the Population Institute, East-West Center, Honolulu warns:

> The increasing urban concentration is an important aspect of demographic change affecting both rural and urban development efforts. Urbanization in the next two decades will bring

about drastic changes in socioeconomic, and political life. The increasing number of people in cities thwarts governmental efforts to improve the quality of life for current and future generations. When such growth becomes unmanageable—that is, when jobs and public facilities lag behind the demand for them—then urbanization becomes a serious concern for public policy.[83]

By any measurement, the impact of overpopulation on the environment is frightening. In Africa we are already seeing the spread of new epidemics such as cholera, the black plague, and AIDS. Millions are starving to death. In Asia and Latin America we witness the rampant denudation of forests, massive soil erosion, and the depletion of natural resources, which are putting a critical strain on the integrity of their ecological systems.

The intractability of the population problem lies in the fact that even if fertility rates in the Third World declined from four births per woman to the replacement level of two, the population would go on climbing in the next century "because the vast numbers of females born on the steepest part of the S curve in the '50s and '60s have generated 'demographic momentum,' a boom in childbearing that will last for some time to come."[84]

How big that boom is and how long it persists is uncertain. It would be tolerable if the world population would stabilize at 10 billion rather than 14 billion. At double the present population, humans will still be able to feed themselves and prevent destructive social, political, and environmental consequences; but at three times the present population, one might fear the possibility of a Malthusian cataclysm.

North American and European countries (with the exception of Albania) that have growth rates of less than 1 percent should not consider themselves as somehow separate from the problems of overpopulation. Though Western population rates may be low, our consumption rates are high, and these are only being satiated at the expense of poor countries, which must trade their precious resources for us to maintain the standards of affluence to which we have become accustomed.

Moreover, because we share a global economy, the increase in numbers in a Third World country is felt worldwide. For example, massive unemployment in Asia and Africa affects the international economy, making it harder for the West to compete with Third World labor markets.

Most ominously, according to a UN report, *The state of the World Population 1991,* migratory pressures will increase as the Third World population rises. "The number of migrants fleeing poverty, political oppression or environmental instability already is growing while the need for unskilled and semiskilled workers is falling in the industrial nations."[85] The phenomenon of the boat people risking all to reach Hong Kong, only to be returned to Vietnam; illegal immigrants from Pakistan, Sri Lanka, and Nigeria being attacked by "skin heads" and neo-Nazis in the streets of Germany; and the rickety armadas of Haitian refugees being shipped back from American ports to their homeland augur more desperate times which developed nations will find more difficult to overlook.

The possibility of such catastrophes occurring was predicted by Aldo Leopold in his classic conservation primer, *A Sand County Alamanac.* According to his studies of deer, when the natural enemies of these animals is removed, their populations grow rapidly. Then, because of crowding and competition for limited space and food, their numbers are decimated by starvation and disease. Leopold reveals a grim similarity between the graphs of the rise in the deer populations and in the present growth of human population. Outcomes are no different for man and beast. The crisis is already bringing the beast out of men.[86]

Religion is at the core of the population crisis. "Of all entrenched values, religion presents perhaps the greatest obstacle to population control. Roman Catholics have fought against national family-planning efforts in Mexico, Kenya and the Philippines, while Muslim fundamentalists have done the same in Iran, Egypt and Pakistan."[87]

U.S. contributions to population control diminished after President Ronald Reagan cut support for family planning programs from $290 million in 1985 to $230 million in 1988. The slash signified his administration's opposition to funding programs involving abortion. When George Bush was the U.S representative to the United Nations, he wrote in 1973 that "success in the population field" might "determine whether we can resolve successfully the other great questions of peace, prosperity and individual rights that face the world."[88] As president, Bush switched to Reagan's policy out of fear of Republican right-wingers who proclaim they are "pro-life." In the realities of the

Third World, that slogan veils a policy that is pro-death. Now with President Bill Clinton in office, the pre-Reagan U.S. policies on family planning are being restored.

The Problem of the Nuclear Epidemic

For forty years the world lived with the constant threat of a nuclear holocaust. Suddenly, with the collapse of the Soviet Union, the world breathed a sigh of relief that the prospects of a doomsday had now ended. The United States was now the only military superpower, and it could be counted upon to keep the world safe from incinerating itself. That reprieve was short-lived. By early 1992, a more ominous threat to planetary survival mushroomed in the form of "the nuclear epidemic." Cover stories in our national magazines shocked us with the news that "the West's attempt to prevent the spread of nuclear weapons has failed, and a dangerous new era of nuclear proliferation has begun."[89]

First, let us trace this epidemic to its source. In an incisive piece, David Doyle, novelist and veteran of the OSS, CIA, and U.S. Foreign Service, observes that the conversion of the fifteen Soviet republics into the Commonwealth of Independent States (CIS) has created some worrisome situations. One problem is "the future of some 33,000 strategic and tactical nuclear weapons, and uncounted amounts of military nerve agents." Another problem is that "a few of the newly independent states, notably Armenia and Azerbaijan, are able and willing to use modern weapons against each other on a scale that can quickly become outright war."[90]

Doyle believes that whereas the prospects of CIS members doing battle with one another in a non-nuclear civil war are horrendous, resort to nuclear weaponry would be devastating for the whole world.

> Some 11,000 strategic (long range) missiles are temporarily controlled by CIS armed forces commander Marshal Yevgeny Shaposhnikov, and the firing codes are presumably in the hands of Russian President Boris Yeltsin. These weapons are mostly in Russia, with some in Ukraine, Kazhakhstan and perhaps Belorus. Hopefully, none of these states seems likely to try to use them before they are destroyed.
>
> But the other two-thirds, some 22,000 tactical nuclear weapons, constitute a different story. These weapons—the

smallest as powerful as the bomb that obliterated Hiroshima—
are spread over the former U.S.S.R. . . .

Despite assurances from the CIS, revelations of theft of
huge amounts of military assets by former Communist Party
leaders (such as the Kola Society) for sale in the private sector
are very unsettling. Also, hungry and disillusioned military
weapons specialists are reportedly already filtering out of the
CIS with their technology if not with actual hardware. There
are a lot of willing buyers out there, ready to pay cash: North
Korea, Libya, Iran, Iraq, Pakistan, India, to mention a few.[91]

In February of 1992, CIA Director Robert Gates told a congressional committee that the North Koreans were only a few
months away from building an atomic bomb. This puts South
Korea and Japan under a potential nuclear threat and jeopardizes
the safety of 39,500 U.S. troops in South Korea. North Korea is
ruled by Kim Il Sung, a dictator who launched the Korean War in
1950, and who has practiced international terrorism. To make
the bomb, he has repeatedly had to deceive the International
Atomic Energy Agency. With the clock ticking on North Korea's
nuclear bomb, interested nations face a dilemma: "They can
either stand by and watch an 80-year-old megalomaniac arm himself with nuclear weapons. Or they can take out Yongbyon and
risk war with North Korea. It is a fateful choice, but it cannot be
avoided."[92]

The Gulf War revealed that the West had seriously underestimated the timetable for Saddam Hussein's atomic program. The
Iraqi Manhattan Project was very close to making Iraq a nuclear
power. As terms of surrender, the United Nations had ordered the
Iraqis to destroy their nuclear plant. Iraq has been denying that it
was trying to produce nuclear weapons, but UN inspection officials have uncovered evidence of an extensive program that was
close to developing a warhead.

The cases of North Korea and Iraq illustrate two points of
international gravity. First, in respect to making a nuclear bomb,
things that were very difficult for great scientists in 1943 are now
relatively easy. Second, the collapse of the economy of the former
Soviet Union has unloaded supplies of uranium ore and other
nuclear materials onto world markets, and inspectors warn that
"it may be only a matter of time before more dangerous products,
including tons of plutonium from spent Soviet reactor fuel and
perhaps even uranium-processing technology from the Central

Asian republics, reach the black market."[93] The stark economy is also driving Russian physicists and multiple warhead specialists to sell their expertise to Third World countries willing to pay several hundred times their former salaries.

Privately U.S. officials concede that their system to prevent the spread of nuclear weapons, based on a strategy of secrecy, export controls, and inspections of civilian nuclear reactors, has failed. Victory in the Gulf War presented an opportunity to make this passive system into an assertive nonproliferation system, but that opening was not seized. Consequently, a new and much more dangerous era of nuclear proliferation has now begun.

HINDU ENVIRONMENTAL ETHICS

In the previous section we examined the current environmental crisis with reference to the biosphere, global warming, waste, pollution, population, and nuclear proliferation. *These are our latest killing fields.* Our devastation of the environment is the result of our fundamental failure to be able to see the planet as "a single abode."

As a result, we have thrown ourselves all the way back to our primitive beginnings, in which the dominant problem on earth was coping with the environment. The only difference between our tribal beginnings and the situation today is that the problems now are of our own making. The killing fields represent our tragic failure to manage this planet. Through our capacity for invention and our sense of creative splendor, we have found little difficulty to make the earth *accessible*, but never *manageable*. Now the price of our survival is the management of our planet.[94]

This calls for a "philosophy of the whole" and for "a new education" in the comprehension and management of our planet.[95] It will be not so much a test of our skill but of our philosophy, for "everything begins—or ends—with a view of life."[96] Conservationist Aldo Leopold argues for the need of a land ethic as the next step toward productive ways of relating to our natural environment.

> The first ethics dealt with the relationship between individuals. The Mosaic Decalogue is an example. Later accretions dealt with the relationship between the individual and society. Christianity tries to integrate the individual to society, Democracy to integrate social organization to the individual.

There is yet no ethic dealing with man's relationship to land and to non-human animals and plants which grow upon it. Land, like Odysseus's slave-girls, is still property. The land relation is strictly economic, entailing privileges but not obligations.[97]

It is the contention of this study that the sort of land ethic Leopold is pleading for may be found in the ecological insights of Hinduism. Hindu philosophy is a rich repository of ideas, attitudes, and values which can furnish the necessary principles for a proper management of our physical environment. We propose (1) to sketch the development of these ideas; (2) to outline the ecological principles derived from them; (3) and then to see how these principles may be applied to the problems of the biosphere, global warming, waste, and so on.

The first glimmers of Indian environmental thinking are suggested by the excavations of the Indus Valley civilization (3000–1500 B.C.). The pre-Āryan religion of this time is captured in figurines of a mother goddess and representations of a horned god accompanied by animals and plants. The prominence given to fertility suggests a religious orientation in which nature plays a central role.

This fecund religion of the Indus Valley was one source of the Hindu tradition as it took root in the Vedic age (1500–600 B.C.). A second source was the religion of the people who spoke the Dravidian languages and whose deities were also zoomorphic. Animals were revered so highly that they were considered fit to symbolize the gods. These precedents contributed to the making of Vedic religion into a terrestrial communion in which nature was alive! Embree explains:

> The agricultural life of the people combined with the special features of the Indian climate—the brilliance of the sunshine, the clarity of the atmosphere, the easy beneficence quickly altering to harsh malevolence—made the people sensitive to the natural world. Much of the imagery of the poetry and religion can be understood as the response of the imagination to a Nature that seemed living and animate.[98]

An example of the poet's sensitivity to the natural world is the compendium of hymns to Uṣas, goddess of Dawn. They typify the resonance felt by the ancient Indians between the phenomenal world and human concerns. "Perhaps at this early stage can be seen the characteristic tendency of Indian literature to see nature as a frame for human emotions. The natural world is not understood as something apart from man, but as a reflection of his moods and passions."[99]

Like Uṣas, Araṇyāni, tutelary goddess of the forest and wilderness, is celebrated and worshiped. The forest (araṇya) is perceived as different from the village (grāma). Life in the forest is seen as harmonious, with songs of many birds and creatures, cattle grazing, wagons carrying heavy loads of harvest, and wood-choppers felling trees. The "Forest Queen" is praised as "sweet-scented, redolent of balm." She is "Mother of all sylvan things, who tills not but hath stores of food." The picture is clearly one of balance and prosperity. "Man eats of savory fruit and then takes, even as he wills, his rest." But though this "Lady of the Wood" is an object of familiar beauty, the element of mystery dominates. Part of the mystery is Araṇyāni's capacity to strike back. "The Goddess never slays, unless some murderous enemy approach."[100]

The heart of Vedic worship was rituals intended to adapt the beneficent powers of nature to human needs. The gods to whom the prayers were addressed granted favors but were, in turn, dependent on humans for offerings in yajña. The picture is one of interrelationship and interdependence between people and the great cosmic forces that were deified. The gods also helped one another and often worked in pairs, indicating the systemic integration of natural forces.[101]

This highlights a significant feature of Vedic religion: the notion of cosmic law. Philosophers were not content to study human nature only, but turned their speculations on the larger world of nature to which humans belonged. They viewed the external world as an ordered whole, presided over by nature gods. Indeed, the gods are invented to account for the cosmic character of the universe.

The ideas of order and unity are strengthened as the religion evolves toward monothesim and monism. The notion of physical order is combined with a belief in ethical order, and both are brought together in the concept of ṛta. It was early recognized that there were certain proper ways of relating, both to people and to animate and inanimate objects, and that these forms of relating merited rewards and punishments. Consequences counted. Cosmogonic speculations entertained theories of creation and evolution. The early notion that the universe was created by the gods was superseded by the effort to find origins in some primary principle.

Among the early cosmogonic hymns, the Hymn to Goddess Earth invites attention. The earth is lauded as a mistress: "the golden-breasted resting-place of all living creatures." No discrimination is made between humans and other species: "The mortals born of thee live on thee, thou supportest both bipeds and quadrupeds."[102] There is also an awareness of conservation: "What, O earth, I dig out of thee, quickly shall that grow again: may I not, O pure one, pierce thy vital spot, (and) not thy heart!"[103] Most profoundly, the Hymn to the Earth (Pṛthivī) expresses the conviction that the land which sustains and supports us is the embodiment of the divine Mother:

O Earth, thy centre and thy navel, all forces that have issued from thy body—
Set us amid those forces; breathe upon us. I am the son of Earth, Earth is my Mother.[104]

The summit of the Vedic age is reached in the teachings of the Upaniṣads. Here, the highest ideal is not living in harmony with the will of the gods or sacrificial rectitude, but self-knowledge. Vedic ceremonialism and caste duties give way to a new spiritual quest which turns inward for the purpose of understanding Ultimate Reality.

The motivation behind this introspective search is the fundamental idea running through the early Upaniṣads that "underlying the exterior world of change there is an unchangeable reality which is identical with that which underlies the essence of man."[105] "Verily, he is the great, unborn Soul, who is this [person] consisting of knowledge among the senses. In the space within the heart lies the ruler of all, the lord of all, the king of all."[106]

The formulation of this ideal was a long time in the making. Summarily stated, the Upaniṣadic sages synthesized two notions which originally had totally different connotations, namely, *Brahman*, or the ultimate source of the external world, and *ātman*, or the inner self of the person. These sages teach that the *Brahman* of

the macrocosm is none other than the *ātman* of the microcosm—
"That self is, indeed Brahman."[107] With *Brahman* equated with
ātman, each term came to signify the eternal ground of the universe, including the ground of the being of humankind and the
being of nature.

The Upaniṣads also witnessed the development of the doctrine
of karma, which, as the law of cause and effect, early attracted the
Indian mind. The Vedic hymns are connected by the conviction
that one thing we can be certain of in this world is that whatever
we do must have consequences. *Ṛta*, or order, is an inescapable
fact of life, which is binding on mortals and gods alike. Herein are
the germs of the doctrine of karma, which, by the time the earliest
Upaniṣads were written, is combined with the idea of rebirths. It is
held that the universe is so structured that the consequences of our
actions are inexorably played out into an unknown and unseen
future.

The Upaniṣads record diverse theories of creation. The most
succinct formulation is found in the Īśā Upaniṣad. Recognizing
the unity that underlies the diversity of the world, the sage
declares: "By the Lord (*īśā*) enveloped must this all be—Whatever
moving thing there is in the moving world."[108]

The epic and Purāṇic literature contain many imaginative theories of creation. In none of these stories are humans exalted over
other creatures. To the contrary, to be created human invests people, not with rights and privileges, but with responsibilities and
obligations.

Paralleling the Purāṇas are the Tantras, the scriptures of the
Śāktas. From the perspective of environmental thinking, it is interesting to note that the Mother Goddess motif we had first encountered in the pre-Āryan religion is here (A.D. 300–750) combined
with Āryan elements, giving prominence to the worship of Śakti, the
Divine Power personified as a goddess. In the form of Durga, the
goddess was identified with the Absolute of Vedānta philosophy.

Hindu environmental thinking reaches its apex in the philosophical sūtras of the six schools called *Darśanas,* or views of life.
We limit our remarks to the ecological insights of the two best-
known schools: Sāṃkhya and Vedānta.

The Sāṃkhya system is ontologically dualistic. It postulates
two uncreated, independent, and eternal principles known as
puruṣa and *prakṛti*. *Puruṣa*, the spiritual principle, and *prakṛti*,

the material principle, are the transcendental essences of our conscious and unconscious experiences. All experiences arise from this duality between *puruṣa*, the knower, and *prakṛti*, the known. Together they form the matrix from which the phenomenal universe evolves.

Prakṛti (nature), the changing object, is the *causa materialis* of the whole world of becoming. Sāṁkhya affirms the reality of matter. The theory of causality explaining this evolution is known as *pariṇāmavāda*. It holds that the effect is only a modification of the cause. The effect resides in the cause in a potential form prior to manifestation.

The existence of *prakṛti* is proved through inferential reasoning, and not by recourse to revelation. The nature of *prakṛti* is also explained by reason. Since the effect is only a modification of the cause, the nature of the cause can be deduced from the nature of the effect. Upon analysis, the physical universe is seen to possess three basic properties called *guṇas* (*sattva, rajas, tamas*); therefore it is concluded that the Unmanifest cause must also be characterized by similar constitutents.

When the *guṇas* are in a state of equilibrium, there is no evolution. The *guṇas* maintain their dynamic character, but do not interact with one another.

Change within unconscious *prakṛti* from the state of dissolution (*pralaya*) to that of evolution (*sarga*) is attributed to the proximity of conscious *puruṣa* (*Sannidhi matra*). Acting like a magnet, the presence of *puruṣa* draws the *guṇas* into a state of excitation, and so starts them off on their evolutionary cycle. By combining in various proportions, the *guṇas* give rise to the manifold variety in the physical world. The union between conscious though inactive *puruṣa* with active though unconscious *prakṛti* is compared to the union that exists between a blind man carrying a lame man on his shoulders. "From this union proceeds evolution."[109]

What is environmentally noteworthy in Sāṁkhya's theory of evolution is that, though the universe is viewed dualistically, spirit and matter are held together in a teleological balance. Further, unlike some systems in which spirit and matter are polarized as good and evil, the Sāṁkhya system suggests no such moral dualism. To the contrary, both the design and function of *prakṛti* are aimed at the liberation of *puruṣa*. The *Kārikā* says: "As the insentient milk flows out for the growth of the calf, so does Nature act towards the emancipation of spirit."[110] Hiriyanna comments:

> The noteworthy point here is the physical accompaniment of man as well as his environment is neither hostile or indifferent to his attaining the ideal of freedom. Through them rather, *Prakṛti* is ever educating him into a fuller knowledge of himself with a view to securing that result. Nature therefore, cannot in the end, be said to enslave spirit. In fact, it behaves towards man as a "veritable fairy godmother."[111]

The second of the *darśanas* to which we turn is the Vedānta system. The chief commentators are Śaṁkara (eighth century A.D.) and Rāmānuja (twelfth century A.D.). They provide us with nontheistic and theistic interpretations of the Vedānta, respectively. Śaṁkara's system is monistic, and is known as Advaita. Rāmānuja follows a qualified monism called Viśiṣṭādvaita.

The purpose of Advaita is the intuitive realization that there is one and only one Reality which is the negation of all plurality and difference. This rigorous monism is the key to Śaṁkara's system. It is capsulized in the well-known phrase: *Brahma satyaṁ jagan mithyā jīvo brahmaiva nā' parah* (*"Brahman* is real, the world is false, the self is not-different from *Brahman"*).

The environmental aspect of this affirmation is that *Brahman* is the sole Reality. It is the ground of all existence, and individuals in their essential being are identical with *Brahman*. To say that "the world is false" does not mean that the Advaitan thinks the world a phantom, something imaginary or nonexisting. The Advaitan is not a subjective Idealist, believing that there is no extramental reality and that all we see and know are only ideas in our mind which are falsely thought to be outside the mind. To the contrary, the world as we see it does indeed exist outside our consciousness and has positive content. Yet it is unreal. How?

For the Advaitan, the test of truth consists in what might be called "unsublatedness." A thing is untrue or unreal when it is sublated by a subsequent experience. That alone is true or real which is unsublated or noncontradicted (*abādhita*) by subsequent experience.

Judged by this test of truth, the world is both real (*sat*) and unreal (*asat*). It is real because it has a positive, concrete existence, and to that extent is not an hallucination. It is unreal because it does not meet the test of Reality, being impermanent and subject to constant alterations. The ecological meaning of this philosophic reasoning is that the truth of Reality lies in its pervasive unity, and therefore to think of the world as separate or independent entity is to indulge in an illusion.

Next, we look at Rāmānuja's qualified nondualism. According to Rāmānuja, *Brahman* is not a characterless identity; it possesses features and qualities. He agrees with Śaṁkara that *Brahman* has nothing different from it, of either a like kind or unlike kind. But he disagrees with Śaṁkara that *Brahman* is without internal differences. He asserts that *Brahman* is the sole Reality. There is nothing besides *Brahman*. But *Brahman* is a determinate being, having internal differences, and it maintains its identity in and through the differences internal to it.

Thus *Brahman* is an organism which sustains, as parts integral to it, the world of matter (*acit*) and the world of souls (*cit*). These two orders are internal to *Brahman*, and though dependent on *Brahman* and grounded in it, cannot ever be resolved away into an indistinguishable identity with it.

Rāmānuja uses various analogies to describe this total integrity called *Brahman*. One is the relation between the soul and the body it animates. *Brahman* is the soul, and the world of matter and the world of individual souls constitute the body which the soul animates. The body is indeed distinct from the soul, and though it is distinct it has only a dependent and subordinate existence because the body cannot survive without the soul.

Another example is the relation between substance and qualities. Qualities are distinct from the substance, and yet they have only a dependent existence and can never have a self-subsistent existence. They are totally dependent on the substance. Substance and quality together constitute a unity—not a simple and bare unity, but the unity of a complex whole. Brahman, the world, and individuals constitute such a whole.

This brief survey has shown that Hindus have reflected long and hard on the relation of God to humans, God to physical nature, and people to the world. These assumptions serve as the backdrop for formulating ethical principles that are both philosophically valid and environmentally sound. First, we shall articulate what these principles are in the context of the current environmental debate; and we shall then attempt to apply them to actual situations.

The Principle of Unity

Indian speculative wisdom is essentially unitive and cosmic. The Upaniṣadic sages behold the Supreme Being as manifest in all creation. "Verily, the Soul is the overlord of all things, the king of all things. As all the spokes are held together in the hub and felly of a wheel, just so in this Soul of all things, all gods, all worlds, all breathing things, all selves are held together."[112]

The cosmic manifestation of the Supreme Being is expressed in evolutionary terms. Evolution is progressive and spiritual. It starts with matter in which the Spirit lies dormant. From a lifeless stone, Spirit rises to the level of life and manifests itself in the vegetable kingdom. It then ascends to the level of consciousness, manifesting itself in the animal kingdom. From consciousness it progresses to the level of intelligence, and takes form in the kingdom of humans. The most perfect state is that of pure Spirit, in which matter lies dormant and Spirit manifests itself as pure bliss in the Supreme Spirit.

Thus all the world is a stage, and each life form is a unique player. They have their exits and their entrances, and the One Spirit plays many parts. Matter is in tension with Spirit, but Spirit, step by evolutionary step, comes into its own. The Bhagavadgītā summarizes this cosmic scenario thus: "Unmanifest is the origin of beings, manifest their mid-most stage, and unmanifest again their end."[113]

That which precedes and succeeds the evolutionary process is shrouded in mystery because it is outside the pale of time. As mortals in this planetary theater, we cannot apprehend how the Divine Actor divided itself into subject and object and commenced this evolutionary show. Nor can we tell how Spirit shall prevail over matter so that the original perfection is finally restored. All that we know at this stage of history is that there is movement, that this movement is progressive and spiritual, and that the divine plan for human life is that we join the creative ascent of the Spirit. To have this knowledge is to be able to distinguish the relative merits of material, biological, intellectual, and spiritual values.

Such is the unitive vision of Hinduism. It is rationally held, but it derives its strength from subliminal springs. The conviction is religious, but it permeates the whole culture, including all the arts and sciences.

The cosmic vision of Hinduism sees humans as an intrinsic part of nature. The fabric of life has many special strands, and human beings are special in their own rights by virtue of their moral character; but this does not place them outside nature or above nature. *Distinction*, not *separation*, is the hallmark of the Hindu view of the· position of humans in nature. The unitive thinking of Hinduism aligns it with a "deep ecology" which places people *in nature*, as opposed to a "shallow ecology" which is anthropocentric and which ascribes to *Homo sapiens* a position of dominance and superiority *over nature*.

The unitive thinking of Hinduism is also attuned to the holographic model, and to the new paradigm of science in which there is a radical shift from the parts to the whole. As described by Fritjof Capra, "In the old paradigm it was believed that in any complex system, the dynamics of the whole could be understood from the properties of the parts. In the new paradigm the relationship between the parts and the whole is reversed. The properties of the parts can be understood only from the dynamics of the whole. Ultimately there are no parts at all. What we call a part is merely a pattern in an inseparable web of relationships."[114]

In the context of the new physics, the Hindu paradigm is clearly holistic, emphasizing the whole over the parts. Yet it would be more precise to describe Hindu ethics as being *ecological* rather than holistic. The distinction is fine, but important. Holistic thinking sees an entity in all of its complex relationships. For example, holistic medicine is sensitive to the body-mind relationship, and to how all parts of the human organism function together. Ecological thinking is also holistic, but it expands the unity to encompass larger systems which are all dynamically related. In Hindu ecological thinking the microuniverse is one with the macrouniverse. The individual is a child both of earth and of the distant stars.

The philosophic contribution of the unitive worldview of Hindu ethics is that it avoids the dichotomies that have characterized Western religious, philosophic, and scientific thinking— dichotomies between God and man, between God and the world, and between people and nature. This split-thinking is now scientifically discredited as being completely dysfunctional in the task of tackling environmental problems.

More positively, the unitive, evolutionary view of Hindu environmental ethics engenders respect and reverence as the *natural* way of looking at things in the world. They are all parts, but none is *apart*, for each is a part of the whole, and just as a spark of fire is the fire, so also each item of nature is instinct with spiritual life.

This awareness of biotic and spiritual connectedness has engendered in the Hindu mind an attitude of noninjury to all living creatures, as expressed in the doctrine of *ahiṃsā*. It is one thing to know of the continuity of humans and physical nature in terms of the biological evolutionism taught by Darwin, and quite something else to be inwardly aware of the fundamental unity of all life. The latter affects the whole person and mobilizes the individual to act responsibly toward the weaker links in the chain of life.

Eliot Deutsch argues that if the unitive thinking of Vedānta were fully assimilated, it "would rule out the possibility of any gross exploitation of nature and of ourselves."

> It is certainly one of the greatest follies of man that he still believes that, as an individual (whether in corporated or not), he has an inalienable right to exploit and destroy nature for his own personal gain, or indeed for the mere satisfaction of his own idiosyncratic taste. But surely nature does not *belong* to anyone. The idea of *possessing* or *owning* nature is utterly alien to Vedānta, as it ought to be to any sophisticated spiritual perspective. "Possession" has no meaning where there is no real possessor. If everything in nature is already one's own basic self, and the self of all others, then clearly no single individual or group of individuals can lay claim to it. God, if he exists, is certainly some kind of socialist. And if the Hindu gods laugh, as assuredly they do, then the skies over India must rock from time to time with hilarity over some men's nonsensical claims to ownership of the universe. The Hindu god Śiva, the god of destruction, is certainly quickening the steps of his cosmic dance, pleased that man has been so cooperative with him in his work of destruction.[115]

The Principle of Interconnectedness

The unitive orientation of the Indian mind has predisposed it to account for natural and human processes in terms of the principle of interconnectedness. The concept of *ṛta* representing the "immanent dynamic order" was an early formulation of this principle that linked cause and effect. Order was not something imposed by the gods from outside, but was the internal function of the universe to which all beings, including the gods, were subject. Later, *ṛta* gave rise to the notion of *dharma*, meaning "what holds together," and thus the basis of all order. The operative element of *dharma* is the law of karma, which, as far back as 1000 B.C., was affirmed thus by Indian *rishis*: "According as one acts, according as one conducts himself, so does he become."[116]

This notion of causality has given to Indian thinking a consequentialist bent which evaluates things in terms of their connectedness. Deutsch deftly brings out the relevance of the doctrine of karma for environmental planning.

> According to the doctrine of *karman*, every deed or act that one performs has its effect in the world and forms a "tendency" (*saṃskāra* or *vāsanā*) within the doer to act in a similar way in the future; to form, in other words, a *habit* of action. This habit of action produces further consequences in the actor and in the world and, accordingly, the wheel of life turns around and around. Whatever one does will have effects not only in the immediate present but in the long future as well: any act, in short, will have consequences that reach out far beyond the act itself. And everything in nature is so interconnected through causal chains and relationships that we ourselves become part of the natural process and are conditioned by it.[117]

The environmental crisis is basically made up of two factors; one, our belief that we are somehow separate from nature, referred to above, and two, our willingness to ignore the consequences of our actions. The latter problem proceeds from our myopic vision that concentrates on current needs and short-term issues. With little faith in the future, we find it difficult to assess the impact of our actions on future generations, and act as if the future is now.

One example is the DDT poisoning, notwithstanding the warnings of pesticide abuse by such brave pioneers as Rachel Carson in her classic book, *Silent Spring*. For a time, government officials refused to look beyond short-term profits for long-term consequences.

Another example of foreshortened thinking was the use of the herbicide Agent Orange in the Vietnam War. The military focus was solely concentrated on the ability of this poison to obliterate the lush groundcover, making it easier to shoot the enemy out in the open. The effects of this herbicide on the soldiers, causing chromosomal damage and producing cancer, were not given a second thought. Particularly painful was the tragedy for the family of Admiral Elmo Zumwalt, who authorized the use of Agent Orange, because it made casualties of his veteran son and grandson. Wary of the fact that all chemicals have extraordinarily powerful effects on the world around us, Al Gore asks:

> How can we be sure that a chemical has only those powers we desire and not others we don't? Are we really taking enough time to discover their long-term effects? Agent Orange, after all, is just one of the better-known examples of a whole new generation of powerful compounds created in the chemical revolution, which picked up speed after World War II; over the past fifty years, herbicides, pesticides, fungicides, chlorofluorocarbons (CFCs), and thousands of other compounds have come streaming out of our laboratories and chemical plants faster than we can possibly keep track of them. All of them are supposed to improve our lives, and hundreds of them have done so. But too many have left a legacy of poison that we will be coming to terms with for many generations.[118]

In addition to the consequential side of interconnectedness, there is the causal side. The ecological standpoint encompasses a view of the whole, and comprehends how the diverse parts of nature interact with one another, reaching toward a balance that is sustained through time.

The principle of interconnectedness demands that we should not compartmentalize the planet from the civilization that exists upon it. Civilization is part of that planetary whole, and when we view the whole we are viewing ourselves as constitutive of the whole. The sun and the sea are among the natural forces which interact with one another, but people, no less than Pinatubo, are a force of nature, and if this feature of human causality is not assessed, then we will not be able to see how the pressures of civilization are throwing the planet off balance.

The Principle of Interdependence

If reality is one, if all parts of the whole are interconnected, then interdependence must define the mode of ecological relationships.

Hinduism's earliest expression of interdependence takes shape within the dynamics of an awesome sense of all-encompassing natural forces, and is ritualized in the magico-religious form of *yajña*.

Through sacrifice the worshiper attempted to secure earthly blessings because it was believed that the generative properties of nature were maintained by the gods, who in turn depended on humans to sustain them through oblations. Offerings to these divinized forms of natural phenomena acknowledged that to ensure fertility, humans must harmonize their lives with the energy of the sun, the wind, water, and fire. Delicate exercises had to be observed to make sure that the mechanisms did not go wrong.

In time, Hinduism outgrew the magical aspects of *yajña*, but its sense of interdependence in the world at large persisted when the gods were seen as multiple manifestations of the One Source of creative energy, diversified in myriad life forms.

The most inclusive declaration of interdependence is found in the notion of *ṛna*. The *ṛnas* represent the congenital debts which each individual owes: to the sages, to the ancestors, and to the gods. These obligations are satisfied by study, by begetting a family, and by offering sacrifices. The underlying ethical principle is to give back what one has received. Through reciprocity, balance is maintained and welfare is assured. Manu warns that the person who seeks liberation without fulfilling his obligations incurs hurtful consequences (*vrajatyadhah*).[119]

We propose that the traditional notion of *ṛna-traya* be made more inclusive by expanding the Hindu's obligations to society to include *obligations to the land*. We may designate this as the fourth debt or *caturtha-ṛna*, and call it *bhū-ṛna*. It should stand for our obligations to the *Bhūmi*, mankind's terrestrial home. This proposal is not as innovative as it appears because the elements essential for reciprocal land relationships are vitally embodied in the ancient theme of the earth as Mother Goddess.

Pṛthivī, the Goddess Earth is generally invoked with Heaven (Dyaus), the parents of the universe. Maurer observes that the concept of Pṛthivī in the Ṛgveda (5.84) "is much broader than ours might be of an Earth goddess, as it includes also the atmosphere or area of the rainclouds just above the earth. Pṛthivī in this extended sense . . . is looked upon as a great animator of all things as well as the physical support of the mountain and the trees of her surface."[120]

In her role as Mother, Pṛthivī is described as Agni's womb (S.B. 7.4.1,8) which receives the embryo of existences (A.V. 5.25,2). Pṛthivī vivifies the earth with her might, but she also undergoes pain when there are too many mouths to feed, extracting from her more than she can supply. And so she cries: "I cannot endure all these people," and beseeches Brahmā to reduce the population. Brahmā creates Death, who, in the form of a beautiful woman, sheds tears of sorrow which become fatal diseases.[121]

The metaphor of Earth as divine Mother is aptly chosen in the Hindu tradition because it fosters ties of kinship and evokes sentiments of care and protection. In fact, there is something elemental about this motif because it reaches back to the Indo-European peoples, and further, to mankind in general.[122]

But beyond the stuff of myths, ecologists have scientifically traced "the complex reciprocities and mutualities among organisms, the food chains linking diverse species, the interlocking cycles of elements and compounds, and the delicate balances that are easily upset."[123] The very concept of the "ecosystem" carries the meaning of the interdependence of all forms of life in biotic communities, and underscores the long-range damage that can be incurred by thoughtless human intervention. Al Gore:

> In distinguishing between what is still uncertain and what is known about this crisis, it is important to emphasize that one thing we know quite well is that nature exhibits a recurring pattern of interdependency among the parts of the ecological system. We should assume with great confidence that if we upset the ecological balance of the entire earth in one way, we will upset it in related ways as well. Consequently, while a given behavior may at first seem harmless in that part of the environment we are able to observe, we are unlikely to know enough about the effects of what we are doing to predict the consequences for other parts of the system—precisely because all its parts exist in a delicate balance of interdependency.[124]

The Principle of Restraint

Ever since the Industrial Revolution, Western societies have made of *pleonexia* a commonplace. This has been expecially true of the United States, which is the world's biggest user of natural resources and a major despoiler of the global environment. Because of the magnitude of its economy, the U.S. consumes one-fourth of the world's energy each year. Yet, for a given amount of energy, it produces less than half as much economic output as

Japan or Germany. Therefore the issue is not just one of size but of greed and waste.

During the oil embargo of the early 1970s and 1980s, when energy was scarce and expensive, Americans tightened their belts and were economically more productive. Between 1973 to 1985, our per capita energy consumption fell 12 percent, and the average amount of goods and services per person rose 17 percent. However, since those lean years, energy prices have been reduced, with a corresponding rise in energy consumption. "Americans, who own more than 135 million cars, or about one-third of the world's total, have been driving more and have resumed their love affair with large gas-guzzling cars."[125]

Such prodigal ways cannot go on indefinitely because our resources are not limitless, and when those that are nonrenewable are consumed or transformed, they can never be replenished. The specter of "Old Mother Hubbard" requires that we redefine economic growth. Time-honored principles of industry, such as economic growth based on increasing expansion and consumption, must now be questioned and corrected.

The problem is not only economic but moral. No nation has the moral right to overutilize the world's resources for its own selfish interests, without thought for future generations and the survival needs of poor people.

Emphasizing the need for a conservation ethic, Kenneth Boulding held that it is "more likely to be found in Eastern religions than in the Judeo-Christian tradition," and therefore he urged Western societies to enter a genuine dialogue with Asian religions.

> It may be that India, for instance, had to adjust to a highly conservationist economy before the West had to do it, simply because the West has always been more expansionist geographically and hence should preserve the illusion of the illimitable plane for a longer period. There is a paradox here, in that the scientific revolution could probably have taken place only in the West, precisely because of the Western expansionism and aggressiveness and the concept of man as the conqueror of nature. The East has never had any illusions about being able to conquer nature, and has always regarded man as living in a somewhat precarious position, as a guest of doubtful welcome, shall we say, in the great household of the natural world.[126]

Actually, India's conservationist attitude is less a matter of exigency as of ethics. The principle of restraint was early built into the Hindu mind's enchantment with renunciation. The hero in Hinduism is not the warrior but the ascetic. This is not to say that the pursuit of wealth is discouraged, but that it is always subject to the concerns of morality. *Artha* is relative to *dharma*.

Hindu ethics therefore does not reject growth, for that would consign the Third World to continued poverty and disease. Rather, it steers a path between "pro-growth" and "no-growth" and advocates a position of selective growth based on equity and quality.

In the name of global justice, the principle of restraint requires that the economic growth of advanced nations be directed toward services that are not resource intensive; and in the name of ecological wisdom the principle of restraint requires that wealthy nations limit their consumption and use their vast resources for research and development to produce technologies for recycling and waste reduction.

Having identified the environmental principles of Hinduism, our next task is to see how these ideas of *unity, interconnectedness, interdependence*, and *restraint* are able to address the environmental problems of biodiversity, global warming, waste, population, and nuclear proliferation.

Biodiversity   On biodiversity, the problem is that people are recklessly exterminating life on earth. It has been predicted that over the next thirty years, humans will force one hundred species into extinction every day. Given its evolutionary outlook, Hinduism accepts extinction as part of life, but such vast killings are *hiṃsā* in its gravest form, for the wiping out of whole ecosystems—nature's laboratories of new life forms—constitutes the "death of birth."

Biodiversity has caught the public attention by featuring high-profile animals such as elephants, tigers and rhinos. But Hinduism's nondiscriminatory view of all lifeforms also calls attention to the plight of the *lowliest plants and insects*. When these species disappear unnoticed, "they take with them hard-won lessons of survival encoded in their genes over millions of years."[127]

Where the war on plants and animals is spurred by simple greed, Hindu morality condemns it as unworthy of human beings.

Where the destruction is caused by poverty and population, as developing nations struggle to feed their burgeoning numbers and raise cash to make payments on international debts, Hindu ethics is sensitive to the moral and practical difficulties of their situation. On the one hand, wealthy developed nations ask the debtor nations to deliver on their interest-laden payments, and on the other hand they want their clients to preserve, for the welfare of the world, the very forests which they chop down to finance those debts. For many Third World countries it is a crisis of survival: they do not have the luxury of being concerned about global biodiversity when they must first feed their children.

Compassion requires that the rich nations reduce the debt burden of the poor countries. This plea was heard repeatedly at the Earth Summit, where poverty was described as the world's "quiet emergency." It was deeply felt that the most difficult aspect of moving toward sustainable development was the divide between North and South. Calls were heard for the North to accept big debt write-offs in the South.

At the same time, the poor countries must become aware of the economic consequences of their short-term expedients, such as deforestation. In the long run this is bound to backfire when their precious resources are depleted and the life forms they support become extinct. They then kill the goose that lays the golden egg. Karmically stated, a quick economic return often has a long fuse.

In order to prevent this from happening, environmental reviews should be conducted at the time when loans are being negotiated in the effort to prevent local banks from supporting projects that wipe out species. Also, governments, businesses, and the general populace need to be educated in the value of genetic diversity, and be shown that when habitats are destroyed the loss of the species living in those habitats is irreversible.

On the constructive side, "gene banks" should be set up in places such as zoos to perpetuate species; and projects should be created to validate the fact that, with judicious planning, endangered habitats can be developed into profitable enterprises, without necessarily incurring their depletion or demise.

Further, the myth must be laid to rest that the preservation of biodiversity is intrinsically opposed to economic returns. This misperception was articulated by Secretary of State James Baker at a forum in Princeton, New Jersey. Defending the decision of the Bush administration not to sign a treaty at the Earth Summit intended to preserve the diversity of plant and animal life, and citing controversial provisions about patents, advanced biological genetic engineering and funding as the reasons, Baker declared, "This so called biodiversity treaty . . . would put people out of business in this country."[128]

The position of Hindu ethics has always been: *artha* and *dharma* can coexist. The experience of the ancient Indian *vaidya* who cultivated exotic plants for the development of a profitable pharmacopoeia demonstrates that there are dividends from diversity. The following are modern examples of the harvesting of unexpected benefits from exotic plants and animals:

- Squibb used the venom of the Brazilian pit viper to develop Capoten, a drug for high blood pressure.
- By transplanting genes from tropical tomatoes, the NPI biotech firm increased the density of U.S. tomatoes 2 percent, promising catsup manufacturers extra profits.
- Scientists believe that arcelin, a natural protein in wild Mexican beans that repels insects, might protect some U.S. crops without poisoning soil and water.
- Future newspapers may be printed on paper from kenaf, an African plant that can produce five times as much pulp an acre than the trees normally cut for newsprint.[129]

In addition to such facts, the position that the preservation of biodiversity can only be purchased at the expense of jobs is at odds with developments in Japan and Germany. These countries are recognizing that a new world order is being born and that in this green revolution there will be an increasing demand for environmentally friendly products, and they are technologically preparing to become leaders in this global market. If this is correct, then the pitting of jobs against the preservation of biodiversity is a false choice. It is antithetical to a major way in which the world is today beginning to think, and tomorrow will begin to buy.

An alarming feature of the Bush administration was the operation of the White House Council on Competitiveness, headed by Vice President Dan Quayle. It had the power to grant exceptions to the Endangered Species Act, and in this capacity was dubbed the "God Squad." In May 1992, over the protests of the administrator of America's Environmental Protection Agency, William Reilly, Quayle's committee gave loggers permission to cut down 688 hectares (1,700 acres) of ancient forest in the Pacific Northwest. Asked by reporters about the "God Squad," Reilly responded, with a touch of bitterness, that it was "a group of people, of which I am a minor divinity, which has the power to blow away a species."[130]

There can be no room for a "God Squad" within the Hindu pantheon. The Vaiṣṇava tradition connects the evolution of animal life forms with divine incarnations, moving upward from fish, to amphibians, to mammals, and to humans. Karan Singh points out: "This view clearly holds that man did not spring fully formed to dominate the lesser lifeforms, but rather evolved out of these forms himself, and is, therefore, integrally linked to the whole of creation."[131]

If indeed there were room for a "God Squad" in the Hindu fold, the strong ones would be obligated to protect the weak ones. Gandhi incorporated this value into his teachings on cow protection. He thought cow protection was "the gift of Hinduism to the world." It symbolized the protection of the weak by the strong. It subsumed everything that feels. Causing pain even to the lowliest creatures on earth was a breach of the principle of "cow protection."[132]

Incidentally, "cow protection" in Hinduism should be seen as illustrative of the combination of utility and sanctity. All animals are sacred, but the cow is held specially so. It is the darling of Lord Kṛṣṇa, and is a goddess who embodies several divinities. Yet all of this veneration proceeds from the utilitarian role of the cow within an agrarian economy.

Global Warming   The second problem Hindu ethics must confront is global warming. The danger looming over our planet is that greenhouse gases could bring about a climatic calamity. The dust from Mount Pinatubo has had the effect of global cooling, but this temporary phenomenon is not expected to exceed 1° F for the next few years, after which the greenhouse warming will again pick up.

Global warming was the second area in which Washington took the heat at the Earth Summit. The Bush administration was roundly criticized because its negotiators succeeded in softening a major treaty to control the emission of carbon dioxide and other gases said by some scientists to cause global warming. Here, too, the reasons given by Washington for its go-slow policy were the costs involved in modernizing business to cut down on gases, the lack of scientific evidence that global warming is now taking place, and the hazards involved in making future projections.[133]

Our argument is that if the levels of greenhouse gases are on the rise, as the 1991 National Academy of Sciences' report attests, then the problem needs addressing. The academy said: "In the absence of greater human effort to the contrary, greenhouse gas concentrations equivalent to a doubling of the pre-industrial level of CO_2 will occur by the middle of the next century.[134]

In keeping with the conservationist element of Hindu ethics, nations should promote energy conservation by implementing energy efficiencies; limiting warming gases at 1990 levels by the year 2000; reducing dependency on coal, oil, and gas; utilizing renewable resources; taxing carbon dioxide emissions in excess of set standards; implementing alternate energy sources such as solar power; harnessing methane gas expelled from landfills and cattle feedlots; banning the production of CFCs used in the manufacture of plastic foam and as coolants in refrigerators and air conditioners; and in general, greening the energy system.

Certainly the least expensive and most benign step to take in controlling greenhouse emissions and slowing global warming is tree planting. This could be done as a companion strategy to the more complex task of deforestation. Trees absorb carbon dioxide from the air and pump moisture into the air by evapotranspiration. Trees are the most effective producers of clouds. Proper placement of trees in cities could reduce energy consumption by 15 to 35 percent. Trees also create "white noise" (rustling noise in wind) which helps block out the more shrill urban noises.

Tree planting can be undertaken by all segments of society, from individuals growing fruit trees in their backyards and municipalities planting trees along city streets, to the governments reforesting hills and valleys with the help of school children or factory workers.

The rationale for tree planting can be found at all levels, but its roots strike deepest in religious soil. Eastern and Western religions attribute sanctity to trees. They represent life, and embody the meeting place of the spiritual and physical. The ideological and cultural roots of reforestation are firmly embedded in Indian soil and provide an optimum rationale.

The Hindu tradition venerates flora with the similar blend of utility and sanctity it expresses for fauna, and both flora and fauna, along with humans, are seen as existing in a state of mutual connections and dependencies. The tradition goes back to the Indus Valley civilization, where the pipal tree is viewed as representing the Mother Goddess. Later it is associated with god Viṣṇu. The banyan tree also stands tall and majestic—Mother Nature's own cathedral. Under its vaulted canopy, Lord Buddha received his enlightenment. The record has it that in his quest for illumination Gautama withdrew to Uruvela, "a pleasant spot and beautiful forest." The Buddha was acting on the Indian belief that Nature speaks with many tongues to the deep levels of the human soul, and hence the practice of locating temples, schools, and monasteries in arboreal settings. So, too, the forest was deemed the appropriate environment for the *Vānaprastha* (forest recluse) and for the *Parivrājaka* (ascetic). Trees provided these aspirants with not only food for the body but sustenance for the soul. Their pristine pillars formed living temples that soothed the senses and brought heaven down to earth. In such all-embracing environments, there was felt continuity between matter and spirit. Boundaries were as indistinguishable as the intertwining of the roots of the trees under the surface. It therefore only took a small flight of the imagination for the Śatapatha Brāhmaṇa to derive the strength, aroma, juices, and color of certain trees from diverse parts of the body of none other than Prajāpati.

In gratitude to the Bodhi-tree under which he received his enlightenment, the Buddha bade all his monks not to harm trees because they, too, possessed sensate existence. Similar sentiments are expressed in the Epic literature. Through intuition Manu appears to have made the discovery, now known to science, that trees and plants, when subjected to injury, exhibit reactions which can be photographed. Manu says: "All trees and plants are full of consciousness within themselves and are endowed with the feelings of pleasure and pain."[135]

The belief that trees have lives of their own and are associated with presiding deities required that one ask reverent permission before felling a tree, even when it was to be made into an image of deity. The wood-chopper prayed: "O tree! you are intended for the making of an image of [such-and-such a deity]. I salute you. Please accept my worship offered according to injunctions. . . . May those beings who reside here arrange for their residence elsewhere after accepting the oblations offered according to injunctions! Let them forgive me. Salutation to them all."[136] One can dismiss this as a relic of outdated animism, or one can see in this scenario of man and environment the *animistic expression* of a *prior and independent* value which is attributed to the tree, and which is then expressed within the spiritual conventions of the times.

Given the perception of continuity and connection between the pipal and people, tree planting was made a dharmic act. There was the promise of the expiation of sin to anyone who planted a neem tree or various fruit trees—all of which possessed nutritive and medicinal properties.[137]

The Institutes of Viṣṇu propounds an environmentally consequentialist theory which, in addition to the rewards for digging wells and giving water, includes rewards for tree planting. "He who plants trees will have those trees for his sons in a future existence. A giver of trees gladdens the gods by (offering up) their blossoms to them. (He gladdens) his guests by (giving) their fruits to them; (He gladdens) travellers with their shade; (He gladdens) the manes [ancestors] with the water (trickling down from their leaves) when it rains."[138]

If tree planting brought inherited rewards, the destruction of trees incurred punishments. Kauṭilya levies the following fines: "For cutting off the tender sprout of fruit trees or shady trees in the parks near a city, a fine of six panas shall be imposed; for cutting off the minor branches of the same trees, twelve panas, and for cutting off the big branches, twenty four panas shall be levied. Cutting off the trunks of the same, shall be punished with the middlemost amercement."[139]

Using a similar calculus, Manu declares: "According to the usefulness of the several (kinds of) trees a fine must be inflicted for injuring them; that is the settled rule."[140] The fines for injuring trees was graduated, with small fines for damaging shade trees, middling fines for damaging flower-bearing trees, and stiffest penalties for the destruction of useful fruit trees. Another factor which had to be accounted for in computing fines was the position of the tree: whether it was a boundary marker, at a crossroad, or in a monastery.[141]

The yardstick applied in these ancient systems of Kauṭilya and Manu is that of utility. The base line is that although all trees and plants are sacred, the human impact upon them is to be measured in terms of their usefulness. This thinking is amenable to the industrialization of forestry, but is averse to its reduction to a commodity, which then justifies the clearance of forests to make room for more jobs.[142]

It must be admitted that the preservation and planting of trees is only a stopgap measure against global warming. But if the major peril faced by global warming is the rapid pace of change which is now going on, then stopgaps can be helpful. Short of other measures, reforestation can slow the pace until other solutions can be found. But there should be no illusions. The battle is with the Goliath of Big Industry, which changes forests into fodder with the appetite of runaway consumerism. For grass-roots communities to withstand this onslaught, they must be empowered with the sort of passion that energized the Indian Chipko movement.

The Chipko movement was born as a result of the reckless destruction of the environment of the Alaknanda catchment area in the mid-Himalayas. Commercial exploitation, aided and abetted by the building of a vast network of roads for border security, involved the slashing of forests in the region. This led to soil erosion, devastating floods, and the reduction of agricultural production. The life of the villagers was perilously affected. As Chandi Prasad Bhatt describes the situation: "It was here that the Dasholi Gram Sarajya Mandal (DGSM), Gopeshwar, . . . stepped in. While doing relief work during the 1970 floods the Mandal realized that forest and land and forest and man were intricately linked. The people were also educated about it and gradually they geared themselves into the movement. Thus was born the Chipko movement."[143]

The sequel is by now well known. When the Forest Department auctioned trees as a means for acquiring foreign exchange, the brave villagers hugged the trees as a nonviolent act to stop their being cut down. The government backed off, and the local

people gained their first victory. Since then the DGSM has organized conservation camps, and has branched out beyond tree protection to wider environmental concerns.

Waste   The third problem Hindu ethics must address is that of
waste. In America it is a dilemma of our affluence; but the scourge
is global. All countries face the question: "how to reduce the gargantuan waste by-products of civilization without endangering
human health or damaging the environment."[144]

The problem is multifaceted. Waste is of several types: municipal solid waste, of which the average American creates some 5
pounds a day; hazardous waste, a by-product of the chemical revolution starting in the 1930s, with approximately 650,000 commercial and industrial sources in the United States; nuclear waste,
which remains toxic for thousands of years; industrial solid
waste, of which 1 ton is created each week for every individual in
the United States and gaseous waste, to which each person in the
United States contributes 20 tons of CO_2 each year.[145] When the
figures are added from around the world, waste becomes an
urgent global dilemma. What can be done to prevent the world
from wallowing in waste?

On the one hand there are policymakers who are only guided
by economic interests and who look for garbage dumps in some
poor fellow's backyard. On the other hand there are those who
oppose development and nostalgically hope for the horse-and-
buggy days. Hinduism's balanced scale of values (*puruṣārthas*)
counsels neither *rape* nor *retreat*. Instead the strategy of Hindu
ethics to control the volume of waste produced involves recycling,
renewal, and restraint.

The waste problem has two aspects: mechanical and human.
On the mechanical side we can discuss the merits of various disposal methods, but prior to the question of disposal is the production process that creates the waste, and therefore it is at that
karmic source where we must begin. In all instances the waste-
generating process must be rethought and reinvented. Forward-
looking companies that have overhauled their operations have
registered success. "The Minnesota Mining and Manufacturing
Co. has cut waste generation in half by using fewer toxic chemicals, separating out wastes that can be reused and substituting
alternative material for hazardous substances. 3M's saving last
year: an astonishing $420 million.[146]

This "ascetic" approach succeeds because it approximates the natural model in which one species' waste becomes another species' means of livelihood. In nature this cycle of *waste* and *want* are held in balance, but in aggressive consumer societies this balance is disrupted and waste becomes *wasted* because nature is not able to sustain its reuse due to an overloaded system. By redesigning our production systems we can curb the generation of waste where it starts.

Next, with the volume of waste reduced, the remainder of waste must be recycled. Recycling is the most effective way to reduce waste. Japan has been most innovative in this area. In many cases it has been a case of creativity born of necessity. For example, up to now, waste from Yokohama, Japan's second largest city, had been ending up in Yokohama Bay, which is filling up fast. The solution was to recycle the sewage waste. Through inventive research, the Yokohama sewage works bureau created a line of sludge products, including fertilizers, bricks, vases, paper, and business cards. Yokohama has declared its sewage system "a treasury of resources."[147]

At the consumer level, governments can prod the public to curb waste by levying a charge according to the amount of garbage they produce; to encourage recycling, households should be required to sort garbage into recyclable and nonrecyclable items.

In terms of *renewal*, there are two kinds of energy: nonrenewable and renewable. The first category includes natural gas, coal, oil, and peat—all being in great demand. Unfortunately, most nonrenewable sources come from fossil fuels that emit gases that contribute to smog, urban air pollution, and acid rain, and that are enormously productive of waste. It is therefore imperative for society to switch to renewable sources of energy by making greater use of water, geothermal heat, solar radiation, and wind.

On the principle of *restraint*, the concept of *bhū-ṛṇa*, introduced in this chapter, elevates conservationism above consumerism. We are to put back into the system what we take out, in order to maintain its ecological balance. Manu makes the point well: "As the leech, the calf, and the bee take their food little by little, even so must the king draw from his realm moderate annual taxes."[148]

Rich countries take more out of the earth than they replenish, and poor countries are playing "catch-up." The United States is the greatest consumer of them all, producing the most amount of waste. Clearly we need to curb our voracious appetite for energy with stringent new energy efficienty regulations and widespread conservation practices. Gandhi maintained that nature's supply is always adequate when demands are managed intelligently.

Population   The fourth environmental problem Hindu ethics must address is the problem of population. The two giants in this area, casting colossal shadows over 40 percent of the world's population, are China, first, and then India. But those standings could be shortly changed, since India is moving toward topping China as the most populous nation in the world by the year 2025. Erling Dessau, representing the United Nations Fund for Population Activities, released the UNFPA's annual report in New Delhi on April 29, 1992, which announced that "medium growth projection shows India overtaking China by 2025 or 2030 as the world's most populous country with a population of over 1.4 billion people."[149] An earlier projection had set China's population by 2025 at 1.5 billion, but that figure has been reduced to 1.4 billion, taking into account China's stringent population control policies.

However, being a democracy, India cannot resort to the strong-arm policies of its neighbor, as the ouster from office of the late prime minister, Indira Gandhi, attests. But democratic pride does not make the requirements for feeding, housing, clothing, and gainful employment by 2025 anything less than staggering. The UNFPA report noted that India's progress toward improving the quality of life had been slower than might have been expected. About 350 million people in India live in absolute poverty—more than its population at the time of independence in 1947.

The UN report also highlighted achievements of the southern state of Kerala, in contrast to the five large states in the north where 40 percent of India's people live. "Where Kerala has matched the human resource development of the very best performers among developing countries, the five northern states have been among the worst. And the place of women is central to the difference," the report said.[150]

We hark back to a speech of the late prime minister, Rajiv Gandhi, on the eve of Republic Day, 1987, in which he said:

The real benefits of development can be had in the long run only if we tackle our population growth effectively. In this task the active participation and cooperation of the people have to be enlisted. Family welfare should be developed into a mass movement. Social and attitudinal changes have to be brought about through sustained endeavors. Voluntary organizations have to supplement the efforts of the Government in this regard.[151]

Responding to Rajiv Gandhi's challenge, the question arises: What part can Hindu ethics play toward supplementing the effort of the government, especially in bringing about necessary social and attitudinal changes?

First, the concept of *dharma* or morality is a dynamic notion in Hindu ethics, open to processes of change as different situations arise. The *dharma* of the Vedas was to beget "ten sons." That made sense in times when warfare, an agricultural economy, and high rate of infant mortality were the order of the day. For most of India's history, these exigencies have prevailed, and hence the practice of having large families has become part of a hallowed tradition. But today the same dharmic principle of welfare dictates a radical shift in attitude, both toward fertility and toward fertility as a requirement of *dharma*. Bluntly stated, yesterday's *dharma* is today's *adharma*. "The rules of *dharma* are the mortal flesh of immortal ideas and so are mutable."[152]

Today it is ethically irresponsible to say, "God sends children into the world," and that "man should not interfere with the will of God." In Hindu ethics, that which distinguishes civilization from the jungle is the capacity of persons to control nature, including their own. Sexual restraint is the infrastructure of the *āśrama* scheme, in which procreation is limited to the householder stage. It is also the rationale for sanctions against sexual intercourse on a number of auspicious days and seasons.

But, having acknowledged the place of restraint in family planning, it is not our purpose to isolate this age-old Hindu virtue as a method of birth control. That was Gandhi's solution to the problem. "I want limitation of population," he declared, "but the method which we adopt is the method of abstinence, austerity, and self-control." Radhakrishnan opposed Gandhi on this point:

> There is no doubt that it [abstinence] is the best method, but, I should like to ask, whether it be by self-control or abstinence, or austerity of living that limitation of population is brought

about, is not that interference with nature? If we do not control ourselves we will produce more, and if we do control ourselves, we will produce less. There is an interference with nature even there, and so far as we are concerned most of us are human beings striving to be saintly, but have not yet become saints.[153]

The last remark of Radhakrishnan reflects the thinking of another Hindu sage, Rabindra Nath Tagore. Opposing Gandhi's plea for abstinence, he said: "I believe that to wait till the moral sense of man becomes a great deal more powerful than it is now and till then to allow countless generations of children to suffer privations and untimely death for no fault of their own is a great social injustice which should not be tolerated."[154]

Indians need control, but they need contraceptives first. Seshagiri Rao correctly states:

> Generally Hindus show little resistance to the idea of birth control. There is no objection to contraception on religious grounds. Bṛhadāraṇyaka Upanishad spells out a method of birth control for a man "who desires a wife, but does not want her to concieve" (VI.4.10). A temperate exercise of sex instinct by the householder is recommended in the shastras . . . ; and contraceptions help in avoiding unwanted and undesirable pregnancies. Hence contraception is generally acceptable to the Hindus and is to be encouraged in the interests of domestic felicity and welfare of society.[155]

Family planning should involve more than the distribution of contraceptives. One mistake of the past has been to rely on contraceptives in isolation. What needs to be emphasized is the integration of family planning with family welfare, environmental sanitation, child nutrition, literacy, and social and economic independence for women. This *"package"* approach versus the conventional piecemeal approach is ethically more sound because it does justice to Hinduism's concern for the whole person and for the environment in which he or she lives.

Two remaining factors that are essential to a population ethic involve marriage and offspring. Traditional Hindu marriage has a fivefold purpose: pleasure (*rati*), parenthood (*prajati*), companionship (*sakhya*), sacrificial service (*yajña*), and spiritual bliss (*ānanda*).[156] Because of the historic need for large families, it is understandable how the primary meaning of marriage developed around the notion of *prajati* (parenthood). This identification of marriage with procreation has tended to define the wife's role as primarily biological. The young bride only becomes a fully fledged member of the husband's family when she produces a child, preferably a son. Traditionally, without this her traditional status has been in jeopardy. Today, with the need to limit the size of families, the social and spiritual purposes of marriage ought to be cultivated around the ideal of *sakhya* or companionship. A wife is a friend, not a factory. This sentiment is expressed in the words of the groom to the bride in the marriage hymn of the Ṛgveda, "I take thy hand in mine for happy fortune that thou mayst reach old age with me thy husband."[157]

Finally, in developing a population ethic, Hindus are obligated to face honestly the issue of equality of offspring. Prejudice and injustice run deep. They are hallowed by religion and flourish in an ethos that is patriarchal to the core. Success in this area could mean not only a moral victory but also a reduction of the birthrate by a substantial percentage. Signs of hope can be read on billboards of family planning agencies that promote the "value of female babies in an effort to open a new perspective for many Indian couples who feel their family is incomplete unless they have at least one male child."[158]

The need for a new perspective grows out of Hinduism's traditional preference for male offspring. The religious basis for this preference is the belief that the son rescues the souls of departed ancestors from hell. Manu says: "By a son one conquers the worlds, by a son's son one attains the infinite, by the son of a son's son one attains the region of the sun. Since a son succours his father from the hell called *Put*; hence, the self-begotten one (Brahma) has called a son, *Putra* (lit., deliverer from the hell of *Put*)."[159]

The status of the eldest son in the family is unique. He has the right to offer the funeral cake (*piṇḍa*) at the time of the *śrāddha* ceremony marking the anniversary of the death of the father and ancestors.

Responsibility for performance of rites for the forefathers stems from the notion that the sins of commission and omission done by parents are visited upon their children. Retribution can be averted by means of the *śrāddha* rites. These household ceremonies are conducted every month for one year after a death. During this time it is believed that the deceased father moves in the air, not having been admitted to the company of the forefathers. At the conclusion of the year, a ceremony is performed by which the deceased is admitted to the assembly of the forefathers and thereby becomes a *pitri*. Manu states that the first-born son on whom the father passes his debt (*ṛnam*) and by whom he gains immortality (*anantyam*) is the only child begotten for the sake of *dharma* (*sa eva dharmajah putrah*); all others are the fruit of passion (*kāmajah*).[160]

The importance of *śrāddha* rites elevates the role and status of the son and devalues the daughter. When the dowry, which the father must give upon the marriage of the daughter, is also calculated, her liability increases as compared with a son, who is an asset to his father in every way—spiritual, social, and economic. No wonder there are always accounts of female infanticide, especially among low-caste families.

It is time that Hindus reevaluated the unethical accretions which have grown around their popular eschatology. Hindu beliefs are held on progressive levels of sophistication, but *śrāddha*, though philosophically low, is not recognized as such because it caters to a host of nonreligious factors that assume male superiority and are therefore difficult to eject in a patriarchal society.

Philosophically viewed, the declared function of a son "as an instrument for cleansing his ancestors in the funeral rites" is purely magical. The private performance of *śrāddha*, done outside the sight of eunuchs, outcastes, heretics, or pregnant women for fear that it might be rendered "unclean," is both magical and superstitious. It demeans Hindu ethics to be associated with beliefs about collective guilt; with the belief that doing good deeds will acquire merit; and with the notion that offerings (excluding "unconsecrated grain or lentils, gourds, garlics, onions, or red vegetable extracts," and salt) somehow nourish the ethereal bodies of the departed ancestors and enable them to perform works of merit that will advance them toward their goal of union with *Brahman*.[161]

Hindu ethics is more rationally served by the philosophic belief in karma, which asserts that each person makes his or her own heaven or hell. Moreover, our deeds are private and therefore cannot transfer for good or ill to other persons. Most importantly, a religion that views life unitively is ethically inconsistent when it elevates the salvific superiority of one sex above the other. It is strange that a religion that establishes the worship of animals and the veneration of trees should discriminate against its own daughters. In today's world of exploding populations there is a more ethical way to affirm the continuity between generations and to honor and immortalize the names of beloved ancestors. This is achieved by performing good deeds—the most dharmic of which may be limiting the size of one's family.

Nuclear Proliferation   Finally, we examine the Hindu ethical perspective on the most threatening of all environmental problems—the danger of nuclear war. On the one hand, it appears that with the dismemberment of the Soviet Union the fear of nuclear catastrophe has ended and there is victory for common sense. At last we have the opportunity to dismantle the giant military-industrial machine, and turn swords into ploughshares. On the other hand, as discussed earlier, various dictators are scrambling to acquire nuclear power for military purposes.

In addition, the demons of nationalism and terrorism threaten international stability. Even in America, we are hearing nationalistic voices calling for the government to put America first by attending to domestic causes instead of dispensing foreign aid. This inward turning is comprehensible, considering the burden of the special role the United States has had to play throughout this century, at immense material and human cost. But America's current dilemma is that she can no more remove herself from her traditional role of global responsibility as she can put her trust in the military might that makes her the only superpower in the world today.

Some argue that it was precisely her swift and massive power in the Persian Gulf War that routed a brutal dictator in "the Mother of all Battles." They want America to be a policeman to the world, using her armed forces to keep rebel nations in their place. Actually, the Persian Gulf War was a victory for the world community, by whose mandate the allied forces joined in battle. The Gulf War served as the defining event of a possible new world order in which the United Nations would assume a new and vigorous role as an instrument for peace.

The Gulf War also demonstrated that there are deep divisions between people that defy easy solutions. It showed the fundamental need for changes in consciousness between people and nations. And the doomsday sight of hundreds of uncontrollable oil fires under blackened skies, with birds and beasts sinking in seas of sludge, served as apocalyptic images of a possible Armageddon that could vaporize the planet. All of this calls for a reassessment of values. As former president Mikhail Gorbachev has revealed, it was "a reassessment of values" that "opened the road for deep transformations" in the Soviet Union.[162]

Hindu ethics is based on a set of assumptions which transcend the natural divisions between people and people, and between mankind and nature. Its *ecumenism* is *existential and environmental*. It sees humanity in nature and nature in humanity.

In his chapter "Vedānta in the Nuclear Age," Karan Singh argues convincingly that humankind is at the crossroads and is groping for a new philosophy to replace the old. This is taking place at a time when the supreme peril people face is not from without but from within. "There has been a tragic divergence between knowledge and wisdom, and from deep within the human psyche there has developed a terrible poison that threatens not only our own generation but countless generations yet unborn; not only our own race but all life on this planet."[163] Singh goes on to delineate Vedāntic insights which provide a framework to support the emerging global consciousness on Planet Earth. These insights are: that *Brahman* is the divine force that pervades the entire cosmos; that Brahman resides in each individual as the *Ātman*; that by virtue of their shared spirituality, all humans are members of a single family; that solidarity must extend beyond human welfare to include all creation.[164]

The principles of *unity, interdependence, interconnectedness*, and *restraint* incorporated in these Vedāntic assumptions might have sounded naively utopian in an earlier age. Even as recently as the forties, when Wendell Wilkie published his *One World*, the notion seemed like a dream. But as we witness nuclear weapons proliferate before our eyes, yesterday's dream becomes today's nightmare. Today's shrunken world cannot permit the luxury of national particularism. The entrenched status quo that has lasted interminably is now being pressured by the forces of modernity. Their message is clear: *interdepend or perish!* Our technological civilization leaves us in no doubt: interdependence is not a theory, but a fact; not an ideology, but a condition. Technologically, economically, politically, and morally, interdependence in international relations is inescapable. No more can any single nation be the master of its own fate and the captain of its own soul.

A dramatic example of interdependence is the current AIDS epidemic. The global spread of this disease confounds national boundaries. It demands global remedies. No single nation or group of nations, no matter how technologically advanced, possesses the capabilities or resources to arrest the deadly virus independently. What was first dubbed as an "African problem," then a "Haitian problem," then a "gay problem," has now surfaced, like a hydra-headed monster, as a global problem.

AIDS is the latest in a long list of other problems—poverty, hunger, environmental decay, resource depletion, population pressure, international terrorism, and nuclear proliferation—that once were neatly and logically discussed within the closed categories of the "life-boat" ethic. But in an interdependent world there are no lifeboats. We either sink or swim—together. Like the king who discovered that his royal command could not stop the tide, no country can place "No Entry" signs upon its national border against any of these problems—most especially the threat of nuclear suicide and terricide.

CONCLUSION

The general idea behind Hinduism's environmental ethics is that the individual *ātman* is one with the universal *Brahman*. This *Brahman* force is manifest uniformly in the divinities of heaven and in human, animal, and plant life on earth. All of these entities live an apparently independent existence, but they all emanate from *Brahman* and are finally reabsorbed into it. *Brahman* itself is infinite, and is therefore greater than the sum of all its manifestations, past, present, and future.

This belief in *Brahman* provides the philosophic basis for the Hindu's veneration of the natural world. The universe appears to be material, but actually it is the universal consciousness or *Brahman*. Since all is one, the conquest of nature cannot be true to reality, and our sense of separateness is the product of ignorance.

This calls for self-knowledge. Humans cannot act ethically toward nature as long as they are ignorant of themselves. Lacking our own sense of universal identity, we cannot identify with the trees and the mountains, nor can we feel empathy for the beasts of the fields. Nature is perceived as empty because we are empty. We manipulate nature because we manipulate ourselves. Our loss of our relation to nature is a corollary of the loss of our own selves. William Wordsworth recognized this correlation between our inner world and the outer world, and expressed it in his sonnet:

> The world is too much with us; late and soon,
> Getting and spending, we lay waste our powers;
> Little we see in Nature that is ours:
> We have given our hearts away, a sordid boon!
> This sea that bares her bosom to the moon,
> The winds that will be howling at all hours,
> And are up-gathered now like sleeping flowers.
> For this for everything, we are out of tune.[165]

The rallying message of Hindu ethics is that harmony is already here: that we do not have to create it—only disover it. Since *Brahman* and Nature are one, we must see the Supreme Being in the whole world, and the whole world in Him.

NOTES

INTRODUCTION

1. Ezra Bowen, "Ethics: Looking to Its Roots," *Time*, May 25, 1987, p. 26.
2. Ibid.
3. Ibid.
4. Jerry Falwell, "An Agenda for the Eighties," in *Moral Issues and Christian Response*, ed. Paul T. Jersild and Dale A. Johnson (Fort Worth, Tex.: Holt, Rinehart and Winston, 1988), p. 28.
5. Quoted in ibid.
6. *Time*, Feb. 19, June 25, 1990.
7. Quoted in "Asian Wave Is Changing U.S. Scene," *Honolulu Star-Bulletin*, November 8, 1990.
8. David Carter and Alice Chandler, "Fostering a Multi-Cultural Curriculum: Principles for Presidents," in *American Association of State Colleges and Universities* (Washington, D.C.: American Association of State Colleges and Universities), p. 3.
9. Ewert N. Cousins, "Interreligious Dialogue: The Spiritual Journey of Our Time," IRF (A Newsletter of the International Religious Foundation), vol. 11, no. 1, January–February, 1987, p. 2.
10. John Cobb, Jr. *Matters of Life and Death* (Louisville, Ky.: John Knox Press/Westminster, 1991), p. 9.
11. John B. Buescher, "Putting Asia in the Core Curriculum," *The NEA Higher Education Journal*, vol. 6, no. 1, Spring 1990, p. 69.
12. Bimal K. Matilal, "Moral Dilemmas: Insights from Indian Epics," in *Moral Dilemmas in the Mahabharata*, ed. B. K. Matilal (New Delhi: Motilal Banarsidass, 1989), p. 8.
13. Ibid.
14. Ibid., p. 9.
15. Ibid., p. 9.
16. Ibid., p. 9.
17. Mbh. Santi. 34.16–32; 109.13–15; 141.39; 142.9.
18. Manu, ll.11–21.
19. M. Hiriyanna, *Popular Essays in Indian Philosophy* (Mysore: Kavyalaya Publishers, 1952), p. 14.

20. See "*Dharma*," in Margaret and James Stutley, *Harper's Dictionary of Hinduism* (New York: Harper and Row, 1977), p. 76.

21. Quoted in Bowen, op. cit., p. 26.

CHAPTER 1. THE ETHICS OF ABORTION

1. "The Battle over Abortion," *Time*, April 6, 1981, p. 20.

2. Ibid., p. 21.

3. "Nothing Less than Perfect," *Time*, December 11, 1989, p. 82.

4. Ibid.

5. Lawrence M. Friedman, "The Conflict over Constitutional Legitimacy," in *The Abortion Dispute and the American System*, ed. Gilbert Y. Steiner (New York: The Brookings Institute, 1983), p. 13.

6. Ibid., p. 16.

7. 410 U.S. at 116.

8. In common law, it was not a crime to perform an abortion before "quickening"—the first recognizable movement of the fetus, appearing usually from the 16th to the 18th week of pregnancy. This appears to have developed from a confluence of earlier philosophical, theological and civil and common law concepts that life begins when the fetus became recognizably human or when a "person" comes into being, that is, infused with a "soul" or "animated." "Although Christian theology and the canon law came to fix the point of animation at 40 days for a male and 80 days for a female, a view that persisted until the 19th century, there was otherwise little agreement about the precise time of formation or animation. There was agreement, however, that prior to this point the fetus was to be regarded as part of the mother, and its destruction, therefore, was not homicide." Because of continued uncertainty about the precise time when animation occurred, quickening was focused upon as the critical point. Ibid. at 132–134.

9. The Fourteenth Amendment provides in pertinent part that no state shall "deprive any person of life, liberty, or property, without due process of law."

10. Ibid. at 153.

11. Ibid. at 159.

12. Ibid. at 160–161.

13. Ibid. at 162–163.

14. Ibid. at 163.

15. For further discussion see John T. Noonan, "An almost Absolute Value in History." In *The Morality of Abortion*, ed. John T. Noonan, pp. 1–59. Cambridge, Mass.: Harvard University Press, 1970.

16. Honolulu Star-Bulletin, July 3, 1989, p. 1.

17. Ibid.

18. Ibid.

19. Cynthia Tucker, "Abortion Decision Furthers Cause of Liberty," *Honolulu Star-Bulletin*, July 6, 1992.

20. Ibid.

21. "Court Backs Abortion but Allows New Limits," *Honolulu Star-Bulletin*, June 29, 1992.

22. "Clinton Cuts Abortion Restrictions," *Honolulu Star-Bulletin*, January 22, 1993.

23. Wade, however, undeniably made abortion acceptable to many, whereas it had not previously been so.

24. Jonathan Glover, *"Matters of Life and Death" The New York Review*, May 30, 1985, pp. 19–23. A review of *The Right to Lifers*, Connie Paige; *Our Right to Choose: Toward a New Ethic of Abortion*, Beverly W. Harrison; *Abortion and the Politics of Motherhood*, Kristin Luker.

25. Julius Lipner, *"The Classical Hindu View on Abortion and the Moral Status of the Unborn," in Hindu Ethics*, ed. Harold G. Coward, Julius Lipner, and Katherine K. Young (New York: State University of New York Press, 1989), p. 42.

26. RV. 4.54.2, in A.C. Bose, *Hymns from the Vedas* (Bombay: Asia Publishing House, 1966), p. 333.

27. RV. 5.4.10, ibid., p. 334.

28. RV. 10.85.45, ibid. p. 139.

29. Ibid., p. 334.

30. RV. 10.85.35–41, ibid., pp. 135–137.

31. Yajurveda vs. 32.4, ibid., p. 301.

32. Ibid. vs. 5.

33. YV. vs. 8.53, ibid., p. 92.

34. RV. 10.85.43, ibid., p. 137.

35. AV. 14. 2.71, ibid., p. 12.

36. Ibid.

37. Atharvaveda 19.67.1–8, ibid., p. 97.

38. Atharvaveda 19.60.2, ibid.

39. RV. 10.85.45, ibid., p. 139.

40. Atharvaveda 2.36.3, ibid., p. 125.

41. Atharvaveda 6.17.2, in *Sacred Books of the East*, ed. F. Max Muller (New Delhi: Motilal Banarsidass, 1987 reprint), vol. 42, p. 98.

42. Atharvaveda 2.25.3, ibid., p. 36.

43. Atharvaveda 1.11.2, ibid., p. 99.

44. Atharvaveda 6.112.3, ibid., p. 165.

45. 6.112 Commentary, ibid., p. 521.

46. Śatapatha-Brāhmaṇa 3.1.2, 21, ibid., vol. 26, p. 11.

47. Śatapatha-Brāhmaṇa 4.5.1, 62, ibid., vol. 43, p. 272.

48. Bṛhad-Āraṇyaka Upanishad 4.3.19, in *The Thirteen Principal*

Upanishads, trans. Robert E. Hume (London: Oxford University Press, 1971), p. 136.

49. Kaushītaki Upanishad 3.1, ibid., p. 321.

50. Yājñavalkya Saṁhitā 3.75, in *The Dharam Shastra: Hindu Religious Codes*, ed. M. N. Dutta (New Delhi: Cosmo Publications, 1978), vol. 1, p. 130.

51. Manu Saṁhitā, 9.8, ibid., vol. 5, p. 316.

52. Ibid. vs. 9.

53. Yājñavalkya 1.14, in Dutta, op. cit., vol.1, p. 4.

54. Gautama Saṁhitā 22, ibid., vol 3, p. 706.

55. Vaśishtha 20.23, in Muller, op. cit., vol. 14, p. 105.

56. Manu Saṁhitā 11.87, in Dutta, op. cit., vol. 5, p. 397.

57. Yājñavalkya 3.298, ibid., vol. 1, p. 159.

58. Vyāsa Saṁhitā 1.7, ibid., vol. 3, p. 508.

59. Vaśishtha Saṁhitā 15, ibid., p. 800.

60. Vishṇu Saṁhitā 24.41, ibid., vol. 4, p. 875.

61. Parāśara Saṁhitā 4.14, ibid., vol. 3, p. 555.

62. Yājñavalkya Saṁhitā 1.68–69, ibid., vol. 1, p. 12.

63. Ibid. 3.79.

64. Vishṇu Saṁhitā 4.130, p. 831.

65. Manu Saṁhitā 3.114, ibid., vol. 5, p. 102.

66. Ibid. 9.9, vol. 5, p. 316.

67. Yājñavalkya Saṁhitā 2.237–240, ibid., vol. 1, p. 104.

68. Vishṇu Saṁhitā 36.1, ibid., vol. 4, p. 891.

69. Manu Saṁhitā 2.27, ibid., vol. 5, p. 39.

70. Yājñavalkya Saṁhitā 1.13, ibid., vol. 1, p. 3.

71. The Bhagavadgītā 16.2.

72. Caraka Saṁhitā, Priyavrat Sharma, ed. and trans. (Varanasi: Chaukhamba Orientalia, 1981), Śārīrasthānam 5.4, vol. 1, p. 440.

73. Ibid., Sa. 2.63–64, p. 403.

74. Ibid., Sa. 1.52, p. 401.

75. Ibid., Sa. 1.39–42, p. 400.

76. Ibid.

77. Ibid., Sūtrasthāna 1.46–47, p. 6.

78. Ibid., Sa. 4.4–7., pp. 428–429.

79. Ibid., Sa. 3.3, p. 419.

80. Ibid., Sa. 4.8, p. 429.

81. Ibid., Sa. 3.8, p. 422.

82. Ibid., Sa. 11.23–27, p. 415.

83. Ibid., Sa. 8.22, p. 469.

84. *Suśruta-Saṁhitā: A Scientific Synopsis,* ed. P. Ray, H. Gupta, and M. Roy (New Delhi: Indian National Science Academy, 1980), p. 22 (Cikitsasthana 15.6–7).

85. O. P. Jaggi, "History of Medical Ethics: India," in *Encyclope-*

dia of Bioethics, W. T. Reich, gen. ed. (New York: The Free Press, 1978), vol. 3, p. 910.

86. Seema Sirohi, "Indians Embrace the Boy-Girl Test," *Honolulu Star-Bulletin*, March 22, 1988.

87. Arvind Kala, "Banning Sex Tests: Unfair, Unworkable," *Times of India*, January 25, 1991.

88. Ibid.

89. Sirohi, op. cit.

90. Caraka Saṁhitā, op. cit., vol. 1, p. 354.

CHAPTER 2. THE ETHICS OF SUICIDE

1. J. Michael McGinnis, "Suicide in America—Moving up the Public Health Agenda," *Suicide and Life-Threatening Behavior*, vol. 17, no. 1, Spring 1987, p. 18.

2. Ibid., p. 19.

3. Martin Buda and Ming T. Tsuang, "The Epidemiology of Suicide: Implications for Clinical Practice," in *Suicide over the Life Cycle: Risk Factors, Assessment, and Treatment of Suicidal Patients*, ed. Susan J. Blumenthal, David J. Kupfer (Washington: American Psychiatric Press, 1990), p. 18.

4. McGinnis, op. cit., p. 20.

5. Ibid.

6. Buda and Tsuang, op. cit., p. 20.

7. McGinnis, op. cit., p. 21.

8. Buda and Tsuang, loc. cit.

9. Ibid., p. 23.

10. Ibid., p. 24.

11. Ibid.

12. Ibid.

13. Ibid.

14. Ibid., p. 25.

15. Ibid.

16. McGinnis, op. cit., p. 21; Buda and Tsuang, op. cit., p. 20.

17. McGinnis, op. cit., p. 20.

18. McGinnis, op. cit., pp. 20, 21.

19. For a survey of contemporary approaches, see Edwin Schneidman, *Definitions of Suicide* (New York: John Wiley, 1985), p. 30ff.

20. Buda and Tsuang, op. cit., p. 26.

21. Ibid, p. 27.

22. Ibid., p. 29.

23. Ibid.

24. Ibid., p. 31.

25. Ibid.

26. Schneidman, op. cit., p. 34.

27. Cited in ibid., p. 35.

28. Ibid., pp. 35, 36.

29. Quoted in ibid., p. 14.

30. A. W. Mair, "Suicide," *Encyclopaedia of Religion and Ethics*, ed. James Hastings, 12 vols. (Edinburgh: T. and T. Clark, 1980), vol. 12, p. 33.

31. Ibid.

32. Ibid.

33. Ibid.

34. Tom L. Beauchamp, "Suicide," in *New Introductory Essays in Matters of Life and Death: Moral Philosophy*, ed. Tom Regan (New York: Random House, 1980), p. 70.

35. Ibid.

36. Ibid.

37. Ibid., p. 71.

38. Ibid., p. 72.

39. Ibid.

40. Ibid., p. 73.

41. Ibid., p. 77.

42. St. Augustine, *City of God,* trans. Gerald G. Walsh et al. (New York: Image Books, 1958), p. 55.

43. Ibid., p. 57.

44. Ibid., p. 52.

45. Ibid., p. 53.

46. Fathers of the English Dominican Province, trans., *The Summa Theologica of St. Thomas*, vol. 11, revised by Daniel J. Sullivan, in *Great Books of the Western World*, ed. Robert M. Hutchins (Chicago: Encylopaedia Britannica, 1952), vol. 20, p. 222.

47. Ibid., pp. 245, 246.

48. Charles E. Norton, trans., *The Divine Comedy of Dante Aligheri*, in Hutchins, ibid., vol. 21, pp. 17, 18.

49. William E. Phipps, "Christian Perspectives on Suicide," in *Moral Issues and Christian Response*, ed. Paul T. Jersild and Dale A. Johnson, 4th ed. (New York: Holt, Rinehart and Winston, 1988), p. 398.

50. Eberhard Bethge, ed., *Ethics*, by Dietrich Bonhoeffer (New York: Macmillan, 1965), p. 166.

51. Ibid., p. 167.

52. Ibid., p. 168.

53. Beauchamp, op. cit., pp. 67, 68.

54. Phipps, op. cit. p. 399.

55. Ann Wicket, "Two Double Suicides Part of a Wider Trend," *The Hemlock Quarterly*, No. 31, April 1988, p. 4.

56. Ibid.

57. Ibid.

58. Dennis J. Horan and Edward R. Grant in Jersild, op. cit., p. 390.

59. Pandurang V. Kane, *History of Dharmaśāstra* (Poona: Bhandarkar Oriental Research Institute, 1973), vol. 4, p. 612.

60. Ibid.

61. Abinash Chandra Bose, *Hymns from the Vedas* (Bombay: Asia Publishing House, 1966), Rigveda 7.66.16, p. 95.

62. Ibid., p. 97.

63. J. N. Farquhar, *An Outline of the Religious Literature of India* (New Delhi: Motilal Banarsidass, 1984), p. 13.

64. Margaret and James Stutley, *Harper's Dictionary of Hinduism* (New York: Harper and Row, 1977), p. 272.

65. Atharvaveda 18.3.2., quoted in R. W. Frazer, "Sati," in Hastings, op. cit., vol. 11, p. 207.

66. Ibid.

67. A. Berriedale Keith, "Suicide (Hindu)," in Hastings, op. cit., vol. 12, p. 33.

68. Ibid., p. 34.

69. Bṛhadāraṇyaka Upanishad 1.3.28, in *The Thirteen Principal Upanishads*, trans. Robert E. Hume, 2d ed. rev. (London: Oxford University Press, 1971), p. 80.

70. Ibid., 4.4.22, p. 143.

71. Keith in Hastings, op. cit., vol 12, p. 34.

72. S. Cromwell Crawford, *The Evolution of Hindu Ethical Ideals* (Honolulu: The University Press of Hawaii, 1982), p. 44.

73. Chāndogya Upanishad 3.16.1.

74. Chāndogya Upanishad 3.17.4, in Hume, op. cit., p. 213.

75. Kaṭha Upanishad 2.7.

76. Chāndogya Upanishad 5.10.7.

77. Parāśara Saṁhitā 4.1–6, in *The Dharam Shastra: Hindu Religious Codes*, trans. M. N. Dutta (New Delhi: Cosmo Publications, 1979), vol. 3, pp. 553, 554.

78. Vaśishtha 23.14, in George Buhler, trans., *Sacred Books of the East*, ed. F. Max Muller (New Delhi: Motilal Banarsidass, 1984), vol. 14, p. 119.

79. Ibid. vs. 19.

80. 4.7 Arthaśāstra of Kauṭilya.

81. W. E. H. Lecky, *History of European Morals* (London, 1946), vol 2, p. 22.

82. Āpastamba 1.10.28.17.

83. Adiparva 179.20.

84. Kane, op. cit., vol. 2, part 2, ch. 27, p. 924.

85. Manu 6.32 in Muller, op. cit., vol. 25, p. 204.
86. Yājñavalkya Saṁhitā 3.55.
87. Manu 11.74, in Muller, op. cit., vol. 25, p. 445.
88. Manu, ibid., vs. 91, p. 449.
89. See Āpastamba 1.10.28.15–17.
90. Benjamin Walker, ed., *An Encyclopedic Survey of Hinduism* (New Delhi: Munshiram Manoharlal, 1983), vol. 2, p. 448.
91. Ibid.
92. Ibid., p. 447.
93. Kane, op. cit., vol. 4, p. 615.
94. Mahābhārata 25.62–64; also Vanaparva 85, 33.
95. Matsya Purāṇa, 186.28–33.
96. Kane, op. cit., vol. 4, p. 237.
97. Naradiya (purvardha 7.52–53)., ibid., pp. 204, 205.
98. Keith in Hastings, op. cit., vol. 12, p. 34.
99. W. Crooke, "Jagganath," in Hastings, op. cit., vol. 7, p. 464.
100. A. F. S. Ahmed, *Social Ideas and Social Change in Bengal 1818–1835* (Leiden: E. J. Brill, 1965), p. 112.
101. Ibid.
102. *The English Works of Raja Rammohun Roy*, part 2, ed. Kalidas Nag and Debajyoti Burman (Calcutta: Sadharan Brahmo Samaj, 1946), p. 96.
103. Pandit Sivanath Sastri, "Rammohun Roy: The Story of His Life," in *The Father of Modern India*, ed. Satis Chandra Chakravarti (Calcutta: Rammohun Roy Centenary Committee, 1935), p. 22.
104. See S. Cromwell Crawford, *Ram Mohan Roy* (New York: Paragon House, 1987), p. 110.
105. Manu 6.45.
106. Bṛihadāraṇyaka Upanishad 1.3.28, in Hume, op. cit., p. 80.
107. Kaṭha Upanishad 5.11.
108. Kaṭha 6.14.
109. Bṛihadāraṇyaka Upanishad 4.4.11, in Hume, op. cit., p. 142.
110. Gautama 14.11, in Muller, op. cit., vol. 2, p. 250.
111. See Kane, op. cit., vol. 11, p. 925.
112. Kane, op. cit., vol. 4, p. 608.
113. Ibid., pp. 609, 610.
114. Ibid., p. 610.
115. Anna Quindlen, "Why Book on Suicide Became a Best-seller," *Honolulu Star-Bulletin*, August 15, 1991.
116. Richard Doerflinger, "Suicide Best Seller Stirs Ethics Debate," *Honolulu Star-Bulletin*, August 12, 1991.
117. Richard A. Knox, "Doctor-aided Suicide Gains Support," *Honolulu Star-Bulletin*, August 11, 1991.
118. Ibid.

119. Ibid.
120. 1.27 in Priyavrat Sharma, ed. and trans., *Caraka Saṁhitā* (New Delhi: Chaukhamba Orientalia, 1981), vol. 1, p. 5.
121. Tom L. Beauchamp, *"Suicide," Matters of Life and Death: New Introductory Essays in Moral Philosophy,* ed. Tom Regan (New York: Random House, 1980), p. 98.

CHAPTER 3. THE ETHICS OF EUTHANASIA

1. "Suicidal Ethics," *U.S. News and World Report,* December 30, 1991–January 6, 1992, p. 93.
2. Betty Rollin, Foreword in Derek Humphry, *Final Exit* (Oregon: The Hemlock Society, 1991), p. 12.
3. Alan Parachini, "The California Humane and Dignified Death Initiative," *Hastings Center Report,* vol. 19, no. 1, January–February 1989, Supplement, p. 10.
4. Richard A. McCormick, "Physician Assisted Suicide: Flight from Compassion," *The Christian Century,* December 4, 1991, p. 1132.
5. Andrew Greeley, "Live and Let Die: Changing Attitudes," *The Christian Century,* December 4, 1991, p. 1124.
6. Ibid.
7. McCormick, loc. cit.
8. The Dryden Translation, *Plutarch,* vol. 14 of *The Great Books of the Western World,* ed. Robert M. Hutchins, 54 vols. (Chicago: Encyclopaedia Britannica, 1952), p. 40.
9. Ibid., Benjamin Jowett, trans., *The Republic,* vol. 9, p. 362.
10. Ibid., Benjamin Jowett, trans., *Politics,* vol. 9, p. 540.
11. H. J. Rose, "Euthanasia," *Encyclopaedia of Religion and Ethics,* ed. James Hastings, 12 vols. (Edinburgh: T. and T. Clark, 1981), vol. 5, p. 600.
12. Jowett, op. cit. pp. 335, 336.
13. Ibid.
14. Hutchins, op. cit., W. D. Ross, trans., *Nicomachean Ethics,* vol. 9, p. 362.
15. Hutchins, ibid., Francis Adams, trans., *Hippocratic Writings,* vol. 10, p. xi.
16. *Epistolae Morales.*
17. De. Ira. 1, 15.
18. *Dissertations* 1, 9, 16.
19. Edwin R. Dubose, "A Brief Historical Perspective," *Active Euthanasia, Religion, and the Public Debate,* ed. Ron Hamel (Chicago: The Park Ridge Center, 1991), p. 20.
20. Asa Kasher, "Jewish Ethics: An Orthodox View," *World Reli-*

gions and Global Ethics, ed. S. Cromwell Crawford (New York: Paragon House, 1989), p. 149.

21. Robert M. Veatch, ed., *Cross-Cultural Perspectives in Medical Ethics: Readings* (Boston: Jones and Bartlett, 1989), notation, p. 44.

22. Ibid.

23. J. David Bleich, "The Obligation to Heal in the Jewish Tradition," in ibid., p. 45.

24. Sanhedrin 37a, quoted in Bleich, ibid.

25. Ibid.

26. Ibid.

27. Basil F. Herring, *Jewish Ethics and Halakah for Our Time: Sources and Commentary* (New York: Ktav Publishing House, 1984), p. 78.

28. Ibid., p. 79.

29. Ibid.

30. Avodah Zarah 18a, ibid., p. 70.

31. Avodah Zarah 18a, ibid., pp. 70, 71.

32. Rema (R. Moses Isserles) on Yoreh Deiah 339:1, ibid., p. 72.

33. Ibid., p. 86.

34. Ibid.

35. St. Augustine, *City of God*, trans. Gerald G. Walsh et al. (New York: Image Books, 1958), p. 49.

36. Ibid., p. 441.

37. Ibid., p. 442.

38. Hutchins, op. cit., *Thomas Aquinas*, vol. 20, p. 222.

39. In Ron Hamel and Edwin R. Dubose, "Western Religious Traditions," in Hamel, op. cit., pp. 50, 51. I am indebted to the authors for their valuable information.

40. Ibid., p. 53.

41. Ibid.

42. Ibid.

43. Ibid., p. 54.

44. Ibid., p. 55.

45. Ibid., p. 56.

46. Ibid., p. 57.

47. Ibid., p. 58.

48. Ibid., p. 59.

49. Ibid.

50. Ibid., p. 60.

51. Ibid.

52. Ibid., p. 65.

53. Ibid.

54. Ibid., p. 67.

55. Ibid., p. 69.

56. Sir Thomas More, *Utopia*, Book 11.

57. New Atlantis (1626).

58. Gerald J. Gruman, "Death and Dying: Euthanasia and Sustaining Life: History," *Encyclopedia of Bioethics*, ed. Warren T. Reich, 4 vols. (New York: The Free Press, 1978), vol. 1, p. 262. I am indebted to the author for his invaluable information.

59. Ibid.

60. Ibid., p. 263.

61. Ibid.

62. Ibid.

63. James Rachels, "Euthanasia," in *Matters of Life and Death: New Introductory Essays in Moral Philosophy*, ed. Tom Regan (New York: Random House, 1980), p. 36.

64. Gruman, op. cit., p. 264.

65. Newsweek, November 3, 1975, p. 58.

66. Ibid., p. 59.

67. James H. Rubin, "Court: States Can Bar Pulling Life Support," *Honolulu Star-Bulletin*, June 25, 1990, p. A–4.

68. Richard Carelli, "Nancy Cruzan Is Dead; Controversy Continues," *Advertiser*, December 27, 1990, p. A–3.

69. Humphry, op. cit., p. 132.

70. Ibid., p. 135.

71. "Suicide Physician," *Honolulu Star-Bulletin*, June 4, 1990, pp. A–14, 15.

72. Beck et al., "The Doctor's Suicide Van," *Newsweek*, June 18, 1990, p. 46.

73. Ibid., p. 49.

74. Ibid., p. 46.

75. Humphry, op. cit., p. 138.

76. Ibid., p. 139.

77. "The Physician and the Dying Patient," American Medical Association, issued December 1973, in Rachels, op. cit., p. 38.

78. "Euthanasia: The Swamis' Views," part 2, *Hinduism Today*, August 1988, p. 5.

79. Surendranath Dasgupta, *A History of Indian Philosophy* (Cambridge University Press, 1968), vol. 2, p. 272.

80. Ibid., p. 403.

81. Ibid., p. 404.

82. *Hinduism Today*, loc. cit.

83. See "Chikitsastanam," 1:1–6, in *Caraka Saṁhitā*, ed. and trans. Priyavrat Sharma (Varanasi: Chaukhambha Orientalia, 1983), vol. 11, p. 3.

84. Chāndogya Upaniṣad 2.17.4.

85. *Young India* (weekly paper), April 11, 1926, p. 385.

86. Ibid.

87. *Young India*, November 18, 1926, p. 395.

88. Raghavan Iyer, *The Moral and Political Thought of Mahatama Gandhi* (New York: Oxford University Press, 1973), p. 207.

89. Frank E. Reynolds, "Death: Eastern Thought," in Reich, op. cit., p. 232.

90. Patrick Olivelle, *Saṃnyāsa Upaniṣads* (New York: Oxford University Press, 1992), p. 33.

91. Bṛihad-Āraṇyaka Upaniṣad 4.4.22, in Hume, op. cit., p. 143.

92. Olivelle, op. cit., p. 34.

93. Kaṭhaśruti Upaniṣad, 39, in Olivelle, op. cit., p. 134.

94. Śātyāyanīya Upaniṣad, 331, in ibid., p. 286.

95. Nāradaparivrājaka Upaniṣad, 138, in ibid., p. 176.

96. Ibid., p. 179.

97. Maitreya Upaniṣad 3.12, 13, 18, in ibid., pp. 167, 168.

98. See Varaha Upaniṣad 1.8–11.

99. Maitreya Upaniṣad 108.

100. Mahābhārata 13.113.9.

101. Ibid. 12.260.22.

102. *Foundations of the Metaphysics of Morals*, p. 422.

103. Rachels, op. cit., p. 44.

104. R. M. Hare, "Euthanasia: A Christian View," *Philosophic Exchange* (Brockport, New York), vol. 2, no. 1, Summer 1975, p. 45.

105. "Sutrasthana," in *Caraka Saṁhitā*, op. cit., vol. 3, 10.7–13, p. 67–68.

106. Ibid. ; "Indriyasthāna" 1.1–2.

107. Glover, op. cit., p. 192.

108. K. N. Siva Subramanian, "Caring for Newborns: In India, Nepal, and Sri Lanka, Quality of Life Weighs Heavily," *Hastings Center Report*, vol. 15, no. 4, August 1986, p. 20.

109. Quoted in *Health Scene*, Winter 1991–1992, p. 3.

110. Iyer, op. cit., p. 207.

CHAPTER 4. THE ETHICS OF THE ENVIRONMENT

1. Thomas A. Sancton, "Planet of the Year," *Time*, January 2, 1989, p. 29.

2. In "A Statement from President Nixon," *The Environment*, editors of *Fortune* (New York: Perennial Library, 1969), p. 11.

3. Ibid.

4. Ibid., p. 12.

5. Max Ways, "How to Think about the Environment," *Environment*, ibid., p. 204.

6. "Reconciling Progress with the Quality of Life," ibid., p. 8.

7. Ways, loc.cit.

8. L. White, "The Historic Roots of our Ecologic Crisis," in *Ecology and Religion in History*, ed. David and Eileen Spring (New York: Harper Torch Books, 1974), p. 23.

9. Sancton, op. cit., p. 27.

10. John C. Ryan, "Conserving Biological Diversity," *State of the World, 1992*, ed. Lester R. Brown (New York: W. W. Norton, 1992), p. 9.

11. Eugene Linden, "The Death of Birth," *Time*, January 2, 1989, p. 32.

12. Madhav Gadgil, "Saving the Subcontinent's Wealth," in *The Hindu Survey of the Environment 1991* (Madras: National Press, 1991), p. 140.

13. Ibid.

14. Ibid., p. 141.

15. Ibid.

16. Ryan, op. cit., p. 10.

17. Ibid., pp. 10, 11.

18. Sancton, op. cit., p. 34.

19. S. S. Chawla, "Punjab-Haryana: Like Woes of Neighbours," in Gadgil, op. cit., p. 53.

20. Sunny Sebastian, "Rajasthan: Digging at Roots of Sanctuaries," in Gadgil, op. cit., p. 59.

21. V. T. Joshi, "Madhya Pradesh: Not Learning from Experience," in Gadgil, op. cit., p. 59.

22. M. S. Prabhakara, "Assam: Public Sector Playing Havoc," in Gadgil, op. cit., p. 63.

23. Anil Bhattacharya, "Tripura: Gunti Dam, of Uprooted People," in Gadgil, op. cit., p. 65.

24. P. K. Roy, "Uttar Pradesh: Heading for Ecodisaster," in Gadgil, op. cit., p. 56.

25. S. S. Chawla, "Himachal Pradesh: The Dying Lake Renuka," in Gadgil, op. cit., p. 51.

26. M. Vannucci, "Mangroves: Saving a Crucial Ecosystem," in Gadgil, op. cit., p. 157.

27. Ryan, op. cit., p. 12.

28. Ibid.

29. Ibid., p. 9.

30. Linden, loc. cit.

31. Ryan, op. cit., p. 13.

32. Ibid., p. 14.

33. Lonnelle Aikman, "Nature's Gifts to Medicine," *National Geographic*, September 1974, p. 424.

34. Ryan, loc. cit.

35. Ibid.

36. Michael D. Lemonick, "The Ozone Vanishes," *Time*, February 17, 1992, p. 63.

37. A.P. Mitra, "The Greenhouse Effect," in Gadgil, op. cit., p. 77.

38. Lemonick, op. cit., p. 60.

39. Ibid.

40. Michael D. Lemonick, "The Heat Is On," *Time*, October 19, 1987, p. 59.

41. Peter Wagner, "Hawaii's Toxic Sins Pale in the Glare of U.S. Problems," *Honolulu Star-Bulletin*, August 17, 1989, pp. A1–2, B1–2.

42. Samuel S. Epstein, "Environmental Ethics, Health and Human Disease," *Encyclopedia of Bioethics*, ed. Warren T. Reich (New York: The Free Press, 1978), vol. 1, pp. 380–381.

43. Ibid., p. 380.

44. Ibid.

45. Ibid.

46. The Harvard Medical School Health Letter Book, ed. G. T. Johnson and S. E. Goldfinger (New York: Warner Books, 1981), p. 367.

47. Ibid., pp. 382, 383.

48. Ibid., p. 382.

49. Ellen Hale, "Communism Is Blamed for Deadly Pollution in Eastern Europe," *Honolulu Star-Bulletin*, August 14, 1990, p. D–11.

50. Ibid.

51. Ibid.

52. Ibid.

53. Glenn Garelik, "The Soviets Clean Up Their Act," *Time*, January 29, 1990.

54. Ibid.

55. Christine Gorman, "Mexico City's Menacing Air," *Time*, April 1, 1991.

56. Indranil Banerjie, "The Invisible Menace," *India Today*, June 30, 1984, p. 142.

57. Ibid.

58. Ibid.

59. Ibid.

60. Ibid.

61. B. B. Sundaresan, "Industrial Pollution: The Main Culprits," in Gadgil, op. cit., p. 99.

62. Angus Denning and Kathy Cheng, "Victim of Its Own Success," *Newsweek*, June 4, 1990, pp. 74, 75.

63. Ibid.

64. Ibid.

65. Edward Flattau, "Japan Has a Split Environmental Personality," *Honolulu Star-Bulletin*, March 19, 1991.

66. Ibid.
67. Eduard Shevardnadze, *The Future Belongs to Freedom* (New York: The Free Press, 1991), p. 171.
68. Ibid., pp. 174, 175.
69. Ibid. pp. 175, 176.
70. "Nuclear Energy," *Honolulu Star-Bulletin,* July 15, 1990.
71. John Langone, "Waste: A Stinking Mess," *Time,* January 2, 1989, p. 44.
72. Ibid.
73. Ibid.
74. Ibid.
75. Dan Grossman and Seth Shulman, "Down in the Dumps," *Discover,* April 1990, p. 38.
76. George J. Church, "Garbage, Garbage Everywhere," *Time,* September 5, 1988.
77. Ibid.
78. Al Gore, *Earth in the Balance: Ecology and the Human Spirit* (Boston: Houghton Mifflin, 1992), p. 151.
79. Church, loc. cit.
80. Gore, op. cit., pp. 154, 155.
81. Eugene Linden, "The Last Drops," *Time,* August 20, 1990.
82. Eugene Linden, "The Last Drops," *Time,* August 20, 1990.
83. Lee-Jay Cho, "The Population Institute," *East-West Center Prospectuses* (Honolulu: 1982–83), p. 1.
84. Strobe Talbott, "How Bush Has Wimped Out," *Time,* December 16, 1991.
85. "UN Rings Alarm on Population Rise," *Honolulu Star-Bulletin,* May 13, 1991.
86. Aldo Leopold, *A Sand County Almanac* (New York: Oxford University Press, 1968), p. 224f.
87. Anastasia Toufexis, "Too Many Mouths," *Time,* January 2, 1989, p. 49.
88. Talbott, loc. cit.
89. Stephen Budiansky, "The Nuclear Epidemic," *U.S. News and World Report,* March 16, 1992, p. 40.
90. David Doyle, "Intelligence Needs Heat Up as Cold War Ends," *Honolulu Star-Bulletin,* March 23, 1992.
91. Ibid.
92. B.J. Cutler, "Foreign Affairs," *Honolulu Star-Bulletin,* March 20, 1992, p. A–16.
93. Budiansky, loc. cit.
94. Norman Cousins, "Cleaning Humanity's Nest," *Saturday Review,* March 7, 1970.

95. Ibid.

96. Ibid.

97. Aldo Leopold, *Readings in Conservation Ecology*, ed. George Cox (New York: Appleton-Century-Crofts, 1969), p. 585.

98. The Hindu Tradition, ed. Ainslie T. Embree (New York: The Modern Library, 1966), p. 9.

99. Ibid., p. 16.

100. RV. 146.5, Ralph Griffiths, trans., *The Hymns of the ṚgVeda*, ed. J. L. Shastri (New Delhi: Motilal Banarsidass, 1973), p. 641.

101. See R. S. Bhatnagar, "The Emergence of Basic Ethical Concepts: First Book of Rig Veda," unpublished paper.

102. Atharvaveda 12.14

103. Atharvaveda 12.35.

104. Atharvaveda 12.12.

105. S. Dasgupta, *A History of Indian Philosophy* (Cambridge: Cambridge University Press, 1969), vol. 1, p. 42.

106. Brh. Up. 4.4.22, in R. E. Hume, *The Thirteen Principal Upanishads*, 2d ed. rev. (London: Oxford University Press, 1971), p. 143.

107. See Tait. Up. 2.8; Maitri Up. 6.17; Brh. Up. 5.15; Īśā Up. 16.

108. Īśā Up. 1.1, in Hume, op. cit., p. 362.

109. SK. 21.

110. SK. 57.

111. M. Hiriyanna, *The Essentials of Hindu Philosophy* (London: Allen and Unwin, 1967), p. 119.

112. Brh. Up. 2.5.15, in Hume, op. cit., p. 104.

113. Bhagavadgītā 2.28.

114. Fritjof Capra and David Steindl-Rast, *Belonging to the Universe* (New York: Harper, 1991), p. 83.

115. Eliot Deutsch, "Religion and Ecology: Ancient India and Modern America," paper presented at conference on Religion and Ecology, Cromwell Crawford, Director, University of Hawaii, Honolulu, 1968.

116. Brh. Up. 4.4.5, in Hume, op. cit., p. 140.

117. Deutsch, op. cit.

118. Gore, op. cit., p. 4.

119 Manu 6.35, 37, also Yaj. 3.56; Bau. 2.34; Apa. 2.24.

120. Walter H. Maurer, *Pinnacles of India's Past* (Philadelphia: John Benjamins Publishing Company, 1986), p. 219.

121. In Margaret and James Stutley, *Harper's Dictionary of Hinduism*, ed. Margaret and James Stutley (New York: Harper and Row, 1977), p. 234.

122. Maurer, loc. cit.

123. Ian Barbour, "Environment and Man," in *Encyclopedia of Bioethics*, vol. 1, op. cit. p. 370.

124. Gore, op. cit., p. 50.

125. Michael D. Lemonick, "Feeling the Heat," *Time*, January 2, 1989, p. 36.

126. Leopold, op. cit.

127. Linden, op. cit., p. 34.

128. Advertiser News Service, "Washington Taking the Heat at Earth Summit," *Sunday Star-Bulletin and Advertiser*, June 1992, p. A25.

129. Linden, op. cit., p. 34.

130. Charles P. Alexander, "On the Defensive," *Time*, June 15, 1992, p. 35.

131. Karan Singh, *Hinduism*, 2d rev. ed. (Delhi: Ratna Sagar, 1990), p. 118.

132. *Young India*, June 18, 1921.

133. Advertiser News Service, loc. cit.

134. Philip Elmer-Dewitt, "Rich vs. Poor," *Time*, June 1, 1992, p. 43.

135. Manu 1.49.

136. Brihatsaṁhitā 59.

137. Varaha Purāṇa 172.39.

138. Vishṇu 91.4–8.

139. 111.19.197.

140. Manu 8. 285.

141. Ibid., note on vs. 285.

142. Michael Weisskopf, "Quayle, Gore Now Point Men for Environment," *The Sunday Star Bulletin and Advertiser*, p. A30.

143. Chandi Prasad Bhatt, "The Hug That Saves," in Gadgil, op. cit., p. 17.

144. Langone, op. cit., p. 44.

145. See Gore, op. cit., p. 146.

146. Langone, op. cit., p. 45.

147. "Japan Gets Creative in Sewage Business," *Chicago Tribune*, June 7, 1992, Section 7–7B.

148. Manu 7.129.

149. Reuters, "U.N.: India Will Top China as Most Populous Nation in World by 2025," *Honolulu Star-Bulletin*, April 30, 1992.

150. Ibid.

151. "President's Message," *Indiagram*, January 26, 1987, p. 2.

152. S. Radhakrishnan, quoted in S. Chandrasekhar, "How India Is Tackling Her Population Problem," *Foreign Affairs*, October 1968, no. 1, p. 145.

153. S. Radhakrishnan, *Planned Parenthood* (New Delhi: Central Planning Institute, 1969), p. 11.

154. H. C. Ganguli, "Religion and the Population Explosion," *Religious Pluralism and the World Community*, ed. E. J. Jurji (Leiden: E. J. Brill, 1969), p. 208.

155. Seshagiri Rao, "Population Ethics: A Hindu Perspective," *Encyclopedia of Bioethics*, vol. 3, op. cit., p. 1271.

156. Manu 9.137, 138 in *Dharam Shastra*, vol. 5, ed. M. N. Dutta (New Delhi: Cosmo Publication, 1979), p. 334.

157. RV. 10.85.36.

158. Burdett, "Ambitious Targets Highlights India's Population Strategy," *Popline*, December 1986, p. 4.

159. Manu 9.137, 138.

160. Manu 9.107.

161. Stutley, op. cit., p. 284.

162. Mikhail Gorbachev, "View from Washington," *Honolulu Star-Bulletin*, April 30, 1992.

163. Karan Singh, op. cit., p. 44.

164. Ibid., pp. 45–47.

165. William Wordsworth, *The Golden Treasury*, ed. F. T. Palgrave (Nelson and Sons, n.d.), p. 310.

GLOSSARY

acit—matter, material
advaita—monism
Agni—god of fire
ahaṅkāra—ego
ahiṃsā—nonviolence
anantya—immortality
anārabdha—karma that has not begun to bear fruit
araṇya—the forest
artha—worldly prosperity; one of four human ends
asat—unreal
āśrama—stage of life
Atharvaveda—the fourth Veda
atithis—chance guests
ātma-ghata—self-killing
ātma-hatyā—self-killing
ātman—the self
avidyā—original ignorance
Āyurveda—the science of longevity

bala—strength
Bhagavadgītā—The Lord's Song; a part of the Mahābhārata
bhrūṇa-hatyā—feticide
bhū-ṛṇa—obligations to the *Bhūmi*, humankind's terrestrial home
Brahmacarya—the stage of the religious student
Brahman—Ultimate Reality
Brāhmaṇas—Vedic texts discussing sacrificial rites
buddhi—intelligence, cognition

caturtha-ṛṇa—the fourth debt
cit—self

dayā—compassion
dharma—duty, law, righteousness

Dharmaśāstras—sacred texts dealing with morality
dīkṣā—consecration ceremony

Gaṅgā—the most sacred river
grām—the village
guṇas—basic properties

hiṃsā—causing pain or killing out of anger

jauhar—rite by which womenfolk of Rajput warriors would col-
    lectively immolate themselves to preserve honor
Jhum—practice of slash-and-burn
jiva—the individual embodied soul
jivadayā—kindness to creatures
jīvanmukti—the state of self-realization while yet in the body

kāma—pleasures of the five senses; one of four human ends
karma—action; the law of cause and effect in the moral sphere

Mahābhārata—one of India's two great epics; discussions of morals
mahābhūtas—gross elements
mahā-makha—great sacrifice
mahāpātakas—atrocious acts
mahāprasthāna—the Great Journey
Manu—the most eminent Hindu lawgiver; teaches the four stages
    and ends of life
mokṣa—liberation

niyoga—levirate marriage

pāpa—evil
pariṇāmavāda—theory of causality
parivrājaka—ascetic
Pārvatī—wife of Siva
piṇḍa—morsel of ritual oblation of food to an ancestor
pitṛ—deceased forefathers, existing in heavenly realms
prajāti—parenthood
prakṛti—the material principle
pralaya—state of dissolution
prārabdha karma—karma that has come to fruition

prāyopaveśa—fasting
Purāṇas—popular moral stories about legendary gods and heroes
Puruṣa—the Supreme Being; the spiritual principle
puruṣārthas—the four supreme values of life

Rāmānuja—eleventh-century philosopher of qualified monism
Rāmāyaṇa-one of India's two great epics; narrating the story of
    Vishṇu's incarnation as Rama
rati—pleasure
Ṛgveda-first of the four Vedas, composed of hymns; essential for
    understanding Hindu thought
ṛnatraya—triad of obligations
ṛta—natural and moral order of the universe

sādhu—a holy man
sakhya—companionship
Śakti—divine Mother; female creative energy
sallekanā—starving oneself to death
Śaṁkara—eighth-century philosopher of nondualism
Sāṁkhya—a philosophy of dualistic realism
saṁsāra-the wheel of rebirth; the world of impermanence and
    suffering
saṁskāras—innate tendencies of a person
sañcita karma—karma accumulated from past lives
sannyāsin—one who has abandoned the world and lives the holy
    life
sapiṇḍa—blood relations
sarga—state of evolution
satī—a virtuous, devoted widow who immolates herself on the
    funeral pyre of her husband
sattva-one of the three basic properties, of the nature of truth,
    purity, and light
satya-rakṣā—protecting the truth
Smṛti—the body of sacred lore remembered and passed on by
    tradition
śrāddha—ceremony honoring dead ancestors
Śruti—scriptures revealed to ancient ṛsis, identified with the Vedas

Upaniṣads-ancient philosophic treatises forming final sections of
    the Vedas

vāhana—the mount of a god
vaidya—physician
vartamāna-karma—karma generated in present life
Vedānta—a system of philosophy based on the Upaniṣads

BIBLIOGRAPHY

Ahmed, A. F. S. *Social Ideas and Social Change in Bengal 1818–1835.* Leiden: E. J. Brill, 1965.

Bethge, Eberhard, ed. *Ethics*, by Dietrich Bonhoeffer. New York: Macmillan, 1965.

Blumenthal, Susan J., and Kupfer, David J. *Suicide over the Life Cycle: Risk Factors, Assessments, and Treatment of Suicidal Patients.* Washington: American Psychiatric Press, 1990.

Bose, A. C. *Hymns from the Vedas.* Bombay: Asia Publishing House, 1966.

Brown, Lester R., ed. *State of the World, 1992.* New York: W. W. Norton, 1992.

Capra, Fritjof, and Steindl-Rast, David. *Belonging to the Universe.* New York: Harper, 1991.

Chakravati, Satis Chandra, ed. *The Father of Modern India.* Calcutta: Rammohan Roy Centenary Committee, 1935.

Cobb, John, Jr. *Matters of Life and Death.* Louisville, Ky.: John Knox Press/Westminster, 1991.

Cox, George, ed. *Readings in Conservation Ecology.* New York: Appleton-Century-Crofts, 1969.

Crawford, S. Cromwell. *The Evolution of Hindu Ethical Ideals.* Honolulu: The University Press of Hawaii, 1982.

———. *Ram Mohan Roy.* New York: Paragon House, 1987.

———, ed. *World Religions and Global Ethics.* New York: Paragon House, 1989.

Dasgupta, Surendranath. *A History of Indian Philosophy.* 2 vols. Cambridge: Cambridge University Press, 1969.

Dutta, M. N., ed. *The Dharam Shastra: Hindu Religious Codes.* 5 vols. New Delhi: Cosmo Publications, 1978–1979.

Eliade, Mircea, ed. *The Encyclopedia of Religion.* 12 vols. New York: Macmillan and Free Press, 1987.

Farquhar, J. N. *An Outline of the Religious Literature of India.* New Delhi: Motilal Banarsidass, 1984.

Fortune, editors of. *The Environment.* New York: Perennial Library, 1969.

Gore, Al. *Earth in the Balance: Ecology and the Human Spirit.* Boston: Houghton Mifflin, 1992.

Hamel, Ron, ed. *Active Euthanasia, Religion, and the Public Debate.* Chicago: The Park Ridge Center, 1991.

Hastings, James, ed. *Encyclopaedia of Religion and Ethics.* Edinburgh: T. and T. Clark, 1980 reprint.

Herring, Basil, F. *Jewish Ethics and Halakah for Our Time: Sources and Commentary.* New York: Ktav Publishing House, 1984.

Hindu. *The Hindu Survey of the Environment 1991 (Annual),* ed. N. Ravi. Madras: National Press, 1991.

Hiriyanna, M. *The Essentials of Hindu Philosophy.* London: Allen and Unwin, 1967.

———. *Popular Essays in Indian Philosophy.* Mysore: Kavyalaya Publishers, 1952.

Hume, Robert E., trans. *The Thirteen Principal Upanishads.* London: Oxford University Press, 1971.

Humphry, Derek. *Final Exit.* Oregon: The Hemlock Society, 1991.

Hutchins, Robert M., ed. *Great Books of the Western World.* 50 vols. Chicago: Encyclopaedia Britannica, 1952.

Iyer, Raghavan. *The Moral and Political Thought of Mahatama Gandhi.* New York: Oxford University Press, 1973.

Jersild, Paul T., and Johnson, Dale A. *Moral Issues and Christian Response.* Fort Worth, Tex.: Holt Rinehart and Winston, 1988.

Jurgi, E. J., ed. *Religious Pluralism and the World Community.* Leiden: E. J. Brill, 1969.

Kane, Pandurang Vaman. *History of Dharmaśāstra.* 6 vols. Poona: Bhandarkar Oriental Research Institute, 1973.

Matilal, B. K., ed. *Moral Dilemmas in the Mahābhārata.* New Delhi: Motilal Banarsidass, 1989.

Maurer, Walter H. *Pinnacles of India's Past.* Philadelphia: John Benjamins Publishing Company, 1986.

Muller, F. M., ed. *Sacred Books of the East.* 50 vols. New Delhi: Motilal Banarsidass, 1987 reprint.

Nag, Kalidas, and Burman, Debajyoti, eds. *The English Works of Raja Rammohun Roy.* Calcutta: Sadharan Brahmo Samaj, 1946.

Olivelle, Patrick. *Saṃnyāsa Upaniṣads.* New York: Oxford University Press, 1992.

Palgrave, F. F., ed. *The Golden Treasury*. London: Nelson and Sons, n. d.

Ray, P., Gupta, H., Roy, M., eds. *Suśruta Saṃhitā: A Scientific Synopsis*. New Delhi: Indian National Science Academy, 1980.

Regan, Tom, ed. *Moral Philosophy: Matters of Life and Death*. New York: Random House, 1980.

Reich, W. T., general ed. *Encyclopedia of Bioethics*. 4 vols. New York: The Free Press, 1978.

St. Augustine. *City of God*, trans. Gerald G. Walsh et al. New York: Image Books, 1958.

Sharma, Priyavrat, ed. and trans. *Caraka Saṃhitā*. 3 vols. Varanasi: Chaukambha Orientalia, 1981.

Shevardnadze, Eduard. *The Future Belongs to Freedom*. New York: The Free Press, 1991.

Spring, David, and Spring, Eileen, eds. *Ecology and Religion in History*. New York: Harper Torch Books, 1974.

Steiner, Gilbert Y., ed. *The Abortion Dispute and the American System*. New York: The Brookings Institute, 1983.

Stutley, Margaret, and Stutley, James, eds. *Harper's Dictionary of Hinduism*. New York: Harper and Row, 1977.

Veatch, Robert M., ed. *Cross-Cultural Perspectives in Medical Ethics: Readings*. Boston: Jones and Bartlett, 1989.

Walker, Benjamin, ed. *Hindu World: An Encyclopedic Survey of Hinduism*. 2 vols. New Delhi: Munshiram Manoharlal, 1983.

INDEX

229